ISLE OF BEASTS AND SHADOWS

THE FORGOTTEN ISLE SAGA
BOOK ONE

MCCAYLEIGH DANIELS

LEGENDARY INK
Publishing Company

First published in the United States in 2018
This edition published in 2025

ISBN-13:
Paperback: 979-8-9915192-0-5
Hardcover: 979-8-9915192-1-2

For the warriors who battle their own demons and rise stronger every time. I see you.

ABOUT THE BOOK

While this book is classified as Young Adult and contains no overly explicit scenes, there are still some topics that may be sensitive to certain readers. For your awareness, a full list of trigger warnings can be found at the back of the book. Please feel free to review them before continuing with Airella's journey.

Shadowspeak
Valoria
Kingdom of Aurian
Oxreach
Aramore
Alverstone
Kingdom of Eldaraya
Mount Vorel
N
W
E
S

Edros
The Isle

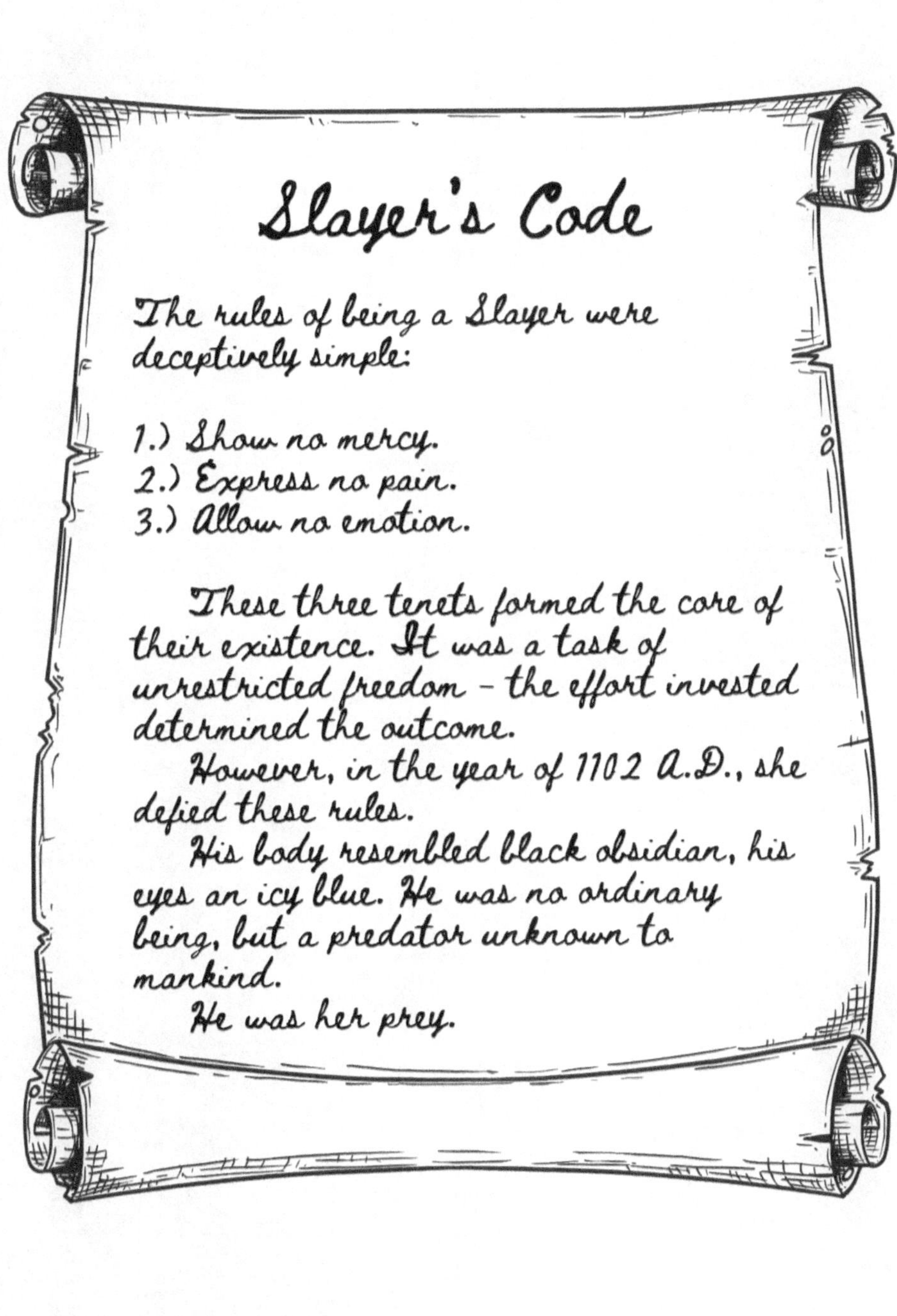

Slayer's Code

The rules of being a Slayer were deceptively simple:

1.) Show no mercy.
2.) Express no pain.
3.) Allow no emotion.

These three tenets formed the core of their existence. It was a task of unrestricted freedom – the effort invested determined the outcome.

However, in the year of 1102 A.D., she defied these rules.

His body resembled black obsidian, his eyes an icy blue. He was no ordinary being, but a predator unknown to mankind.

He was her prey.

256 YEARS AGO

The deep voice of Emmaline's father echoed through the cottage, his words sharp as they bounced off the walls. This was all too familiar. Every time she protested her arranged marriage to Rowan, her father, bound by tradition and guild hierarchy, erupted in frustration.

Rowan, the famed Miscreant Slayer, had earned the title of Champion, giving him the right to choose his bride—a path that would lead him to head the guild. And fate had chosen her. As her father delivered his well-worn lecture, she listened without really hearing, already knowing every word by heart.

Emmaline slipped on her brown cloak, pulling it from the wall hook. As her father finished his speech on duty and honor, she pulled the hood over her head, stepping out into the thick snow blanketing the ground. A chill seeped into her bones. The cold spell was unnatural for their island, where flowers should have been in full bloom. Yet, like everything else, they lay buried beneath the snow.

She and her father entered the guild hall, its wooden interior bustling with chatter. Though the guild called itself a family, she always felt like an outsider. Even as the guild master's daughter, she struggled to belong. At sixteen, most members were older, reinforcing her isolation. Rowan was among them, his arms wrapping around her from behind. She stiffened before shrugging him off.

"Still so feisty," he chuckled, the scent of liquor clinging to him.

"You're disgusting," Emmaline snapped, resisting the urge to shove him harder.

Rowan, arrogant and entitled, was used to her defiance. He wanted to marry her not for love, but to cement his place as guild leader. Without another word, he staggered off toward the council chambers.

The guild hall resembled a lively tavern, its candlelit walls filled with laughter and the clinking of tankards. Ignoring the noise, Emmaline moved to the Quest Board. Their island was plagued by Miscreants, and the guild thrived on hunting them. Villagers offered hefty rewards for their extermination, making slaying a lucrative business. Her eyes scanned the parchment pinned to the board.

"Bloodsucker – 500 gold pieces. Lycan – 250 silver pieces. Reaper – 800 gold pieces..."

For over a year, Emmaline had been saving every coin, desperate to escape before she was bound to a fate she despised. She had a plan—under the cover of night, she would sail away on her own. No one had ever left the island and returned, but she would take the risk. Any life was better than the one waiting for her here.

A tap on her shoulder startled her.

"What are you doing?" a sharp voice asked.

"Anya! I, uh..." Emmaline turned, fidgeting.

Two years ago, she had found Anya, as a thief struggling to survive, and offered her a job at the tavern. Now, Anya was her closest friend, her sleek black hair cropped at her chin, her porcelain skin flawless.

Before she could speak, Anya pulled her into a hug. "I just want what's best for you. If leaving is what you need, I'll support you."

Relief flooded Emmaline. Anya always understood her in ways others never could. She returned the embrace.

"Thank you, Anya. I—"

Anya pulled out a slip of paper and handed it over. "This bounty posted this morning might interest you. Remembering our chat last week, I thought it might interest you. It's worth a fortune."

Emmaline unfolded it, reading aloud. "Ice Hellion – 10,000 gold pieces. Crimes: Freezing temperatures, missing townsfolk."

Her heart pounded. This was it. If she could claim the bounty, she could finally afford her escape. Large rewards like this were rare, usually snapped up by veteran guild members. This was her chance.

Anya gave her one last squeeze. "Please, be careful. I'll be here if you need me."

Determined, Emmaline wasted no time. She adjusted her hood, tucked the parchment into her pocket, and slipped out into the cold night with her weapon strapped at her waist.

At least an hour had passed since she ventured into the dense forest. Snowflakes clung to her lashes as the wind howled through the trees. She was alone. Her father had always insisted she take partners on dangerous hunts, but this time, she had no choice.

Kneeling, she examined a trail of footprints. They ended abruptly at a thick thicket.

A low voice rumbled through the stillness. "Źēćmœł."

Emmaline's pulse spiked. That had to be the Ice Hellion.

"Dïmłëmźał!"

A massive figure burst through the underbrush. Seven feet tall, clad in obsidian armor, the beast lunged at her. Emmaline spun, raising her metal rod to block its attack. With a sharp kick, she sent it sprawling, but the creature retaliated swiftly, encasing her feet in ice. She gritted her teeth, shattering the frost with a crack of her weapon.

Sparks danced along the rod's metallic surface. The hellion hesitated, its icy blue eyes locking onto hers. A fog rolled in, thick and unnatural. For a split second, something held her back from delivering the final blow. Why did she hesitate?

The Miscreant seized the moment, freezing the ground beneath her. Ice shards shot toward her in rapid succession. She dodged, but one cut across her cheek, a sharp sting in the freezing air. The real threat, however, was the frost creeping toward her boots.

With a fierce swing, she broke free, only to find the hellion had vanished, leaving behind only faint tracks in the snow.

Pushing her tangled blonde curls back, she followed its trail, her breath misting in the air. Snowflakes swirled around her as she emerged from the woods to find a vast frozen lake stretching before her.

Through the storm, she spotted a small cave on the distant shore. Was that where the beast was hiding?

She stepped onto the ice, her every movement cautious. The lake groaned beneath her weight, cracks forming with each step. The storm raged on, blurring her vision. She forced herself to move forward, ignoring the creeping sense of unease.

Then—

CRACK.

Panic surged through her as the ice beneath her feet splintered into jagged veins.

"No," she whispered, heart pounding.

She ran.

Desperation seized her as she sprinted, her movements deftly avoiding the expanding fault lines that threatened to swallow her whole. The thunderous cacophony of breaking ice echoed around her, a symphony of danger propelling her toward the safety of solid ground.

Another crack. Then another.

With each heart-pounding stride, the cave loomed closer, a beacon of hope amid chaos. Victory tantalizingly close, she pushed herself to the brink, the promise of sanctuary urging her onward. Just as the mouth of the cave came into view, a flicker of determination ignited within her, a beacon of resilience in the face of the unknown.

And then, the world dropped out from beneath her as she plunged into the freezing abyss below.

1

256 YEARS LATER

Airella's world shattered when the Plague took her father, leaving her to navigate life at just seven years old. With her mother battling a chronic illness, she became their anchor, shouldering the weight of survival. By eighteen, the burden of providing for her small family—her ailing mother and her spirited younger brother, Arii—had only grown heavier.

Arii dashed down the narrow hallway of their cottage, his untamed blond hair bouncing with each step. Airella watched him with a mix of exasperation and fondness.

"Arii, it's too early, and you stink." She wrinkled her nose. "When was your last bath? What trouble have you gotten into this time?"

"I was practicing my sword skills," he declared proudly. "I'm going to be the best swordsman in all of Edros."

"Arii," Airella's voice softened, though her words were firm. "We've talked about this."

"I know, I know. But how else will I protect you and Mama

from the villains?" he asked with the unwavering determination of an eleven-year-old.

"That's my job," she reminded him, ruffling his hair. "Papa's weapons stay locked away. Lay a hand on them again, and you'll be eating pig slop for dinner."

"No, please don't!" Arii whined, dashing off. Airella chuckled, shaking her head. He had once dared to taste pig slop out of curiosity—it had not ended well.

Stepping into her room, Airella caught her reflection in the small, cracked mirror. Her mismatched eyes—one icy blue, the other a vivid emerald green—stared back at her, a stark reminder of the father she missed dearly. His teachings, his wisdom, his unwavering love—gone. But she still had Arii. She still had her mother. And she would protect them at any cost.

The floorboards creaked under her weight as she moved toward her nightstand. The cottage was crumbling around them, a victim of time and poverty. A rusty tin can in the center of the room collected water from a leaking ceiling, a reminder of the storm that had battered their home the night before. No matter how hard she worked, there was never enough money for repairs.

Winter had made everything worse. The animals had gone into hibernation, making hunting nearly impossible. With fewer hides to sell at the market, their already meager funds were dwindling. The thought of turning to desperate means lingered in the back of her mind, but she quickly shoved it away. There had to be another way.

A sudden knock at the door made her jump.

"Yes?" she called, her pulse quickening.

The bedroom door creaked open, revealing her mother's frail figure. Elizabeth's once-bright eyes were clouded with exhaustion, her illness weighing heavily on her.

"Airella," her mother's voice was barely above a whisper, "they're outside… They're coming."

Dread settled in Airella's stomach like a stone.

"Who?" she asked, stepping closer.

Elizabeth's eyes filled with urgency. "Listen to me, child. There are things you do not yet understand. Take your father's axe. It will protect you."

Airella's breath caught in her throat.

Before she could question her mother further, the sharp command of men's voices cut through the air, followed by the crash of their front door being forced open.

Panic surged through her as Elizabeth shoved a golden, dual-bladed battle axe into her trembling hands.

"There is no time," her mother said, voice shaking. "Hide! I'll find Arii."

Airella barely had time to react before Elizabeth pushed her away, locking the door behind her. Footsteps pounded against the wooden floor, accompanied by harsh orders barked by men who had no right to be there.

Clutching the axe, Airella crouched behind her bed, heart hammering. The weapon was heavy, its jeweled handle glinting even in the dim light. She had never wielded Dawnbreaker before. Her father's most prized possession. A weapon of legend. Now, it was all she had.

"No, don't hurt him!" her mother's voice rang out, raw with desperation.

Airella's blood ran cold at the response.

"Then tell us where the girl is. If we don't find her, the boy will suffice."

"No," another voice interjected, sharper, crueler. "We need the one who takes after their father."

Airella's hands clenched around the axe handle. They knew. They knew about her.

"Search the house," the leader commanded. "Burn it down if you have to."

Airella barely had time to steel herself before the door to her room burst open. Boots stomped inside. She held her breath as shadows passed over the floorboards.

Just when she thought they might leave, a hand clamped around her ankle and yanked her out from under the bed.

"Let go of me!" she snarled, kicking and thrashing. With reckless strength, she swung Dawnbreaker, narrowly missing her captor's head. The blade lodged deep into the wooden floorboards instead.

The soldier staggered but didn't let go. More hands grabbed her, pinning her arms and forcing her onto her feet.

Bursting into the main room, her heart twisted at the sight before her—Arii in a soldier's grasp, struggling, and her mother kneeling before their intruders, her face a mask of fear and defiance.

"Wait! Don't hurt them!" Airella cried. "What is the meaning of this?"

Another soldier stepped forward, unfurling an aged parchment. His uniform bore the crest of Eldaraya. His voice rang with unshakable authority as he read:

"Airella Devereaux. By decree of the King of Eldaraya, you are to be promptly escorted to the palace. Any resistance will be met with force."

Airella struggled harder, her fury blinding. "You can't just take me!"

The soldiers paid her no mind. One hoisted her over his shoulder as if she weighed nothing. She screamed and kicked, but their grip was ironclad.

Outside, villagers peered from their homes, watching in stunned silence as she was dragged away. The relentless downpour mixed with her tears, her golden locks heavy with rain.

Her mother's voice cut through the storm. "Hold on to it, Airella!"

Airella turned her head just in time to see a soldier carrying Dawnbreaker away. Her heart clenched. She wasn't just losing her freedom—she was losing everything.

Lightning split the sky, thunder roaring in her ears as she was forced into a waiting carriage. The door slammed shut, sealing her fate.

And as the wheels began to roll, she realized—there was no one left to protect her family now.

2

The soldiers forced Airella to her knees before King William. Chains bound her wrists, ensuring any thoughts of escape remained futile.

The throne room was unlike anything she had ever seen. Tapestries of ancient battles and noble victories adorned the towering walls, their intricate designs illuminated by the flickering glow of candlelight. The marble floors gleamed beneath her, a stark contrast to the rough wooden boards of her home. Airella felt out of place yet strangely captivated by the grandeur surrounding her.

Her gaze drifted to King William, his piercing eyes locked onto her, their depths unreadable. She quickly averted her gaze, her heart pounding.

"What do you want from me?" The words tumbled from her lips before she could stop them. She fought to keep her voice steady, but a slight tremor betrayed her fear. All she wanted was to return home—to her mother, to Arii. They needed her.

"That is no way to address the king, commoner," a sharp voice cut through the air.

Airella turned to see a man standing beside the throne. His golden armor gleamed in the dim light, his posture rigid with authority. He circled her like a predator appraising prey.

"Your father left a mark before his passing, Airella Devereaux," he continued, his voice a mixture of condescension and amusement. "It's only natural that his offspring would inherit his strength and talent. Your reputation precedes you—speed, power, resilience. Traits your father was known for. Traits that make you valuable to us."

Her father's involvement in the King's Royal Army had always been a mystery to her, but she knew his duties provided for their family. The envy of the village children for her possessions had never bothered her much, as she had grown accustomed to their way of life. It wasn't until her father's passing that the reality of their situation hit hard. With the income gone, her mother's illness only added to the burden. Their cottage, once a place of comfort, now showed signs of neglect. The struggle to put food on the table and afford her mother's medicine weighed heavily on Airella's mind.

Airella's jaw clenched. The weight of their expectations settled on her shoulders, suffocating and unwanted.

"What makes you think I'd help you?" she asked, forcing confidence into her voice.

A sudden blow sent her reeling. The sharp sting of leather against her cheek burned, her head snapping to the side. Her vision blurred with unshed tears, and she tasted blood.

"Know your place," the scarred man sneered, crouching beside her. His eyes were cold, void of empathy. "We offer you a place in our military, and you resist? This is why women belong in kitchens, not on the battlefield."

Airella's hands curled into fists.

"We considered your brother," he added, his tone dripping with mockery. "But he lacks your... advantages."

"Duran, that's enough." King William's deep voice cut through the air. The man—Duran—stood, but his smirk remained.

King William rose from his throne, his regal presence commanding the room's attention. "Child," he began, "we have discovered an island off the coast of Edros. A land of mystery, untapped potential. We seek to claim it, to turn it into a refuge for our people should Aurian invade. But first, we must understand its dangers. We need warriors, those who possess the strength to endure the unknown." His gaze never wavered. "You would be generously compensated. Your family will want for nothing."

Airella's mind raced.

If she accepted, her mother would receive the medication she desperately needed. Arii would be safe. Their struggles would be over. But at what cost?

She had no reason to trust these men. They had taken her from her home, treated her like a criminal. And yet, refusing them could mean worse—Arii in their hands, her mother left to suffer.

Could she abandon them? Or was this the only way to save them?

She took a steadying breath. "I... I accept."

King William's lips curled into a satisfied smile. "A wise decision."

He turned to Duran. "Ensure she is equipped for the journey."

Duran wasted no time. He yanked her to her feet by the chains, unlocking them with a sharp click.

"You will do as I say," he hissed, his grip bruising as he pulled her close. "You may have your father's blood, but you've yet to prove yourself. Until then, you are nothing. Just a foolish girl playing soldier."

Airella bit the inside of her cheek, swallowing the rage burning in her chest. Duran wanted her to react, to break. She wouldn't give him the satisfaction.

Instead, she met his gaze, unflinching.

Duran scoffed. "Find your armor. You have one hour."

He shoved her toward the armory and disappeared down the hall.

Airella exhaled, pressing a hand to her throbbing cheek. Her thoughts swirled, doubt gnawing at her resolve.

Was this really the right choice?

She pushed the thought aside and turned her attention to the rows of weapons and armor before her. Most were too large, designed for men. The silver breastplates were worn, dented with past battles. She found the smallest set she could, fastening the rusted buckles as best as possible.

Then, she saw it.

Dawnbreaker.

Her father's golden battle axe lay beside her discarded clothes. Airella's breath caught.

She wrapped her fingers around the handle, the weight both familiar and foreign. The gleaming jewels embedded in the hilt shimmered under the torchlight.

Airella tightened the strap around her waist, securing the axe. Whatever came next, she would be ready.

A knock at the door startled her.

"We leave in an hour," a soldier announced.

Airella followed him onto the docks, the wooden ship looming before her. Soldiers murmured as she passed, their gazes a mixture of curiosity and doubt. A woman among them was unheard of.

A red-haired man in golden armor approached, his confident stride easy and assured. Light stubble framed his strong jawline, and a small, genuine smile softened his otherwise commanding presence.

"You must be Airella."

She tensed, distrust still fresh in her mind, but Jonathan's demeanor lacked the hostility she had come to expect.

"I'm Jonathan, second-in-command. We'll be working together."

Airella hesitated before nodding slightly.

He held out a wooden box, offering it to her. "I was instructed to give this to you," Jonathan continued. "King William had his own blacksmith forge it while we waited for your arrival." He placed it in her arms with deliberate care.

Taking it cautiously, she lifted the lid to reveal a set of finely crafted golden armor, tailored perfectly to her size. The sight of it left her momentarily speechless.

"I figured you'd rather keep your own weapon," Jonathan said, nodding toward Dawnbreaker at her hip.

Airella met his gaze, the weight of the past pressing against her. "Did you know my father?" she asked, curiosity pushing aside her hesitation. "Would you mind sharing what you know?"

Jonathan's smile faltered slightly. "You don't know?" he asked, then sighed, rubbing the back of his neck. "I suppose that makes sense. You were just a child when he passed." He hesitated before continuing. "Your father—he was known as The Executioner. He led the Great War on Aurian."

Airella felt the words settle over her like a thick fog. Her mother had never spoken of such things. How could she have been kept in the dark about something so significant? The realization cast new light on the weapons her father had once owned, the hidden cache he had left behind.

"Are you sure you're talking about the same Lysander Devereaux?" she asked, shaking her head. "It seems impossible."

Jonathan held her gaze. "The proof is there. Your strength is rumored to mirror his, your agility too. Even your eyes..." He stepped forward, placing a steady hand on her shoulder. "I would know. I was his apprentice."

Airella's breath hitched. "If that's true, then why aren't you first-in-command instead of Duran?" She cast a glance toward Duran, who stood across the upper deck, barking orders at soldiers.

Jonathan's jaw tightened slightly before he answered. "Duran was second-in-command when your father retired. He positioned himself to take over, and that's how it's been ever since. The succession never changed."

Airella absorbed his words, understanding but not entirely convinced.

"I have to make sure everything is in order now," he said, stepping back. "I'll be seeing you."

With a final warm smile, he turned and disappeared into the crowd of men loading the ship.

Airella lingered for a moment before carrying the box to her assigned cabin. She placed it on the cot, her fingers carefully lifting the lid once more. The golden armor gleamed under the dim light, perfectly shaped for her frame.

She traced the edges of the plates, her thoughts heavy. The gesture was thoughtful, but it didn't erase the unease that had settled deep in her bones.

Far from Alverstone, far from the life she had known, she realized just how alone she truly was.

3

onathan gazed across the vast waters of the ocean's horizon, the soft hues of the setting sun painting the sky in breathtaking shades of orange and pink. The ship, a magnificent vessel with billowing sails that caught the evening breeze, had just set sail. His unexpected encounter with the one and only daughter of Lysander Devereaux, a moment filled with a mix of curiosity and intrigue, had caused a flood of memories to rush through his mind.

Amidst the bustling activity on deck, men moved with purpose and determination. Each soldier, clad in weathered uniforms that bore the marks of countless voyages, carried out their designated tasks with precision. Some diligently scrubbed the upper deck, while others manned the helm, guiding the ship towards its mysterious destination—the island that had captured the imagination of many.

Whispers of the island's recent discovery had spread like wildfire through the kingdom, igniting a sense of wonder and curiosity among the inhabitants of Eldaraya. It had been only a month since one of the king's intrepid travelers stumbled upon its shores during a perilous voyage, returning to the kingdom with tales of uncharted lands and untold treasures waiting to be uncovered.

As the red-haired man turned his back to the sea, the sun cast a warm, golden glow over his freckled face. He caught a glimpse of Duran, the wrinkles around his eyes deepening with concern. Jonathan felt a pang of guilt as their eyes met briefly before he averted his gaze, focusing on the weathered wooden floorboards beneath his feet. Duran's once warm demeanor had turned frosty ever since The Executioner's departure from this world. Jonathan remembered his first experience with the great war hero, each detail etched into his memory like a haunting painting.

His first encounter with the man took place 15 years ago.

Untrimmed and scarlet red hair fell into the boy's dirtied face, the strands clinging to his cheeks as if seeking solace from the chaos surrounding him. Amidst the debris, one could discern the beautifully soft skin that contrasted with his glistening eyes and defined cheekbones. His green eyes, wide and unblinking, reflected a mix of fear and sorrow as he witnessed his village engulfed in flames.

As tears welled up in his eyes, blurring his vision, the ten-year-old boy scrambled to his feet. Despite his tender age of 10, he had witnessed a level of death and destruction that no child should ever experience, serving as a grim reminder of the cruelty of war that had engulfed his home.

"Mother!? Father!?" His voice pierced through the pandemonium, a desperate cry amidst the cacophony of panic and destruction that engulfed the once-serene village of Oxreach.

The air reverberated with the sounds of anguish and terror as the Eldarayan soldiers unleashed their wrath, sparing none in their path. The onslaught shattered the serenity of the small town, replaced by the harrowing symphony of screams and crackling flames consuming homes and hopes alike.

"Jonathan? Where are you?" The sound of a familiar yet concerned female voice rang out.

Jonathan's eyes, filled with a mixture of panic and confusion, desperately scanned the sea of scrambling people, his attempts hampered by his petite stature.

And then, as if a beacon in the chaos, a gentle hand enveloped his shoulder.

"There you are!" The voice, now tinged with relief, belonged to Scarlet, his older sister.

"Scarlet!" Jonathan's voice wavered with a mix of fear and relief as he embraced his sister tightly.

At that moment, amidst the crowd and the uncertainty, they found each other, realizing they had become separated from their parents in the midst of the bustling crowd.

"Follow me!" She gripped his hand, her fingers interlacing with his as she turned to run with urgency.

Her silky hair, a mirror to his own, cascaded behind her like a vibrant flame, dancing in the chaotic air of the burning town. She led him towards the ancient well that stood solemnly at the heart of the fiery chaos.

As they reached the well, a sense of foreboding crept over Jonathan. His sister swiftly secured the wooden bucket to the well's edge, ensuring it hung steadily from the rope that dangled ominously in the darkness below.

"Hold on to this," she instructed him, urgency lacing her words. Jonathan obeyed, his hands gripping the weathered rope while he tentatively placed his feet into the bucket.

"I'll come back for you, okay? I'm going to find Mother and Father. You'll be safe down here. I love you, Jonathan," his sister's words tumbled out hurriedly.

Before he could utter a word of protest or farewell, she

planted a quick kiss on his forehead and began lowering him into the shadowy depths of the well.

Jonathan clung to the rope with a desperation that mirrored his fear. Tears welled in his eyes as he watched the blue sky recede further with each passing moment.

And then he fell.

The slack in the rope grew, giving the eerie sensation that there was no one above to guide his descent. In that heart-stopping moment, Jonathan grappled with the realization that his sister had either lost her grip on the rope or had fallen victim to the Eldarayan soldiers who haunted their village.

Jonathan hit the shallow water below with a splash. Unfortunately, the water lacked so much depth that he hit his head against the stone ground beneath the murky water, causing a sharp pain to shoot through his skull. Emerging from the water, he gasped loudly for air.

With a bloodied face, the boy's eyes frantically scanned the dark abyss he found himself in, the dim light barely illuminating his surroundings. His head throbbed with pain, but his immediate concern was the chaos unfolding above him. Eldarayan soldiers were attacking Aurian, the sound of battle echoing through the air. The declaration of war resulted from a breach in a treaty the two territories once agreed to, shattering any semblance of peace that once existed.

Now, the boy was stuck in the heart of the conflict. Alone with his fears and a cracked skull, the 10-year-old felt a sense of hopelessness creeping in. His mind spiraled with visions of the worst probable outcomes his family might be enduring.

Above, the battle raged on. Eldarayan soldiers shouted commands. The metallic clang of swords echoed through the air. Then—nothing. The screams faded. The fire crackled. And the silence that followed was far worse.

Hours seemed to drag on as the screams faded into the

distance, leaving him alone in the cold, murky waters of the well. A sense of surrealism washed over him as he teetered on the edge of consciousness.

Torchlight flickered above. Shadows loomed over the mouth of the well.

"He's the last one," a soldier muttered.

Soldiers clad in Eldarayan armor lifted his limp body from the well. Jonathan flinched, but there was nowhere to run. Rough hands pulled him from the depths, his body too drained to resist. His vision blurred, and as he sagged in their grip, the world around him shifted.

One moment, he was watching from above—his own lifeless body being hoisted into the arms of an armored soldier. The next, he was standing beside them, shouting at the top of his lungs.

"I'm alive! I'm right here!"

No one reacted. He reached out, grasping at the shoulder of the nearest soldier—his hand passed through them like mist.

Jonathan stumbled back, horror creeping up his spine. His body lay still in the arms of the Eldarayan warrior. A deep voice cut through the night.

"Are you sure he's dead?"

Jonathan turned, his gaze locking onto the soldier who stood apart from the rest. He wore intricate black armor, his presence commanding, his strangely colored eyes piercing in the torchlight. Even now, Jonathan could still remember the way his gaze had unsettled him.

A soldier knelt beside his limp body, pressing fingers to his throat. A moment later, the man exhaled. "He's alive. Barely."

Jonathan felt something tug at him—an invisible force dragging him back, pulling him toward his body. He gasped, cold air filling his lungs as he coughed violently, the world snapping back into focus.

Pain shot through his ribs. Blood trickled down his face. He barely had the strength to lift his head, but his eyes found the strange eyed man once more.

The stranger extended a gloved hand.

Jonathan hesitated. These were the people who had destroyed his home. The ones who had taken everything from him. And yet... his fingers moved of their own accord, reaching out, grasping onto something solid.

That was the moment everything changed.

Jonathan now stared into those same multi-colored eyes that resembled those of Lysander Devereaux. The girl, Airella, was cautious, and being the only woman on a boat full of men, she was smart to be. Her wariness was a shield in this volatile environment. However, no man would be courageous enough to approach her, since they knew who her father was.

What he was.

Lysander Devereaux commanded a fearsome reputation that even the most reckless soldier wouldn't dare challenge.

"Can I help you?"

Airella kept a hand on the door to her private cabin held within the confines of the lower deck of the ship. Her posture was defensive, eyes narrowing slightly as a strand of blonde hair fell into her face.

Jonathan felt a magnetic pull towards her. He wasn't afraid. He had grown up learning to be her father's shadow, navigating the complexities of loyalty and danger that came with it.

"I just wanted to see how you were holding up. I haven't seen you around much the last couple of days," Jonathan gave her a soft smile. The only times he had seen her mostly was when everyone lined up to get their meals on one of the upper decks of the ship.

"I'm good, thanks," she began to close the door, but Jonathan was fast enough to reach out and stop her before it could shut. She looked at him in confusion, her brows knitting together as she tried to read his intentions.

"Sorry, I, uh…" Jonathan couldn't make out his words. He didn't want to sound like he was pitying her, but he also couldn't ignore the fact that she was alone on this journey. And after all her father had done for him, he felt like he owed it to him to aid her in any way he could. Her solitude on this voyage weighed on him—she seemed so strong, yet so isolated.

"Listen, Airella… do you know how to use that?" He pointed at Dawnbreaker, which she had kept strapped to her side the entire journey. The axe's hilt gleamed in the dim light, a symbol of protection and power.

She had thought little of it, but it'd probably be best if she knew how. It'd be hard to determine when she may need the skill to fight with a weapon, especially on a journey filled with unknown perils. Her eyes followed his gesture to the weapon, a flicker of uncertainty crossing her face before hardening into resolve.

"No, not really. I suppose I have a lot more training to do," Airella took a glance down at the floorboards, her mind already racing with the daunting task ahead.

"Well, if you're up for it, I could help train you when we have the time. I mean, how much different could a sword be from an axe?" He chuckled, gesturing to his sheathed blade. Airella's eyes widened in surprise.

"Really? You would do that for me?" After everything that

had gone down since being stripped from her family, it was a breath of fresh air to find kindness in someone.

Jonathan nodded, a small smile on his face.

"Yeah, I think it'd be good for both of us. Gives us something to do during this long journey," he replied. He had trained recruits in the past. "Are you free right now?"

She gave him a nod and stepped out of her cabin and into the hallway, her heart pounding with a mix of excitement and nervousness.

Jonathan led her to an open space on the upper deck, where they would have enough room to spar without the risk of knocking over anything or anyone. The deck was mostly vacant, except for a few crew members who were too engrossed in their tasks to pay much attention.

"First things first," Jonathan said, unsheathing his sword with a practiced ease. The metal caught the dying light, reflecting it with a sharp gleam. "Let's see how you handle Dawnbreaker."

"You know its name?" Airella grasped the hilt of her weapon and drew it from its sheath. The gold metal gleamed in the fading light, and she could feel its weight, not just physically but emotionally. It was more than just a weapon; it was a connection to her past and a symbol of what she had lost and hoped to regain.

"I'd recognize Lysander Devereaux's axe anywhere. He won many battles with that at his side. It was forged in the fires of Mount Vorel, tempered by the hands of master smiths who infused it with their skill and dedication. It has a soul of its own, a searing purpose that burns as brightly as the morning sun. Now, keep a firm grip," Jonathan instructed, positioning himself opposite her. His stance was steady and confident, a testament to his experience. "And remember, it's not just about strength. It's about balance and precision."

Airella took a deep breath, trying to steady her racing heart. She mirrored Jonathan's posture, feeling the cool metal of the hilt under her fingers. She recalled all the times her father would show her Dawnbreaker, memories that had been etched into her mind. It was his most prized possession, and she was far too young to understand why at the time.

As they began, Jonathan's voice was calm and guiding, offering corrections and encouragement. She focused on Jonathan's words and the feel of Dawnbreaker in her hands, determined to learn and grow stronger.

She mimicked his stance, legs apart, knees slightly bent. The first clash of their blades sent a shiver down her spine.

Jonathan was a patient teacher, guiding her through the basics with a steady hand and calm voice. Each swing, each block, was a small victory, a testament to her determination to survive in a world that seemed hell-bent on breaking her spirit.

As twilight turned to dusk, they practiced relentlessly; the air filling with the sharp sound of clashing steel and their labored breaths. There were moments when she faltered, her inexperience showing, but Jonathan was always there to correct her, to offer a word of encouragement. His eyes, sharp and focused, never missed a detail—adjusting her grip, repositioning her stance, ensuring every movement was precise.

"You're doing great," he said after an intense round. Sweat trickled down her face, but there was a light in her eyes, a fire that hadn't been there before.

"Thanks," she panted, wiping her brow. "I never thought I could actually do this."

"You have the heart of a warrior, Airella. With practice, you'll only get better," Jonathan gave her a nod of approval.

As they continued, Jonathan corrected her grip and posture with a patience borne from experience. With each swing of the axe, Airella felt a growing connection to the weapon—and to the man who taught her its secrets.

"Your father," Jonathan began during a lull in their training, "he had a way with the men. He led with strength, but also with heart."

"Was he... was he a good man?" Airella dared to ask.

Jonathan hesitated.

"He was the best of us," he finally admitted. "To me, he was more than just a leader. He was the father I lost."

"Lost?" Airella probed gently, sensing the depth of his sorrow.

"Before Eldaraya became my home, I was from Aurian. Your father spared my life after my village..." Jonathan's green eyes clouded over, his words trailing off as he grappled with the memory. "After they razed it to the ground. My family didn't survive."

Airella's grip on Dawnbreaker tightened, the revelation connecting them through shared loss.

"Yet you stayed," she murmured, understanding the complexity of his emotions.

"I had nowhere else to go," he confessed, his gaze flickering to the churning waters below. "Lysander saw potential in me. He trained me, made me his apprentice. But Duran..." Jonathan's expression hardened. "He and your father were close before... Before everything changed."

"Changed how?" Airella pressed, eager to understand the shadows that lingered behind Jonathan's eyes.

"Let's just say Duran's heart seems to beat to a different drum now." Jonathan's jaw clenched. "Be wary of him."

"Thank you," Airella said softly, feeling the weight of his trust. "For sharing that with me."

"Trust goes both ways," Jonathan replied. "And so does learning. Now, show me that strike again. Remember, with Dawnbreaker in your hands, you're not just fighting—you're continuing a legacy."

Airella nodded, the knowledge of her father's impact on Jonathan, and the soldiers at large, strengthening her resolve. With renewed vigor, she lifted the axe, the blade singing through the air as she repeated the motion, her movements becoming surer under Jonathan's watchful eye.

Jonathan shared more stories about her father, painting a picture of a man who was both a fierce warrior and a compassionate leader. Airella listened intently, each tale adding to her understanding of the legacy she was part of. The stories were not just about battles and victories but also about moments of kindness and wisdom, lessons that her father had imparted to those he led.

"Your father once said," Jonathan recounted, "that true strength is not just in the arm that wields the blade, but in the heart that guides it. It's that heart, Airella, that will make you a prominent leader."

Airella felt a surge of pride and a deep sense of responsibility. She was not just training to fight, but to uphold the values her father had lived by.

As the following day turned to night, the stars twinkled above them. The bond between teacher and student strengthened with each passing moment, forging a partnership that would be crucial in the battles to come.

With each strike and parry, Airella's confidence grew, her movements becoming more fluid and powerful. Jonathan's encouragement and guidance were unwavering, his belief in her evident in every word and action.

Finally, as exhaustion set in, Jonathan called an end to their session. "That's enough for tonight," he said, sheathing his sword. "Rest now, Airella. Tomorrow we continue."

Airella nodded, her body aching, but her spirit invigorated.

She knew that with Jonathan's help, she would be ready to face whatever challenges awaited them on the isle. As she walked to her cabin, she replayed the day's lessons in her mind, each detail etched into her memory.

And so, under the watchful stars and the gentle lull of the sea, Airella and Jonathan prepared for the dawn of a new chapter in their journey. The path ahead was uncertain, but they faced it together, their hearts and spirits united by a shared purpose and the knowledge that they were stronger together.

5

Airella leaned on the ship's railing, her gaze tracing the endless horizon. The morning sun cast a golden hue across the waters, painting a picture of tranquil beauty. A gentle breeze played with her hair, carrying the salty scent of the sea.

Suddenly, the clank of armor approached, breaking her reverie. Marcus Thornfield, a seasoned soldier with weathered lines of experience etched into his tanned face, stopped beside her. His armor, though worn from countless battles, gleamed in the sunlight, each scratch and dent a testament to his past struggles.

"Miss Devereaux," he greeted, his voice bearing the weight of many battles, each syllable a testament to his years of service. "I'm Marcus. Thought it time we spoke."

She turned towards him, noting the respectful nod he offered.

"I overheard you and Jonathan sparring the other night. Your father," he began, the mention of Lysander softening his features. "He saved more lives than just Jonathan's. He was a beacon for us all," Marcus paused. "But this war," he sighed, the words heavy with unspoken sorrow, "it took its toll on us, on both kingdoms. Even though it ended years ago, Eldaraya has yet to put its guard down."

"What did the war cost you?" Airella urged gently, sensing the depth of his reflection.

"More than coin can repay. Many of us were farmers, blacksmiths... fathers," Marcus continued, his hazel eyes clouding with the weight of loss. "My brother fell at the Siege of Shadowspeak. Many of us have lost kin. We fight not just for Eldaraya, but for those whom we've buried. But the truth is, the war changed us. It left voids where families and friends once stood." His voice faltered, a tear glistening at the corner of his eye, quickly wiped away with a rough hand.

"Is that why you still fight?" she asked, her heart aching for the pain she saw reflected in his eyes.

"Partly," he admitted, his voice a gravelly rumble that seemed to echo the weight of his past. "But I also fight for the hope of peace, so no one else has to endure what we did. So my niece, who is about your age, can live freely." His gaze turned towards the horizon, where the last light of the day was fading. "Yet there are those among us who wonder," Marcus continued, his eyes meeting Airella's with an intensity that took her breath away. "What fuels Aurian's fire so fiercely? What drives men to war against neighbors they once traded with?"

"Questions that haunt us all," Airella nodded, understanding blossoming within her.

Their shared loss was the silent undercurrent connecting them all. Their gazes locked, and in that moment, a silent understanding passed between them—a recognition of shared pain and the possibility of redemption that lay ahead.

In the days that followed, Airella spent increasing hours with Jonathan, their conversations ebbing and flowing like the tides of the vast ocean. She diligently practiced with Dawnbreaker until her arms ached from the exertion, but amidst the training sessions, it was during the serene moments when the ship creaked beneath them and the stars sprinkled the sky like a shimmering tapestry that their bond deepened.

"Did you ever think of leaving?" Airella's voice carried a hint of curiosity one evening.

"Every day," Jonathan admitted with a touch of vulnerability. "But Lysander, my mentor, instilled in me the values of duty and purpose. Those teachings have become an intrinsic part of me," he confessed, his voice gentle, brimming with respect for the man who had shaped his path.

"Like how my father's absence has shaped me," Airella pondered aloud.

"Exactly," Jonathan affirmed, offering her a reassuring smile. "Our identities are forged by the crucible of our experiences, Airella. It is these trials that render us resilient."

"Resilient and wary," she added wistfully, her mind drifting to Duran and the lingering unease that nestled in the recesses of her heart, the shadows of doubt that stubbornly refused to dissipate.

"True," Jonathan nodded in agreement. "Yet, together we stand stronger."

"Stronger together," she repeated, the words resonating within her like a soothing melody, infusing her spirit with a renewed sense of purpose and unity.

As the ship sailed through the nights and days, Jonathan and Airella's alliance flourished, each finding solace and camaraderie in the other's presence.

The wooden ship cut through the waves, its timbers groaning under the strain of the relentless sea. The crew, seasoned by countless voyages, moved with practiced precision, their faces etched with the salt and sun of many journeys.

Marcus leaned heavily against the railing, his gaze distant.

"I've seen too many young men go to their graves for this cause," he murmured, the salt air whipping at his tousled hair. His voice carried the weight of years spent in battle, each loss a scar etched into his soul. "And I fear the isle may be the end for many more."

Jonathan stood beside him, his arms crossed, the weight of his second-in-command mantle palpable.

"We knew the risks when we swore our oaths, Marcus. But it's not just about survival. It's what we're searching for that counts," Jonathan replied.

"Is it worth it, though?" A soldier named Darian piped up from behind them. "Our homes, our families… they're all a world away because of this endless voyaging. Always searching for a place to expand just so we have a place to run to when Aurian ignites a war again." The young soldier's eyes reflected the weariness of countless nights spent away from home.

"Home…" Marcus echoed softly, his thoughts drifting to the warmth of hearth and kin. Memories of laughter and love flitted through his mind, bittersweet in their absence. "But if we don't stand against the darkness, there won't be a home left to return to."

"My father believed in Eldaraya—its people, its future," Airella pitched in, "he fought to preserve that future, even if he didn't live to see it. Each of you has witnessed and experienced more than I, but let us not forget that his endeavors have not been in vain."

"Your father was a great man," another soldier, Brenner, added, respect lacing his words. "His legacy is the reason many of us still hold fast, despite the shadows that threaten to engulf us."

"Yet, what awaits us on this isle?" Darian questioned, his hand resting on the hilt of his sword. "What if it's just another failed voyage and more wasted time?"

"Whatever it is, we face it together," Jonathan declared, meeting each soldier's eyes. His gaze was steady, a beacon of resolve amidst the rising tide of doubt. "We carry the strength of Eldaraya in our hearts. That unity is our greatest weapon."

"Let's hope that's enough," Marcus sighed, turning his hazel eyes toward the darkening sea. "Because I want to believe we can return to tell tales of victory, not lie beneath foreign soil as whispers of defeat."

"Then let's make sure those tales are worth telling," Jonathan's steely resolve hardened his features as he looked upon the isle. The land ahead held secrets, yes, but also the promise of answers. "For Eldarayans present and future, we will prevail."

Their voices melded with the creak of wood and the rush of wind, a chorus of fears and aspirations carried across the open waters. As night fell, the isle grew ever closer, its secrets shrouded in darkness, waiting to be unearthed by those brave enough to step ashore. Every crewmember felt the weight of the moment, their collective breath held in anticipation of what was to come.

The ship's bow cut through the frothing waves, each crest they surmounted bringing them closer to the isle's sinister silhouette. Airella tightened her grip on Dawnbreaker, feeling its weight a reassuring presence at her side. Beside her, Jonathan scanned the horizon, his keen eyes reflecting the moonlight that danced upon the water.

"Look at it," Airella whispered, her gaze locked onto the looming darkness of their destination. "It's like nothing I've ever seen."

"Aye," Jonathan agreed, his voice low and steady. "And nothing we have seen can prepare us for what lies on those shores."

Around them, the soldiers busied themselves with preparations, the sound of whetstones sliding along blades into a grim lullaby. The rhythmic sharpening was a ritual they had perfected.

She watched as Duran moved among them, his confidence bolstering their spirits despite the palpable tension that clung to the salted air.

"Remember what we're searching for," he called out, his words carrying over the din of clanging metal and creaking timber. "Not just for glory, but for peace—for a future where our children won't know the horrors of war."

A murmur of agreement rose from the men, their faces set in grim determination. Airella felt a surge of warmth for these soldiers, united under the banner of hope. Their shared experiences, the battles they had weathered, forged a bond stronger than any blade.

As the ship neared the island, the smell of decay wafted over them, mingling with the brine. The stench was a stark contrast to the freshness of the sea air, a harbinger of the corruption that awaited. Jonathan returned to Airella's side.

"Are you ready?" he asked, his hand reaching out to steady her.

"More than I've ever been," she replied, meeting his gaze.

Her fingers brushed against his, a silent vow passing between them.

Together, they turned to face the encroaching darkness, their hearts pounding in unison. Dawnbreaker gleamed at Airella's side, a beacon of light amidst the shadow that enveloped the isle. The axe seemed to pulse with an inner light, as if responding to the courage that filled her heart.

"Whatever awaits us, we'll confront it head-on." Her words were a declaration, a promise to face whatever challenges lay ahead with unwavering courage.

Jonathan nodded, his eyes alight with the fire of anticipation.

"For our past and our future," he added, his hand now resting on the hilt of his sword.

As the ship drew closer, the first tendrils of mist reached out toward them like ghostly fingers, beckoning them into the isle's embrace. The fog swirled around the ship, creating an eerie atmosphere that heightened their senses.

In the distance, faint shapes moved within the mist, shadows of the unknown challenges that awaited them. But as long as they stood together, they knew they could face anything.

The soldiers, now fully prepared, gathered behind them in silent solidarity. As the ship's hull scraped the shore, Airella stood firm, Dawnbreaker ready to blaze a path through the darkness.

6

It had taken three weeks filled with a whirlwind of emotions and challenges before the soldiers finally arrived at their awaited destination. Airella, amidst the camaraderie of her fellow soldiers, wrestled with waves of homesickness that gnawed at her heart, aching for the familiar warmth of her family.

As the ship neared the island, relief washed over her. When she stepped off the vessel alongside her comrades, her boots sank into the soft embrace of the sandy shore. The sensation grounded her in reality—they had finally arrived.

"Land sweet land," Airella whispered, savoring the salt-kissed air and the temporary sense of freedom it carried.

The beach bustled with movement as the crew disembarked. Airella's gaze drifted to Duran. Though she had kept her distance since their first encounter, she found an unexpected solace in the silence between them.

Duran, ever the commander, wasted no time asserting his authority. "We make camp for the night," he announced. "At dawn, we begin scouting in assigned groups. Clear the area and remain in your armor." His tone left no room for argument, and the soldiers moved swiftly to follow his orders.

Airella and Jonathan worked in tandem, their combined strength and skill making quick work of the tents. Though space was limited, she was relieved to be granted one to herself.

Slipping inside, she removed her boots and sat on the rough fabric lining the floor. The night air was thick with the scent of the sea, the distant crackle of the campfire lulling her into drowsiness. She shifted uncomfortably in her armor but made no move to remove it. Instead, she closed her eyes, listening to the sounds of the island as she drifted into uneasy sleep.

A lone figure stood atop the rocky cliffs, his silhouette blending with the shadows of the night. Cloaked in black, he surveyed the island, his golden eyes gleaming like embers in the darkness. The land before him, once teeming with life, was now void of human souls—until now.

Sirius clenched his fists, unease prickling at the edges of his mind. For over two centuries, not a single human had set foot here. He had drained the last of their kind long ago, consuming their souls to maintain the delicate balance between good and evil. But something—someone—had disrupted that fragile equilibrium.

The wind played with his silver-white hair as he made his way toward the island's edge, his steps soundless on the uneven terrain. His gaze locked onto the unfamiliar glow beyond the dense foliage. A fire, flickering against the night.

Camp.

His lips curled into a knowing smirk. Humans had returned.

Sirius slipped through the trees, his movements fluid as shadows. The scent of burning wood mixed with something unexpected—rosemary. He frowned. A weak attempt at repelling Miscreants? If so, it had failed miserably, for he was already here.

The camp was modest but well-constructed. A ship rested on the shore, its towering masts slicing through the moonlit sky. Soldiers moved in the fire's glow, setting up for the night. He watched them from a distance, his sharp eyes assessing every detail.

Then, something—or rather, someone—caught his attention.

A tent, smaller than the others yet somehow different. He moved closer, brushing the fabric aside with slow deliberation. Inside, bathed in the warm flicker of firelight, lay a woman.

Sirius's breath hitched.

She was young but battle-ready, clad in golden armor that reflected the fire's glow. Strands of blonde hair framed her face, her features delicate yet strong. Even in sleep, she exuded quiet defiance, her lips parted slightly as if whispering secrets to the night.

Something about her stirred an unfamiliar feeling deep within him. Recognition. But that was impossible. He had long forgotten the faces of those he once knew. And yet, as he took in the soft rise and fall of her chest, the steady rhythm of her breath, a strange sensation curled in his gut.

Déjà vu.

Sirius stepped back, his pulse unsteady. He had not felt anything like this in centuries.

The fire outside crackled, casting shifting shadows against the tent's fabric. He hesitated, his gaze lingering on the curve of her jaw, the faint scar along her brow. A warrior, but not yet hardened by time. Not yet consumed by darkness.

She should have been nothing more than another soul,

another whisper of life waiting to be extinguished. But something about her made him pause.

His grip tightened around the handle of his scythe, the blade buried deep in the sand outside. He had come here for one reason—to reap. Yet, for the first time in centuries, hesitation clawed at him.

Fresh souls for the taking.

And yet, as he looked at her, something inside him whispered—

Not hers.

A rustle in the underbrush made him stiffen. He turned sharply, golden eyes narrowing as the night stirred around him. The island, long abandoned by men, seemed to breathe anew. The presence of humans had disturbed the equilibrium, awakening something long buried.

His gaze flicked back to the tent, to the woman who lay just beyond reach.

"Humans…" he murmured, the word foreign on his tongue. "It's been so long."

With a final glance at her sleeping form, he turned, melting back into the night. The weight of his scythe pressed against his palm, but for the first time, it felt heavier than before.

He had seen countless mortals come and go. None had ever made him pause.

Until now.

irella's eyes fluttered open, a strange stillness pressing down on her. A chill crept up her spine, her limbs frozen in place as if something unseen held her captive. A deep unease pooled in her chest, a nameless fear lurking just beyond the edges of her consciousness.

She forced herself to sit up, her movements sluggish, heavy. Fingers trembling, she reached for the lantern beside her, coaxing a flame to life. The dim glow cast flickering shadows across the fabric walls, but the warmth did little to ease the tension wrapping around her like an iron vice.

Had someone been in here?

Her heartbeat pounded against her ribs. If it had been a fellow soldier, they would have spoken. And Duran—Duran wouldn't bother sneaking. The thought of him checking in on her sent a shudder through her body, but the unease pressing against her skin told her this presence was something else entirely.

Slipping from her tent, Airella inhaled the cool night air, its crispness biting at her skin. Sand clung to her boots as she took careful steps forward, her fingers tightening around Dawnbreaker's hilt. The fire at the center of camp crackled softly, illuminating the empty space between the tents. Yet something was off.

Fresh footprints trailed across the sand, leading toward the forest.

Airella's breath hitched. The steps weren't from a soldier—they were too light, too deliberate. She followed them without hesitation, her pulse hammering with each step toward the tree line. The deeper she ventured, the thicker the shadows became, the air heavier, charged with something unnatural.

A rustling sound made her halt. She pressed herself against a tree, extinguishing her lantern's flame to avoid being seen.

"Who goes there?"

Duran's voice slashed through the silence, sharp and commanding.

Airella swallowed hard. If he caught her outside her tent, there would be consequences. She edged backward, careful not to step on anything that might betray her presence.

Then, movement—a figure ahead of her, barely visible in the darkness.

Airella's breath left her in a sharp exhale.

He stood just beyond the fire's glow, wrapped in a dark cloak, the fabric shifting around him as if alive. His presence exuded something dangerous, something otherworldly. But it was his eyes that locked her in place—golden, luminous, cutting through the shadows like burning embers.

She barely dared to breathe.

Had he heard Duran? Or had he sensed her?

As if in answer, the man tilted his head, and before she could react, he vanished. The wind carried a whisper, just for her ears.

"Run."

Airella's heart slammed against her ribs. She barely registered the brush of air against her cheek before she obeyed, turning on her heel and sprinting through the underbrush. Her pulse roared in her ears, her breath sharp and ragged. She barely had time to register the scythe flashing toward her before instinct took over.

She twisted, Dawnbreaker's hilt meeting the attack in a violent clash of metal. Sparks flared between them, illuminating his face for the briefest moment.

A pale complexion, sharp features, those golden eyes drinking her in with something akin to fascination.

Then he was gone.

Airella stumbled backward, panting, gripping Dawnbreaker with white-knuckled intensity. A cold sweat dampened her skin. The dark fog that had coiled around her dissipated, leaving her standing alone, bewildered.

"But… how?" she whispered.

A hand grabbed her by the hair, yanking her head back with brutal force. A sharp cry left her lips as she reached for the grip, but her assailant's fingers tightened.

"What do you think you're doing out here?"

Duran.

His voice was thick with fury, each syllable a blade slicing into her resolve. Before she could react, he wrenched her forward, dragging her out of the brush and shoving her toward the camp. Her boots scraped against the dirt as she fought to steady herself.

"You just can't follow orders, can you?" His grip found her collar, hauling her up so their faces were mere inches apart. His breath was hot against her skin, his gaze a volatile mix of rage and something darker. "Do you have any idea what would have happened if I hadn't found you first?"

Airella glared up at him, her defiance sparking despite the danger. "I can take care of myself."

Duran let out a short, humorless laugh. "That so? Because from where I'm standing, you look like a lost little girl playing warrior." His free hand grabbed her chin, forcing her to meet his gaze. "I should teach you what happens to soldiers who disobey."

Airella clenched her jaw, refusing to look away. "It won't happen again."

His grip tightened for a moment, as if debating whether to strike her. Then, with a sharp shove, he released her, sending her stumbling to the ground. "Damn right it won't."

The fire crackled in the suffocating silence that followed. Duran loomed over her, his shadow stretching long against the dirt.

"Get to your tent," he growled. "Now."

Airella pushed herself up, swallowing the bitter taste of humiliation, and stalked toward her tent. Every muscle in her body screamed for her to fight back, but she knew better. Not now. Not when she was still figuring out what had just happened in those woods.

She crawled onto her cot, gripping Dawnbreaker like a lifeline. Her mind replayed the stranger's golden eyes, the way his voice had curled around her like smoke.

Run.

She didn't know who he was.

But somehow, she knew this wouldn't be the last time they crossed paths.

8

The morning sun burned through the mist, casting long shadows over the camp. Airella blinked against the harsh light, her body aching from an unrestful sleep. The events of last night still lingered in her mind like fragments of a half-remembered nightmare. The golden-eyed stranger. The chilling whisper. Duran's brutal grip. Had it all been real? It felt impossible in the clarity of daylight.

Jonathan's voice cut through her thoughts. "Alright, gentlemen, we're splitting into three groups." His commanding tone carried easily over the gathering soldiers. "Group One will scout the coastline. Group Two will gather supplies—food, water, anything useful. Group Three will head deeper inland." He cast a glance toward the towering trees. "We'll move as far as we can before making camp."

"The more advanced scouting will be done with Group Three," Duran interjected, his voice sharp and to the point.

Airella subtly shifted closer to Jonathan's side, placing herself in Group Three. If she had to deal with Duran, she preferred to have an ally nearby.

Duran led the group of twenty soldiers into the dense forest, their path quickly swallowed by vines and thick undergrowth. Soldiers swung at the foliage with their blades, clearing the way.

"How'd you sleep?" Jonathan asked, stepping beside Airella. His voice was light, but his concern was real. "First nights on missions like these are always rough."

Airella hesitated. "Oh, you can say that again."

Jonathan chuckled. "Yeah, the bugs are crazy, right?" He grinned, but his expression turned comical as a branch swung back and smacked him square in the face. Airella clapped a hand over her mouth, stifling a laugh.

"Are you alright?" she asked, trying to keep her voice steady.

Jonathan blinked a few times, rubbing his forehead. "Yeah. Just testing my reflexes. Guess I failed."

Airella let out a small, genuine laugh, and for a brief moment, the tension lifted. But then she lowered her voice. "Jonathan… I think I saw someone last night."

Jonathan's brow furrowed. "Someone? Who?"

Before she could answer, Duran barked, "Get a move on!"

Airella gritted her teeth. "I'll tell you when we're alone."

Jonathan gave her a short nod, his expression unreadable.

Hours passed, and the weight of the heat pressed down on them. The soldiers' complaints filled the air:

"So thirsty…"

"Can we take this armor off?"

"My boots are melting."

Airella shook her head. So much for the King's finest. The amusement faded when Duran ignored them, pushing forward without rest.

Finally, they arrived at a peculiar sight—a village, eerily untouched yet unmistakably abandoned.

"Spread out. Check every house. Look for anything useful," Duran ordered.

"Sir," Marcus called, kneeling near the entrance of a dilapidated home. He picked up a tattered piece of dark cloth, rubbing the frayed fabric between his fingers. "This looks like it was left here recently."

Duran snatched the cloth, his expression darkening.

Airella, eager to get away from him, veered toward a small wooden house that hadn't yet been searched. The structure, though still standing, bore the weight of time—collapsed roofs, dust-covered beams, silence pressing in like an invisible force.

Her hand hovered over the door handle. An inexplicable hesitation gripped her, as though some unseen force urged her to turn back.

"Going in?" Jonathan's voice startled her.

She exhaled. "Yeah."

Together, they pushed inside, the air thick with the scent of decay. Dust swirled in the dim light as they climbed the creaking stairs to the second floor.

Airella froze.

In the corner of the room, a pile of skeletal remains lay haphazardly stacked, the bones gleaming unnaturally in the low light. A thick, viscous substance clung to them, dark and oily, filling the air with a faint, sickly odor.

Jonathan stiffened beside her. "What the hell happened here?" His voice was low, but Airella could hear the edge in it.

Neither of them moved.

Jonathan knelt beside the bones, inspecting them with a trained eye. "These aren't just old remains. Something preserved them. This village wasn't abandoned—it was wiped out."

Airella swallowed hard. The weight of her discovery pressed against her chest. "Jonathan... about last night."

$\mathcal{A}$irella's breath was shallow as she stood frozen in the decayed village house, her heart hammering in her chest. She and Jonathan had come searching for answers, but instead, they had found something far worse. Something lurking, something waiting.

From above, a figure watched. Piercing yellow eyes gleamed in the dim light filtering through the cracked wooden beams. The man—or whatever he was—stood motionless in the rafters, his presence a shadow that had gone unnoticed until now. Yet, he had been there, observing, learning.

Airella's fingers flexed around Dawnbreaker's hilt as an unsettling awareness crawled over her skin. She could *feel* something watching her, but she didn't know where from. The silence in the room was deafening, save for the slow creak of settling wood.

Then, in an instant, their gazes locked.

Her pulse stuttered, a shiver racing down her spine as golden eyes bore into her mismatched ones. The stranger's expression was unreadable, his gaze a challenge wrapped in dark curiosity. And yet, for a moment, something flickered there—recognition.

"Airella." Jonathan's voice came out tense beside her, his sword rising instinctively. "Who the hell is that?"

She swallowed. "He was watching us."

The stranger didn't move, his skeletal fingers still gripping the hilt of the scythe slung over his back. His dark cloak draped around his lithe frame, swaying gently with the breeze sneaking through the broken walls. There was something both mesmerizing and terrifying about him, a lethal grace coiled beneath the surface like a predator waiting to strike.

Jonathan took a step forward. "Are you one of the island's inhabitants?"

The man tilted his head, amusement flashing in those unholy eyes. "You ask questions when you should be running."

Then, without warning, the air shifted.

He moved—*fast*. Too fast.

Jonathan barely had time to react before the figure materialized in front of him. Skeletal fingers clamped over his face, and with a flick of unnatural strength, he hurled Jonathan backward through the window.

"Jonathan!" Airella shouted, her voice strangled as she saw him vanish from sight. The sickening crash of his body against the ground below made her stomach drop.

Rage surged through her veins like wildfire. Without thinking, she lunged, Dawnbreaker arcing through the air toward the stranger's throat.

But he was ready for her.

Their weapons clashed, the force of impact sending vibrations up her arms. He smirked, a knowing gleam in his eyes as their faces hovered inches apart.

"Bold," he mused, his voice low, rich, and taunting. "But you're untrained."

Airella gritted her teeth, shoving against him with everything she had. He barely budged. Instead, he pressed forward, his body impossibly close, his scent—a strange mix of ash and something almost *electric*—coiling around her senses.

A slow smirk curved his lips. "But not weak."

Heat surged through her, but not from anger alone. It was the way his breath ghosted over her cheek, the way his fingers flexed against her wrist as he twisted, forcing her off balance. He wasn't just playing with her; he was *studying* her.

Airella growled in frustration, using the momentum to duck beneath his grip and sweep her leg out. He let her move him, but only just, his body reacting like he was indulging her rather than defending himself.

"You fight like someone who hasn't had to before," he murmured as he caught her wrist again, twisting her back against the cracked wall.

"And you talk like someone who needs to shut up," she snapped, jerking her head forward in an attempted headbutt.

He dodged just in time, a low chuckle vibrating through his chest. "Fiery."

Airella wrenched herself free, panting, heart racing for reasons she couldn't quite place. He was toying with her, yet something in his stance had shifted. There was an intensity in his gaze that went beyond the fight.

A crashing sound shattered their focus.

"Airella!"

Duran and Marcus burst into the room, weapons drawn. Airella felt a rush of relief—until Sirius turned, his golden eyes flashing with something unreadable.

"Miscreant!" Duran spat, charging forward without hesitation.

Sirius didn't flinch. Instead, he moved with eerie grace, side-stepping just as Duran's sword came down. The reaper's skeletal hand shot out, seizing Marcus before he could react.

"No!" Airella's scream tore through the room as Sirius's bony fingers pressed against Marcus's face. The soldier's body convulsed, his eyes rolling back as his skin rapidly aged, his veins darkening as his very essence was pulled from him.

Marcus let out a ragged gasp, his voice strangled in his throat.

"Marcus!" Airella lunged forward, but Duran grabbed her arm, holding her back.

Airella's throat tightened. *Marcus had family. A niece. A home to return to.*

And now he never would.

The soul-eater exhaled slowly, as if savoring the energy surging through him. A faint hue returned to his once-pallid skin, his form appearing stronger, more solid. But the hunger in his eyes remained.

He turned to Duran, lips curling. "Care to join him?"

Marcus—what was left of him—let out a guttural groan before charging at Duran. The first-in-command barely managed to raise his sword before the undead soldier tackled him, pushing him through the window and towards the ground below.

Airella barely had time to register what had happened before she felt Sirius's attention snap back to her.

The room was silent, save for her heavy breathing. She clenched her fists, grief twisting into fury.

"You..." she seethed. "You monster."

Sirius tilted his head, as if considering her words. "Monster?" he mused. "I suppose that's fair."

White-hot fury ignited inside her. She turned back to the golden-eyed reaper, gripping Dawnbreaker so tightly her knuckles turned white. "You think you're Death?" she hissed. "Let's see how you handle facing it."

She lunged, this time not holding back. Their blades clashed again, but there was no amusement in his eyes now. She drove him back, striking with an unrelenting fury fueled by loss, by grief, by *vengeance.*

He caught her wrist mid-swing, twisting her into another sharp hold, but this time, she was ready. She hooked her leg around his, knocking him off balance, and they tumbled together. He twisted mid-air, and when they hit the rooftop of the next building, he landed on top of her, arms bracing on either side of her head.

For a moment, neither of them moved. Their chests rose and fell, breaths mingling in the cool night air.

He was solid and warm, despite the eerie coldness that clung to his presence. His grip on her wrist loosened, but his gaze bore into hers with something unreadable—something dangerous.

His lips parted, his voice a rasp of something unspoken. "Who *are* you?"

Airella's breath hitched. She didn't know why her heart was pounding so violently, whether it was fear or something else entirely.

She shoved against his chest, but he didn't move, just watched her with that maddening intensity. He reached down, brushing his fingers against her cheek where sweat and dirt clung to her skin.

Before she could react, he was gone.

Leaping from the rooftop, he vanished into the darkness, his whispered final word lingering in the air—

"Sirius."

irella recovered swiftly, peering over the rooftop's edge to trace Sirius's descent. Frustration bubbled within her, compelling her to drive Dawnbreaker's hilt forcefully into the rooftop in her vexation.

"Ugh!" Airella called out in frustration, slamming Dawnbreaker into the rooftop.

A deafening rumble filled the air, followed by the ominous cracking of stone and wood. With wide eyes, she watched in horror as the once sturdy roof below her began to splinter and give way.

In a split second, the structure groaned under the strain, then succumbed to the force of gravity. Airella plummeted through the collapsing floor, the sensation of free fall gripping her stomach in a vice-like hold. The impact of each level she crashed through was jarring.

Finally, as the descent came to an abrupt halt, Airella lay still amidst the chaos. Slowly, she pushed herself upright, wincing as she coughed up a cloud of dust and dirt that hung thick in the surrounding air.

Her eyes stung from the lingering dust, making it difficult to see clearly as she fumbled through the debris, searching for Dawnbreaker amidst the ruins of the once-grand building.

"Help!" She heard Duran's voice, a mix of desperation and fear echoing through the wind.

Reacting instinctively, Airella abandoned thoughts of her lost weapon and sprinted towards the source of the distress call. As she approached, the scene unfolded before her and her heart plummeted—it was Marcus who now was a decayed form twisted in a grotesque display of menace, cornering Duran against the rugged stone wall. Marcus' gnarled hands reached out, poised to inflict untold harm on Duran.

With a surge of adrenaline, Airella launched herself at him, her fingers finding purchase on the silver armor. She wrenched Marcus away from Duran with a swift and practiced motion, sending him crashing to the ground with a resounding thud.

In that brief pause, Airella's gaze fell upon Marcus at her feet. Once a man, now a twisted shell of his former self, the soldier lay squirming on the cobblestones. Marcus had served in the King's Army for over a decade and had a loving family waiting for him back home. The thought of reuniting with his family kept him going through the toughest times, and now his niece, who he cared so much for, will never get to speak to him again.

As she retrieved Duran's sword, a pang of sorrow tugged at her heart.

Marcus lunged at Airella with what she thought to be some type of battle cry, but she swung the unfamiliar sword in a horizontal motion with significant force, slicing off his mummified head. His head rolled, and she closed her eyes as she listened to his body make a thud when it hit the ground.

Airella's eyes continued to sting, and not just because of the dust from bringing that house down. Knowing that he was undead, she wasn't sure if cutting off his head would have worked. But now, he was unmoving. That was until she took a glance at his severed head.

With horror, Airella stepped back. Marcus was staring at her, making noises as he gnawed, growled, and clicked his teeth together. She held her breath, doing what she could to keep herself from vomiting.

She pulled herself together and raised the sword, sliding the blade into his head and finally reuniting him with the brother he had lost at the Siege of Shadowspeak.

Airella's heart raced as she turned towards Duran, who had been leaning against the building in agony.

"My ankle, damn it!" He roared.

Many of the soldiers swarmed in her direction. Airella's heart raced as she wondered where they had been all this time.

Her eyes fixed on Jonathan, who lay motionless on the ground. A soldier leaned over him, desperately searching for signs of life.

The tension in the air was thick, suffocating, until a voice pierced through, "He's breathing!"

Airella felt a wave of relief wash over her.

Her gaze shifted to Duran, his pained cries echoing in her ears. Men surrounded him, their hands working quickly to mend his injured foot.

Airella watched from a distance, her grip on the unfamiliar sword she held loosening as she dropped it to the ground.

As she turned to walk away, her eyes fell upon the remains of the fallen building, a stark reminder of the devastation that had unfolded. Dawnbreaker, glinting faintly under the debris, seemed almost out of place in the rubble. It lay there as if waiting for her to reclaim it.

Beside her weapon, a piece of tattered black cloth caught her eye, its edges frayed and worn from the violence of the day.

Airella bent down, her fingers tracing the rough fabric. A surge of determination rose within her. With a solemn resolve, she tied the dark cloth around Dawnbreaker's hilt, a silent vow of retribution for the pain inflicted on Jonathan.

As she walked away, the eyes of the soldiers followed her, their silent scrutiny weighing heavy on her back. Airella kept her gaze lowered, her steps steady but filled with purpose, each footfall a resounding echo of the battles yet to come.

"Airella Devereaux, you have some explaining to do," Duran glared at Airella from his cot. His eyes bore into hers, as if demanding answers that only she could provide.

It had been about a day since their harrowing encounter with the reaper who she had now come to know as Sirius.

The decision to retreat to the safety of the base camp had been unanimous among the soldiers, except for Duran. His unwavering determination to explore the uncharted territories of the island clashed with the caution that now lingered in the air.

"I overheard Jonathan mention you were familiar with that Miscreant." Duran grabbed her arm in frustration.

"No, I only saw him that first night—" Airella explained, but Duran cut her off abruptly.

"Don't you lie to me, girl!" His grip on Airella's arm tightened as he pulled her closer. "If you had seen him, why didn't you say anything? He could've turned us into those things while we slept. Yet you endangered us all! Marcus is dead because of you." With a forceful shove, he pushed her away.

"How was I to know he was capable of such things?"

"We're even." Duran's tone was firm. "I don't owe you anything. I saved you in that building while you were tangling with that Miscreant."

Sirius. His name was Sirius

With a heavy heart, she turned and stormed out of the tent where Duran was recovering.

As she trudged her way back to her tent, the weight of the situation sank in, and she collapsed onto her small cot. Miscreant. Those things were just myths, weren't they? But what other explanation could there be for today? Despite her fatigue, she couldn't shake off the feeling of unease that lingered in the air. The mysterious occurrences in the camp had put her on edge, urging her to remain vigilant.

High-pitched, maniacal chirps of laughter that echoed through the camp abruptly shattered the eerie silence, stirring a sense of dread in her. The sound seemed to pierce through her thoughts, overwhelming her senses as she struggled to maintain composure. She instinctively sat up on her knees, hands pressed firmly against her ears, mirroring the reactions of the other soldiers in their respective tents.

A wave of dizziness washed over her, the laughter blending with the chaos in her mind. As the world spun around her, she teetered on the edge of consciousness before succumbing to the darkness that enveloped her, the haunting laughter fading into silence as she blacked out completely.

11

"Sirius! You should be more observant of your surroundings," stated a shadowy figure on the outskirts of the soldier's base camp.

It had been hours since the fight, and the shadowy figure was actually his father. Well, that was what Sirius knew him as. The strange humanoid shadow took him in as a child and has cared for him ever since.

"You shouldn't be doing this to the humans, Father. They need their peace," Sirius said firmly, crossing his arms amongst the shadows.

He listened intently to the pained screams resulting from Father's high-pitched squeal. The setting sun cast an eerie glow, enhancing the ghostly atmosphere as Father's victims fell under his haunting wail.

"Need their peace? The last thing I remember, you were struggling to fight a little girl!"

It was true. He had indeed found it challenging to combat her. It seemed like a strange weakness had crept over him in her presence, as if something mysterious had taken hold of his entire being. A peculiar crinkle formed in his stomach as Father passed through him, dissipating into a cloud of black mist before coalescing once more.

"This could have waited until nightfall, when they fell asleep. I need to delve deeper into the motivations of these humans and understand why they have ventured here. It's crucial not to startle them prematurely. They were not meant to catch a glimpse of me today," Sirius expressed with concern.

"But they did," was Father's only reply.

Sirius took a deep breath as dim light surrounded his body, allowing him to take the form of the soldier that he had absorbed earlier. The soldier's comrades knew he was dead. However, the second-in-command didn't watch the end of the battle unfold. Perhaps if he could maintain this form, he could get the answers he sought with ease. Although the maniacal cries of Father's lullaby had temporarily knocked the soldiers out, Sirius decided that disguising himself would provide an extra layer of security.

As Sirius stealthily made his approach to the campsite, an eerie silence shrouded the scene. The people who were previously bustling around had now succumbed to exhaustion, their weary bodies collapsing where they stood.

Sirius swiftly closed the distance to Jonathan's hammock. Taking on the guise of the soldier, he leaned over the sleeping man. As Jonathan's eyelids fluttered open, they met Sirius's unwavering pair of golden eyes. Despite the transformation in appearance, Sirius's eyes remained a telltale sign of his true identity.

"You're not Marcus..." Jonathan's voice quivered. "Soul-eater. You killed Marcus. Why have you taken his form?" Jonathan reached for his knife.

"I need answers," Sirius loomed over him. He must have been notified that his fellow soldier had fallen by Sirius's hand.

The Miscreant crossed his arms and gave an emotionless stare once he settled next to Jonathan's hammock. "What is your kind doing here?" Sirius asked. "If you refuse to answer, I will slice off each of your fingers until you talk," he threatened, the weight of his words emphasized by an intimidating growl.

Jonathan gulped hesitantly. He slowly reached over the side of the hammock for his skinned canteen, his hands slightly trembling in the face of the imminent threat that lingered in the air.

"We are here by the order of King William of Eldaraya," Jonathan declared. "Our mission is to scout this island and evaluate its potential for habitation by our people. The expansion of our kingdom relies heavily on us. Our citizens need somewhere to live should our kingdom fall to our rival, Aurian, if they attack," pausing for a moment, he raised his canteen to his lips, taking a refreshing sip of water to quench his thirst.

Sirius found himself lost in contemplation, reflecting on his earlier encounter with the lone female soldier in their group. Airella. The memory of her remarkable strength during their recent battle lingered in his mind, prompting him to ponder the significance of her presence among them.

Her eyes stood out vividly in his mind—one icy blue, the other a captivating green. The mere recollection of those striking eyes stirred a mix of fascination and intrigue within Sirius.

"Why is that woman here?" the question slipped effortlessly from his lips.

Jonathan gave him a worried look, concerned he may hurt her next. He turned his head to the tent she slept in. "You mean Airella?"

Sirius leaned back against a log. He was determined to hear what the red-haired soldier had to say.

"She's just some girl," Jonathan clenched his fists, squeezing tighter to the knife in his palm.

Sirius just stared, not buying his answer. Sirius waited for Jonathan to continue, his golden eyes peering into his soul. Jonathan clenched his teeth in nervousness.

"She was called upon by our king. She is the daughter of a deceased war leader. It's believed that her family lineage shares some sort of supernatural abilities."

Jonathan's bones shook underneath his sun-kissed skin. Yet, the Miscreant felt remorse for him. Unlike Airella, he gave him the feeling of mercy, to let him live, to continue doing what he did long before traveling to the island.

"Supernatural? You do not know? What of the rest of the Miscreants on your lands?" Sirius questioned.

"Miscreants on our lands? Oh, no. Airella is not a Miscreant. All the Miscreants were wiped out years ago from Eldaraya. Perhaps the entire continent of Edros. We've only ever known them as myths. But now that we've found this place and the likes of you… I simply do not know anymore," Jonathan's quivering voice grew calmer with each breath. However, something about Jonathan's tone and demeanor gave him pause. There was fear hidden beneath the calm facade, and it made Sirius wonder just how much he truly knew about Miscreants. "So, you do not know of what lies beyond these shores?"

Jonathan then made him feel more interested in learning about this king, this kingdom. Not for just the souls to devour, but for the sake of learning. Sirius had never left the isle and was curious to know what lied beyond the ocean. He became more intrigued by the thought of markets, agriculture, different languages, and most of all… no Miscreants.

As Sirius pondered on the notion of a life beyond the island, his mind wandered to envisage bustling markets filled with vibrant goods, the sight of vast fields ripe with crops swaying in the wind, the sound of diverse languages mingling in the air, and above all, the absence of malevolent forces like Miscreants. The desire to explore these unknown lands grew within him, fueled by a curiosity that burned brighter with each passing moment.

"Tell me more about your people," Sirius's voice brimmed with eager curiosity. Lost in the tales of Edros and the unsettling conflict between Aurian and Eldaraya shared by Jonathan, he seemed to drift into a realm of imagination.

As time passed, an hour slipped away unnoticed, blurring the lines between strangers. A sense of camaraderie sparked between Sirius and Jonathan, yet a chill in the air hinted at a watchful presence—Father's silent vigil.

"What are you exactly?" curiosity laced the man's voice as he turned to Sirius.

The Miscreant, with a hint of weariness, let out a light sigh. The soldier facade dissolved, revealing Sirius in his cloaked, slender form. His gaze fixated on his bony hand, swathed in worn fabric.

"I'm not entirely certain. This guise has been my constant for as long as memory serves. However, through the ages, humanity has given me various monikers. Death, Miscreant, soul-eater, reaper... You see, mortals have always feared death. But what they cannot realize is that there is beauty in the unknown. A finality that brings closure and peace. And it is my role to ensure that this transition is peaceful and graceful for those departing. I am sorry your friend became collateral."

Jonathan sat in awe as Sirius spoke, his heart heavy with newfound understanding. However, he departed his gaze from Sirius at the mention of Marcus.

"And the humans," Jonathan shifted, "what happened to them? The abandoned village was proof enough that they once lived here." Curiosity piqued, he trailed behind Sirius, his voice tinged with skepticism.

"The humans were pests. Always hunting us down. So, the Miscreants wiped them out. It was a mistake, and we've been suffering for centuries because of it." Sirius spoke, a coldness lacing his words.

"So, what you did to Marcus back at the abandoned village," Jonathan began, his tone hesitant and sad, "how are you able to take his form?" He couldn't shake off the unnerving feeling that lingered after witnessing Sirius's uncanny ability.

Sirius met Jonathan's gaze before glancing down at his skeletal hands, their bony structure partially concealed by the cloth wrappings.

"It's not something I can fully control," Sirius confessed, a hint of remorse in his voice, "but I keep my hands covered to avoid any unintended consequences. I siphoned the life out of him and absorbed his essence."

Jonathan's features tensed, a wave of unease washing over him as he processed Sirius's chilling explanation.

Sirius entered a large, weathered tent, its flaps billowing gently in the breeze. Jonathan, his footsteps echoing softly against the canvas floor, eventually caught up with Sirius.

Inside, a makeshift desk stood at the center, adorned with a large piece of parchment. Resting beside it was a delicate feather and a small glass jar filled with a dark, viscous liquid.

Sirius approached the writing materials, stepping over the snoring form of Duran. His brow furrowed in confusion as he examined the unfamiliar tools.

Jonathan followed, watching with quiet curiosity. "You don't know how to read or write?"

Sirius shook his head, his voice a whisper. "No."

Jonathan huffed a small laugh, shaking his head. "You're something else."

Sirius ignored him, stepping back out into the night. He turned to Jonathan, his golden eyes flickering with thought. "I do not wish to harm your people. They intrigue me. Tell Airella... I am sorry."

Jonathan frowned. "For what?"

Sirius didn't answer. In a blink, he was gone, swallowed by the shadows.

$\mathcal{A}$irella woke up in her tent, the early morning light filtering through the fabric walls. As she sat up, a dull ache throbbed in her temples, a lingering reminder of the night's events.

She stepped outside and watched as the other soldiers emerged from their tents, each wearing a similar expression of confusion and disorientation.

As she walked, a wave of dizziness washed over her, causing her to sink down onto the sandy ground. Watching her comrades, she observed the growing anxiety etched on their faces, mirroring her own inner turmoil.

"This island is haunted. Let's get out of here!" Darian yelled out. He ran in frantic circles, his hands grasping at the shoulders of every man he passed. "We'll all be dead! This place isn't good for humans! Let's board the ships!" His words were punctuated by a laughter filled with a crazed intensity.

Amidst the chaos, Airella remained composed, her gaze unwavering as she observed Darian's escalating panic. As the commotion reached a fever pitch, a sudden cry pierced through the air.

"Duran is gone!"

The proclamation drew the attention of all, their eyes turning towards Brenner, who had just emerged from Duran's supposedly vacant tent. Airella's expression remained impassive, a mask of contemplation settling over her features as she made a silent decision to investigate the mysterious disappearance for herself.

With purposeful resolve, she approached the tent, the cloth entrance swaying gently in the night breeze. Stepping inside, a sense of foreboding washed over her as she confirmed the chilling truth—Duran was nowhere to be found.

"What's going on? What do we do?"

The scrambling soldiers seemed frightened and confused. Airella felt a surge of responsibility as she scanned the surrounding faces, seeking guidance and finding none.

"Jonathan," she whispered his name under her breath before she maneuvered through the crowd of men.

Her steps quickened as she made her way towards his hammock. To her dismay, Jonathan's hammock was empty.

This moment offered Airella an opportunity to embody the leadership qualities her father was known for in the past. She deliberated on her options—she could take charge, rally the soldiers, and seek a resolution to the madness unfolding, or she could succumb to the overwhelming pressure and retreat to the safety of the kingdom. Despite her inner doubts, a glimmer of determination flickered within her. She knew she possessed the potential to lead, to guide, and to protect the remaining soldiers from the impending crisis.

As she pondered her next move, the weight of the decision bore down on her, causing a momentary hesitation. Airella could feel the eyes of the soldiers on her, waiting for her command. In that fleeting moment of uncertainty, self-doubt crept in, clouding her thoughts. She turned away from the expectant gazes and took a deep breath, grappling with her conflicting emotions.

"Jonathan!" a man yelled, drawing attention to a familiar face emerging from the thick brush.

His disheveled red hair caught the sunlight as he jogged up to Airella with a wide, cheerful smile.

Airella, taken aback by this sudden encounter, stood frozen in place, her mind racing to comprehend the unexpected turn of events. His carefree demeanor completely stumped her, and she found it slightly unsettling.

With a swift motion, he scooped her up by the waist, spinning her around with an infectious enthusiasm that was hard to resist. Airella, though appreciative of the gesture, couldn't shake off the feeling of unease lingering at the back of her mind. She awkwardly waited for some semblance of an explanation, her eyes silently pleading for clarity amidst this whirlwind of emotions. After all, he had just appeared out of the woods, seemingly out of nowhere.

"I have so much to tell you, to tell all of you," Jonathan exclaimed.

Airella, noticing his sudden burst of enthusiasm, voiced her concern, "Jonathan, are you okay—"

But before she could finish, he interrupted, "Never been better, actually." His declaration caught the attention of the men nearby, who stared at him with mouths agape, unsure of what to make of the situation unfolding before them.

As the soldiers scattered in different directions to search for Duran, Jonathan locked eyes with Airella.

"I'll take care of him," she assured the concerned soldiers nearby, her unwavering focus on Jonathan.

He beamed at her, jabbering, "It'd probably be best if I told you first, anyway."

Intrigued, Airella pressed for more information, "Tell me why—"

"I met him, face-to-face. He is like nothing you'd expect," Jonathan revealed, the seriousness creeping into his voice as he mentioned Sirius.

Airella halted him mid-explanation.

"Is that where you've been?" Her fists clenched in a mix of emotions.

She wasn't just angry; she was also taken aback by the situation unfolding before her. Contemplating the implications of Jonathan's association with Sirius, a known threat, she struggled to reconcile his actions with his higher rank. Despite her own encounters with the stranger, she couldn't shake off the unease of aligning with someone perceived as a danger to their world.

"He's kind, yet misunderstood. You'll have to see for yourself. Come on, I'm sure we can find him," he began tugging on her arm, but Airella stood her ground with wide eyes.

In this moment, she couldn't help but think if Duran had to deal with this type of nonsense all the time. Perhaps it's why the old man had built up such an enormous wall meant to keep out any emotion and do what he always thought was best for his people, even if everyone else disagreed.

"You realize he killed Marcus?" Airella grimaced. "He brought him back from the dead to rip you and Duran to shreds. That thing, Miscreant, Sirius, whatever he is, engaged in battle against us. He even threw you out of a window from a two-story building," she recounted, her eyes welling up with tears. However, as Jonathan's words echoed in her mind, a flicker of doubt crept in—maybe there was some truth to it all, maybe she was simply letting fear cloud her judgment.

"We found him!" A group of men rushed out of the woods, assisting Duran as he limped on his hurt ankle.

Airella's heart raced as she sprinted in their direction, her mind filled with worry and relief intertwining in a chaotic dance. Meeting them halfway, she scanned Duran's pale face, a mix of concern and fear reflected in her eyes.

"Where was he?" Her voice trembled, her gaze shifting between Duran and the soldiers. Despite the dirt and bruises marring his features, he seemed fine.

"We found him wandering around along the border of the camp. We think he saw something." The soldiers' words were a lifeline in the sea of uncertainty. With gentle urgency, they carried Duran into his tent, their movements swift and practiced as they began their healing ministrations.

"He was in our camp last night, I'm telling you! He was in my tent, I just know it." Duran's voice carried through the camp.

Airella's eyes flicked back to Jonathan. His stillness spoke volumes. Determination etched in her features, she strode purposefully towards him.

"Jonathan, do you know anything about this?" Her voice was a mix of accusation and desperation, her hand gesturing in an arc before his unfocused gaze.

He hesitated, the lines of his face etched with conflict before straightening his posture.

"He wanted to let you know that he's sorry." Jonathan's words hung in the air.

Airella's expression wavered, a kaleidoscope of emotions swirling in her eyes. Shock, disbelief, and a glimmer of hope danced across her features, a storm brewing on the horizon of her soul.

"But that's not all," he began. "He wants to learn about us. He wants to know—" Jonathan tried to explain, but Airella's focus remained fixed on proving him wrong.

"Jonathan," she interjected, "we can't just trust this stranger right now, okay? Much less one who has tried to kill us. Our key priority is to scout the island and ensure our survival. Dealing with Miscreants around us constantly won't make it any easier. I'm in no place to give you orders, but if I were in your shoes, I'd keep this encounter to yourself." Airella rested her hand on his golden armor. She couldn't deny that she was adopting Duran's pragmatism.

Jonathan gazed at the ground for a moment before meeting her eyes again. "You're right, I guess I don't know what's come over me," he said, though his voice betrayed a hint of uncertainty that didn't escape Airella's notice.

Exhaling a sigh, Airella took a step back, leaving Jonathan to shoulder the responsibility in Duran's absence. Looking up at him, she suggested, "Perhaps we should explore further. There must be more to this island than meets the eye. Duran's reluctance to return to Eldaraya is clear, but it's a decision we need to respect. I can't mess this up, Jonathan. Being here means my family is going to be taken care of."

Jonathan nodded in agreement, his demeanor serious and devoid of his usual joviality. Airella couldn't ignore the absence of his usual smile and laughter, and she wondered if her lack of faith in him was the cause.

Biting on her lower lip in uncertainty, she wrestled with her desire to trust Jonathan completely. Yet, an unspoken doubt lingered, preventing her from fully committing to that trust.

"Attention, everyone," Jonathan's voice rang out, commanding authority. "We can't afford to waste any more daylight. Half of us will remain here to safeguard the camp and care for Duran, while the rest will venture further into the southern region of the island." His directive spurred the group into action, each member preparing for their respective tasks with a sense of purpose.

13

***

256 YEARS AGO

He had no intent to attack anymore. He only wanted her to leave so that she wouldn't die. However, when he saw her walking across the weak ice of the lake, his heart sank. Her panicked huffs of fear grew closer as they echoed throughout the snowy mountains. He now faced the decision of either watching her freeze to death or saving her after her body went under the chilling waters.

He let out a deep, rumbling growl that reverberated through the icy landscape. With a powerful leap that seemed to defy gravity, he soared from the shadowy entrance of his cave with a grace that belied his massive form. As he landed gracefully on the crystal-clear frozen lake, the ice beneath him shimmered with a delicate dance of light, reflecting the cold beauty of the winter moon.

Summoning his ancient powers, he focused his mind on the girl as her body fell through the ice. He channeled the essence of frost and snow, willing the elements to obey his command. Quickly, a large pillar of ice rose from the frozen depths, its form taking shape beneath the girl's limp body. The pillar grew steadily, reaching towards the starlit sky like a frozen sentinel standing guard over the icy waters.

As the pillar reached its full height, it swiftly lifted the girl's body above the shimmering expanse of the frozen lake. With a tender touch, he scooped her up in his arms, cradling her gently against his obsidian-covered chest. She lay motionless, her skin chilled by the icy water, her breath forming delicate clouds in the frigid night air. Her features, once flushed with life, now grew paler by the second.

The dilemma weighed heavily on his mind as he pondered the unfamiliar territory of this situation. How was this challenge different from the foes he had conquered in the past? The answers seemed to dance just out of reach, cloaked in the enigma of his conflicting emotions and thoughts.

He carefully positioned her on a massive rock that stood prominently within his cavern's depths. Thick stalagmites, covered the floor beneath them, while the walls displayed intricate engravings of his ancient language—a language that echoed tales of a long-forgotten era.

Intrigued by the presence of the girl before him, he leaned in closer, studying her features with a mix of curiosity and fascination. His trembling obsidian-covered hand reached out, brushing aside the strands of disheveled hair that veiled her face, a gesture laced with both uncertainty and tenderness.

Noticing her shiver from the chill that permeated the cavern's air, he swiftly retrieved a tattered brown blanket he had acquired from a distant village in times long past. He wrapped the worn fabric around her frame, aiming to provide a shield against the biting cold that lingered in the shadows of the cavern.

As time trickled by, each passing second stretching into minutes and hours, he remained unwaveringly vigilant by her side. Her restless slumber was punctuated by shivers, her head tossing from side to side in a rhythmic yet troubled dance, as the days slipped past like ghosts in a silent vigil.

An undercurrent of nervousness gripped him, his heartbeat echoing in the quiet cave. His eyes never strayed from her form, the flicker of concern evident in the furrow of his brow. It was in this suspended moment of anticipation that her eyes fluttered open, her consciousness emerging from the depths of sleep.

A soft moan escaped from her lips, followed by a gasp that filled the cavern's air, as she found herself in the dimly lit, damp cave. Momentarily disoriented, she gazed around, half-expecting the surroundings to dissolve like a mirage. Across the cavern, the ice hellion observed her with an inscrutable gaze, his presence looming in the shadows.

"Ciíñßæł," his voice reverberated against the rugged walls of the cave. His eyes shifted between her and the metal rod that he had carefully separated from her as she slept.

The blonde-haired girl couldn't remember anything that had happened. How did she end up in here, and how long had she been unconscious? Thoughts clouded her mind as her eyes scanned the interior of the cave, the dim light casting eerie shadows on the walls. The last thing she remembered was the sound of cracking ice.

She watched the hellion toss away his daggers with a cautious gesture. He wanted to prove to her that he meant no harm, his movements slow and deliberate. She flinched instinctively, pulling the rough blanket closer to her nose as if seeking solace in its familiar touch.

The tension in the air seemed to thicken as he continued to unsheathe his daggers, the metallic sound echoing in the confined space of the cave before they clattered to the ground. After he finished, he raised his hands above his head in a gesture of surrender.

As she tilted her head ever so slightly, her eyes, a striking shade of blue, showed a hint of trust in them.

"You don't want to hurt me, do you?" she asked softly, her voice barely above a whisper.

He shook his head in agreement, his expression softening slightly. "Mĕñtĕźł mœñdæžĕrį! Žîź î Zol…" his words trailed off, a sense of urgency in his tone as he glanced towards the entrance of the cave, as if expecting something or someone to appear.

Her gaze followed his, landing on her metal rod which lay a distance away from her.

She removed the warm, woolen blanket from her shivering body and rose unsteadily, relying on the damp cave wall for support as she sought to steady herself. She felt a wave of weakness wash over her, and a gnawing curiosity crept in, making her wonder how long she had been confined within this murky cavern.

"You can't speak my language, can you?" she inquired wearily, her fingertips tracing the uneven surface of the wall for balance. The horned, obsidian-covered figure before her slowly lowered his hands.

"Rætü," he grunted cryptically.

She furrowed her brow, interpreting his response as a negative. Continuing to explore the wall, her hand brushed against strange markings etched into the rough surface. With a sense of intrigue, she withdrew her hand, revealing a series of unfamiliar engravings, each telling a story unknown to her.

She couldn't help but ponder if the mysterious symbols before her were indeed his language. Her curiosity piqued. As her gaze shifted towards the cavern's deeper, darker recesses, a shiver of anticipation ran down her spine, wondering about the secrets concealed within.

With a determined sigh, she tore her attention away from

the ominous depths, back to the looming figure of the hellion, now mere steps away. Emboldened, she took a tentative step forward, away from the security of the cave wall. Yet, her legs, weakened by both fear and fatigue, betrayed her, causing her to stumble. Before she could plummet to the ground, the hellion's swift reflexes intercepted her fall, his touch unfamiliar and strangely coarse against her skin. With a final reassuring glance, the hellion let go of her arm, revealing eyes that glowed with an otherworldly intensity beneath his obsidian helmet, captivating her with their piercing blue light.

"Thanks," she whispered softly.

Her gaze shifted towards the cave's entrance, revealing a world blanketed in pristine snow. The urgency to return home pulsed within her; she knew loved ones would be concerned. Her father was likely in a state of panic by now. Yet, the task seemed daunting in her current state—each step a struggle against her unsteady footing, making the journey back home a seemingly insurmountable challenge.

The hellion gave a subtle nod. Perhaps there was a glimmer of understanding in his gaze, or maybe he merely nodded out of a sense of familiarity.

She studied him intently, noting the intricate spiraling of his horns that framed his head and the obsidian helmet that veiled his features. In that moment, she realized she had never been in such proximity to a Miscreant without facing imminent danger.

She gently placed her palm against her chest. "I'm Emmaline," she introduced herself, her voice tinged with uncertainty, unsure if her words would bridge the gap between them.

As he attempted to repeat her name, she nodded encouragingly, relishing the hint of his accent from his native tongue. He then echoed her actions, placing a hand over his chest and uttered, "Zol."

14

256 YEARS LATER

Hours had passed, and exhaustion clung to the group like a heavy fog. The soldiers pressed onward, their footsteps sluggish against the uneven terrain. The once-dense jungle had begun to thin, giving way to jagged rock formations that jutted out of the earth like the bones of a long-dead beast.

Airella trailed slightly behind, adjusting the weight of Dawnbreaker at her side. The thick cloak wrapped around her armor did little to ward off the damp chill that clung to her skin. As she pushed forward, something flickered in the corner of her vision—just beyond the towering rocks that led into the mountainous region ahead.

She froze.

Her pulse quickened as her gaze locked onto the shadowy figure slipping between the stone outcroppings. A trick of the light? A figment of her fatigued mind? Whatever it was, it had moved fast.

Airella's first instinct was to call out, to alert the others, but before she could open her mouth, a sharp voice shattered the eerie silence.

"Did you see that?" Brenner's voice rang out, tense and alert.

The young soldier's hand shot to the hilt of his sword, his knuckles turning white. His eyes, wide with unease, flickered toward the darkened cave entrance ahead.

Despite the creeping sense of dread clawing at her insides, Airella hesitated. There was something deeply unnatural about the cave ahead of them—it seemed to breathe, exhaling cool air that sent an involuntary shiver down her spine. It smelled of damp stone and something else—something foul and ancient.

"I think there's something over there," Brenner added, stepping closer. His words carried an unspoken dare, a challenge to anyone who might disagree.

Airella clenched her jaw, feeling the weight of their unspoken expectations. There was still time to turn back. They could pretend they had seen nothing, leave whatever was inside that cave undisturbed, and move on. That would be the logical choice.

But logic rarely dictated the actions of men who sought glory.

Jonathan, who had been walking a few paces ahead, turned back and frowned. "Brenner, what exactly did you see?" His voice remained steady, but there was a flicker of apprehension in his gaze.

Brenner shook his head, as if unsure himself. "I don't know. A shadow, maybe. Something moving. Could've been a trick of the light, but..." His eyes darted back to the cave. "I swear it was real."

Another soldier let out an irritated sigh. "We don't have time to go chasing shadows. We keep moving."

But before he could take another step, the ground trembled beneath their feet.

Airella's breath hitched.

It was subtle at first—a faint vibration, almost imperceptible. Then it grew stronger. Pebbles scattered across the earth, trembling as though in anticipation. The wind, which had been eerily still just moments ago, howled through the trees.

A deep, guttural sound echoed from within the cave.

Not the wind. Not the shifting of rocks.

A growl.

The soldiers instinctively raised their weapons. Jonathan stepped in front of Airella, shielding her without a second thought.

Airella tightened her grip on Dawnbreaker, her instincts screaming at her to prepare for a fight. The weight of the axe was familiar, reassuring, yet an unsettling truth settled in the pit of her stomach.

They were not alone.

The sound of shifting stone filled the air, followed by the unmistakable scrape of claws against rock. Something was waking. Something that had been waiting.

Airella swallowed hard. "We should go," she whispered, barely audible over the rising wind.

But it was too late.

Sirius called the place he had hidden in his humble abode, though in reality, it was nothing more than a secluded hollow beneath a canopy of intertwining vines, nestled deep in the heart of the island's dense woodlands. It stood at the edge of the frozen region, where the warmth of the jungle met the icy grip of the mountains—a contrast as stark as the worlds he and the humans came from.

He knew Father would come looking for him.

And sure enough, the shadowy figure emerged from the darkness, his voice a low, menacing growl.

"What are they doing here?"

Sirius didn't look at him, keeping his golden gaze locked on the distant glow of the humans' campfires. "They wish to claim the island as their own." He exhaled slowly. "And they are not alone in their ambitions."

Father's form wavered, shifting like smoke in the wind. "So they'll bring more?"

Sirius nodded. "An entire kingdom waits for them. Soon, more ships will come. More people. They intend to build a new home here."

Before he could continue, a bloodcurdling scream shattered the night air.

Both Sirius and Father turned toward the sound.

"The humans."

Sirius vanished into the shadows, his form dissolving into the darkness.

The moment he arrived, he knew they were in trouble. The soldiers had pushed too far into the unknown, their boldness leading them straight into the claws of a Miscreant.

Perched behind the thick trunk of a tree, the winged beast lay in wait, its gleaming talons flexing in anticipation. It had chosen Jonathan as its prey. The red-haired soldier stood oblivious, gripping his sword tightly.

The Miscreant moved like a ghost, silent, patient—then it lunged.

The soldiers screamed for Jonathan to move, but fear had locked his limbs in place.

Sirius leaped from the trees, his scythe flashing in the moonlight. He met the beast mid-air, their gazes locking in a moment of stunned realization before he brought his blade down.

A shriek of agony erupted from the creature as its wing was severed, feathers and blood raining down around them.

"Run." Sirius's voice cut through the chaos.

Jonathan didn't hesitate.

The soldiers, stunned into inaction, stood frozen in place. They had never seen anything like this.

The winged Miscreant, now grounded, let out a guttural snarl. Its glowing red eyes burned with fury as it turned its attention to Sirius.

With a deafening roar, it lunged.

Sirius barely raised his scythe in time, deflecting its slashing claws. The impact sent him skidding backward, his boots digging into the dirt. The creature was fast—too fast.

It struck again, but Sirius twisted away, spinning his scythe in a graceful arc. He slashed at its chest, but the beast caught the blade in its claws, its talons sinking into the metal. Blood seeped from its grip, but it refused to let go.

Sirius narrowed his eyes. "That was a mistake."

With a sudden surge of strength, the Miscreant shoved him back, sending him sprawling. Sirius hit the ground hard, the wind knocked from his lungs. He barely had time to roll before the beast was on top of him, pinning his arms down with its monstrous claws.

It raised one massive talon, ready to rip out his throat.

Then—a sharp whistle through the air.

A blur of gold and steel flashed in Sirius's vision. The

Miscreant howled in agony, its severed claw tumbling to the ground.

Sirius's eyes darted up.

Airella.

She stood over him, Dawnbreaker raised, her chest rising and falling with labored breaths. Drops of blood—Miscreant blood—splattered across her face, her blue and green eyes burning with fierce determination.

For a moment, he simply stared.

She had saved him.

His instincts screamed at him to push her out of the way—and so he did.

With a sharp shove, he threw her down, his body shielding hers as the Miscreant lunged again. He felt the beast's claws slice through his cloak, raking across his chest. White-hot pain lanced through him, but he ignored it.

Instead, he grabbed his scythe and with one swift, clean motion, he severed the creature's head from its body.

Blood sprayed the ground as the beast's body collapsed.

For a long moment, the forest fell silent.

Sirius finally allowed himself to fall to his knees, his breathing ragged. The pain in his chest flared, and he glanced down, grimacing at the sight of liquid gold seeping from the deep gashes across his torso.

Damn.

He heard a rustle behind him and turned just as Airella shoved him hard in the shoulder.

"You threw me?" she hissed, glaring at him.

Sirius exhaled sharply, rolling his eyes. "You're welcome."

"I had him!" Airella shot back.

Sirius raised an eyebrow, amusement flickering in his golden eyes. "You mean the part where you stood there looking shocked? Yes, that was very intimidating."

She let out an exasperated growl, stepping closer. "You're insufferable."

Sirius smirked despite himself. Even with her face streaked in blood, hair wild and breathing heavy, she was... entirely captivating.

"And you're reckless." His voice lowered, his gaze locking onto hers. "You could have been killed."

Airella scoffed, stepping closer still. "So could you. And yet, here we are."

For a moment, neither of them moved.

They were too close.

Sirius could feel the heat radiating from her, could see the fire in her mismatched eyes. She was still gripping Dawn-breaker so tightly that her knuckles had turned white.

She wasn't afraid of him.

She should be.

Sirius's smirk faded. His injuries burned, reminding him of the real danger here.

Not her. Him.

He tore his gaze away, dragging himself to his feet with a pained grunt.

Airella followed suit, studying him carefully. "You're bleeding gold."

Sirius clenched his jaw. "Yes, thank you for your observation."

Her lips pressed together, and to his utter disbelief, she reached out, brushing her fingers along the edge of his torn cloak.

"Does it hurt?"

Sirius swallowed. "No."

Airella raised an eyebrow, her skeptical gaze unwavering. "Liar."

Before he could respond, the sound of rushing footsteps snapped them both out of the moment.

Jonathan and the remaining soldiers burst through the underbrush, weapons raised, their eyes darting between Airella and Sirius.

Sirius stiffened, his golden gaze flickering over the gathered soldiers, then back to Airella.

She took a slow step away from him, her grip tightening on Dawnbreaker.

But she didn't raise it.

She hesitated.

She wasn't sure which side he was on.

Neither was he.

The edges of his vision blurred, the weight of his wounds finally crashing down on him. His limbs grew heavy, the world spinning as the pain burned hotter, sharper.

Then—everything went black.

15

Sirius awoke to a cacophony of shouts, voices laced with anger, confusion, and heated accusations rattling the air outside the tent. His ears rang from the commotion, but one voice stood out—a desperate plea slicing through the noise.

"Release him!"

Airella.

His eyes fluttered open, vision swimming as he tried to make sense of his surroundings. A sharp pull at his wrists made him realize they were bound, thick, coarse ropes digging into his skin. He attempted to move, but his arms were tethered to a wooden pole, leaving him utterly restrained.

The metallic scent of blood and sweat filled his nostrils. The red fabric lining the tent blurred into focus, the rich color almost mocking him. He let out a slow breath, head throbbing from what he assumed was the aftermath of the fight.

Then a low chuckle cut through the chaos outside.

"Finally awake, Miscreant?"

Sirius lifted his head, and there he was—Duran, standing before him, smug and triumphant.

Duran's scarred face twisted in amusement, but the amusement didn't reach his cold eyes. He looked Sirius over like he was something to be toyed with.

"How was your nap?" His voice dripped with condescension.

Sirius gave him a slow, lazy smirk. "I had better accommodations in the dirt, but thanks for the hospitality."

Duran's jaw ticked. He took a step closer, his armor clanking, casting a long shadow over Sirius. Up close, Sirius could see the faint gray threading through his dark hair, the weathered lines of age cutting across his tanned skin.

Sirius tilted his head. "You look tired, old man. Is it the stress? It must be exhausting being an insufferable bastard all the time."

Duran's fist lashed out, striking Sirius across the face. The impact snapped his head to the side, a sharp sting blooming across his cheek. A coppery taste filled his mouth, but Sirius merely rolled his jaw and smirked, licking the blood from his split lip.

Duran crouched, getting in close, his breath hot and sour. "Listen closely, filth. I don't know what the hell you are, but you are my prisoner. And when we return to Eldaraya, you will be paraded like the monster you are."

Sirius arched a brow. "A parade? How thoughtful. Will there be snacks?"

Duran sneered. "You'll be caged, experimented on—maybe displayed in the royal gardens for amusement. Perhaps we'll let the children throw stones at you. Does that sound fun, Miscreant?"

Sirius's expression darkened, his golden eyes flashing dangerously.

"You talk too much," he said, before slamming his forehead into Duran's nose.

A sickening crack filled the tent.

Duran stumbled back with a roar, clutching his face as blood gushed from his nose.

Sirius grinned, despite the throbbing pain in his own skull. "Oops."

Duran's eyes blazed with fury as he lunged, grabbing Sirius by the chin, forcing him to meet his gaze. "You're going to regret that, creature."

Sirius's lips curled in a mockery of a smile. "Oh, I highly doubt that."

And then he bit down on Duran's hand—hard.

A howl of agony tore from Duran's throat as Sirius's teeth sank deep, tearing through flesh and bone. Duran yanked his hand away, but it was too late—Sirius spat a chunk of his index finger onto the ground, the severed piece landing with a wet plop.

He licked his lips, tilting his head. "You taste disgusting."

Duran staggered back, staring at his bleeding hand in horror. For a long moment, there was only the sound of his ragged breaths, his body trembling in pain and rage.

Then he snapped.

With blinding fury, he drew his sword and lunged—only for a voice to bark from outside the tent.

"Duran! That's enough!"

Jonathan.

Duran froze, his sword hovering inches from Sirius's throat. He let out a ragged breath, then sheathed his weapon with a snarl, his entire body trembling with barely restrained fury.

"Lock him down. Double the watch." His voice was cold, lethal.

Then he stormed out, blood still dripping from his mangled hand, his curses trailing behind him.

For a moment, Sirius simply sat there, rolling his aching jaw, the warmth of his own blood cooling against his skin.

Then two nervous-looking guards entered, eyeing him like a caged beast. One of them shifted uneasily. "What do you think it is?"

His partner swallowed, glancing at Sirius's golden eyes, his skeletal hands, the way he sat too still, too unbothered by what had just happened. "I... I don't know. He looks human, but he's not."

The first guard nodded quickly. "Yeah. I think we should—uh—go stand outside. Just in case."

The second didn't argue. They both backed away, their faces pale, before scurrying out of the tent like frightened rabbits.

Sirius sighed, tipping his head back against the pole, a smirk playing at his lips despite the throbbing pain in his body.

That had been fun.

Along the serene shoreline of the camp, Airella took a moment to cleanse her face, rinsing away the remnants of dried Miscreant blood with water from a nearby spring. In a rare moment of respite, she had shed her battle-worn armor, opting instead for the comfort of a white blouse, layered with a brown leather vest, pants, and sturdy boots. It was a change of pace, considering Duran rarely allowed them out of their armor.

As she strolled back into the camp, Airella observed a flurry of activity in the darkness, with men scurrying in various directions, clutching wood and supplies.

Rumors circulated that Duran had instructed the construction of a makeshift cage to transport their captive, unwilling to leave him unguarded while the others were out surveying. The fear of his potential escape loomed large among them.

Airella watched as the team hastened to piece together the prison wagon. In that moment, Duran trudged past her, his hand wrapped in a blood-soaked rag, a trickle of blood staining his purple-hued nose.

"Duran, what happened to you?" Airella inquired, not solely out of genuine concern, but also driven by an insatiable curiosity.

His response was grim, laced with a mix of pain and resentment, "That Miscreant—no, that pest—bit my finger off and broke my damn nose!" The intensity of his words matched the fury in his eyes as he forcefully pushed Airella aside, his relentless stride reflecting a determination untamed by the recent altercation.

She felt an unsettling twist in her stomach, unsure of Sirius's true allegiance. His actions seemed to oscillate between saving lives and committing the unthinkable. Still, a part of her believed that Duran may have had it coming. As she nibbled nervously on her lower lip, her gaze fixed on the imposing figures of the armored guards stationed at the entrance to the tent Duran had just exited.

Seating herself on a rough tree stump near the crackling campfire, she found herself locked in a staring contest with the tent. She willed herself to move, only to halt abruptly. This internal debate dragged on for what felt like an eternity until a surge of determination finally urged her to rise from her seat and traverse the sandy ground towards the tent's entrance.

Just before she could step inside the tent, a pair of soldiers clad in polished armor stood guard, their imposing presence halting her progress.

The soldier on her left spoke first, "No one is to enter. Duran's orders."

Airella couldn't help but notice a subtle tremor beneath his stoic facade, a glimmer of fear betraying his outward composure.

Pondering the soldier's reaction, Airella's thoughts meandered. Was he scared of her?

As she stood at the threshold, a hushed whisper reached her ears from the soldier on her right.

"Just let her through, Daniel. She's The Executioner's daughter." The soldiers shared a quick glance with one another, weighing the consequences of denying her or Duran.

Airella caught wind of his words, stirring a sense of unease within her. She grasped fragments of her father's legacy, aware that he once commanded the king's military forces with great power. However, the finer intricacies of his reign remained elusive, evading her grasp like a fleeting shadow.

With a steely resolve in her gaze, she countered the soldiers' apprehension with a measured response.

"In case it has slipped your notice, I possess the same formidable abilities as my father once wielded," she asserted, her voice carrying an air of undeniable authority. "Should you dare to question my capabilities, I invite you to put them to the test."

With a graceful movement, she navigated past the two soldiers, leveraging their trepidation to her advantage as she breezed through the tent's billowing flaps.

irella's breath hitched as she stepped closer to the bound figure before her. Sirius.

Even tied to a post, his presence commanded attention. His silver-white hair was disheveled, strands sticking to his forehead, and fresh streaks of golden blood trailed from the corner of his mouth. His cloak had been stripped away, revealing the battered expanse of his chest, the gray hue of his skin marred with dried, glimmering wounds.

He should have looked defeated. But he didn't.

Sirius met her gaze with a slow, deliberate smirk, his golden eyes glowing beneath the dim torchlight. "I'm just getting a lot of visitors lately, aren't I?" His voice, deep and teasing, sent an involuntary shiver down her spine.

Airella crossed her arms, narrowing her eyes to mask the unease curling in her stomach. "Funny. I didn't take you for the entertaining type."

Sirius tilted his head, amusement flickering in his gaze. "Depends on the company."

She rolled her eyes, willing away the warmth creeping up her neck. "Why did you help us? Why did you help me?"

Sirius exhaled through his nose, the flickering torchlight catching the subtle twitch of his jaw, as if the answer wasn't one he was used to giving.

"Why did you cut off that beast's claw for my sake?" he countered, his voice smooth, challenging.

Airella blinked, caught off guard. "That's not the same."

"Isn't it?" His voice was low, almost seductive in its quiet intensity.

She clenched her jaw, unwilling to play into whatever game he was spinning. "I'm not the one tied to a post," she said pointedly.

Sirius's smirk deepened. "And yet, here you are, standing so close. Tell me, Airella… are you here because you're curious? Or is it something else?"

Her heart stuttered, pulse quickening. His voice—his eyes—they pulled at something inside her, something dangerous.

"I couldn't just let you die," she said finally, quieter than before.

"And neither could I," Sirius murmured.

Airella exhaled, trying to regain control of her thoughts. She pulled a roll of bandages from her belt. "Your chest—those wounds need to be wrapped before they get worse."

Sirius arched a brow. "Concerned for me?"

Airella didn't answer. She simply stepped closer, kneeling beside him. His breath hitched when she pressed the bandages against his chest, wrapping them carefully around the deep wounds. He was warm. Warmer than she expected.

Her fingers brushed against his skin as she worked, and a jolt of something sharp and electric shot through her.

Sirius inhaled slowly. "Your hands are soft."

Airella swallowed. Damn him.

She kept her focus on securing the bandage, even as the heat between them became unbearable.

Sirius watched her, his golden eyes half-lidded. "Tell me, Airella... what will you do when you realize I'm not your enemy?"

She froze for half a second.

Then, she tightened the bandage just a little too much.

Sirius hissed sharply.

"Oops," she murmured, feigning innocence.

Sirius let out a low, breathy laugh, his teeth flashing in the dim light. "Oh, you are going to be trouble, aren't you?"

Airella finally stepped back, shaking off the feeling of his skin beneath her fingers. "You're coming with us when we go further into the island," she stated, avoiding his gaze.

Sirius smirked lazily. "Ah, so I'm a prisoner and an asset?"

She glanced over her shoulder before leaving the tent. "Try not to bite anyone else before morning."

Sirius grinned, leaning his head back against the pole. "No promises."

The moon cast a soft glow over the campsite, illuminating the fluttering shadows of the surrounding trees as a gentle breeze rustled the leaves. As she walked, she couldn't help but overhear the sounds of commotion going on inside of Duran's tent. Being as curious as she had been to see Sirius just moments before, she peeked into the entrance of the tent.

"Duran, we have to go back." Jonathan pleaded, but Duran remained steadfast, his eyes unwavering.

"Shut up. You don't have the authority to give me orders." Duran's retort echoed through the tense atmosphere.

"We can't afford to linger here any longer, can't you see that?" Jonathan implored, frustration evident in his gestures. "It's too perilous for our people to stay."

Duran's confidence surged. "We possess the means to triumph over these creatures, Jonathan. We must strategize, understand our foes' vulnerabilities. Then, we'll rally our forces from Eldaraya and—"

"Stop trying to be Lysander! What are you trying to achieve? You're not him, so cease this pursuit of an unattainable ideal. Your tactics are turning you callous, not formidable." Jonathan interjected firmly.

Duran looked at him, and his gaze eventually turned into a deadly stare. By this time, his broken nose had swollen and turned purple. His hand had been carefully tended to, the bandage neatly wrapped around his hand.

"Get out of my tent," Duran spoke with coldness wrapped in his voice.

Jonathan, feeling a surge of disappointment, shut his eyes for a moment, taking a deep breath to steady himself, before he turned to walk out of the tent. Airella, sensing his dismissal, stamped out of his path, feeling invisible in his presence.

As she gathered her thoughts, she turned back to the entrance of the tent, a mix of determination and fear swirling within her. She knew that now was the opportune moment to seek answers about her father, to unravel the secrets shrouding her past.

Summoning her courage, she took a tentative step forward and ventured inside. Upon entering, she noticed Duran had his back turned to her, his imposing figure dominating the space.

"Now what, Jonathan?" He growled, his voice dripping with disdain as he glanced over his shoulder. Realizing that the intruder was not Jonathan, he swiftly adopted a more menacing demeanor. "What do you think you're doing in here? I didn't give you permission to enter. And where is your armor? We have a Miscreant captive in our camp and you're not wearing your armor? Just get out of my sight." Duran's eyes blazed with fury, a storm brewing behind his intense gaze.

"I need answers," Airella asserted, her gaze unwavering as she met Duran's fiery stare. Despite her inner turmoil, she masked her trembling voice with a facade of bravery, determined not to show weakness.

Duran advanced towards her, his massive frame looming over her, casting a shadow of intimidation.

"I said get out," he snarled.

Airella refused to yield this time. She silently vowed that things would change, that she would no longer be fearful of this ill-tempered man. In a defiant gesture, she stood her ground as Duran seized her shoulders, his forceful grip propelling her towards the exit.

"Wait!" She squirmed, feeling the urgency rising within her. "I need to know more about my father."

Duran let out a sigh, his grip loosening as he looked at her intently. "Why, you little rat... eavesdropping, eh?"

"Please, Duran. I have to know." She heeled him as he made his way to a worn chair.

Duran, with a nostalgic look in his eyes, reached for a rag dampened with cold water and pressed it gently against his bruised nose.

"That man," he began, a faint smile tugging at the corners of his lips. "He was a legend, a friend, and Jonathan's mentor. Lysander Devereaux was what every ordinary man dreamed of being. His strength was extraordinary, unmatched, and his willpower was akin to that of a god."

Airella listened intently, captivated by the image being painted of this remarkable figure.

"His nickname, The Executioner," she inquired with genuine curiosity, her eyes reflecting the desire to uncover the missing pieces of her father's tale. This was the part of the story she felt had eluded her for so long, and now she was on the brink of unraveling its secrets.

"A master of war and an inspiration to Eldarayan soldiers everywhere," he began, his voice carrying a weight of history and reverence. "During the War of Aurian, he single-handedly turned the tide of battle, felling thousands of enemy soldiers with just one swift stroke of his legendary battle axe. Dawnbreaker. It was astonishing and the most inhuman thing anyone had ever seen." His eyes shifted to the axe strapped to her back.

Pausing for a moment, Duran's eyes seemed to drift into the past, lost in contemplation of the events that had unfolded. "He proved himself not just as a warrior, but as a leader of unmatched skill and courage, earning the esteemed title of the king's hand and war general. As his closest confidant," Duran's voice softened, "I couldn't help but become envious of my best friend. What had he possessed that I lacked? What secret to success had eluded me for so long?"

Turning to face Airella, Duran's demeanor shifted. "The both of you... initially, many believed it to be the work of dark magic, myself included," he confessed. "But now, with the truth laid bare about the secrets hidden on this island, I realize it's something far more profound, far more extraordinary." Rising from his seat, Duran loomed over Airella, casting a shadow that seemed to stretch beyond the confines of the room. "You, Airella Devereaux, are no mere mortal."

Airella, taken aback by the gravity of his words, felt a surge of defiance rise within her.

"What do you mean?"

"Your lineage," he began, his voice barely above a rough whisper, "it's not of this world. The blood that flows through your veins carries a legacy far older, far more powerful than you can imagine. You, my dear, are a being of legend, a Miscreant born of ancient myths and forgotten truths."

Airella's disbelief was palpable, her voice tinged with uncertainty. "No, that can't be true. My mother is human, and so was my father." Her words faltered, her arms rising in a futile gesture of defense as Duran drew closer.

"I will not let you or anyone else get in my way of my duties. I will surpass your father and bring glory to Eldaraya with the civilization of this island. As for you, you'll just end up like your father. Locked away and left for dead along with the rest of the Miscreants that lurk upon this island," he spat, his words filled with venom, causing Airella to stumble and fall to the floor of the tent, the weight of his threats crashing down on her.

Her eyes filled with tears, reflecting the turmoil within her. What if it was all true? What if she really was one of those things the elders spoke of in hushed tones? The thought sent shivers down her spine as she scrambled to her feet, a sense of dread pushing her to flee the tent, leaving Duran standing alone in his place, his cruel intentions echoing in the air behind her.

17

"Get in there!" yelled a burly soldier as he ushered Sirius forward into the cramped confines of the prison wagon.

As Sirius was pushed inside, he kept a stoic countenance

A sense of foreboding lingered in the air, causing Jonathan to bow his head in silent regret.

Beside him stood Airella. Sparing a moment of eye contact with Sirius, she secured the cage door with a resounding click.

"Get moving!" Duran demanded.

Several men, their faces grim with determination, heeded his command and began pulling on the heavy wagon, their boots sinking into the muddy ground with each tug. The strained grunts of effort mingled with the squelching sounds of the wheels turning, marking their slow progress forward.

What felt like endless hours dragged on as the group of soldiers navigated through the thick, tangled forestry of the island. A creeping sense of unease gradually enveloped Sirius, casting a shadow over his thoughts. The once impenetrable forest thinned out, allowing slivers of light to filter through the canopy. It was in this moment that Sirius felt a sudden chill in the air.

As the surrounding trees grew sparser, a wave of dread washed over Sirius, sending a shiver down his spine. The realization dawned on him like a bolt of lightning, sparking a surge of panic within him. Frantically, he pulled at his restraints, desperation etched across his face, silently pleading for a glimmer of hope from the men encircling him.

"We have to turn back," Sirius's voice rose in urgency, his heart pounding in his chest as the gravity of the situation sank in. His usual stoic demeanor cracked, revealing a raw emotion he now struggled to contain.

Fear.

As the group of soldiers pressed onward, the air grew colder, wrapping around them like a sinister cloak.

Sirius's breath misted in the icy air, his muscles tensing with a sense of foreboding. With a defiant growl, he strained against his bonds, desperation flickering in his eyes as he sought a way to avert the looming danger.

"Quiet in there!" shouted a nearby guard.

In rebuttal, Sirius's frustration took over. He pulled on his bindings. Though, without his scythe, a weapon that he used to channel his power, he was almost as weak as the humans surrounding him.

"What are you on about? We haven't come across any threats." Duran, annoyed but curious, hunched his back in front of the prison wagon. He held his hands on his hips as his purple nose stared back at Sirius.

"If you keep going, you will all be at the mercy of an ice demon. You will all freeze," Sirius tried to warn them of the ancient ice hellion that lived in the snowy, treacherous area of the island they had just crossed into. It was Zol's territory, a place where legends of icy terror thrived and nightmares became reality.

Duran merely responded with a quizzical look, skepticism etched on his face. He thought that the prisoner's words were absolutely insane, impossible to believe.

"We'll freeze? Did he just say we'll freeze?" Asked Darian, his hand trembling as he drew his sword.

"It's nothing but nonsense." Duran's voice boomed, his frustration clear. "This scoundrel doesn't even know the meaning of fear. Look at him, devoid of any emotion." His words reverberated through the tense air as the soldiers exchanged uneasy glances, some nervously scratching their heads while observing Sirius in the cage.

"I don't know, Duran," Jonathan chimed in, his voice tinged with uncertainty. He had edged closer to the cage, weapon at the ready, like the rest of the group. An uneasy atmosphere enveloped everyone except Duran, who seemed unfazed by the unfolding events.

"I suggest you run," Sirius's voice cut through the tension, his brows furrowed.

Suddenly, a rustling in the trees captured the soldiers' attention, making them jump in alarm. A dark figure leaped down from the tree, landing behind a group of soldiers in a swift, calculated move. The aberration swiftly plunged two long daggers into two different chests simultaneously.

"Żîłćaæł ßîbłîś rävičh! Get out of my forest!" The hellion known as Zol bellowed with fierce intensity. Clad in obsidian armor, a large helmet obscuring his face, and eyes glowing ominously, Zol's menacing presence underscored that fear was not exclusive to humans but also instilled in the hearts of Miscreants.

The beings who inhabited this secluded island for centuries

were well-versed in the legend of the dynamic couple. Emmaline, a Miscreant Slayer, found an unlikely mate in the form of the ice hellion, Zol. Their clandestine companionship evolved into a deep bond, eventually leading to their mating shrouded in secrecy. Tragedy struck when Emmaline died, triggering a descent into madness for Zol, who laid claim to the expansive territory they once shared harmoniously. This poignant tale was etched into the memory of Sirius, resonating with the complexities of love, loss, and the haunting echoes of a once idyllic existence.

"Holy sh—" Duran exclaimed, but his words became drowned out as a wave of panic swept through the group. A few men, overwhelmed by fear, seemed to freeze in place, their bodies turning into statues with just a touch from Zol's palm. Chaos ensued as Duran's lack of understanding of karma led to disastrous consequences.

Amid the commotion, Airella's eyes widened with fear as she hurried towards Sirius's cage. Despite her trembling hands, she skillfully wielded Dawnbreaker, effortlessly slicing through the thick rope that bound the door of the prison wagon shut.

With a swift motion, the door swung open, allowing Sirius to scramble out of the wagon. Airella wasted no time, grabbing his clothed hand firmly and leading him into the dense forest, their figures quickly disappearing into the shadows.

18

Airella's breath came in shallow pants as she leaned against the rough bark of a nearby tree. Her legs trembled beneath her, exhaustion settling deep in her bones.

Across from her, Sirius stood watching, his golden eyes burning like embers against the frigid air. Even bound and battered just hours before, he still carried himself with an unnatural grace, his scythe balanced effortlessly in his hand.

"Why save me? Again?" he asked, voice low, laced with something Airella wasn't ready to name.

She met his gaze, searching for an answer she didn't have. Wasn't it obvious? She had freed him because…

Because what?

Before she could say anything, she felt it—a presence. Cold and unnatural.

Airella gasped as a hand landed on her shoulder.

The chuckle that followed was wrong. Twisted. Chaotic.

She spun around—and froze.

Jonathan stood before her, but he was not Jonathan.

His face, usually so full of warmth and kindness, had been

hollowed out by something sinister. A shadow curled beneath his skin like an infection.

"Father." Sirius muttered, his voice barely above a whisper as he recognized the malevolent presence that had haunted him for years.

The shadow that had taken residence in Jonathan seemed to revel in the fear that emanated from both Sirius and Airella.

"This is the girl?" The shadow's voice resonated with a hint of amusement. "She's too small to be defeating someone like you in battle, Sirius."

"Jonathan?" Airella's voice trembled with confusion as she searched Jonathan's eyes for recognition, but found none.

Father, with an enigmatic tilt of his head, flashed a crazed smile.

"No, this is Father," Sirius declared. "Well, he's not my biological father, and that's not his name. His real name is—" Father silenced any further revelation by gently pressing his finger against the reaper's lips, abruptly halting Sirius's words.

"No, no, you must tell no one my little secret." Father chided, giving Sirius a pat on the head. Despite the playful scolding, there was a hint of malice in his eyes.

"I suggest you exit my friend's body," Sirius responded nonchalantly.

Father then shifted over to Airella. As he placed a hand on her head, a surge of energy seemed to pass between them. She fidgeted at his touch, her mind racing with a myriad of questions and doubts.

"Not her," Sirius stated. At his words, Airella took an immediate step backward, accidentally bumping into the tree she had been leaning on just minutes before.

"Hmph," the voice came from Jonathan's body as they watched him turn back to Sirius. "It's been quite a while since I've had any contact with humans. So many years."

Airella watched with wide eyes as a dark essence escaped from Jonathan's mouth, swirling and forming into a humanoid figure. It almost resembled a shadow, but with a strange three-dimensional quality.

Jonathan's body collapsed as soon as he returned to himself, and Airella caught his upper body before he hit the ground. She landed on her knees, cradling Jonathan's head gently in her lap.

"Jonathan? Jonathan?" Her voice echoed softly as she gently shook him by the shoulders.

"Oh, he'll be fine." A faint smirk played on Father's shadowy lips.

She shot a wary glance at the figure, her eyes narrowing with suspicion. Her fingers reached for Dawnbreaker, only to realize it wasn't there. She realized she must have dropped it when they were ambushed. She then glanced back to see that Father appeared to morph into nothing more than a swirling black fog.

Jonathan took a quick gasp of air seconds later, quickly capturing everyone's attention. His heart raced as he frantically shot up straight, his eyes darting in every direction, searching for any sign of familiarity.

"Where am I?" he uttered in a mixture of confusion and urgency. "Where are the others?"

"I'm not sure," Airella responded, her gaze shifting around, only to realize that the dark figure known as Father was no longer in their presence.

Sirius remained silent, his expression unreadable as he observed Jonathan's every move.

Airella's mind jumbled with questions, the encounter with the ice hellion leaving her unsettled. How many more Miscreants like him lurked among them? The urgency of finding the others weighed heavily on her mind, knowing that being separated was far from ideal in their current situation. Despite her reservations, she couldn't shake the feeling that Sirius held the key to some answers. For now, she allowed him a chance to slip away, focusing instead on regrouping with the rest of their party.

"We have to find the others before the sun goes down," Airella informed Jonathan as she rose to her feet.

Recognizing the importance of the task at hand, Jonathan nodded in agreement.

With a shared determination, Jonathan and Airella set off, their steps guided by hope of discovering even the slightest clue to the whereabouts of their missing companions. As they ventured forth, a sudden interruption halted their progress.

"Wait."

The voice pierced through the air, causing both the redhead and the blonde to freeze in their tracks. Airella turned around, her eyes meeting Sirius, who stood steadfastly in the same spot they had left him.

In the aftermath of their encounter with the obsidian hellion, Sirius appeared to have reverted to his usual composed demeanor, concealing any trace of emotion that might betray his inner thoughts.

"You never answered my question."

Airella stared at him for a moment as she replayed the memory of breaking him out of the confines of the prison wagon. The image of them escaping into the dense forest lingered in her mind.

"You've proven to have a good heart, Sirius," she finally spoke. "That's why I saved you." She grappled with the weight of her decision to put her trust in a Miscreant, realizing the gravity of the risks they were taking. Airella felt like she owed him a further explanation, but finding the right words felt like an impossible task at that moment.

Turning away, she resumed her steps, her gaze evading any

contact with the reaper trailing behind her. Despite her efforts to focus on the path ahead, she couldn't shake off the lingering sense of his presence hovering over her and Jonathan.

"Are you coming with us?" Airella asked Sirius. Sirius, with an air of nonchalance, gazed blankly at her for a moment before finally speaking.

"I might as well," he said, his tone carrying a hint of amusement. "You humans manage to find trouble pretty effortlessly. I suppose I could offer my assistance. Not to mention I also need my scythe back." With a casual stride, he caught up to their pace.

Jonathan raised his eyebrows and flashed a knowing smile at Airella. "He could prove quite handy if we encounter any unforeseen challenges."

Airella, though accustomed to Jonathan's unwavering positivity, couldn't shake off a sense of unease. She exhaled slowly, anticipating the reactions of the soldiers once they realized they were accompanied by Sirius.

As they continued their journey, the familiar sound of distress reached their ears, prompting Airella to scan the surroundings. Her gaze settled on Duran, who kneeled on the ground, visibly exhausted and struggling to catch his breath.

He looked up at the trio, disgust filling his eyes once his gaze landed on Sirius. "Why, you... you knew! You knew about that ice Miscreant... he caught at least half of our men!" Duran unsheathed his sword and charged at Sirius, who stood there in silence, a flicker of defiance in his eyes.

Jonathan quickly stepped into Duran's path, his hands held up in a calming gesture. "Duran, calm yourself. Violence won't solve anything here."

Duran's chest heaved, and he fell to his knees as exhaustion seeped through his every pore. Sweat dripped from his brow, mingling with the dust of their surroundings. He looked up at the vast expanse of the sky, his breaths ragged, and a deranged chuckle escaped his lips.

"We're going to die out here, all of us," he muttered. Shaking his head in disbelief, he covered his face with a trembling hand.

"What are you talking about?" Airella's voice carried a note of concern as she approached Duran. She reached out a hand to steady him as he leaned against a large rock.

"All our supplies, at least half of our men. It's gone," lamented Duran. "We're going to be stranded in this hellhole."

"That's right... we abandoned everything in our haste to escape that ice Miscreant," Jonathan interjected.

"Zol," Sirius murmured.

"Alright, let's retrace our steps and retrieve what we lost. We know what to expect now. We can be careful and just take back what we need," Airella proposed. She was fully prepared to do whatever she needed in order to be reunited with Dawnbreaker. She recalled dropping it while freeing Sirius from his confinement, a moment of oversight that now weighed heavily on her mind.

"Are you stupid?" Duran's voice growled with an edge of urgency. "Just take a moment to look around. The situation we find ourselves in is dire! If we backtrack to retrieve our supplies now, the odds of us facing slaughter are alarmingly high!"

"He's not wrong, Airella," Jonathan chimed in reluctantly.

"Do you honestly believe we could safely navigate the journey back to the ship without essential provisions, such as food, water, and our limited arsenal of weapons? Sirius is without his scythe, I'm without my axe, and Jonathan is without his sword. Returning to camp without our gear would be risky. Our best bet is to reunite with as many soldiers as possible, regroup, and strategically retrieve our belongings." Airella's impassioned plea resonated through the group.

Duran and Jonathan exchanged uneasy glances.

Even Sirius, known for his stoic demeanor, couldn't conceal the hint of fear in the presence of the mysterious obsidian creature. Despite the trepidation hanging in the air, the task at hand was clear, a necessary mission that weighed heavily on every member of the small group.

Throughout the rest of the day, the team diligently scoured the area in search of survivors. By day's end, they had located a small fraction of the men they set out with. They found some huddled together, others wandering alone, and unfortunately, a few could not be accounted for.

The sky was darkening, painting streaks of orange and pink across the horizon as the sun started its descent. Despite the fading light, a sense of urgency lingered in the air. They knew they had to act fast to retrieve their supplies before nightfall.

As they set off toward the spot where they last encountered the elusive ice hellion, each step seemed to echo louder in the encroaching silence. The biting cold crept in, causing the men to huddle closer and exchange uneasy glances.

Jonathan, being his optimistic self, tried to reassure them, "It's okay, he may not even be around anymore."

With every passing moment, the wind picked up strength, whipping through the air and sending swirls of snowflakes dancing around them. Soon, a sprinkling of snow dusted Airella's blonde locks, causing her to wrap her arms around herself to ward off the chill. Her gaze shifted to Sirius. Despite the freezing temperatures, he stood resolute, his focus unwavering as they ventured further into the icy unknown.

The prison wagon, which had been torn to bits at Airella's doing, came into view. Everyone kept their distance, and Duran stood before them all as they waited for him to give the queue. They all waited in silence, spreading out so no one would get in someone else's way.

Duran waved his hand in the air after giving a quick scan of the area, signaling to everyone that it was okay to head out for the supplies.

The remaining soldiers, their breath visible in the cold air, moved swiftly and silently towards the barred wagon. Each step seemed to echo the weight of their mission.

Airella felt uneasy as she snuck her way through the soldiers that had become frozen statues, their faces twisted in expressions of fear and surprise. Her heart plummeted when her gaze fell on two familiar faces she knew all too well.

Her eyes stung at the frozen sight of Brenner, his loyal companion Darian at his side. She tried to reach out, her hand trembling, but found herself unable to move, paralyzed by grief and shock. The dreadful realization filled her mind that it was too late for them. They were dead, their lives snuffed out in an instant, leaving behind only these cold, unmoving shells.

As they reached the wagon, the soldiers stooped to collect their bags of weaponry, armor, and meager rations. The fallen bodies of their comrades served as stark reminders of the peril that surrounded them, driving home the reality that danger lurked at every turn.

Airella turned her gaze towards the wagon, her breath forming frosty puffs in the frigid air. She bent down to retrieve Dawnbreaker where she had dropped it when freeing Sirius from his confining cage. As her fingers closed around the worn handle, a chill ran down her spine, a sense of foreboding settling over her like a heavy shroud. Suddenly, a wave of paralysis washed over her, freezing her in place as if she had stepped into a waking nightmare. Her mind raced with a thousand unspoken fears.

The glowing icy blue eyes glared straight into hers, piercing through the darkness. His obsidian helmet, etched with intricate patterns, concealed his facial features as he lay motionless on his stomach atop the creaking wagon. His intense gaze seemed to search her soul, questioning her very existence.

"Em...ma?" The hellion's voice was a whisper as he inclined his head slightly, drawing closer to Airella. With a fluid motion, he shifted onto his hands and knees, his eyes never leaving her face.

Surprised, Airella instinctively took a step back, her heart pounding in her chest.

"Sirius." Her voice quivered. In this moment of uncertainty, she called out to him before comprehending why his name escaped her lips.

The ice hellion stood menacingly on the rooftop of the prison wagon. His intense gaze surveyed the bewildered men below. Slowly, he drew his twin daggers, each blade glinting in the dim light. As he prepared to strike, a chilling transformation overtook him—icy crystals materialized around his helmet and the horns on his head, radiating an otherworldly aura.

With a deafening screech that pierced the air, he unleashed a primal cry of anger and frustration, the words foreign yet filled with malice.

The men, paralyzed by terror, barely had time to react before Duran's urgent warning shattered the silence.

"Run!" he shouted, his sword raised defensively as he retreated towards the safety of the forest.

Airella witnessed the hellion's ruthless pursuit, his speed and savagery unmatched. With a firm grasp on Dawnbreaker, she steeled herself for the impending confrontation. However, a sudden tug on her arm diverted her attention, pulling her focus away from the unfolding chaos and towards an unknown force beckoning her away from the impending danger.

"You can't fight him. He's too dangerous." Sirius, who now had his cloak and scythe in hand, warned.

"Airella, we have to follow the others. We can't lose them

again!" Jonathan's voice cut through the panic and chaos. He dashed towards her, his footsteps leaving imprints in the freshly fallen snow.

Sirius and Airella exchanged a glance, a silent agreement passing between them. With a nod, they followed Jonathan's lead, their steps steady but determined as they trudged through the snow-laden landscape. Each of them carried bags of supplies, the weight a physical reminder of the challenges ahead.

At that moment, amidst the swirling snowflakes and the distant echoes of danger, it became clear. Airella's resolve was unwavering; she was determined to leave this island, even if it meant defying Duran's wishes.

19

Homeward bound to Eldaraya, the ship's sails billowed as it cut through the sea.

The soldiers on board, previously watchful and ready for battle, now found themselves slumped against the railings or sprawled across the deck, their bodies clad in armor rising and falling in sync with their deep, tired breaths.

Airella leaned on the prow, her gaze firmly fixed upon the distant horizon where the skyline of Aramore would eventually emerge. Her thoughts were a whirlpool of emotions, stirred by the rhythmic sound of the waves crashing against the hull. Each wave seemed to carry with it a piece of her past, stories of battles fought and won, of friends lost and memories created on the treacherous isle they now left behind.

As she watched the waves, a shadow fell beside her. Sirius stood there. His golden eyes reflected the vastness of the ocean, mirroring its endless mysteries and depths.

The soldiers gave him a wide berth, their wariness palpable in the space they left around him. But it was not fear that filled

Airella's mismatched eyes; it was a cautious intrigue, a puzzle yet unsolved.

"Are you glad to be leaving the isle?" Airella asked. The question hung in the air, delicate, like a glass orb that could shatter with the wrong answer. The isle had been a place of trial and tribulation, of heartache and hardship, but it had also been a crucible in which she had forged her strength and resolve.

"Leaving? Yes," Sirius replied, his gaze never leaving the horizon. His voice was calm, yet layered with an undercurrent of suppressed emotion. "I have no desire to remain tethered to Father's whims."

Jonathan approached, his green eyes bright and alert. "You helped us instead."

A faint smile ghosted Sirius's lips, his expression softening as he glanced at Jonathan. "Our paths are intertwined now," he softly replied. "Eldaraya's fate is mingled with my own, whether by chance or destiny. On the isle, I was only Father's prisoner. I can't believe it took until meeting you before realizing it."

Jonathan nodded. The trust wasn't whole, not yet, but they had sown the seeds and watered them through the shared experience of survival and escape. The camaraderie that had formed through their shared struggles showed faint glimmers of hope.

As the night fell, stars sparkled in the expansive sky, silently witnessing their journey. Guided by the shared resolve of its passengers, the ship continued on its course. The future was uncertain, but together, they would face whatever challenges lay ahead, bound by their newfound unity and the promise of a brighter tomorrow.

"Father will not relent easily," Sirius continued. There was a quiet intensity in his eyes, a flicker of determination that burned brightly despite the shadows of doubt that lingered at the edges. "He desires control over the Miscreants and humans alike. I cannot abide by such tyranny."

Airella's heart thrummed at his confession, the gravity of his decision to turn away from such power resonating deeply within her. She felt the weight of their journey, the burden of what lay ahead, and the strange comfort found in this unlikely companion who, like her, sought to defy the darkness that threatened their world.

"Then we stand together," Jonathan affirmed, clasping Sirius's shoulder in a gesture of camaraderie.

"Indeed, we do," Sirius said, meeting Jonathan's grasp with a nod, his eyes reflecting a shared determination.

Airella turned back to the sea, the spray of saltwater lightly caressing her face. The isle, with its shadowy threats and hidden dangers, was behind them now. Ahead was Eldaraya, her home, her duty. And beside her stood new allies—unexpected, perhaps, but no less bound to her cause.

"Your mother," Sirius said quietly, breaking the comfortable silence that had settled over them, "and your brother, Arii—do they know of your exploits?"

Airella's mismatched eyes shimmered with unshed tears as she turned to him, a soft smile curving her lips. He must have overheard her countless conversations with Jonathan about how she wanted nothing more than to see them again, to feel the embrace of her family once more.

"I hope to tell them myself," she confessed. "Though I miss them more than words can express."

"You'll like them," Jonathan chimed in, his voice full of warmth and sincerity. "If they're anything like Airella, they'll be brave and kind." He glanced at Airella, admiring her strength and grace.

"Speaking of bravery," Sirius interjected, a rare lightness to his tone, "tell me more about this." He nodded toward Dawnbreaker, strapped securely to Airella's back.

"Ah," Airella breathed, her fingers tracing the gem-encrusted hilt. "Dawnbreaker is more than mere metal. It's my heritage, my father's legacy, passed down through generations. The blade was forged in the fires of Mount Vorel, tempered by the hands of master smiths who infused it with their skill and dedication. It has a soul of its own, a searing purpose that burns as brightly as the morning sun." She recalled Jonathan's words from their first training sessions.

She paused, lost in the reverie of her father's stories, his voice echoing in her mind. "My father always said that Dawnbreaker chose its wielder. Its power is not just in its blade, but in the hope and strength it symbolizes. When I hold it, I feel connected to my past, to my family, and to the legacy that I must uphold."

"Your father," Jonathan said softly, his green eyes meeting hers, "he would be proud of you, Airella. Proud of the warrior you've become. He always spoke of you with such admiration, and now, seeing you wield his axe, I can understand why."

Her vision blurred, Airella blinked rapidly, fighting the tide of emotion. "Thank you, Jonathan," she murmured. "Every time I draw Dawnbreaker, I feel his spirit guiding me, giving me strength."

As the trio shared stories of Lysander's valor and their own hopes for the future, darkness fell upon the ship, wrapping the deck in shadow.

Unseen by the three companions, a dark fog moved with ghostly silence below deck. Father slid from shadow to shadow, his presence a malignant whisper in the chill night air. His movements were deliberate, calculated—the grace of a predator stalking its prey.

He halted briefly, listening intently to the muffled sounds of camaraderie above. The corners of his mouth twitched into a sinister smile—undetectable, unseen—as he continued his clandestine mission. His eyes gleamed with malevolent intent as he reached a hidden compartment below deck.

"Soon," he whispered to himself, "they will know the true meaning of fear." His sinister grin widened as his every movement was a calculated step toward an unknown, but undoubtedly perilous, future.

Father's shadowy movements were near-silent, his translucent cloak brushing against the rough wood without a sound. With each careful movement, he slipped further into the heart of the ship, weaving through the labyrinth of crates and barrels like a wraith.

The soldiers were exhausted, their senses dulled by relief and the promise of home. None noticed the ominous presence that had invaded their sanctuary, none sensed the peril that now lurked among them. The gentle sway of the ship mimicked the calm before a storm, a deceptive peace that masked the brewing danger. And so Father advanced, one stealthy step at a time, his malevolent plans unfolding with each passing moment.

Below deck, Duran's silhouette loomed in the gloom, his posture once rigid, now slumped in defeat. The first-in-command's haunted gaze, usually sharp as a falcon's, had dulled to a listless stare that saw nothing beyond the wooden planks at his feet.

In the shadowed corner, Father's essence stirred, a malignant breeze slipping through the air. It wound around Duran, silent as the night, and seeped into him like ink spilling across parchment. Duran's frame stiffened, his eyes snapping to attention with an unnatural glint. He rose, movements suddenly fluid, purposeful. A predatory smile played upon his lips—a cruel mimicry of his former self—as Duran turned to leave the hold, now a vessel for Father's will.

Above, Jonathan rambled on with sailors, his laughter cutting through the heaviness that lingered in the air. The surrounding men clung to his lightheartedness, using it as a shield against their own fatigue and fear.

Airella leaned against the ship's railing, her mismatched eyes reflecting the churning sea. Sirius approached her.

"We must warn King William," Sirius said, his voice barely above a whisper. "The isle is no sanctuary; it's a prison."

Airella nodded, her heart heavy with the gravity of their secret. "I fear for my people. If he sends them there…"

"Then we must ensure he understands the peril," Sirius insisted, his hand brushing hers in a gesture of reassurance. "As an inhabitant, my word may carry the weight needed to dissuade him. But I worry that if your people learn I am a Miscreant, they will fear me or lock me away for good."

"Your secret is safe with me. We'll convince everyone onboard to keep your secret as well." Airella's eyes shone with conviction. "You've shown more humanity than many who claim it."

Their hands lingered for a moment longer, bound by shared purpose and unspoken emotion. The bonds they forged on the isle were not easily broken, and they discovered a kindred spirit in each other—a beacon of hope as the darkness closed in.

Yet, as they parted ways, the unease that clung to the air was impossible to ignore. Duran's changed demeanor had not gone unnoticed. His sudden confidence, his newfound ruthlessness— it spoke of an influence far darker than mere madness. The transformation seemed almost supernatural, as if something or someone had taken hold of his very soul. His eyes, once filled with warmth, now glinted with a cold, calculating malice.

20

As the ship sailed closer to Eldaraya, the looming threat that Father posed became more palpable. His sinister machinations were hidden within the mind of one they once trusted, a puppet master pulling the strings of an unsuspecting marionette.

The crew's conversations grew quieter, their laughter more subdued, as the weight of their mission pressed down on them.

Jonathan clasped arms with a fellow soldier, his grip firm and reassuring. "We weathered the storm together," he said, his voice carrying over the creak of weathered wood beneath their boots. "And now we'll see Eldaraya's shores once more."

The surrounding soldiers nodded, their faces etched with fatigue but alight with the shared triumph of survival. As their gazes drifted to where Sirius stood apart from them, the camaraderie fractured into unease.

"Hard to believe that one aided us on the isle," muttered a grizzled veteran, thumbing the hilt of his sword apprehensively.

Jonathan followed his gaze, his eyes narrowing slightly. He could sense the tension, the unspoken questions swirling among the men. "Sirius has proven himself an ally," he countered firmly, "and allies are exactly what we need against threats like those on the isle."

"An ally who's a Miscreant?" another soldier interjected, skepticism lacing his tone. The soldier shifted uneasily, his fingers tapping rhythmically against the rough leather of his belt. "What if it's a ruse?"

"Then it is one that saved our skins," Jonathan replied, clapping the man on the shoulder with a reassuring grip. "Trust isn't given lightly, but look at what we've accomplished by extending it." His words seemed to settle some nerves, but the lingering distrust was as palpable.

Days stretched into a tapestry of azure skies and rolling waves, each passing hour weaving Airella and Sirius closer together. Conversations flowed easily, their laughter mingling with the sound of the sea, creating a harmony that felt timeless.

Under a canopy of stars, Airella found Sirius standing alone at the ship's railing that night, his face illuminated by the silver glow of the moon.

She joined him, the wood cool beneath her fingertips as she leaned in. Their arms brushed briefly, and though neither moved away, the contact sent a shiver through her spine.

Sirius smirked. "If you wanted an excuse to get closer to me, Airella, you could've just asked."

Airella scoffed, rolling her eyes. "Trust me, the last thing I need is an excuse."

Sirius chuckled, low and smooth. "Strange, isn't it," she

murmured, tilting her head toward the sky. "How quickly the world can shift beneath our feet?"

Sirius hummed. "And yet, some things remain constant."

She turned to him, curiosity flickering in her eyes. "Like what?"

He met her gaze, his golden irises shimmering like molten fire. "Like the courage you show in facing adversity," he said softly. "Like the care you display, even toward those who do not reciprocate it."

Her breath hitched.

For the first time in a long while, Airella felt seen.

"I do what must be done," she said, trying to sound casual, but her voice betrayed her.

Sirius leaned in slightly, his voice a low murmur. "That's not true."

Her lips parted, but she had no retort.

He tilted his head. "You didn't have to save me on that island."

"Then why did I?"

Sirius's lips twitched into a knowing smirk. "That's what I'd like to know."

Airella scoffed, looking away to regain control of her heartbeat.

Then, Sirius did something unexpected.

He reached for her hand.

Not forcefully, not teasingly—just enough for his fingers to brush against hers. He hesitated, as if unsure of himself, and then he slowly wove his fingers through hers.

Airella swallowed hard.

"Together," he said, voice steady, "we will warn King William of what lurks on the isle."

Airella nodded, her throat suddenly dry.

A whisper of a smile ghosted over her lips. "Thank you,

Sirius."

The gratitude in her voice was undeniable.

His thumb traced over the back of her hand absentmindedly, as if memorizing the feeling.

Their gazes locked.

The tension wasn't just there anymore.

It was suffocating.

Airella was not naive. She recognized the pull between them, the fragile thread that had been stretched and tangled since the moment they crossed paths.

But this?

This was undeniable.

Sirius was the first to break the silence.

"Before you," he murmured, his voice quieter now, almost... vulnerable, "I knew nothing but the cold tutelage of Father. He taught me to reap, not to feel."

Airella exhaled sharply.

She had suspected as much. But hearing it—the weight of those words—it carved something deep inside her.

Her hand moved on its own.

She brushed her fingers along his clothed hand, her touch light yet deliberate. "You're not alone anymore," she whispered.

Sirius stilled.

His golden eyes flickered with something she had never seen before.

Something soft. Something terrifying.

Something real.

"With you, Airella," he said slowly, deliberately, "I am learning what it means to be... more than a reaper." His voice dropped to a near whisper. "You see me as a person, not the monster I was made to be."

Her heart squeezed painfully.

"Because that's not who you are."

The words left her before she could even process them.

And then she did something reckless.

She squeezed his hand.

Tightly.

Sirius's breath hitched.

For all his teasing, his sarcasm, his sharp wit—this caught him off guard.

Airella felt it, too—the shift, the way the ice inside him melted, drop by drop.

Sirius exhaled slowly.

His free hand lifted slightly, as if he wanted to touch her face —to trace the slope of her cheek, to push a loose strand of hair behind her ear.

But he hesitated.

And then—he pulled away.

His fingers ghosted over hers before he let go entirely.

Airella felt the loss immediately.

Sirius smiled at her, but it was softer now. "You should get some rest," he murmured. "We'll need our wits about us tomorrow."

Airella nodded, but she lingered.

She wasn't sure why.

Finally, she took a slow step backward, her eyes never leaving his.

And Sirius?

He watched her go.

And for the first time in centuries, he let himself wonder…

What if he had met her sooner?

What if, instead of cold hands and a scythe, he had known warmth?

What if she was the one thing he couldn't afford to lose?

He closed his eyes.

Too late now.

As the ship sliced through the gleaming azure waters toward Eldaraya, Jonathan kept a watchful eye on the crew. The uneasiness about Sirius had not abated, and he feared whispered doubts could unravel the delicate trust they had woven over the course of their journey. He would stand by Airella and Sirius, come what may, his loyalty to them as steadfast as the tides that guided their vessel.

Days unfurled like the sails above, each one marked by the steady progress towards home. Amidst the rhythm of sailing, a disquiet settled over the men. Whispers snaked through the ship's underbelly, carrying fragments of concern about Duran's odd behavior.

"Have you noticed Duran lately?" one soldier murmured to another as they coiled ropes on deck.

"His eyes... It's like he's looking through you, not at you," came the hushed reply.

Duran, who had always been a pillar of strength and discipline, now moved with a distracted air, his commands tinged with an uncharacteristic sharpness that set the men on edge.

Unseen by all, Father wove his dark intent through the ship's very timbers. He whispered to Duran in the dead of night, his spectral touch guiding Duran's hand to sow seeds of discord among the men. Each subtle manipulation twisted the atmosphere onboard, turning trust into suspicion, camaraderie into isolation.

Airella approached Duran with measured steps, searching his form for clues to the discord he seemed to breed amongst the crew. She noted how the twilight cast long shadows across the deck, playing tricks on the eye—shadows not unlike the ones lurking in Duran's gaze.

"Duran," she began, her voice steady despite the unease coiling in her gut, "you've been distant since we left the isle. Your orders are... scattered. Is something wrong?"

Duran turned slowly, his eyes narrowing as they settled on her. The once-bright spark in his gaze had dimmed, replaced by a shadow of weariness that Airella had never seen before. "Your concern is misplaced, Airella," he said, his voice a low growl that did not invite further query.

"Perhaps," she conceded, stepping closer, emboldened by an inner fire that sought to mend frayed bonds. "But we cannot afford disunity—not when what awaits us in Eldaraya could change everything."

His lips twisted into a semblance of a smile, cold and devoid of humor. "Worry not about me, girl. Focus on your Miscreant friend and the tales you'll spin to sway the king."

Airella held his gaze, recognizing the sting of his words but choosing empathy over retaliation. Her thoughts wandered back to the isle, to the moments of camaraderie and the shared struggles that had forged them into a unit. Now, those bonds seemed to unravel.

"We all bear scars from the isle, Duran. Some visible, some

not. If you ever wish to speak of it..." Her voice softened, offering him an olive branch amidst the storm of his turmoil.

"Enough," he snapped, turning his back to her, the conversation severed like a rope cut by a sharp blade.

She sighed, watching his retreating figure. Her heart ached—for Duran, for her people, and for the uncertain future that loomed ahead. The journey to Eldaraya was fraught with peril, and the dissonance among their ranks only amplified her fears. With a heavy heart, she resolved to bridge the chasm that had opened between them, for the sake of their mission and the lives that depended on their unity.

Jonathan watched the horizon, where the silhouette of Eldaraya emerged from the morning mist. He stood at the bow, his hands gripping the weathered rail as the ship sliced through the gentle waves. Airella and Sirius approached, their faces set with a shared determination that had become familiar over the course of their harrowing journey.

"Never thought I'd find myself in league with a Miscreant," Jonathan said, breaking the silence. His voice carried a lightness, but his eyes were earnest as they shifted from Sirius to Airella. "Nor did I imagine witnessing such bravery as yours, Airella."

"You keep saying that. Bravery is often just another word for recklessness," Airella replied, though her lips curved into a half-smile.

"Reckless or not," Sirius chimed in, "it's gotten us this far." His golden gaze was intense as he clapped a hand on Jonathan's shoulder. "And we owe much of that to your guidance, my friend."

"Guidance?" Jonathan gave a self-deprecating chuckle. "I've merely followed where you two have led. But I must admit, it's been an honor."

"An honor that will soon be tested," Airella said as she scanned the approaching coastline. The sight of Aramore's majestic towers filled her with a mix of anticipation and trepidation. She turned toward them, her expression solemn. "We'll need each other more than ever once we reach the king."

"Whatever awaits," Jonathan replied, his voice steady with resolve, "we face it together."

They sealed their pact with a nod, a silent understanding that bound them as a trio against the impending challenges. The ship continued its journey toward Eldaraya, the city of their destinies looming ever closer. The bond they shared felt like an unbreakable shield, ready to face whatever trials lay ahead.

Deep within the ship's underbelly, Duran stared into his reflection, his features warped by the rippling surface of a tarnished mirror. The dim light caused shadows to dance across his face, accentuating the lines of tension etched into his skin. His eyes, usually so sharp and commanding, now flickered with an unfamiliar darkness, a haunting void that seemed to consume the surrounding light.

"Your resistance is futile," a voice hissed through him, one that clawed at the edges of his consciousness, insidious and cold. It was a voice he had heard many times, one that carried the weight of ancient authority. Father's essence swirled within Duran, gripping tighter with every passing moment, like icy tendrils wrapping around his mind, squeezing out his own will.

"They think they can prevent the humans from coming to the isle," Duran spoke, his voice no longer entirely his own. "Fools. They do not understand the hunger that drives us, the necessity of our survival. We need the humans to thrive again."

"Indeed," the dark whisper agreed through Duran's lips. "The

Miscreants require sustenance, something to reign over. Centuries ago, we indulged too freely, and our prey vanished. But now... now the feast shall begin anew." The voice within him seemed to grow stronger.

"More souls will come," Duran continued, his eyes glinting with malice. "They must. The isle thirsts for lifeblood, and I will permit no one to disrupt the flow."

"Ensure the king remains pliable," Father commanded, tightening his hold. The pressure in Duran's mind increased, and he felt his own thoughts slipping further away. "The humans will settle the isle, whether or not they wish it."

Duran's hand clenched the edge of the table before him. "It will be done," he affirmed, his resolve as cold and hard as the sea below. The future was set in motion, and Duran knew there was no turning back.

22

"Are you ready?" Jonathan held out his gloved hand to Sirius. Sirius responded with a slight grin, his anticipation evident. Their three-week journey to Eldaraya had finally ended. As Jonathan gathered the articles of armor, he playfully remarked, "Put this on. You'll fit right in with the crowd."

Sirius willingly traded his tattered cloak for the silver chest plate, though he couldn't help but express his uncertainty, "Yes, but this armor…"

"Feels odd, right?" Jonathan interjected, sensing Sirius's hesitation. Sirius glanced over at Airella, who couldn't contain a small chuckle at Sirius's new appearance. With a reassuring smile, Jonathan continued, "As an inhabitant of the island, Sirius, you must explain to the king that it is unfeasible for our kingdom to establish civilization there. Just maintain your composure and avoid giving him any reason to lock you away."

Jonathan took the lead, his confident stride echoing through the wooden ship as Sirius ducked his head while stepping out of the inner chambers. Airella trailed close behind.

The soldiers, clad in armor, couldn't hide their unease as Sirius locked eyes with Duran. The intensity in Sirius's gaze spoke volumes, a constant undercurrent of anger simmering beneath the surface.

A significant portion of Duran's men had fallen victim not only to Zol, but also to other malevolent creatures that prowled the island. As Sirius addressed Duran, his words carried a weight of both promise and threat.

"As we agreed, I will refrain from harming your people and will aid in preventing them from settling on the island. In exchange, I seek to understand your kingdom's ways and you will maintain secrecy about my presence," Sirius concluded before breaking his intense gaze.

With a deliberate step, Sirius disembarked from the ship onto the weathered dock. His eyes scanned the bustling marketplace of Aramore, the towering structures, and the distant silhouette of the grand castle that dominated the skyline.

"Just follow my lead, Sirius. We'll guide you straight to King William. It's only a matter of time," Jonathan reassured.

Sirius followed behind him, weaving through the crowd as he pushed past citizens who shot him deep glares or shivered in fear. The peasants whispered amongst themselves, their voices gradually rising in curiosity and concern as they trailed the large group of soldiers. Soon, a ripple of gasps spread through the crowd like a sudden gust of wind, each gasp a testament to the shock that gripped the citizens.

In a swift and dramatic turn of events, it was Duran who deftly maneuvered behind Sirius, pressing a dagger against his throat. With a deft motion, Duran removed Sirius's iron helmet, revealing his golden eyes and silver hair to the astonished onlookers of Eldaraya. Though Sirius gripped his scythe tightly, an unfortunate twist of fate caused it to slip from his grasp as Duran presented him before the stunned crowd.

"This Miscreant," Duran declared in a booming voice that echoed across the square, "has taken the lives of our own people, and who knows who else! If we do not act now, he may come for your children next! He will devour them whole, just like this witch!" His accusatory tone pierced the air, adding Airella to the chaos that unfolded. As Duran pointed towards her, she involuntarily took a step back, her eyes wide with disbelief and fear.

Sirius then cocked his head back with a sharp and sudden motion, showing that he had knocked a tooth from Duran's mouth once he heard the successful sound of a loud crack.

The citizens, as well as many of the soldiers, trembled with fear as Sirius picked up his scythe from the ground. Sirius paused and scanned over the people. He took a moment before he pulled the rest of his armor from his body; the pieces clanging softly as they fell to the ground. The people surrounding him confirmed their suspicions as they beheld the dark, decaying flesh of his chest.

Jonathan watched as Sirius took his cloak from Airella and draped it behind him with a sense of finality. Then, Jonathan took ahold of Airella's left shoulder as he guided her through the towering kingdom gates.

Sirius looked back to Duran, who was being helped back up to his feet by concerned onlookers. The man, despite his injuries, emitted a sinister and bloody smile towards Sirius.

"No use, it's over," Sirius murmured as Airella glanced in his direction.

Now, as the weight of responsibility settled on his shoulders, it was time for them to confront the king and the challenges that lay ahead.

23

The grand doors of the throne room swung open, revealing King William, seated atop his resplendent golden throne. His jewel-encrusted crown gleamed under the torchlight, a stark contrast to the dark stone walls that loomed behind him.

His sharp, calculating gaze landed on the trio approaching—Jonathan, Airella, and the pale, golden-eyed stranger they had brought before him.

"Who is this you bring before me?" the king inquired, his voice laced with curiosity and quiet authority.

Jonathan took a measured step forward. "Your Majesty, this is a resident of the island. He bears vital information that could determine the future of our kingdom."

King William leaned forward, his keen gaze sweeping over Sirius. He descended from his throne, each step slow and deliberate as he circled the reaper, assessing him like a predator watching prey.

Sirius, unreadable as ever, held his ground.

"That island, Your Majesty, is not fit for human settlement,"

Sirius began, his voice smooth but firm. "The Miscreants who remain there—they do not sleep, they do not die, and they will not share."

The king chuckled, low and mocking.

"Miscreants?" he mused, tilting his head. "I thought they were nothing more than stories. Boogeymen conjured by frightened children. And yet, here you stand, expecting me to believe they wiped out an entire civilization?"

Sirius's golden eyes narrowed.

"They did not wipe out a civilization," he corrected. "They took back what was theirs."

The smirk on the king's lips faltered.

Sirius took a step forward, voice unwavering. "The humans on that island—your people, centuries ago—arrived with the same arrogance you now display. They believed the land was theirs to claim. They saw the Miscreants as lesser creatures, ones to be conquered."

His voice turned sharp. Cold.

"They were wrong."

King William scoffed, folding his arms. "And what of you? What makes you so different?" He eyed Sirius with scrutiny. "If you are one of them, why bring me this warning?"

A long silence stretched between them.

Airella watched Sirius carefully, sensing something shift in the air.

Finally, he answered. "Because I am not like them."

The words carried weight—an unseen burden pressing against his shoulders.

"I am not one of them, yet I am not one of you. I am something else entirely," Sirius said, voice quieter but no less sharp. "And if you do not heed my warning, your people will share the same fate as the last humans who stepped foot on that island."

King William's lips curled in amusement. "Is that a threat?"

Sirius exhaled through his nose. "It is a fact."

The king chuckled again, the sound grating against Sirius's patience. He turned his back to him, waving a dismissive hand.

"I do not take orders from creatures who lurk in the shadows," he said. "My kingdom is built on strength, on order, on conquest. I will not be frightened by some ghost story."

Jonathan shifted uneasily beside Airella. He could feel Sirius's rage like a storm building on the horizon.

The reaper stiffened, his hands curling into fists.

It was always the same.

Humans, standing atop their golden pedestals, believing they could do as they pleased.

The humans from centuries ago had believed the same thing —until they were nothing but bones buried beneath the earth.

"You think you are invincible," Sirius murmured, his voice barely above a whisper.

The king stopped mid-step.

"You sit in your gilded throne, wrapped in luxury, surrounded by men who would die for you." Sirius's golden eyes darkened, his voice turning lethal. "But I wonder—how many would die because of you?"

King William turned, face twisting with irritation. "You dare speak to me that way?"

"You think your soldiers stand a chance against what's coming?" Sirius continued, undeterred. "Do you have any idea what Miscreants are capable of? Have you seen their hunger? Their wrath?"

His voice was rising now, filled with something sharp and unforgiving.

"You send your men to claim land that is not theirs, and you expect the island to simply bend to your will?" Sirius scoffed, a sharp, bitter sound. "You will not conquer that island, Your Majesty. You will die on it."

The room fell silent.

Airella saw it—the way Sirius's hands trembled at his sides, the way his chest rose and fell with barely contained fury.

The king grinned.

And then he spoke the words that broke something inside Sirius.

"I do not fear the unknown." The king tilted his head. "And if the isle is as dangerous as you say, then it will be my soldiers who will turn the tides. We will wipe the Miscreants out and make Eldaraya's kingdom greater than it has ever been."

The room blurred.

Airella barely registered what happened next.

One moment, Sirius was standing still.

The next—he lunged.

His exposed hand—*the one that could steal life with a single touch*—shot forward, aiming straight for the king's throat.

Gasps erupted across the chamber.

And then—he was stopped.

A hand clamped around his wrist.

Airella.

Her fingers seared into his skin, a warmth that cut through the suffocating darkness.

Jonathan had grabbed his other arm, both of them holding him back, their faces stricken with urgency.

"Sirius, don't!" Airella's voice pierced through the red haze clouding his mind.

The weight of her grip was startling—solid and real in a way nothing else in this room was.

Sirius struggled, chest heaving, his pulse hammering in his skull.

The king's face twisted into disgust. "He's feral."

Jonathan shot the king a glare. "You're not helping!"

Sirius gritted his teeth, his mind spinning. His pulse slowed. His vision blurred.

The anger was too much. It burned too hot.

And then—his body gave out.

His knees buckled. The edges of the world tilted.

Airella's worried expression was the last thing Sirius saw before darkness took him.

24

When he finally awoke, his gaze slowly focused, meeting the familiar pair of sparkling multicolored eyes staring down at him.

"Sirius, are you insane?" Airella's voice trembled. She leaned over him, her heart racing as she assessed his condition, relieved to see him awakening from unconsciousness.

Jonathan and Airella had just narrowly escaped from the relentless pursuit of the castle guards, bringing Sirius along with them, but the danger still lurked close behind, their footsteps echoing in the shadows.

"Airella, we have to go right." Jonathan whispered urgently, his grip firm as he pulled her up by the arm, his eyes scanning their surroundings for any sign of escape.

"No, we should go left." Airella's voice filled with conviction as she stood her ground, mapping out their path through the passageways of the castle.

They found themselves enveloped in a maze of twisting tunnels. Vigilant guards had sealed every known exit from the king's throne room off, leaving them with no choice but to navigate the labyrinthine passages in search of a way out. Voices of men and loud footsteps echoed off the walls, coming from behind them.

"We have to move, now!" Jonathan urgently shoved both Sirius and Airella ahead of him.

They dashed in random directions, no longer concerned about the trivial arguments about whether to turn left or right. The relentless sounds of footsteps were gaining on them.

"Dead end," Airella declared in defeat as she halted the group, her eyes fixed on the seemingly impenetrable brick wall that stood before them.

"We can't turn back now, they'll catch us," Sirius muttered, his voice tinged with a sense of resignation, mirroring Airella's growing despair.

But amidst the suffocating fear, Jonathan's sharp eyes caught a glimmer of hope. He pointed towards a crumbling hole in the top corner of the tunnel's ceiling, where a faint stream of light beckoned from the outside world. The passageways were shrouded in darkness, but the dim glow guided them towards potential freedom, albeit through a perilous crawl upwards.

"How are we supposed to reach up there?" Airella's gaze shifted upward towards the small opening. Before she could voice her doubts, a pair of hands grasped her waist, lifting her effortlessly onto Jonathan's sturdy shoulders. "Whoa! What are you doing?"

"You're going to crawl out," Jonathan stated as he lifted Airella toward the opening. She hesitated, realizing that the gap was only wide enough for those slimmer than Jonathan's muscular build.

"No, are you crazy? I'm not leaving you. We can help fight them off!" Airella's fists clenched as she looked down at him with determination.

"We don't have time for this," Jonathan's voice was firm. It was a tone she had never heard from him before. With no other option, she crawled through as he nudged her forward. "Don't worry, I've picked up a thing or two from your father back when I was a kid," Jonathan reassured her, trying to lighten the tone of the situation.

Next, he turned to Sirius, who was also hesitant to leave. Before coaxing Sirius to crawl through, Jonathan whispered something inaudible, a moment that piqued Airella's curiosity. However, her focus shifted as the voices of the approaching men drew nearer, urging them to hurry.

Airella sat beside Sirius, their figures silhouetted against the castle walls as the lush green grass surrounded them. She gazed down the gaping hole, her heart pounding in her chest as Jonathan, arms raised in surrender, kneeled before the soldiers who swarmed around him. The clatter of weapons being confiscated echoed in the air, while the search for the remaining two fugitives intensified.

As Jonathan was led away in chains, his eyes met hers one last time, and Airella felt a knot form in her stomach. She turned to Sirius, whose expression mirrored her concern. Their next move was critical, but Airella's thoughts lingered on rescuing Jonathan.

"We have to save him," she whispered, her voice trembling with emotion as she remained on her knees.

Sirius hesitated, his gaze scanning their surroundings before he spoke. "We need to handle a few matters first."

Airella's eyes bore into his, silently demanding answers, but Sirius remained cryptic. With a resigned sigh, she wiped away a tear, knowing their current location was far from safe.

As uncertainty clouded her mind like a dense fog on a moonless night, Sirius took the first step, setting off in a direction unknown to both him and Airella. Intrigued and wary, Airella hesitated for a moment before deciding to follow him.

"Where are you going?" Airella's voice was hushed as she trailed after Sirius.

Sirius remained silent, but a glint of determination flickered in his eyes, hinting at a deeper motive driving him forward. Airella sensed a hint of revenge in his demeanor, a resolve to fulfill the promises and threats he had made in the heat of the moment towards Duran.

"Stop." Airella's hand shot out, grasping the sleeve of Sirius's cloak, bringing him to an abrupt halt. "We can't leave Jonathan behind. We must go back for him; everything else can wait." Her voice was urgent, laced with a sense of responsibility and loyalty to their friend. "We have to find Jonathan."

Sirius regarded her for a moment, his expression softening slightly as he processed her words. With a nod of acknowledgment, he signaled his agreement, a silent promise to stand by her side on this precarious journey they had embarked upon.

Rather than attempting to retrace their steps through the labyrinthine passageways, Airella and Sirius opted for a different approach, seeking out a clandestine back entrance into the palace. Their footsteps were soundless as they navigated the hidden corridors, avoiding the grand rooms and evading the vigilant eyes of the palace guards.

"Shh." Sirius brought his finger to his pale lips as they hid behind a wooden door, side by side, their breaths synchronized in anticipation.

After ensuring the coast was clear, he gently seized her hand with his clothed one, guiding her into the open hallway with a silent urgency. Airella could feel a rush of heat creeping up her cheeks, but she willed herself to focus on the task at hand, pushing aside the self-consciousness that threatened to overwhelm her.

"Who goes there?" the booming voice of a soldier, accompanied by others, shattered the stillness behind them.

With a shared glance of determination, Sirius and Airella wordlessly agreed on their next move and bolted in the opposite direction.

"Go, go, go," Airella chanted inwardly, her mind a whirlwind of fear and adrenaline as they sprinted through the corridor. They reached a junction with two diverging stairways, one ascending and the other descending.

"Find Jonathan." Sirius's urgent command cut through the chaos, directing her towards the path leading downward, presumably to where the dungeon lay hidden. Despite her reluctance to part ways with him, the urgency of their escape left her with no choice but to comply.

With a last look over her shoulder at Sirius engaged in diverting the guards, Airella descended the worn brick steps, the distant sounds of muffled moans and echoes of distant grunts growing louder with each passing moment.

Airella froze in surprise as she collided with a taller, brunette-haired girl who appeared slightly older than her. The brunette's wide-eyed gaze met Airella's, who then noticed a black-haired maid standing beside her. Strangely, Airella sensed an air of difference about the maid, with her pale skin and a mysterious smile playing on her blood-red lips as she fixed her gaze on Airella.

Feeling a mix of curiosity and caution, Airella drew Dawn-breaker from its holster, ready to defend herself.

"Step aside," she commanded, trying to exude confidence.

The brunette girl, clad in a loose cloak and a silky purple gown adorned with gems, crossed her arms defiantly. It was clear from her attire that she was of noble birth, far removed from the life of a commoner.

"Who do you think you are?" she retorted, her tone haughty and dismissive.

Airella's gaze hardened as she avoided the question, her

suspicions growing. "What is someone like you doing down here?" she challenged, her voice tinged with defiance.

The brunette's response was cutting, her words laced with condescension. "That's none of your concern. Do not raise your weapon against me! Are you some poor excuse for a palace guard? How unladylike of you," she scoffed, rolling her eyes in disdain.

Reluctantly, Airella lowered her weapon, deciding to gather more information about this unexpected encounter. As she observed the girl more closely, a realization dawned on her—this could very well be Princess Thea, the king's daughter, disguised and exploring incognito.

"I apologize, Your Highness," Airella muttered with a deep bow. Princess Thea's piercing gaze lingered on her, and Airella could sense the weight of disapproval in the air.

"Hmph. Come, Anya." Princess Thea's tone was dismissive as she motioned for her handmaiden to follow. Anya's gaze lingered on Airella, a subtle smile playing on her lips, hinting at hidden meanings and unspoken alliances.

Feeling a surge of frustration, Airella clenched her teeth and closed her eyes briefly, steeling herself for what was to come. With a determined resolve, she turned on her heels and made a beeline for the dimly lit corridor leading to the prison cells.

As she navigated the maze of narrow passageways, the haunting pleas of the incarcerated echoed around her, their desperate voices tugging at her heartstrings. She pressed on, her steps quickening as she neared the cell that held the key to her mission.

"Jonathan?" Airella's voice cut through the somber air, causing a ripple of anticipation among the other prisoners. Their eyes, filled with a mixture of hope and longing, followed her every move as she approached Jonathan's confinement.

Jonathan, with his back turned towards her, froze at the

sound of her voice. As he pivoted to face her, the dim light revealed the weariness etched on his features.

"Airella, you were supposed to get out of here! Where is Sirius?" Jonathan's words spilled out in a rush, his worry palpable as he took a step closer to the cell bars.

"He stayed back as a distraction," Airella replied, her gaze scanning the surroundings in search of a means to free him. The absence of keys left her momentarily stumped, but a flicker of determination sparked in her eyes as a daring plan took shape in her mind.

With a silent prayer, Airella gripped the cold iron bars of the cell, her muscles straining with the effort as she exerted all her strength. The metal groaned in protest, but gradually yielded to her relentless tugging. Inch by inch, the bars bent, creating a narrow gap.

Breathless and exhilarated by her small victory, Airella turned to face Jonathan, whose eyes held a mix of admiration and disbelief.

"Can you squeeze through?" She asked tentatively, unsure if her strength would bend the bars any further.

"I might," he replied, his voice strained as he contorted his body to squeeze through the narrow gap. With his hands still bound behind his back, he wriggled through, narrowly escaping the confines. Upon emerging on the other side, she swiftly severed the rope binding his hands with Dawnbreaker, granting him freedom despite the raw rope-burn etched into his wrists.

"Maybe Sirius has lost the guards. We have to find him and escape this place for good," Airella urged Jonathan, tugging at his arm.

"Hold on, we can't just leave. We have to convince the king about the dangers of the isle." Jonathan declared adamantly.

"They won't listen to us. Perhaps the soldiers will challenge Duran and convince the king to not venture back to the isle," she exclaimed passionately, pivoting and leading the way out of the dungeon in a race to find Sirius before he encountered further peril.

Airella and Jonathan navigated the labyrinthine corridors of the dungeon. The flickering torchlight cast fleeting shadows, causing their anxiety to spike at every turn. They were so close to the exit—freedom was almost within reach. But suddenly, a soldier emerged from the darkness, a glint of malevolence in his eyes as he charged towards Airella with a raised dagger.

Jonathan didn't hesitate. With a swift, desperate move, he thrust himself between Airella and the assailant, their bodies crashing together with violent force. The dagger found its mark, plunging deep into Jonathan's chest. He gasped, a harsh, wet sound escaping his lips as the pain seared through him. His knees buckled, but he maintained his stance long enough to meet Airella's horrified gaze.

As the soldier withdrew the blade, intending to strike again, Airella's shock transformed into a raw, primal rage. With an almost inhuman speed, she clutched Dawnbreaker and swung it with all her might. The axe connected with the soldier's skull, a sickening crack echoing through the dungeon. He collapsed lifelessly to the ground, his own dagger clattering beside him.

The moment of triumph was fleeting. Airella lowered Dawnbreaker, her hands trembling violently as she stared at the fallen soldier. Guilt and revulsion washed over her, the reality of what she had done sinking in. Her breaths came in frantic gasps, eyes widening in panic as she turned her attention back to Jonathan.

He was on the ground, hand pressed weakly against his wound, blood seeping through his fingers.

"Jonathan!" Airella screamed, dropping to her knees beside him. "No, no, no, Jonathan, stay with me!" Her voice broke, and she tore at her cloak, trying to fashion it into a makeshift bandage.

Jonathan's eyes fluttered open, his breath shallow and labored. "Airella," he whispered, his voice barely audible over her sobs. "You have to… keep going…"

She shook her head violently, refusing to accept his words. "I won't leave you," she insisted, her hands desperately working to stop the bleeding. But deep down, the horrifying realization that she might lose him was taking hold.

25

Sirius wielded the handle of his scythe, striking a patrolling guard on the head, causing him to crumple to the ground.

As the footsteps of soldiers drew nearer, a guard bellowed, "Halt! We have you encircled, traitor! Where is the girl?"

Sirius turned to face the advancing soldiers. With a measured calmness, he raised his scythe.

"Stop this at once," a guard beside the first soldier demanded, his voice tinged with authority.

Sirius couldn't help but notice a flicker of recognition in the royal guard's eyes, a sense of unease creeping over him. Memories intertwined with the present, blurring the lines between past betrayals and present dangers. As he stood there, a rush of emotions flooded Sirius—a mix of fear, confusion, and a sliver of hope. The weight of unresolved emotions lingered in the air like a haunting echo, enveloping him in a shroud of uncertainty.

"Father?" Sirius uttered.

Finally, everything made sense, connecting the dots between Duran's peculiar behavior and the mysterious presence of

Father. Father had indeed followed them off the island, embarking on a covert mission to ensure the humans' journey to the isle.

The strange guard sneered, a subtle twitch in his eyes betraying the darkness that lurked within. Sirius recognized the familiar pattern of manipulation, a tactic he had seen before in the eyes of those under Father's influence. Slowly, the man opened his mouth, his voice a chilling command that echoed through the narrow passageway. It was Father's voice.

"End them, Sirius."

Sirius's scythe met the leg of an older guard, the clash of metal against flesh reverberating through the tense silence. As the guard fell, others surged forward, a chaotic wave of bodies and weapons converging on Sirius. He moved with fluid grace, a dance of survival and restraint, his movements a delicate balance between defense and the primal urge to strike back.

One young boy, barely a teenager, lunged at Sirius with a heavy sword, his eyes wide with fear and determination. Sirius deflected the clumsy attack with a swift movement, guiding the boy into the unforgiving stone wall.

Amidst the chaos, the cries of pain and anguish filled the air like a haunting melody, echoing through the palace hall. The clash of steel carried on as Sirius engaged in combat. Each strike he delivered was not merely an act of violence, but a strategic move aimed at disarming his foes rather than delivering a fatal blow. The fallen guards, their bodies strewn across the polished floor, bore the marks of battle—wounds severe yet miraculously not mortal—a testament to Sirius's exceptional skill and the restraint he exercised against Father's ruthless commands.

Father had augmented his power through sinister means— the unrestrained consumption of countless souls. His strength had swelled to unparalleled levels. This self-imposed limitation had rendered Sirius vulnerable, his own power waning. Unable to confront Father directly in terms of sheer might, Sirius found himself at a disadvantage.

As he surveyed the aftermath, his gaze lingered on the guard who had now become Father's vessel. There was a complexity in those haunted eyes, a reflection of the past and present colliding in a silent plea for redemption.

"Father!" Sirius yelled angrily as he twirled his scythe during his march towards the possessed figure.

A crazed smile washed over Father's face. Father had possessed the soldier almost entirely; it was clear from the black veins that clouded his eyes and forehead.

"Long time no see, Sirius." Father growled as he pushed Sirius backward with a force that almost knocked him off balance. Father swung down upon Sirius, but the handle of his trusty scythe deflected the soldier's sword. "Tell me, why care for these men? Why don't you just kill them like you used to all those centuries ago? Do you not recall how you felt when you wiped out that Miscreant Slayer village on the isle? Consume these souls, and you will be filled with more power! There are so many souls here. We will not repeat our last mistakes. Join me, Sirius, and you will see." Father's voice resonated with a chilling tone as he swung his sword down upon a fallen palace guard.

Sirius cursed under his breath as he swiftly blocked the oncoming attack, saving the already dying man's life. He then froze as the sound of Jonathan's yelling voice echoed down the long corridors.

Sirius gave the possessed soldier one last glance before leaving him behind to find Airella and Jonathan.

"Airella! Jonathan! Where are you?" The yellow-eyed reaper called out, his voice echoing through the now empty corridors.

He retraced his steps back to the stairwell he had sent Airella down, but they were nowhere to be seen. His heart raced as he scanned each corridor, desperately searching for any signs that could lead to them. Yet, the trail of blood leading down one passageway seemed a bit too obvious, raising more questions than answers in Sirius's mind.

The trail wasn't extremely noticeable, but the blood was fresh. It almost appeared someone had been through a struggle, leaving behind this eerie trace.

"Sirius? Where are you?" A faint groan accompanied by a voice filled with fear echoed through the corridors. The castle's complex hallway system felt like a labyrinth, disorienting even to those familiar with its layout.

Racing through the twisting maze of dimly lit corridors, Sirius hastened his steps. The distant echoes of voices guided him through the labyrinthine paths, drawing him closer to a chilling discovery. A vivid trail of crimson droplets painted a macabre path on the cold stone floor, leading him to a scene of unimaginable horror.

As Sirius neared the source of the blood, a scene of despair unfolded before his eyes. There lay Jonathan, his once vibrant eyes now clouded with pain and fear, an open wound causing blood to coat his chest. Airella kneeled beside him, her hands bloody from trying to stop the bleeding.

"Sirius," Airella's voice trembled, "he shielded me from a soldier."

"I..." Jonathan's voice, barely a whisper, struggled to convey his final thoughts as blood stained his lips, his strength waning with each passing moment. Sirius kneeled beside him.

"Don't speak," Sirius uttered in a hushed tone, his eyes shifting to Airella. Tears cascaded down her cheeks as she gently leaned Jonathan against the wall, ensuring his comfort. "Watch the corridor. Alert me if anyone approaches," Sirius directed her, extending a delicate pendant from beneath his cloak. Jonathan, his gaze trembling, peered at the necklace curiously, a silent question in his eyes. "This will safeguard you, though the process may not be pleasant. I plan to transmigrate your soul into a new vessel once I locate a suitable one. For now, your essence will live within this pendant. Do you understand?"

"What are you suggesting?" Airella's voice resonated with disbelief as she confronted Sirius. With a swift motion, she knocked the glass pendant from his grasp, the ornament clinking against the stone floor, but remaining unscathed. "You can't take his soul! There must be another way."

"There is no alternative, Airella. The wound is fatal, and even with attempts to mend him, he will succumb before any recovery can take place." Sirius's eyes blazed with unwavering determination as he spoke.

The two paused as Jonathan, his once powerful voice now reduced to a weak and raspy whisper, made a profound statement, "I would rather be a... soul... than dead. If Sirius... says he can save me... then I trust him."

Despite the sharp pain from the wound in his chest, Jonathan's determination to fulfill his purpose burned fiercely within him. As the second-in-command of Eldaraya's military, his duty to safeguard his people was unwavering. The prospect of allowing civilization to flourish on that island was inconceivable to him; failure was not an option.

Sirius turned to Airella and posed a pivotal question, "Do you trust me, Airella?"

Her mind raced as she grappled with the gravity of their predicament. After a moment of contemplation, she met Sirius's eyes with a resolute expression, "Yes. Yes, I trust you."

With a nod of acknowledgment, Sirius advanced towards Jonathan, placing his hand gently on the injured man's chest. A mystical energy enveloped them as their eyes radiated with otherworldly hues—Jonathan's eyes shimmering in emerald brilliance while Sirius's gleamed in their natural gold. A surge of vitality passed through Sirius's hands, manifesting as a luminous blue orb that emanated from Jonathan's being. Mesmerized, Airella watched as the ethereal sphere hovered before Sirius, who carefully guided it into the pendant with deft precision.

"He is safe," Sirius declared softly, his touch soothing as he tenderly closed Jonathan's eyes.

Drawing closer, Airella kneeled beside them, her gaze fixed on the radiant necklace in Sirius's hands. With a gentle smile, Sirius encircled the glowing blue pendant around Airella's neck. The magic she had just witnessed stirred a whirlwind of emotions within her—the cold, luminescent glass against her skin sparking wonder and curiosity.

"Let's go," Sirius urged, his eyes focused ahead as he started a brisk jog towards the nearest exit.

Airella hesitated for a moment, stealing a final glance back at Jonathan's lifeless body. Reaching up to clutch the pendant tightly in her hand, she sprinted to catch up with Sirius.

Together, they navigated through the castle corridors. Pausing behind a towering stone statue, they observed Princess Thea's regal procession pass by, flanked by vigilant palace guards. Airella's breath caught in her throat as she watched the entourage disappear from view, her pulse echoing loudly in her ears.

As they finally escaped the heavily guarded palace grounds, a sense of relief washed over Airella. Gasping for air, she leaned over, hands on her knees, marveling at the speed at which they had fled.

"We need a horse," she said between breaths, her eyes scanning the nearby horse stalls reserved for palace steeds. Seeing agreement in Sirius's gaze, Airella swiftly led them to a sleek black horse, their only option amidst the vigilant soldiers patrolling the area.

With Sirius holding onto her waist, Airella seized the reins, her childhood memories of horseback riding flooding back. Instinctively, she guided the horse as they galloped, the looming threat of King William's pursuit urging them forward.

"Where are we headed?" Sirius's voice broke through the rush of wind.

"I'm taking you to my home in Alverstone. It's not terribly far from here," she told him. Despite her reassuring tone, doubt gnawed at her. They had found her once before; what would stop them from finding her again? However, they had no money and nowhere to go. She also knew that King William would find Arii and her mother and make them pay for her betrayal. She had to be there to warn and protect them.

"Airella, there's something I need to tell you. It's about Father. And Duran," Sirius said, each word dripping with urgency.

Airella's hands gripped tighter to the reins. "What about them?"

"Father's possessed Duran and others. He plans to convince the King to send the humans to the isle. If that happens..." Sirius trailed off, the severity of his unspoken words hanging heavily in the air.

Airella's eyes widened. Duran's strange behavior on the ship now made sense. She should have known.

"We need to stop him," she finally said, determination hardening her voice.

"We will. But first, we need to get out of Aramore," Sirius said, holding tighter to Airella.

26

The night stretched long and quiet as Airella and Sirius rode through the dense forest, the moonlight barely piercing through the thick canopy above. The scent of damp earth and pine clung to the air as their horse moved in a steady rhythm. Airella sat in front of Sirius, her back pressed against his chest, every shift of the horse forcing their bodies closer. His arms bracketed her, his hands resting protectively against her waist.

Neither of them spoke, but the tension between them was palpable, a slow-burning fire waiting to ignite.

Jonathan was gone.

The memory of the castle's halls filled with blood haunted Airella's mind. He had fought beside them, protecting her until the very end. And then, just before his last breath, Sirius had done something she never thought possible—he had trapped Jonathan's soul in the pendant she now wore around her neck. It pulsed faintly against her skin, a reminder of the life lost, of the friend she couldn't save.

She swallowed hard, gripping the pendant between her

fingers as the guilt settled deep in her bones. "We should have saved him," she whispered.

Sirius's arms tightened slightly around her. "We did what we could. This way, he's still with us."

It wasn't enough. It would never be enough.

After what felt like hours, they finally found a secluded clearing near a large lake. Sirius slid off first, then turned to help Airella down. His hands found her waist, lingering for just a moment too long, his fingers pressing into the soft leather of her tunic.

"We should rest here," he murmured, his voice rough from exhaustion and something deeper—something unspoken.

Airella nodded, pulling her cloak tighter around herself. They set up a small camp, the fire crackling low, casting flickering shadows that danced across Sirius's sharp features. She tried to focus on anything other than the way his gold eyes followed her every movement.

But when she finally settled down against the tree beside him, their proximity became impossible to ignore. His breathing was deep and measured, but she knew he was not asleep.

"We have to convince the king," she said quietly. "The isle isn't safe for humans. We can't let him send more people there."

Sirius exhaled sharply. "He won't listen. Not while Father is pulling the strings."

Airella scoffed, shifting so she could see his face better. "Then we make him listen."

Sirius let out a low, humorless chuckle. "You say that like it's easy. Like you can just walk into the throne room and demand he changes his mind. Sounds familiar."

"I wouldn't have snapped like you did," she shot back, tilting her chin up defiantly.

He arched a brow. "Oh, of course. Should I start preparing a speech for your execution now or later?"

Airella narrowed her eyes. "You think I can't handle myself?"

"I think you're reckless."

She huffed, crossing her arms. "Look in the mirror. I'm not reckless. I'm determined."

"You're impossible," he muttered, raking a hand through his white hair. The firelight illuminated the frustration in his gold eyes. "You always have to push back, don't you?"

"If you weren't so damn stubborn, I wouldn't have to," she shot back.

Sirius exhaled a sharp breath, his expression unreadable as he studied her. Then, before she could process it, he leaned in slightly, his voice dropping to a low murmur. "You drive me insane."

Airella felt the warmth of his breath against her skin, her pulse quickening. "Likewise," she whispered, though her voice betrayed her, softer than she intended.

His gaze flickered to her lips, then back to her eyes. "Tell me you don't want this."

Her heart pounded. "I—"

Then he was closer, their noses nearly touching. His hand reached up, brushing a lock of hair from her face, lingering at the curve of her jaw. "You should push me away," he murmured.

"I should," she breathed, but she didn't.

And then his lips were on hers.

It was slow at first, tentative, as though he were giving her time to pull away. But Airella had no intention of stopping. She pressed into him, her fingers tangling in his hair as the kiss deepened. He made a sound low in his throat, his hands finding her waist again, but this time, there was nothing hesitant about his touch. He pulled her flush against him, and suddenly, the heat between them was unbearable.

The world beyond their small clearing faded away. There was no kingdom, no danger, no isle—only this. Only him. Only the way his mouth traced fire along her skin, the way his hands anchored her to him as though she might slip away.

"Sirius—" she whispered against his lips, her voice barely a breath.

He groaned softly, his forehead resting against hers, their breaths mingling in the cool night air. "Airella, tell me to stop."

She didn't.

A small smile curved his lips before he kissed her again, slow and deep, as though memorizing every inch of her. His hands moved with purpose, trailing over her arms, her back, leaving a trail of warmth in their wake. She melted into him, her body betraying every logical thought screaming in the back of her mind.

Time passed in a haze of heat and longing, the fire burning low as they lay together beneath the stars. The weight of grief was still there, still present, but for a moment, it was pushed aside. Replaced by something else entirely.

And then, just as she felt herself completely lost in him, the fire crackled behind them, sending a sharp pop into the night. The sound dragged her back to reality, and she forced herself to pull away, her breathing uneven.

She swallowed hard, trying to steady herself. "I should take first watch."

Sirius studied her for a long moment, then nodded. He exhaled, running a hand through his tousled hair, looking as wrecked as she felt. "Wake me when you need rest."

She nodded, standing to put some much-needed distance between them.

The hours stretched on as Airella sat near the fire, keeping her senses sharp despite the exhaustion pressing in. The wind rustled through the trees, and the distant hoot of an owl filled the silence. She ran her fingers over the pendant, Jonathan's presence lingering just beyond her reach.

With a heavy heart, she gazed at Sirius, his scythe a constant reminder of his identity as a reaper. Despite the ominous title, he carried himself with a human-like grace that defied conventional expectations. Lost in contemplation, Airella pondered her own identity and the legacy of her father's enigmatic past. Was she truly just a mere mortal, or was there more to her lineage than she dared to imagine?

Her mind drifted back to the kiss, to the way she had let herself get carried away in the moment. Embarrassment flared hot beneath her skin. What had come over her? Grief, exhaustion, or something deeper? She told herself it had been a distraction—a way to momentarily forget the weight of everything—but she wasn't sure she believed that.

She shook her head, forcing herself to focus. She had a job to do.

And then, somewhere between the flickering fire and the whispering trees, Airella's eyelids grew heavy. She fought against it, gripping the hilt of her weapon tighter. The air around her seemed to hum, an unnatural stillness settling over the forest.

Before her senses could fully grasp the danger, a cloth descended upon her, stifling her protests and plunging her into a moment of peril. Her vision blurred, the world tilting sideways. She gasped, reaching for her weapon, but her limbs felt sluggish, weak. Panic flared in her chest. She had let her guard down. The scent was thick, acrid, making her stomach turn. She tried to cry out, but her voice barely left her lips.

Sirius.

She barely had the strength to call his name before her legs buckled.

Through the haze, she saw movement—dark figures

emerging from the treeline, their footsteps barely audible over the sound of her own heartbeat. A shadow lunged forward, but before they could reach her, Sirius sprang into action, his scythe a glinting arc of protection against the looming threat. The shadows of the thieves from the ambush dissipated in the wake of his swift defense, their surprised cries cutting through the night.

"I didn't see them coming," Airella coughed, the bitter taste of whatever drug they had used still clinging to her tongue.

She knew there was something more than just the cloth that she had inhaled from. The thieves were trying to drug them, she was sure of it. Though she inhaled little, the effects certainly didn't feel great. Her body felt distant, slow, like she was sinking into the earth itself.

Sirius moved like a storm, each swing of his scythe deadly and precise. One attacker barely had time to react before the curved blade caught him, sending him collapsing into the underbrush. Another lunged with a dagger, but Sirius twisted effortlessly, parrying the attack before striking his opponent down with swift finality.

The remaining thieves hesitated, wary of the reaper before them. One turned to flee, but Sirius was faster, his blade cutting through the night with lethal grace. The last attacker, perhaps too desperate or foolish, made a final attempt to grab Airella, but Sirius was there in an instant. His arm wrapped around her protectively as he drove his scythe forward, cutting through the thief with a single, brutal stroke.

Silence fell once more, save for the ragged breaths of the fallen.

Sirius knelt beside Airella, gently brushing damp strands of hair from her face. "Stay with me," he murmured, his voice softer now, edged with something almost tender. "You're alright."

She blinked up at him, still struggling against the drug's effects. "You… you saved me."

He huffed a tired chuckle. "I always do."

Airella tried to smile, though it was weak. "You know… I totally had that under control."

Sirius arched a brow, amusement flickering in his golden eyes. "Oh, of course. I could tell by the way you collapsed dramatically into the mud."

She scoffed, managing a half-hearted glare. "I was lulling them into a false sense of security."

He smirked, shaking his head. "Right. Next time, I'll let you handle it."

She groaned, burying her face in his chest. "I hate you."

His arms tightened around her, his warmth steadying. "No, you don't."

She sighed, her exhaustion settling in again. "Maybe just a little."

Sirius chuckled, pressing a light kiss to the top of her head. "Rest," he whispered, holding her close as he kept watch over the darkened forest. "I've got you."

$\mathcal{A}$irella awoke the next morning with a start, feeling the rhythmic movements of the horse beneath her. Startled, she realized she had been leaning against Sirius while unconscious. As she straightened up, she took a moment to gather her thoughts, reflecting on the events of the previous night.

"About time," Sirius remarked, his voice low, a trace of amusement in it.

Airella remained silent, her attention drawn to the gentle patter of rain around them. Then she noticed the dark cloth billowing around her. Sirius had given her his cloak. A protective gesture, one that sent an unfamiliar warmth curling in her chest. She swallowed, shaking away the feeling, and turned her focus back to the familiar trail they traveled.

Yet, an inexplicable sensation swept over her, setting her nerves on edge. She scanned the surrounding tree line for any signs of movement. Birds darted between branches, the forest thick with life, but still, the eerie feeling of being watched clung to her.

"Sirius—"

"I know," he responded, his voice carrying a growl of unease.

That alone sent a shiver through her. There were few things that unsettled Sirius, and she knew only one person had the power to elicit such a reaction besides Duran.

"Are you sure we're heading in the right direction?" Sirius asked, guiding the dark horse along the winding trail.

Riding wasn't his preferred method of travel—evident by the tightness in his grip on the reins. He did it because she had been weakened by the effects of the drug, and without hesitation, he had taken control, his body solid and steady behind her.

"We're here!" Airella cheered as she slid off the horse with practiced ease.

Sirius followed, landing a bit less gracefully. Airella removed his cloak from her shoulders and quickly handed it back, her fingers brushing his in the exchange. A flicker of something passed between them, an awareness that neither of them acknowledged.

Together, they approached the weathered old door of a small cottage. Before Airella could knock, a raspy voice called out from within, announcing the imminent arrival of its occupant.

The woman, her faded blonde hair swept into a loose braid, swung the door open, green eyes widening with disbelief as they landed on Airella.

Sirius stepped back, watching as the woman enveloped Airella in a crushing embrace.

"Oh, Airella! We were so worried! It's a blessing to see you safe and sound," she exclaimed.

Before Airella could reply, a blur of movement shot past Elizabeth. Arii, her younger brother, ran straight into her arms.

"Airella!" he shouted excitedly, wrapping his arms around her waist. "I missed you so much! You were gone forever! Did you fight any bad guys?"

Airella laughed, ruffling his sandy blonde hair. "More than you can imagine."

Arii gasped. "I knew it! Did you use your axe? Were they scary?"

She crouched down to his level, lowering her voice to a playful whisper. "Terrifying. But you know me—I handled it."

Arii beamed, nodding in admiration before glancing past her. His green eyes landed on Sirius, widening in curiosity. "Who's he?"

Sirius arched a brow, watching the boy with mild amusement.

"This is Sirius," Airella said, standing again. "He's... a friend."

Arii looked between them, then back at his sister, grinning mischievously. "He's haaaandsome," he playfully sang that last word, poking fun at his sister.

Airella groaned, covering her face. "Mother, control your son."

Elizabeth chuckled, ushering them inside. "Come in, both of you. You must be exhausted."

Inside, the warmth of the small home wrapped around them. As the evening stretched on, Airella recounted their journey, her voice carrying the weight of every battle, every loss. When she spoke of Jonathan, she clutched the pendant at her throat, her fingers white-knuckled around the glass.

Sirius said nothing, but he felt her pain like his own.

After she finished, Airella turned to her mother, her tone more serious. "We can't stay here. Soldiers will come looking for us once they realize we're no longer in Aramore. This will be the first place they search."

Elizabeth paled slightly but nodded. "Then we will leave at first light."

"I know it's sudden," Airella said, reaching for her mother's hands, "but we don't have a choice. We need to be somewhere safe."

Elizabeth exhaled shakily before squeezing Airella's hands in reassurance. "Then we'll pack what we can tonight."

Sirius, meanwhile, found his gaze drifting. Just as he let his thoughts settle, an overwhelming vision crashed over him.

A cavern—dark, damp, and reeking of mildew. The walls dripped with moisture, the air thick with something oppressive.

A boy stood in the center, small and frail, his black hair hanging in unkempt strands over his face. He was barefoot, his thin frame dressed in nothing but ragged trousers. His yellow eyes reflected exhaustion, a life spent surviving on scraps.

A towering figure loomed before him, shrouded in a mist of black shadow. Tendrils of darkness curled and writhed around it, and within the depths of the mist, glowing violet eyes stared down at the boy.

"Are you afraid?" the figure asked, its voice hollow, cold.

The boy shook his head slowly.

"Is that so?" the figure chuckled darkly, stepping closer, its form moving with an unnatural glide. "Tell me, are you afraid of Miscreants?"

Again, the boy shook his head. Silence hung heavy between them.

Then, the shadow reached forward, the mist curling against the boy's shoulder in an unnatural caress. "You are something else, boy," it mused, its voice dripping with intrigue. "What is your name?"

The boy hesitated. Then, barely above a whisper, he answered. "Alikad."

The creature chuckled, its violet eyes gleaming. "You may call me Father."

Sirius gasped, the vision tearing away as quickly as it came. He blinked rapidly, his breath unsteady, his mind reeling.

"Sirius?" Airella's voice pulled him back to reality. She frowned, her hand hovering over his arm. "Are you alright?"

He exhaled, trying to shake the lingering remnants of the vision. "Yeah. Just... tired."

Airella studied him for a moment but didn't press further. Instead, she let out a quiet sigh. "Come on, let's get some rest."

She led him to a small, familiar room. The scent of aged parchment and lavender drifted around them. She settled onto the bed, running her hands over the old quilt. After a moment, she glanced up at him, hesitating.

"You don't have to sleep on the floor, you know," she said softly. "There's enough room."

Sirius stiffened slightly, glancing between the bed and the small amount of space it provided. "Are you sure?"

Airella shrugged, feigning nonchalance. "It's not like we haven't shared worse conditions."

He hesitated for only a moment before finally nodding. Quietly, he moved to sit on the bed, feeling the mattress dip unevenly beneath their weight.

The space between them was small. Too small. Her scent wrapped around him, warm and distracting, the faintest trace of pine and steel lingering beneath the lavender.

Minutes stretched into an eternity.

Then, without thinking, Airella shifted, her fingers brushing his.

A sharp breath caught in Sirius's throat. His instinct was to pull away—but he didn't. Instead, he let his fingers curl around hers, slow and deliberate.

The touch was electrifying, charged with something deeper than either of them dared to voice.

Airella turned her head slightly, her breath fanning against his jaw. "Sirius…"

His name on her lips was almost his undoing.

He turned to face her, his golden eyes locking onto her mismatched ones in the dim candlelight. The tension crackled between them, unspoken words lingering in the silence.

"You should sleep," he murmured, his voice rough.

She swallowed hard but didn't pull away. "So should you."

Sirius exhaled sharply, his fingers tightening around hers for just a moment before he forced himself to close his eyes.

Airella, however, remained wide awake, feeling the steady rise and fall of his breath beside her. The knowledge that he was there—that he had chosen to stay—sent a warmth through her she didn't fully understand.

And as the night stretched on, she realized one undeniable truth.

She wasn't afraid.

Not of him.

Not of this.

28

As Airella lay asleep, a strange disturbance suddenly crept over her, stirring her from her slumber. In the depths of a dream, a flash of piercing blue eyes startled her, sending an icy chill through her entire being.

Startled awake, she sat upright in bed. Beside her, Sirius also awoke. His golden eyes gleamed in the darkness.

"We know you're in there!" A commanding voice echoed from outside.

Airella's heart raced with fear.

"We have to leave, now," Sirius urged.

Peering cautiously through the window, Airella spotted a group of well-armed soldiers converging on the home's entrance.

It's happening again, she thought, a sense of déjà vu washing over her.

Opening the bedroom door, Airella and Sirius cautiously descended the staircase. From a vantage point above, they observed as Elizabeth greeted the uninvited visitors in the dead of night.

"May I assist you, gentlemen?" Elizabeth's voice quivered slightly, her robe tightly secured around her.

"You are hiding fugitives, wanted by the king himself," Duran accused firmly, his face etched with determination.

"Sir, I assure you, I know nothing of this absurd claim," Elizabeth retorted, a forced laugh betraying her anxiety.

"Search the premises," Duran commanded.

The large group of soldiers, clad in armor and determination, surged into the home.

Airella's heart raced as they rushed back into the bedroom. When Sirius gestured urgently towards the window, a glimmer of hope sparked in her eyes—the window, their only feasible route to freedom. As they made a desperate dash across the room, the creak of the bedroom door shattered the fragile silence.

In a blur of motion, she was pulled into the depths of the wardrobe, her breath catching in her throat as she pressed against Sirius's chest. The stillness of the moment was deafening, the only sound of her own heart pounding in her ears. The soldiers' heavy footsteps echoed through the room.

"Someone's been here, sir," a soldier's voice broke through the tension.

"So it seems," the voice of Duran, cold and commanding, sliced through the air like a blade. "Burn it down. Let's not give them a place to run back to."

The order to burn down the cottage sent a wave of dread crashing over her, the heat of the flames licking at her skin even before they engulfed the wardrobe. Sirius forced the door to the wardrobe open and quickly searched for an escape.

As the fire roared around them, Airella's mind raced with memories of the home she was about to lose—the familiar creak of the floorboards, the soft glow of the hearth, the laughter that once filled the halls now silenced by the flames. She steeled herself against the rising panic, her resolve hardening at the thought of preserving her past amidst the chaos. The painted family portraits that hung from her walls seemed to watch her with accusing eyes, urging her to fight against the destruction that threatened to consume everything she held dear.

Just as despair threatened to overwhelm her, the sound of Arii's screams cut through the chaos.

"Let's go!" Sirius's urgent call rang through the loud flames, the crackling fire creating a chaotic symphony around them.

"Arii!" Her heart pounded with a mix of fear and adrenaline, the rush of emotions overwhelming her senses.

As she hurried towards Sirius to peer out the window, her eyes strained through the swirling smoke. She stood frozen, watching in anguish as the soldiers ruthlessly seized a screaming Arii.

Through the haze, she caught a fleeting sight of her mother lying motionless on the ground. Standing over her was the possessed Duran. He shifted his gaze to meet Airella's, and he smiled.

The soldiers vanished into the night, disappearing into the darkness with Arii in their clutches. Airella was consumed by a surge of helplessness and desperation. She was frozen, unable to move as her mind tried to process the events unfolding before her. The acrid smoke enveloped her, each breath a painful reminder of the chaos surrounding her.

With the flames encroaching, threatening to devour everything in their path, Sirius, acting on instinct, swiftly gathered Airella in his arms.

In a moment of pure determination, he made a daring decision and leaped through the window, the heat of the flames fading as they escaped into the cool night air.

The ground rushed up to meet them as they landed from the 2-story fall, the impact jolting through their bodies. Adrenaline coursed through Airella as she took in her surroundings, her eyes darting to her mother lying still on the ground.

In that suspended moment, time seemed to stand still, the world holding its breath as the gravity of the situation sank in. The thought that her mother might be lost to her forever weighed heavily on her.

"Mother?" Airella fell to her knees next to her mother, shaking her by the shoulders. She could feel the coldness of her mother's skin and the weightlessness of her body. "Sirius!" She turned her gaze up to Sirius, desperation clear in her voice and tears welling up in her eyes. "Bring her back, like you did to Jonathan. Please!" Airella's voice cracked as she begged.

Sirius, his face a mask of stoicism, closed his eyes and shook his head slowly. "It's too late. Her soul has already departed from her physical form," he stated softly, his words heavy with finality. "I also only have one pendant to use, and Jonathan's soul is currently occupying it," Sirius attempted to explain, but Airella was lost in her grief, unable to fully grasp the magnitude of the situation. Tears streamed down her cheeks unchecked, blurring her vision.

"No!" Airella's cry echoed. It was then that she discovered the bloody stab wound implanted in her mother's chest. The sight of it made her heart lurch with a mix of horror and sorrow. Elizabeth must have been fighting for Arii, sacrificing herself to protect her son. This was Father's doing.

Tears continued to stream down Airella's face as she stood amidst the chaos, her fists clenched in frustration. The soldiers had taken Arii away, leaving her feeling helpless. Airella's gaze darted around, noticing that they had even taken the horse they used to get here. The sense of defeat threatened to overwhelm her, tempting her to give up then and there. But she couldn't. Arii needed her; he needed to be rescued. She wouldn't give up on him.

Covered in smudges of ash, Airella couldn't contain her sobs as her home continued to burn in the dead of night. It all felt like a surreal nightmare, as if she would wake up at any moment and find everything restored to normal.

"She's gone..." Airella whispered, her fists tightening in grief as she held her mother's lifeless body.

Neighboring villagers crowded around the scene. Some whispered accusations in hushed tones, pointing fingers at the young woman before them.

"I knew she was a witch!"

"Murdered her own mother..."

"Who is that strange man?"

Anger seared through Airella as she absorbed their misguided assumptions. These people did not know about what had just happened. Her heart ached for her lost mother, but she knew she had to focus on the immediate challenges ahead. With Arii's safety hanging in the balance and the looming threat of the kingdom's soldiers, Airella steeled herself for the arduous journey ahead.

"Let's go," she muttered under her breath, determination shining in her bloodshot eyes as she turned away from her mother's lifeless form, ready to face the uncertain path that lay before her.

29

To Sirius, the humans on this land appeared far more merciless compared to the old Miscreant Slayers of the island. As he reflected on his own past destructive actions, a fierce glare crept across his face as he surveyed the surrounding villagers.

Lifting his scythe above his head, he made a swift diagonal slash, creating a striking flash of black and twilight hues that forced Airella to shield her eyes.

Startled by the dazzling display, Airella shouted over the crackling flames, "What is that?"

Before she could receive an answer, she noticed the pitch-black portal with jagged white lines resembling a tear in fabric. Ignoring her inquiry, Sirius clutched her hand, swiftly pulling her through the mysterious portal that beckoned behind him.

"Hmph, I remember the world of Limbo being a lot less dark," Sirius spoke aloud as he scanned the area.

The house they had been standing in front of was now a darkened black and was engulfed in white flames. Even the people surrounding them were darkly colored as they shuffled around. Airella attempted to touch her lifeless mother with her hand, but her physical form never made contact with her. The two were completely oblivious to everyone and everything outside of Limbo.

"Where are we?" Airella turned to face Sirius, her eyes wide with curiosity as she surveyed their surroundings. Sirius met her gaze, his expression calm and knowing.

"This is Limbo. It's the place where lost spirits find themselves when they lose their way." He gestured toward a transparent humanoid spirit nearby, its translucent form gripped with disbelief as it gazed upon Airella's burning home.

Airella's thoughts drifted to her mother, but Sirius anticipated her unspoken question.

"Your mother isn't here," he reassured her gently, his words carrying a sense of understanding. "If she were, we would have seen her by now. She must have transitioned smoothly to her next life." Turning back to Airella, he reached out and took her hand in his. "Jonathan. Release him from the necklace. In this realm, his essence will manifest as a transparent figure."

Airella bowed her head slightly, her fingers delicately retrieving the glowing necklace from beneath the collar of her white blouse. Sirius nodded in approval as she presented the pendant to him, his hand hovering over the glass surface. After a brief pause, the locket opened with a soft click.

A radiant blue light enveloped Airella, a shimmering aura of energy as Jonathan's form emerged from the jewelry. He embraced her, the blue figure of his soul holding her close before stepping back. His armor still adorned his ethereal blue shape, every detail preserved from the moment Sirius had transferred his essence into the pendant.

"Jonathan?" she shuttered slightly, a hint of fear flickering in her eyes as she took in his appearance from head to toe. "It's really you," she breathed, relief flooding her features as she returned his embrace warmly.

Meanwhile, Sirius tightened his grip on the scythe's hilt, a shiver running down his spine as a mysterious presence enveloped him.

"We've got company," Sirius muttered grimly, his eyes scanning the shadowy tree line warily as he twirled the scythe in his hands.

Airella's grip on Dawnbreaker tightened at Sirius's words. "What is it?" she questioned, anticipation and concern evident in her voice.

"Miscreant," Sirius replied.

A rustle in the nearby shrubbery caught Jonathan off guard. In a swift motion, Sirius turned to Airella, his fists clenched in determination. "Protect Jonathan. He's vulnerable to most Miscreants that have access to Limbo in his current condition," he commanded, bracing himself as the dark figure leaped towards them. As the malevolent being swung its scythe, Sirius's quick reflexes deflected the attack with a resounding clash.

The mysterious figure, shrouded in a hooded cloak that concealed all features, stood imposingly taller than Sirius. Every movement exuded a sense of foreboding, from the intricate scythe in hand to the enigmatic, black-wrapped hands that hinted at a hidden purpose. The scythe itself was a marvel of craftsmanship, its dual-bladed design unlike anything the trio had encountered, its blackened edge gleaming ominously in the dim light of Limbo.

"I regret to inform you, Sirius, that your existence must end," declared the figure in a chilling tone, preparing to strike with lethal intent.

With a fierce determination, Airella attempted to shield Sirius from the impending danger, but the hilt of the stranger's weapon forcefully pushed her back. As she stumbled to the ground, clutching her chest in pain, Jonathan hurried to her aid.

Amidst the chaos, Airella's startled realization echoed, "I thought Miscreants only existed on the isle." Her grip tightened on Jonathan's arm as he kneeled beside her, his gaze fixed warily on the cloaked figure.

"How do you know me?" Sirius questioned. "Are you a reaper as well?" As he spoke, he clenched his teeth in determination, ready to fend off his foe's relentless attacks.

"I am not just some soul-eater, Sirius," the cloaked figure retorted, his words dripping with disdain. With a deliberate motion, he plunged his scythe into the dark earth. There was an intensity in his voice—harsh, deep, and pristine.

"If you're not like me, then what are you?" Sirius exclaimed, finally landing a blow on his opponent.

A gold stream of blood trickled from the wound on the stranger's chest. Realization dawned on Sirius, widening his eyes as he acknowledged his grave error.

The stranger's retaliation was swift and powerful, launching Sirius towards the nearest tree with such force that it uprooted upon impact. Agony engulfed Sirius as he collided with the trunk, the world spinning around him.

Amid the chaos, Airella's gasp resonated alongside the stranger's unwavering stance and Jonathan's stunned reaction. As the tree crashed to the ground, darkness enveloped Sirius, consciousness slipping away.

With deliberate slowness, the cloaked figure raised a hand to lower his hood, revealing a startling reflection of Sirius himself, with jet-black hair cascading around his face.

"I'm not like you, Sirius. I am you," he declared with a chilling certainty.

Sirius envisioned a new scenario within the depths of his unconscious mind. A feeling, a strange mix of curiosity and fear, washed over the older boy, compelling him to explore this altered reality further.

As he gazed upon his changed form, he realized he was like an entirely different person compared to the child he last envisioned. This transformed version of himself appeared older, the missing skin on his hands now replaced by a web of intricate bone structure. Draped in a long, tattered, black hooded cloak, he felt a sense of unfamiliarity shroud his existence.

The once dark-haired boy had metamorphosed into a mere recreation, a specter of his former identity. His hair, now a ghostly shade of white, stood in stark contrast to his eyes, which gleamed a haunting yellow, reminiscent of the moon on a cloudless night.

A largely built man, towering before him, emanated an aura of formidable strength. Crimson blood drenched his graying beard, creating a stark contrast against the lifeless bodies scattered in all directions, remnants of the fallen Miscreant Slayers. Some figures resembled mere husks, drained of vitality, and had lost limbs. Their once expressive eyes now glazed over in a haunting milky white hue.

Standing alone, the leader of the Slayers faced the soul-eater. The charred remnants of what were once the cottages and homes of the Slayers now lay in ruin, their former warmth replaced by ash and destruction.

"You are mad!" the burly man yelled as he attempted to lift his war hammer from the ground. "You may have destroyed the barrier, killed my people, and destroyed our village, but there is at least one thing you can't destroy, and that would be my daughter! Mark my words, Miscreant... the day you cross paths with her is the day you'll cease to exist! She will avenge us all!"

"Daughter?" Sirius pressed his clothed hand against the man's old bushy chin. "What is the name of your daughter?"

"It's none of your concern, soul-eater! As long as she is far away from you, she's better off with that ice hellion." The man's words sparked interest in the young reaper.

Sirius turned around to walk away, intending to spare the old man's life, that was until the Slayer quickly stood to his feet and raised his war hammer over the reaper's head.

A stunned pause seized the man as a shadow loomed above the reaper, halting him in mid-stride. His weapon slipped from his grip as a colossal shadowy hand, twice his size, ensnared him. With a firm hold on the Miscreant Slayer, the shadowy hand exerted its crushing force. A shadowy humanoid figure materialized beside the young reaper, emitting a chaotic chuckle.

"Do you even realize who you're addressing, boy?" the shadowy figure, Father, bellowed, hovering close to the bearded man struggling against the hand's grasp. "This is Emmaline's father! Never underestimate that cunning rascal, Sirius. The ice hellion she dwells with wields power almost comparable to mine. I cannot afford to exhaust all my might shielding you from him."

"Why did you attack, fool?" the reaper inquired, diverting his gaze from Father toward the towering man. "I spared your life, yet you chose to strike. Are you simply foolish or driven by the honor of slaying Miscreants? Your actions reek of selfishness, as if you wish to discard your own life—"

"It's not about honor or folly," the old Slayer interjected, seizing the reaper's attention abruptly. "It's about family, safeguarding your loved ones. That's my purpose... protecting my daughter! As long as Zol ensures her safety until she reunites with me in the afterlife... it seems my job here is complete." With a last gasp and a crushing squeeze of Father's shadowy hand, blood trickled from the corners of his mouth.

Sirius took his scythe, its blade glinting in the dim light, and gazed into its polished surface for a fleeting moment. Amidst the tension, an unexpected wave of sympathy washed over him for the man before him. Father stood beside him, his shadowy arms now back to their usual size and folded across his chest in impatience. Sirius, with a determined yet conflicted expression, raised his weapon high before delivering the decisive final blow.

30

*I*n that heart-stopping moment of realization, Airella's chest tightened as she watched the tree crash down.

"Sirius!" her breath caught in her throat as the word escaped her lips in a panicked scream. With adrenaline coursing through her veins, she dashed towards his fallen form, Jonathan hot on her heels.

As they kneeled by Sirius's motionless body, a chill settled over Airella as she registered the severity of the situation. The sense of urgency intensified, but she fought to maintain a facade of calm, even as the specter of death loomed in the form of the black-haired stranger before them. The sight of gold blood seeping from Sirius's wound sent a shiver down her spine.

She turned to Jonathan, whose ethereal appearance matched her own disbelief and fear. Airella's mind raced with the realization that this stranger, so eerily similar to Sirius, held the power to claim Jonathan's essence. The urgency of the situation pressed upon her, urging her to act swiftly. Fingers trembling, she retrieved the pendant from beneath her shirt.

"Jonathan, you have to go back!" Airella implored, her voice laced with desperation as she clutched the pendant tightly. Jonathan's bewildered response only fueled her resolve, each moment ticking by fraught with uncertainty.

"I don't know how!" Jonathan's voice wavered.

Airella's fingers gripped tightly to Dawnbreaker, the cool metal providing a sense of grounding in the eerie world of Limbo. Dark, shadowy figures of villagers ambled past her with an unsettling nonchalance, as if the surreal events unfolding around them were of no consequence. Among them, the reaper who bore an uncanny resemblance to Sirius made his way towards Airella. The shock of his appearance rippled through her, for he was a mirror image of Sirius, save for his jet-black hair and imposing stature.

"Who are you? How did you escape the isle? And why do you look like Sirius?" Airella stood her ground in front of Jonathan, her grip firm on her weapon.

Uncertainty knotted in her stomach at the thought of facing a Miscreant who had effortlessly bested Sirius.

"My name is Alikad. Why do you aid this traitor? He is loyal to Father." Alikad's accusation sliced through the tense air as he surged forward. Airella deftly sidestepped his initial strike, her mind racing to decipher the cryptic connection between them. "Return to your realm or join your fallen comrades." With a deft motion, he cleaved through the fabric of reality, a shimmering portal materializing before them, much like the one Sirius had manipulated upon their arrival.

The portal felt as if it were a voracious entity, greedily pulling air into its swirling depths like a hungry vacuum. Airella hesitated, knowing that once she crossed over, returning would be impossible without Sirius by her side.

"Airella, go... you can't beat this guy," Jonathan murmured softly.

"And abandon both you and Sirius? I'll at least try to hold my ground," Airella replied, a surge of determination flooding her senses. It reminded her of the fierce resolve she felt the first time she clashed with the Sirius she once knew. It was a potent mix of courage and strength that fueled her now. With a resolute gaze towards Alikad, she silently signaled her decision to remain.

"You humans always complicate matters," Alikad remarked with a hint of disdain as he lunged towards her. Airella braced herself for the impending strike. His scythe sliced down swiftly, but she parried his blow as their weapons clashed in a symphony of metal. His movements were swift, almost blurring in their speed, testing her limits.

A rivulet of gold liquid seeped from the wound on his chest, bearing a striking resemblance to the hue of Sirius's blood. Airella couldn't help but notice Jonathan's anxious expression in her peripheral vision, wincing with each assault the assailant unleashed upon her.

"Check on Sirius!" she yelled to him, making a swift swing at Alikad. Despite her effort, the blade of her weapon only grazed through the fabric of his cloak, leaving a faint mark. Pausing briefly, she vividly recalled the intense anger that engulfed Alikad when Sirius had inflicted a wound on him. The fear of facing a similar wrath from him gripped her.

Alikad halted his advance, his gaze shifting towards Jonathan, who was frantically attempting to rouse Sirius from his unconscious state. With a last glance in Airella's direction, he pivoted swiftly, charging towards the ethereal blue spirit. Airella's eyes widened in a horror.

"No!" her voice resonated with desperation as she pushed her legs to match his pace, her heart racing at the thought of losing Jonathan to Alikad's clutches.

She hurled Dawnbreaker towards Alikad, the blade finding

its mark squarely in his back, propelling him to the ground in a swift motion. As she sprinted past him, she swiftly retrieved her weapon from its lodged position, a sense of urgency pushing her forward. The mission to secure Sirius and ensure the safety of all consumed her.

Before she could finish her last thought, Airella felt a hand wrap around her ankle, causing her to trip and lose her grip on Dawnbreaker. She flipped over onto her back so she could get a better view of her attacker, who was in the process of climbing over her in pain.

Rage burned in his yellow eyes, reflecting the fury raging within him. His knees pinned Airella's wrists to the ground, rendering her arms useless. She clenched her teeth in pain. He pulled back his fist, the muscles tensed with unrestrained anger, and threw a punch aimed straight at her face.

Airella moved her head away from the impending blow just in time, narrowly avoiding the impact that cracked the ground beneath him. With a fierce determination, he launched a second punch from the opposite side; the force leaving the same shattered ground in its wake, yet she continued to evade his strikes with swift precision. Fueled by anger, he seized her by the collar of her shirt, pulling her face closer to his with a menacing glare.

"You should be dead already. Unless..." Alikad snarled, his menacing figure towering over Airella as he stood.

With a swift motion, he flung Airella across the ground, causing her to gasp in pain as she collided with the unforgiving earth. As she struggled to regain her breath, Airella tasted a metallic flavor in her mouth and felt a sense of dread as she realized her own blood stained her palm.

"You're that half-breed girl," Alikad taunted as he picked up his scythe.

With a menacing grin, he raised the weapon, the sharp edge glinting as he brought it down with lethal precision, the ground shuddering beneath the force of the blow. Airella's quick reflexes saved her from a fatal strike as she rolled to the side, narrowly evading the deadly blade.

"Well, aren't you going to save the day?" Alikad's words dripped with mockery as he relentlessly attacked Airella, descending upon her with his scythe in an unrelenting onslaught.

Airella had no respite between his brutal strikes, each blow forcing her to roll and dodge to avoid a fatal hit. She felt like a cornered prey, her movements driven by sheer survival instinct.

With a surge of anger, Alikad grabbed a fistful of Airella's blonde hair, yanking her to her feet with a cruel grip. Airella's heart pounded in fear as she struggled against his strength, her eyes wide with desperation.

"There is hellion blood running through your veins, Airella," Alikad hissed, the words a chilling reminder of her cursed lineage. With a final display of his brutal power, he threw her to the ground, the impact sending shockwaves of pain through her body.

"I suppose your inner Miscreant hasn't been awakened just yet... but trust me, I'm trying to spare you the agony." Alikad's taunts echoed in Airella's ears, his cryptic words adding to her confusion and fear.

Her thoughts tangled in a web of confusion, each thread leading back to the same unanswered questions—how did he know who she was, what she was?

Just as a surge of fear threatened to wash over her, the reaper standing before her let out a malevolent snicker, his eyes gleaming with an unsettling gleam as he poised himself to deliver what seemed like a final, crushing blow.

But in that precarious moment, a sudden inexplicable calm descended upon the scene. Airella stood, almost suspended in time, as the world surrounding her seemed to freeze in a surreal stillness, as if time itself had momentarily ceased to flow.

As she teetered on the edge of consciousness, a haunting question echoed in her mind—was this the end? Had she suffered defeat? The darkness seemed to close in around her, suffocating and all-encompassing.

Suddenly, a blinding flash shattered the darkness, revealing an ominous presence—an obsidian-like Miscreant pacing restlessly in an icy cavern. A sense of déjà vu washed over Airella as she gazed at the figure. His dark, obsidian-like skin and piercing icy blue eyes stirred a flicker of recognition within her.

"Zol? From the island?" Airella's thoughts raced.

Questions swirled in her mind—hadn't they already departed? Why was she back here? Tentatively, she reached out towards Zol, only to find herself met with an unsettling realization—she was invisible, a mere specter in this frozen realm.

As Zol turned his gaze towards the cave's entrance, a voice shattered the silence, freezing Airella in place. The familiarity of the voice sent shivers down her spine, resonating deep within her being. It was a voice she knew all too well—her own.

The young girl entered the dark, foreboding cave, her eyes brimming with tears that reflected the dim light within. Airella, standing there in stunned silence, couldn't help but notice the uncanny resemblance between them. It was as if looking into a twisted mirror that distorted reality just enough to create an unsettling familiarity. Despite the similarities, subtle differences set them apart—delicate freckles dusting one's cheeks, variations in facial structure, and a cascade of curls tumbling down the other's shoulders. Yet, their silhouettes, body shapes, and even their height mirrored one another.

One other thing that immediately caught Airella's eye was the delicate blue pendant dangling from the girl's neck. As she locked eyes with it, a rush of memories flooded her mind. It was

Jonathan's pendant—a cherished memento that now found its place around her own neck.

"Zol!" The girl exclaimed as she collapsed into Zol's embrace, her voice trembling with emotion.

Airella's mind swirled with confusion and questions. Why Zol? Why in this enigmatic dream? And why did this mysterious girl bear such a striking resemblance to her? The weight of unspoken inquiries crowded her thoughts, leaving her bewildered and unable to make sense of the unfolding scene.

"Emmaline, what happened?" Zol's words carried a hint of an unfamiliar accent.

Tears glistened in Emmaline's eyes as she recounted her harrowing encounter in the woods. "I stumbled upon a dying man in the woods. He warned me to stay away from the village, saying that it had been engulfed in flames," her voice quivered as Zol enveloped her in a comforting embrace.

"Do not weep, Emma," he murmured softly, holding her close.

At that moment, amidst the shadows of the cave, their intertwined fates stood shrouded in mystery, leaving Airella to ponder the depths of their connection and the untold secrets that bound them together.

31

Realization dawned on Airella as Alikad swung his scythe down upon her. With every ounce of energy she could muster, she rolled out of the blade's path, but her efforts were in vain. The sharp edge of the scythe lightly grazed her side, leaving behind a searing crimson mark that slowly welled with fresh blood. Airella winced in agony, struggling to rise to her feet amidst the throbbing pain.

"Enough of this, children," Father's commanding voice resonated through the realm of Limbo.

Alikad cursed silently, his eyes darting around, searching for any trace of the shadow demon. While the reaper's attention was diverted, Airella hurried to where Jonathan kneeled and Sirius lay unconscious. Jonathan's eyes widened as he noticed the wound on Airella's side.

"You're hurt!" Jonathan exclaimed in shock.

"It's just a scratch, I'll manage. You've faced worse." Airella's words carried a reminder of Jonathan's sacrifice for her. "Let's go while he's distracted."

"Right," Jonathan began, but his words trailed off as Sirius spoke with closed eyes, his voice barely a whisper.

"Emmaline..." Sirius muttered.

Airella's body tensed, her muscles contracting involuntarily, a searing pain shooting through her like a bolt of lightning as she mustered the strength to stand up straight. The wound on her side throbbed with an intensity that seemed to echo through the desolate realm of Limbo.

As she struggled against the unseen forces at play, she realized Limbo was not a welcoming abode for the living, its very essence rejecting their presence. Yet, amidst the chaos, a realization struck her—Sirius, the reaper by her side, endured Limbo's influence as well. Deprived of his usual sustenance of human souls, the unnatural grip of this realm seemed to twist and distort his being, just as it did hers.

"Airella, what's wrong?" Jonathan's voice was tinged with confusion as he regarded Airella.

"I... I don't know," Airella stammered, her gaze darting back and forth between Alikad and Sirius.

"Emmaline?" Sirius's eyes fluttered open, his consciousness returning.

For a fleeting moment, Airella was rendered speechless, a confirmation dawning upon her that these were not mere illusions. Collapsing to her knees, she hovered over Sirius, gripping his shoulders.

"Emmaline. That name. Where did you hear that name?" Airella's eyes searched his for any flicker of understanding.

"Airella!" Jonathan's cry pierced the tense atmosphere.

"Tell me," she demanded, her gaze drilling into Sirius.

"Father?" Sirius's vision was a blur, the world around him hazy and unfocused. He struggled to comprehend Airella's words as they echoed in his ears. His head spun, a whirlwind of confusion and pain clouding his thoughts.

The moment Alikad ceased moving, a strange sensation washed over Sirius, freezing him in place.

As Airella and Jonathan came to a sudden halt, their expressions of shock mirrored each other's as they turned to face him.

"You have a lot of nerve showing up here, Father." Sirius uttered through gritted teeth, his voice strained with effort.

Clutching his side, he cast a wary glance towards Alikad, his eyes narrowing in agony as he discovered the fresh wound etched upon his skin. The opposing reaper's strike had been swift and merciless, the searing pain radiating through Sirius's body like a raging inferno. Overwhelmed by the intensity of it all, Sirius sank to his knees, his strength failing him.

Airella rushed to his side, her concern palpable as she reached out to support him, but Sirius raised a trembling hand, warding her off. Was it fear that gripped him now, or simply the excruciating pain that threatened to consume him whole? Even Jonathan, standing nearby, failed to perceive the flicker of fear that danced in Sirius's eyes, masked by a facade of determination.

As Sirius struggled to rise, he slowly peeled back his cloak, revealing the extent of his injuries. Alikad's attack had inflicted far more damage than he had initially realized. The gaping wound snaked its way from his stomach, curving towards his back before terminating at his right hip.

"It looks like you're wounded," the now possessed Alikad spat and cracked his neck, making it pop loudly as he turned. "I thought you were tougher than this. Now, look at you. Pathetic."

Sirius watched him as he laughed at his pain. He stood and hunched himself over his own scythe for support while gold blood seeped from his large wounds. His breaths came in ragged gasps, the metallic tang of blood heavy in the surrounding air.

Father exerted control over Alikad's body, manipulating his

movements. With a forceful gesture, he pivoted Alikad around, unveiling a face contorted with a blend of insanity and rage. Though he concealed his fury outwardly, a flicker of anger gleamed unmistakably in his eyes. Sinister black veins snaked across Alikad's form, his skin taking on a ghastly gray hue as if his very vitality was being drained by Father's malevolent presence.

Father traced a finger along his chin as he circled before the trio. "You're fortunate to still draw breath," he spoke with a hint of disappointment. Grasping the scythe nearby, his expression twisted into another maniacal grin. "Once I finish with you, you'll no longer impede my plans."

Sirius leaned in, his jaw clenched in frustration. "What twisted scheme are you orchestrating, Father?" Then, the realization hit him, prompting a surge of anger that made him clench his fists until his nails dug into his palms. "This was all part of your design from the very start, wasn't it?" Sirius erupted, his voice laced with fury.

Father's smile widened with a sinister gleam as his gaze shifted to Airella. "A perceptive one, indeed," he taunted, reveling in the unfolding drama with chilling satisfaction. Sirius had finally pieced it all together. Father had meticulously orchestrated every moment leading up to this point, from the very inception of their plan.

"You've been plotting this since they first set step on the isle. Are you really aiming to reintroduce human existence to the island just for the sake of the Miscreant food chain?" Sirius muttered under his breath, struggling as he attempted to rise.

His gaze shifted to Jonathan, and with a swift motion, he snapped his fingers. Jonathan's form shrank until he transformed back into an orb-shaped soul. "Get Jonathan back into the pendant! We have to—"

Airella's piercing scream cut Sirius's words off.

A numbness enveloped him. Looking down at his stomach, Sirius's eyes widened in horror. As he glanced up, he met the sinister gaze of the possessed Alikad, his hand resting on Sirius's shoulder. Sirius's eyes locked onto the blade that had pierced through his chest, emerging from his upper back. The scythe narrowly missed his spine, and searing pain surged through him, surpassing any he had ever known. Struggling to remain upright, he confronted Father, hatred burning in his eyes. Sirius defiantly spat his gold blood onto Father's face. Gruesomely, Father wiped away some of the blood from his mouth, a chilling smile fading into darkness. Sirius fought to stay conscious, but his legs gave way beneath him.

Father withdrew the blade from Sirius's body, watching him crumple to the ground. Curling into a ball, Sirius clutched his wound as Airella hurried to his side. The glowing pendant around her neck indicated Jonathan's safety. Sirius attempted to speak, but his thoughts were a whirlwind, rendering his words incoherent.

"Don't talk," Airella sobbed, her voice quivering with emotion. "Everything will be fine."

"Oh, my dear, nothing is going to be fine," Father's words cut through the tension. "Now that he's out of my way, I can now proceed with my plans." With those chilling words, he exited Alikad's body in a dark fog.

"Airella, take my scythe... create a portal... get us out..." Sirius whispered as he clenched his wounds, his gaze locked on Airella with urgency and trust.

Without hesitation, she quickly lifted the heavy scythe, its weight unfamiliar in her hands. Alikad's body lay motionless on the ground beside her, until suddenly, he jerked back to life and reached for her. Airella's heart raced as surprise took her, her next move uncertain.

In a swift and desperate attempt to defend herself, she

swung the scythe over her head, the blade meeting Alikad's arm with a sickening thud. Pain seared through him, and he let out a guttural cry before seizing the weapon. Their struggle intensified amidst the chaos.

On the ground, Alikad and Sirius, locked in a moment of intense pain and emotion, exchanged a gaze that spoke volumes, their fates intertwined in a cruel twist of destiny.

"I had taken upon myself the duty to kill you, Sirius, and perhaps in doing so, I would free myself from here. However, now that even Father is trying to kill you, I believe it would be best for him not to have his way." He ripped a piece of cloth from his cloak and wrapped it around his injured arm, a golden stain blooming through the fabric. "I now know that killing you won't make much of a difference, but you must defeat Father." With a heavy sigh, he then stood and just simply eyed down Airella, his gaze piercing yet filled with a hint of sorrow.

"Why do you look so much like Sirius?" She questioned.

"Father removed a piece of my soul with a spell when I was young and created the Sirius you know today. He took a piece of me that could be easily manipulated. He can't be trusted. Father has complete control over him, whether or not he realizes it. I watched from Limbo as he mercilessly slaughtered most of the humans on the isle. I have been trapped here for centuries, locked away. However, I saw a chance to retreat from the confines of my cage once Father became distracted with this mess. But no matter how many times I've tried, I can't step foot outside of this world." He stared at her, a flicker of desperation dancing in his eyes.

"I'll help you... but here's the deal." He crouched next to Sirius. "When the time comes and we're merged once again, you will obey me. Got it?"

Sirius nodded in response to the pact that was being sealed between them.

"What are you going to do, then?" Airella raised Dawn-breaker in Sirius's defense. Her heart raced as she faced the looming threat before them, her grip tightening on the weapon she wielded with skill honed through countless battles.

"You have to do the rest, half-breed. I'm just going to get you out of here." Alikad's voice held a steely determination. With a swift motion, he swung his dual-bladed scythe through the air.

In that next moment, Airella's inner strength manifested in a way that even surprised her. Despite the odds stacked against them, she swiftly secured Sirius's scythe to her back as they emerged from the ethereal portal that connected Limbo to the realm of the living. With a sense of purpose driving her every step, she carried him, his weight a burden she bore with unwavering determination.

Together, they navigated the treacherous path to Aramore, towards a village nestled just outside the city gates of the imposing castle that loomed in the distance.

"Hopefully there is a healer there," Airella whispered, her gaze fixed on the flickering lights in the distance. She knew Sirius had a deep wound, too grievous for a mere flame to cauterize.

As she trudged along the path, a heavy darkness enveloped her heart, weighing it down with the burden of sorrow. The memory of not bidding a proper farewell to her mother, let alone lay her to rest beside her father's grave, cast a shadow on her spirit. Tears welled up in her eyes, reflecting the pain and longing that tugged at her soul.

Returning to her own village was not an option, not while the accusing whispers of murder lingered in the air. Determined to seek aid for Sirius, she understood she could not find the solace she sought within the familiar confines of her village. With resolve in her heart, they journeyed forth towards the unknown, hoping to find the help that had eluded her so far.

"Airella, thank you..." Sirius's voice trailed off, his eyes closing in a moment of respite as he leaned into her.

The journey ahead was uncertain, but in that fleeting moment of gratitude, a silent vow passed between them—a promise to stand together against whatever challenges awaited them beyond the village.

32

Airella trudged forward, her footsteps echoing softly on the dirt path as she approached a village.

As she knocked on each weathered door, the sound reverberated through the quiet streets. Finally, after what felt like an eternity, an elderly woman opened her door with a creak. The woman, with wisps of silver hair framing her face, peered at Airella with kind, yet curious, eyes.

"Please, can you help us? Do you know of a healer nearby?" Airella's voice quivered with desperation, her eyes filled with worry as she held Sirius close.

The elderly woman, her wrinkled hands clasped together, looked at the peculiar sight before her.

"Oh, my... I know of many remedies myself. Please come in," the old woman said, her voice filled with a sense of urgency. She gestured for them to enter.

Airella stepped inside, taking in the sight of the small run-down cottage. The room was dimly lit by a flickering candle casting dancing shadows on the walls. The scent of herbs and earth filled the air, creating a soothing atmosphere.

The old woman lived alone, surrounded by books and jars of various liquids. Airella couldn't help but wonder why someone of her age and standing would welcome two strangers, armed and in need, into her humble abode. But in that moment, the urgency of Sirius's condition took precedence over her thoughts.

"Lie him on that bed there. I'll go gather my supplies," the old woman said as she hurried to the cabinets.

Airella carefully carried Sirius, her movements gentle as she settled him onto the single bed nestled in the room's corner. A sense of immense relief washed over her as she did so, yet a heavy burden still lingered on her back—the scythe that seemed to weigh not just on her shoulders, but on her very soul. With a deep exhale, she unstrapped the ominous weapon, letting it drop to the floor with a dull thud. Standing upright, she experienced a sense of relief. The journey had been arduous, spanning at least a day's worth of travel, but she had finally arrived.

Gazing down at Sirius, Airella couldn't shake the comparison to Alikad. The notion that Sirius was some kind of missing piece of Alikad lingered in her mind.

"Jonathan," she murmured softly to herself, fingers absently tracing the intricate design of the necklace adorning her neck. Seeking solace in the familiar trinket, she grappled with the uncertainty looming over them amidst the island's enigmatic circumstances. Fatigue crept upon her, her thoughts muddled as the elderly woman approached.

"Hold this," the old woman commanded, pushing a bucket brimming with what appeared to be a concoction of herbs and remedies into Airella's hands. With a deft motion, she then removed Sirius's cloak, unveiling his gray chest. The woman, unfazed by the sight before her, hovered her wrinkled hands over his battle-scarred body. "What happened here?"

Airella, uncertain whether she referred to Sirius's wounds or his reaper-like appearance, observed as the woman gingerly plucked a few herbs from the bucket and applied them to Sirius's injuries while he lay unconscious.

As Airella stood by, a mixture of concern and weariness clouding her thoughts, a heavy sigh escaped her lips, drawing the old woman's attention. With a sudden intensity in her gaze and her gray hair frizzed in disarray, the woman turned towards Airella, her finger pointing out the weariness etched on Airella's own features.

"You look pretty rough around the edges too," she remarked, prodding Airella's chest lightly with her finger. "Go freshen up. I've got this under control."

She felt so drained she couldn't bring herself to do anything but nod her head reluctantly, her mind filled with a mix of curiosity and apprehension about what might unfold in her absence. She set the bucket of medicinal supplies down gently before tentatively making her way towards the door leading to the compact washroom.

As she walked into the room, the dim light revealed a shattered piece of glass hanging on the wall, casting a distorted reflection. Airella's eyes scanned the fragmented mirror, revealing her face marred with splotches of mud and dirt. She took a step back, her gaze shifting to the wooden tub dominating the washroom. The tub brimmed with steaming water, enveloping the room in a warm, inviting aura that left her feeling oddly comforted. It was almost as if the mysterious host had expected her arrival.

Shrugging off the peculiar sensation, Airella shed her dirty garments and eased herself into the tub, enveloped by the soothing embrace of the soapy water. As she submerged herself, a sharp jolt of pain shot through her left side, a stark reminder of her recent clash with Alikad.

Her mind swirled with a myriad of concerns, from ensuring

Sirius's safety to grappling with the weight of unresolved issues. The looming shadow of Father's presence, her mother's demise, Arii's abduction, Jonathan's tormented soul, Sirius's injuries, and the burden of her own struggles crowded her thoughts, threatening to overwhelm her.

Alikad had explained to Airella that she wasn't human. Duran had somewhat done the same back on the island, leading her to question her own identity and origins. She had always felt different, her exceptional strength and appearance setting her apart from others. Despite knowing her mother was human, the mystery of her lineage lingered.

As she soaked in the soothing warmth of the steaming water, memories of the past few months flooded her mind. Weeks filled with revelations and encounters had reshaped her understanding of the world. The discovery of Miscreants and the dark secrets of the island had shattered her perception of reality, opening her eyes to a hidden realm of danger and intrigue.

Amidst these tumultuous thoughts, Airella found herself plagued by strange flashbacks and visions, remnants of her time in Limbo. The ethereal echoes of that otherworldly place lingered within her. Were these visions a clue to her true heritage, a link to the mysterious girl she resembled in her mind's eye?

Sirius's cryptic words and the mention of a name, Emmaline, added another layer of mystery to her already complicated existence. The connection between her visions and the enigmatic Emmaline tugged at her curiosity. How was it that Sirius had Emmaline's blue pendant all this time? She needed answers.

Closing her eyes against the pain of her wound, Airella found solace in the thought of her parents' peaceful reunion beyond the mortal realm. However, the urgency of rescuing Arii from the clutches of the soldiers weighed heavily on her mind. The bond between them drove her to embark on a perilous journey, determined to reclaim him from the shadows that threatened to consume their fragile peace.

The sharp stinging sensation shot through her torso, abruptly interrupting her contemplations and jolting her back to the present with a gasp.

"Agh!"

Grimacing, she hoisted herself out of the water, the lingering effects of the battle with Alikad clear in the large cut marking her skin.

After dressing herself and drying off, she exited the washroom, her eyes immediately drawn to the old woman tending to Sirius's wounds in the main room.

"How is he?" Anxiousness crept into her voice, concern etched across her features as she awaited the news on Sirius's condition.

"He will be fine," the woman began. With a pause, she added, "Though he is in critical condition... no human could ever survive these wounds."

Airella felt a shiver run down her spine at the woman's words. The way she casually mentioned the severity of the situation sent chills through the room.

"I suppose he's just a lucky one, isn't he?" The woman's grin seemed almost sinister, and Airella couldn't shake the feeling that she was onto them. Perhaps she had just figured out that Sirius wasn't human after all.

"Right," Airella replied, playing along but with a hint of nervousness in her voice.

As the woman continued, her tone shifted. "Your side. It looks like you'll be needing stitches." She began rummaging through a bucket of supplies, the clinking of metal tools filling the room.

"Oh?" Her confusion turned to alarm when the woman retrieved a needle and thread from a nearby drawer. Airella's eyes widened as she glanced down to see blood staining the side of her once white blouse.

"Come here, dear," the woman's voice was almost sing song as she approached Airella. "You wouldn't want an ugly scar on that pretty skin of yours, would you?"

"O—Oh, I don't know about that." Airella stammered, attempting to mask her unease with politeness.

"I've already patched up your friend. Let me fix you up as well. It won't take but a moment," the woman assured with a smile. Airella, feeling a mix of relief and apprehension, took a deep breath before giving a hesitant nod.

She lowered herself onto a creaking wooden chair, the rustic scent of aged wood filling her senses, while the woman settled beside her. As the woman carefully lifted the hem of Airella's shirt, the dim light of the room revealed the extent of the nasty gash that marred her skin.

"Oh my, you sure took a beating," the old woman remarked with a sympathetic shake of her head.

"It's nothing compared to Sirius," Airella replied, bracing herself for the discomfort that followed as the woman deftly began the meticulous stitching process. Each prick of the needle sent a sharp jolt of pain through her, causing her to clench her jaw and squeeze her eyes shut against the sensation.

"Sirius is his name, eh? What about yours?" inquired the woman, her focus unwavering on her task at hand.

"I'm Airella," she responded, mustering a grateful smile despite the discomfort. "And yourself? Thank you so much for taking us in, by the way."

"Odelle," the woman introduced herself, her hands skillfully finishing the last stitch with practiced ease. "Now tell me, Airella, do you believe in Miscreants?" Odelle inquired, her gaze keen as she observed Airella's reaction.

Airella's heart skipped a beat as she felt the weight of the old woman's piercing gaze upon her.

"Miscreants?" Airella chuckled nervously, her fingers fidgeting with the edge of her cloak, trying to ease the tension that seemed to thicken the surrounding air. She was determined to go to great lengths to safeguard Sirius's true identity, knowing the potential risks that loomed ahead. "That sounds a bit far-fetched, doesn't it?"

"Sometimes being far-fetched can lead to unexpected outcomes," the woman remarked before pivoting away from Airella's gaze. Airella, surprised, remained silent, processing the woman's words. "Listen, you and your friend can hang around until he's back on his feet. But once he's good to go, I need you both out of here, understood?"

"Yes, of course. Thank you…" Airella nervously responded as the woman exited the room.

Glancing over at Sirius, she noticed him lying on the bed, his chest swathed in bandages, still unconscious. Airella wished she could've provided more help, but felt uncertain about what more she could do. Pulling a creaky wooden chair closer to the bedside, she settled down, resting her head on one of his makeshift pillows.

Airella knew that once they were both ready, she would need to locate Arii. She understood the importance of returning to Aramore to warn everyone about the dangers of revisiting the island. Despite their prior attempts being futile and resulting in tragedy, Airella was determined to prevent further losses like Jonathan's.

33

During his moments of unconsciousness, a barrage of vivid images tormented Sirius. The lingering effects of Limbo twisted through his mind, manifesting in relentless flashes of a mysterious woman.

Clad in a flowing silk gown of the softest pink, she exuded regal elegance. Her hands glowed with an ethereal light, radiating a power beyond comprehension. Sirius's memory struggled to place her, recalling ancient tales of sorcery—long thought extinct. The last known sorcerers had met a grim fate, their existence reduced to mere whispers among the witches of today.

The princess turned toward the door, instinctively hiding her arms behind her as it creaked open. Stepping into the lavishly adorned bedroom, King William entered, holding an exquisite purple gown draped over his arm. Without ceremony, he tossed the dress onto the bedspread before turning to his daughter.

"Yes, Father?" Princess Thea inquired, a touch of sarcasm dancing in her tone.

"My daughter," King William began, his voice filled with grandiosity. "I regret not informing you sooner, but I have been preoccupied." With a dramatic clap of his hands, he declared, "We are to have a grand ball." A rare, genuine smile softened his normally imposing features.

"A ball?" Thea's eyes widened with intrigue. She folded her slender arms, her gaze drifting to the large portrait adorning the wall—a depiction of herself alongside her parents.

Her mother's absence was a shadow that never faded. The beloved queen had been taken too soon, her untimely demise forever etched into the kingdom's turbulent history. The plague that had ravaged the land, stealing countless lives, haunted Thea's thoughts. She exhaled slowly, shaking off the heaviness of the past.

King William continued, oblivious to her moment of reflection. "This is to celebrate the newest addition to our kingdom," he announced with infectious enthusiasm. "Consider it a—how shall I put it—a sailing away party! The ships will set sail once the ball reaches its grand finale."

Just before the vision warped and faded, Sirius caught something that made his gut twist—unease flickered across Princess Thea's expression.

Then, the dream crumbled into darkness. A wave of dizziness overtook him, pulling him back to reality. With a sharp inhale, Sirius jolted awake.

His breath was unsteady as his eyes adjusted to the dimly lit room. He blinked rapidly, his surroundings slowly coming into focus. The first thing he saw was *her*.

Airella.

She was seated beside his bed, her head resting on her arms atop the mattress. Strands of her hair cascaded over her face, rising and falling gently with each steady breath she took. The soft glow of candlelight danced across her skin, illuminating her delicate features.

Sirius exhaled, a mixture of relief and awe swelling in his chest. She was here. *She was safe.*

His throat tightened as he realized the full weight of it—she had saved him. The battle, the pain, the nightmare of Limbo—it all could have consumed him, but Airella had pulled him back from the abyss.

Gratitude, fierce and unwavering, burned through him. He ached to reach out, to brush his fingers against her skin, to reassure himself that she was real. But instead, he simply watched, allowing himself this stolen moment of peace.

She had risked everything for him. And gods help him, but he had never seen anything more beautiful than the woman who had fought to protect him.

Carefully disentangling her hand from his, Sirius rose. He winced from his bandaged wound, but kept his movements slow and deliberate as he tiptoed towards the backdoor for a breath of fresh air.

As he pushed the door open, a tranquil sight greeted him—a small hot spring with steam lazily rising into the cool air, carrying the scent of damp earth and wildflowers. His gaze drifted to a small table, weathered by time and bearing the marks of past use. There, various poisonous herbs and other items lay neatly arranged: nightshade with its deep purple hue, devil's fruit with its ominous red skin, and a vial of blood-colored liquid that seemed to pulse with an otherworldly energy.

"Witch." Sirius muttered, the word sapping the air from his lungs. A witch, just like the girl he had envisioned while sleeping. The princess. Sirius turned around to face an old woman who looked at him with a growl escaping from her lips.

"The name's Odelle, child," she introduced herself with a

hint of amusement in her voice. "Though I'm sure you're far older than me."

"I had a vision just now," Sirius pressed on, his tone filled with curiosity. "What did you do?"

"Oh, dear," Odelle replied nonchalantly, a small smile playing on her lips. "I wouldn't call that anything but a few side effects of the potions I had to use on you."

Sirius delved into his thoughts, recalling any information about the few witches that used to patrol the isle.

"Magic used by witches is personal," he mused aloud. "What ties do you have to the princess and the king?"

Odelle let out a soft chuckle, a twinkle in her eyes. "Wow, I'm impressed," she remarked. "What vision did you see, exactly?"

"Answer my question," Sirius insisted, his gaze unwavering.

With a graceful gesture, Odelle waved her hand in the air. "Stubborn child," she teased lightly. "We all have our secrets. You keep mine, and I'll keep yours, Miscreant." Her words carried a hint of warning, laced with a touch of familiarity. "Princess Thea is my granddaughter. My daughter, the late Queen Elara, married the king, and I stayed here. I couldn't be caught with my potion-making in the castle, could I?"

"I need something of you." Sirius narrowed his eyes and brushed past her, walking back inside the dimly lit cottage.

"Oh, and what's that?" She asked in a raspy old voice, curiosity piqued as she followed Sirius back inside.

"I need a masking potion for Airella," Sirius uttered with urgency. In his vision, he saw King William conversing with Princess Thea about the imminent ball set to take place that very night. "She's a magic wielder, you know," he added as he took a seat.

"I've witnessed these visions as well. Our bloodline pulsates with magic. My dear Thea has remained veiled to the truth for years. I see her lost and adrift, unaware of the immense power she holds, trapped within the confines of that castle." Her voice carried a weight of sorrow and determination as she spoke. "I'll brew the potion for you, but not without an exchange," Odelle declared firmly, her hands resting on her hips.

"What do you need?" Sirius crossed his arms. He winced as a sharp pang shot through his side.

"Your blood, the blood of a Miscreant. Not a lot, but enough to make a good potion. Grab that bottle right next to you and I'll get the knife." Odelle finished her demand as she reached for a knife that gleamed malevolently in the candlelight.

"Why didn't you just take my blood while you were stitching me up?" Sirius questioned.

"Had I done that, you wouldn't be alive right now. You needed time to heal, to regain your strength from within." She motioned for him to offer his hand.

Sirius, though feeling a sense of unease creeping up within him, extended his left hand towards her. As the sharp blade met his skin, a moment of discomfort flashed across his face, quickly replaced by a stoic resolve.

The witch deftly guided him to clench his fist, urging the gold liquid to flow forth, each droplet cascading into the awaiting glass bottle below. The vessel gradually filled to its brim.

"I've needed Miscreant blood for a long time. They are becoming scarce in these lands. The few we encounter are often like me, veiled in secrecy, concealing our true nature." A subtle chuckle escaped her lips as she carefully stowed the filled bottle into a satchel.

Wrapping his hand with a bandage, Sirius winced slightly from the fragrant herbs interwoven within the fabric, their soothing aroma mingling with the metallic tang of blood. As he exhaled a weary sigh, he couldn't help but ponder the mysteries that lay shrouded in the shadows of the witch's cryptic words.

"Now, this potion has a limited use," Odelle explained in a hushed tone. "It will only last for about an hour." With careful steps, she reentered the room, the glass bottle clutched in her slender fingers, its contents swirling like liquid fire. "Use it wisely," Odelle advised. She presented him with a small satchel. Sirius handled the precious potion with great care.

Sitting down beside Airella, whose peaceful slumber painted a serene picture, Sirius felt the weight of the impending task ahead. The air outside carried the whispers of a setting sun, signaling the approaching dusk. The royal ball awaited them.

Gently rousing Airella from her sleep, Sirius whispered her name with a tenderness that belied the urgency in his voice. Her eyes, vibrant and multicolored, widened in surprise as they met his gaze.

"Sirius? You're okay?" Airella's voice carried a mix of relief and joy as she threw her arms around him in a heartfelt embrace.

Sirius winced, a reminder of his tender chest, causing her to retreat apologetically. He let out a pained chuckle, his eyes crinkling with amusement. Airella's smile, bright as a sunbeam, put him at ease despite the looming mission ahead.

"Listen," Sirius began, "we need to infiltrate a royal ball."

"A ball? Why?" Airella's eyes widened with curiosity.

"This king of yours intends on sending innocent people to the island tonight," Sirius explained, his voice tinged with urgency. "This is what Father had been planning this whole time. He wants human life back on the island."

Airella felt a knot form in her stomach, realizing the gravity of the situation.

"We need to get to the palace and talk to the king's daughter," Sirius continued, his grip on her hands firm. "I suspect she will be the only person able to talk some sense into him."

Airella's mind raced with worry. "How do you know that? Also, the guards know what we look like, Sirius, and they have my little brother. We need to save him first." Her voice trembled.

Sirius paused, his eyes reflecting the weight of their predicament. "I had a vision. I'll explain on the way. And Arii will be safer in the dungeon than he will be with us, constantly fighting and on the run," he spoke, his words heavy with sorrow. As he gently brushed a tear from Airella's cheek, a mix of emotions flickered across his face.

"That's unacceptable..." Airella's voice faltered, a sense of helplessness washing over her as she gazed into Sirius's comforting eyes.

He gently wiped away her tears. With a warm smile, he silently conveyed a promise of hope amid uncertainty, a pledge that resonated deep within her heart.

"Trust me," Sirius spoke softly, his tone unwavering. "I swear on my undying life I will rescue him when the time comes." Leaning in, he pressed a tender kiss to her forehead, his eyes meeting hers to reassure her once more. The shock in her expression softened, replaced by a flicker of belief.

"We have to," he repeated.

Airella, though still grappling with her emotions, wiped her remaining tears away and mustered a smile through the pain that lingered. "Okay, but how are we going to get into this ball? Disguises?"

"Here," Sirius reached into the satchel, retrieving a strange concoction enclosed in a glass bottle. "Wait to drink it. It won't last long."

Curious, she inspected the contents of the bottle—an orange liquid sloshing within. "What is it?"

"It's a masking potion," Sirius explained, his gaze fixed on her with a sense of assurance. "It's supposed to change your form to something more appropriate for the situation at hand. At least, that's my understanding." He observed as she carefully returned the glass bottle to the satchel.

"Thank you, Sirius," she expressed sincerely, a glimmer of resolve shining through her gaze.

34

Sirius and Airella stood behind the castle gates, hidden from view. Airella felt a swarm of butterflies flutter nervously in her stomach, their delicate wings creating a whirlwind of emotions within her.

"Wait a second," Airella began, "can't we just travel through Limbo to reach the princess? I mean, we would essentially be invisible to everyone while we're there, right?" She shot a puzzled look at Sirius, hoping for some reassurance.

"In our previous encounter with Limbo, we came face-to-face with Father," Sirius responded, his tone thoughtful and measured. "Having spent considerable time with him, I've gained insights into his ways. I believe entering that realm signals to him somehow. Infiltrating the ball this way might be our best bet." He leaned towards the safer side of their plan, aiming to mitigate any risks they might encounter. "Ready?"

"Yeah, of course," Airella replied, nodding her head slowly as she glanced down at the newly opened potion in her hand.

Bracing herself, she swallowed the bitter liquid as quickly as possible, trying to evade its sour taste. Standing with her eyes shut, she pondered whether the potion had taken effect. Opening her eyes, she searched for Sirius, only to realize that he had vanished without a trace. Curiosity piqued, she exhaled a sigh and mentally prepared herself to venture into the ball alone.

Steeling her resolve, Airella made her way towards the palace entrance. As she pushed past the towering doors and stepped into the resplendent ballroom, a spectacle of grandeur greeted her. Golden streamers adorned the walls, shimmering in the ambient light, while a multitude of guests mingled and conversed animatedly. Overwhelmed by the opulence surrounding her, she turned her gaze, pondering her next move amidst the bustling crowd.

As she continued walking through the crowded room, navigating through the clusters of chattering guests, she almost collided with a buffet table that seemed out of place in the elegant setting. The punch bowl on the table caught her eye, its crimson liquid shimmering in the soft light. As she leaned in for a closer look, her reflection in the glass bowl surprised her—she saw a red-haired young woman with freckles, wearing a delicate sky blue dress.

Lost in this moment, Airella felt a gentle tap on her shoulder, pulling her back to reality. She turned around swiftly to face a stranger, a dashing young man in formal attire. His deep gray eyes met hers, a hint of gold betraying them, framed by his stylishly swept brunette hair.

He extended a hand with a charming smile and a bow. "May I have this dance?"

Airella felt her cheeks flush with a mixture of surprise and delight at the unexpected invitation.

"Is that how it's done?" the man continued, a hint of amusement in his voice as he mirrored the movements of the other guests around them.

"Sirius!" she whispered urgently, her tone tinged with reproach. "Why did you vanish like that?"

Just moments earlier, Sirius had briefly disappeared from Airella's side, yielding to his insatiable appetite as he claimed the soul of a wayward guest. However, instead of consuming it, he wrestled with his inner hunger, knowing the consequences of succumbing to it.

I can be good, Sirius reassured himself silently, a mantra he repeated to maintain control.

In his encounters with Father, Sirius had learned how to inhabit the bodies of the deceased, a skill that set him apart from Father's malevolent abilities. While he couldn't manipulate the living, he possessed the eerie capability to dominate the empty vessels of the dead.

Sirius carefully placed the stranger's soul underneath his cloak, ensuring its safety. He cradled the empty husk in his arms, surrounded by the eerie silence of the abandoned hall. Gently, he covered the stranger's eyes with his fingers, his own eyes glowing a mesmerizing yellow. A rush of air escaped his lips as Sirius transformed into a swirling black mist that merged effortlessly through the stranger's parted mouth. As he opened his eyes, they were now housed in the unfamiliar body he had chosen.

Standing before Airella, Sirius felt the urge to explain his clandestine actions. "I seized a moment to gather intel on the ball from a couple of unsuspecting soldiers. Now, here's the plan." Sirius grasped Airella's arm, leading her to a secluded spot for their conversation. "The king will seat the princess beside him on the throne. When she takes to the ballroom floor, a queue of eager suitors will form. I will position myself to dance with her, and that's when I'll explain the circumstances we're stuck under. We can't take long because as soon as this party is over, that ship is sailing."

"What do we do? Wait?" Airella whispered into Sirius's ear, her voice barely audible over the jubilant sounds of the dancing crowd. Sirius observed Duran, noticing how he nervously toyed with his fingers while engaging in small talk with a group of women. Their eyes met, and suddenly, time seemed to slow down, enveloping them in a cocoon of silence.

"Airella, stay composed and act natural," Sirius reassured her, linking his arm with hers as Duran approached. A forced smile played on Duran's lips, betraying his irritation at their presence.

"Hello. I don't believe we've met," Duran greeted them, extending his hand in a gesture of welcome. Sirius took it and gave him a firm handshake.

Duran's expression turned slightly stern as he shifted his focus to Airella. "And you, Madam, what might your name be?" His gaze was intense, almost predatory. Sirius sensed Airella's unease and swiftly responded for her.

"Her name is Isabella," Sirius said softly. "She's very reserved."

"I apologize for the inconvenience, but I must know your name as well before I depart. We can't simply allow uninvited guests to stroll into the palace as if it were a common occurrence." The man seemed insistent on learning Sirius's name. Sirius could sense the tension but remained composed for Airella's sake.

"Hugh Regaldi," Sirius replied, his voice firm.

Duran shot Sirius a menacing look before strolling away nonchalantly. Even as he disappeared into the swirling crowd, unease coiled in Sirius's gut. Duran was not to be trusted. Whether he was merely scheming or under Father's influence, Sirius couldn't be sure.

His thoughts were interrupted as Airella turned to face him, her dark lashes casting delicate shadows over her flushed cheeks—a shade deep and rich, reminiscent of aged wine.

"Are you alright?" he asked gently, watching the emotions flicker in her gaze.

She inhaled sharply, her expression tight with barely restrained fury. "No, Sirius, I'm not alright," she bit out, her voice trembling. "My mother is dead. Arii is being held hostage. Because of *him*."

Sirius's grip on her hand tightened, a silent promise that he understood. That he would stand by her. "I know," he murmured. "But if we don't dance, we might start attracting unwanted attention. The guards are already watching."

Airella hesitated, but the reality of their situation left little room for protest. With a reluctant nod, she allowed Sirius to take her hand, guiding her toward the heart of the ballroom where couples twirled in perfect synchronization.

The music swelled around them, soft yet commanding. Sirius had never danced before. He had spent his entire life in the shadows of the isle, fighting, surviving. But as he observed the dancers, their graceful movements painting a picture of practiced elegance, he mimicked their steps with surprising ease.

His gaze met Airella's, a quiet storm swirling behind her uniquely colored eyes—eyes that still shone through the illusion of the potion. To him, she was as she always had been. And tonight, she was breathtaking. The blue ball gown hugged her form in a way that made his breath catch, accentuating the fierce beauty that had captivated him since the moment they met.

"Do you even know how to dance?" she teased, her voice barely audible through the music.

Sirius smirked. "How hard could it be?"

Before she could protest, he swept her into his arms. His touch was firm yet impossibly gentle, his grip steady as he led her into the dance.

Airella gasped softly at the closeness of his body, the heat of him seeping through the thin layers of fabric that separated them. His scent—something dark and untamed, yet subtly warm—wrapped around her, sending an unexpected shiver down her spine.

"I suppose you're a fast learner," she admitted, tilting her chin up to meet his gaze.

Sirius's lips curled at the edges. "Or maybe I just needed the right partner."

Her pulse stuttered at the way he said it, his voice low, intimate, dangerously smooth.

They moved effortlessly, the space between them disappearing inch by inch. His hands, rough from battle but impossibly tender in their guidance, rested against her waist. Airella felt the warmth of his palm pressing against the small of her back, urging her closer until there was nothing but the rhythm of their breathing and the electric charge in the air between them.

"Careful, Sirius," she murmured, her voice barely above a whisper. "Someone might think you actually enjoy this."

He leaned in, his lips just shy of grazing her ear. "And what if I do?"

Airella's breath hitched. The world around them blurred, the music fading into the background. His lips hovered dangerously close to hers, their breaths mingling, the heat between them an unspoken challenge, a temptation neither dared give into—but neither wanted to resist.

Her fingers curled into the fabric of his jacket. "Then you'd be even more reckless than I thought."

Sirius chuckled, the sound deep and velvety. "You say that like you don't want me to be."

Airella barely had time to form a retort before his hand slid just a fraction lower, pressing her even closer against him. Her heart pounded against her ribs. Every nerve in her body was aware of him—the strength beneath his touch, the way his fingers skimmed her waist, the way his breath fanned against her lips.

For a fleeting moment, she thought he might actually kiss her. And gods, she might let him.

But then, just as quickly as it came, Sirius smirked and spun her effortlessly under his arm, breaking the spell. Airella exhaled sharply, eyes narrowing as she readjusted herself.

"You're enjoying this way too much," she accused, her lips twitching.

"Am I?" He pulled her back against him with deliberate slowness, reveling in the way her breath caught once more. "I hadn't noticed."

Airella glared, but it lacked heat. "You're insufferable."

His smirk softened just slightly, his eyes dark with something far more dangerous than amusement. "And yet, you're still here."

The music swelled to its final note, and for a moment, neither of them moved, still locked in the invisible pull between them. Sirius tilted his head, watching her through half-lidded eyes, as if daring her to do something reckless.

Airella swallowed hard, the heat in her chest unbearable.

If this had been a fairy tale, this would be the moment where the two lovers sealed their fate with a kiss.

But this wasn't a fairy tale. And the world was watching.

So instead, Airella took a step back, severing the invisible tether between them. Sirius let her go, but the knowing look in his eyes told her that this wasn't over.

Not even close.

The small orchestra, with their instruments poised, gradually faded into silence as a diminutive man, adorned in ostentatious attire, confidently strode to the forefront before the resplendent throne, effortlessly capturing the attention of the assembled guests.

"Ladies and gentlemen, I present to you His Majesty, King William, and Her Highness, Princess Thea!" the announcer's voice resonated through the grand hall, drawing all eyes towards the imposing figures who entered through the magnificent doors. Princess Thea gracefully took her seat, a vision of elegance, while King William remained standing, his presence commanding the room.

"Loyal citizens of Eldaraya," the king announced proudly, his voice carrying across the crowd, "I am thrilled to share a momentous discovery with you all. We have stumbled upon a pristine island nestled off the coast of our beloved kingdom. This newfound land shall serve as an extension of our realm, a sanctuary for those seeking a new place to call home."

As the monarch's gaze swept over the assembled crowd, his expression darkened, and he locked eyes with Sirius, a sense of disappointment clear in his features. Sirius felt a lump form in his throat as tension gripped the air.

"Regrettably, I must address a pressing concern that has breached our kingdom's defenses," the king continued, his voice tinged with gravity. "Two fugitives are among us, threatening our peace and security. One of them is known as Sirius, his surname unknown to us, while the other goes by the name Airella Devereaux."

A sharp intake of breath rippled through the crowd at the mention of Airella's name, the daughter of the esteemed Lysander Devereaux.

"Airella's associate," the king continued, his tone unwavering, "is a peculiar, slender figure with alabaster hair and piercing yellow eyes. Should you encounter either of these individuals, I urge you to report their whereabouts at once."

Seating himself beside his daughter on the ornate throne, the king raised a goblet of wine to his lips, the flicker of determination in his eyes unmistakable. "These malefactors seek to disrupt our harmonious existence and impede our journey to the new land. But let us not dwell on their mischief tonight. I cordially invite all eligible gentlemen to partake in a dance with my daughter." With a resounding clap of his hands, the king signaled the commencement of the evening's festivities.

As soon as he said to line up, Sirius did so, leaving Airella behind. As the guests gathered, Sirius felt a surge of determination coursing through him. It propelled him to swiftly navigate through the crowd, ensuring no time was wasted.

The dance began, following the tradition of circling the area seven times. As Sirius awaited his turn to take Princess Thea's hand, the rhythm of the music perfectly synced with the beating of his heart. Observing the other men conversing with the princess as they danced, Sirius mentally prepared himself for the imminent interaction.

Moments later, Princess Thea's gaze met his, a warm smile gracing her lips as she extended her hand towards him. Locking eyes with her, Sirius felt a mix of nerves and determination swirling within him. As they began their first circle around the dance floor, he reminded himself of the mission at hand, focusing on the task ahead while cherishing the fleeting moments of the dance.

"I need to speak with you," Sirius spoke quietly as they continued to move to the beat of the music. They had just finished their second circle, the ornate ballroom bathed in the warm glow of flickering candles casting dancing shadows around them.

"About what, Miscreant?" She questioned, her voice tinged with a mix of curiosity and suspicion.

Somehow, she could see right past Sirius's facade, her keen intuition picking up on the seriousness of his demeanor. It shouldn't have been a surprise to him, either, the weight of his words pressing on him as they now had four more circles to go.

"The island. I've tried explaining to your father, but I believe he'd be more reasonable when listening to you," Sirius spoke quickly, his words urgent as he raised his hand, placing his palm against hers gently as they continued to rotate in their usual circle, the rhythm of the dance swirling around them. "The island he speaks of, it's not safe." They were now on their fifth circle, the music guiding their movements with a hypnotic allure.

Her stare tensed as they passed by the king, a silent acknowledgment passing between them. They danced more slowly, the urgency in Sirius's voice prompting her to focus, for she wished to hear what he had to say. They had completed their fifth circle, with two more to go, and each step brought them closer to the key aspect.

"How so? What's wrong?" Princess Thea's face filled with concern, her brows furrowing in confusion as she tried to grasp the gravity of Sirius's words. She was completely unaware of the situation that had been unfolding, her thoughts racing as they had one more rotation left.

"Your Highness," Sirius began. "I've lived on that isolated island for what feels like an eternity. The humans who once called it home met a grim fate at the hands of the Miscreants that roam its cursed grounds. They were ruthless, claiming lives for sustenance. I am ashamed to admit, I took part in its ending. But now, I find myself in a role of protector, striving to shield the unsuspecting from meeting the same tragic end." They completed their seventh and final circle.

A heavy silence draped over the ballroom as Sirius's revelation sank in, the air thick with disbelief. All eyes fixated on him, their expressions a tapestry of shock and horror. The scythe he wielded caught the light, its blade gleaming ominously, contrasting against his now-pale complexion.

His gaze drifted downward, only to find the form of the man he had inhabited sprawled at his feet. A bizarre twist of fate had seen the man's soul escape the confines of his cloak and reclaim its vessel, leaving Sirius exposed in his true form.

Turning his attention to Airella, Sirius fought to maintain composure amidst the chaos unfolding around them. With a sense of urgency, he began planning an impromptu escape strategy.

Gripping the scythe tightly, he swung his weapon through the air. But before any plan could take shape, a sudden blur of motion disrupted the scene as Duran lunged towards him, propelling both of them into the yawning maw of the portal to Limbo.

35

Airella stood in the shadows, her heart heavy with the weight of what she had witnessed. As the connection between Sirius and his borrowed body frayed, Airella's illusion faded, revealing her true form.

"Cease them!" King William's voice boomed over the cacophony of gasps and murmurs that filled the room. The crowd of astonished onlookers recoiled in fear, unsure of what to make of the sudden turn of events. But Duran was the first to react, his instincts kicking in as he lunged towards Sirius with a determined resolve.

In a swift and daring move, Sirius opened a portal to the world of Limbo, pulling Duran along with him as they both tumbled into the unknown abyss.

"Sirius!" Airella's anguished cry pierced the air.

As the portal shrank, threatening to disappear entirely, Airella knew she had to act fast. With a desperate resolve, she sprinted towards the dwindling gateway. But as she strained to reach the portal, Airella found herself abruptly seized by the guards, their iron grips clamping firmly onto her arms.

"No! Let me go!" Airella's voice rang out in a desperate plea, her eyes desperately scanning the throng for any glimmer of aid amidst the swirling chaos that engulfed them.

At that moment, King William slowly advanced towards Airella, while the guards unceremoniously pushed her down to the ground in deference to the king. She winced in agony from the rough treatment.

"You've got a lot of explaining to do," King William cast a steely gaze towards the guards. "Escort the guests out. We're putting an end to this celebration. Direct everyone to the waiting ships." The soldiers swiftly carried out his orders. "And another thing, bring the girl's brother along. If memory serves me right, he's languishing in the dungeon. He might appreciate the chance to behold these expansive lands. Also, ensure that all the prisoners are properly accounted for. This could be an opportunity to free up space in the castle's underground cells. Now, Airella, daughter of Lysander Devereaux, I'm certain the former commander of my forces would be utterly disappointed by your actions. You've flagrantly defied me and committed treason." King William's voice dripped with disdain as he glowered down at Airella, the guards nudging her face closer to the cold stone floor.

"Your Highness..." Airella struggled to voice her thoughts. "The isle is dangerous. It's filled with Miscreants. Please, believe me!"

"My first-in-command, Duran, says otherwise. Why would he feel the need to lie to me about such a thing?" King William's booming voice echoed through the grand hall. "This is nonsense. I'm just going to make things simple."

The guards surrounding Airella eased their grip slightly, allowing her a glimpse of the imposing figure of the king as she strained to peer past him. Behind the monarch, a few guards huddled around the almost closed portal.

"You've become quite a nuisance. I believe a proper hanging is in order," declared King William. "However, it's a special night tonight, with our sailing away celebration in full swing. Leaving you here in the dungeon would leave my castle vulnerable, with many of my guards accompanying me. You, along with the other prisoners, shall sail back with us to that island. It is there that justice will be served, and you will face the consequences of your treason."

Desperation etched on her face, the princess hurried to her father's side. "Father, please, allow me a moment to speak with you," she implored, her voice tinged with urgency.

"Not now. Get on the ship," King William commanded, his eyes cold and unyielding.

Princess Thea and Airella shared a moment of eye contact as the guards hoisted Airella to her feet. The disintegrated portal loomed behind her, now heavily guarded, extinguishing any hope of slipping back in to find him.

"Sirius..." she murmured softly.

Trapped and desolate, Airella's spirit teetered on the brink of despair. Her eyes, once filled with determination, now brimmed with unshed tears. The guards led her through the castle's grand doors, each step echoing her inner turmoil.

The loading docks beckoned, bustling with activity as people boarded ships in search of new beginnings. Airella, however, knew the harsh reality awaiting them—death disguised as opportunity.

Among the vessels, the fifth ship awaited, destined for the prisoners' journey. Airella stood, now stripped of Dawnbreaker and other possessions. Vulnerability gnawed at her resolve, igniting a fire of defiance within. She refused to be the helpless maiden awaiting rescue; her path to salvation lay in her own hands.

Gazing back at the grand palace, hope flickered within her

as she yearned for Sirius to emerge like a beacon of deliverance. Time seemed to freeze, the air thick with uncertainty, as she clung to the belief that their reunion was on the verge of happening.

Yet, there was nothing.

Worry crept through the girl. Could Duran have bested him? Airella attempted to push away thoughts of the worst-case scenario. No, that seemed nearly impossible. After all, Sirius had the advantage of familiarity since they were in Limbo. He was capable, but if he remained hidden, the prospect of reuniting seemed increasingly challenging...

Airella lifted her gaze towards the massive ship while standing on the dock. The guards swiftly secured heavy metal cuffs on her wrists and ankles, linking her chains to a lengthy line of drowsy prisoners awaiting to board the vessel.

Once all the prison guards loaded the prisoners, they escorted them to the upper deck. Among them were close to a hundred prisoners, clad only in their undergarments and bound in chains. This ship was designated exclusively for their transport, indicating that it would only house them, the guards, and lower-class individuals. The prisoners found themselves vastly outnumbered and filled with a sense of desperation.

A muscular man stepped onto a podium in front of the prisoners as they were all forced to sit on the deck. His shaggy brown hair, tousled by the wind, danced around his face.

"Ladies and gentlemen, boys and girls, welcome aboard this vessel," his voice carried over the murmurs of the captives. "I'll be your overseer from this point on. Throughout this voyage, you shall receive rations equivalent to those provided at the castle. Expect fair treatment—no more, no less. Your station is here on the upper deck; no requests to venture elsewhere will be entertained. Eat, sleep, and linger here. No exceptions. Given your current circumstances, confined as you are by the chains that bind you, we'll all grow quite familiar with each other over the course of this journey."

As the ships set sail, Airella's gaze lingered on the vast expanse of the ocean before her. Her vessel, trailing behind the others, cut through the waves with a sense of determined purpose.

Thoughts swirled in her mind, contemplating the hierarchy of the ship's order. It seemed that the first ship bore the Royals, with social standing descending according to the ships' sequence. Restless with an unyielding spirit, Airella refused to accept this predicament as her ultimate fate.

A glimmer of hope sparked within her as a plan formed in her mind. The island marked the destination where her resolve would be put to the test. Three weeks lay ahead, time that she knew held possibilities for change. Escape, seeking aid, or some unforeseen course of action—options brimmed in her thoughts as she steeled herself for the challenges to come.

"Airella!" A familiar voice rang out from behind her, causing her body to freeze in place.

"Arii?" Airella whipped her head around, her eyes locking onto a head full of tousled blonde hair. "Arii!"

His whitened smile, contrasting with his dirtied face, sent a wave of emotions through her body, despite the distance that separated them. Chained to many other people, she knew reaching him was an impossible feat.

"I'll get us out of this. I promise," Airella's words carried a sense of reassurance. A promise made in the darkest of times, one she vowed to keep.

The first night dragged on endlessly, filled with unpleasant smells and the biting cold of the frosty air. The overcrowded space left Airella gazing up at the dark expanse above, mentally counting the stars for solace. Alongside the rest of the dirtied prisoners, they lay haphazardly on the upper deck, their heads resting on one another to find comfort amidst the chaos. The guards, taking shifts to stay vigilant, maintained a watchful eye over the captives.

Airella brushed her blonde hair away from her face, the metal cuffs on her wrists serving as a constant reminder of her captivity. As she exhaled a heavy breath, a voice pierced through the silence, one that she hadn't heard in what felt like an eternity.

"Airella, are you awake? Can you hear me?" Jonathan's voice reached her ears, prompting Airella to retrieve the necklace tucked beneath her shirt, a hidden possession the guards had overlooked during their search.

"Jonathan!" Airella's voice, a whisper filled with relief, cut through the tense air. "I'm so happy to hear your voice! How are you able to speak? We have to be quiet, or the guards will hear."

Jonathan's response was hushed yet concerned. "Are you okay? It seems you may be in a bit of trouble. If only I were there to help," as he spoke, the necklace around her neck emitted a soft, reassuring glow, casting a warm light. Airella quickly shielded the light from the prying eyes of the guards with a swift movement of her hand.

"Oh, come on now, Jonathan," she sighed.

"Where is Sirius?"

Airella hesitated, her mind racing to find the right words. "He—Well, I'm not sure. He and Duran... they went into Limbo, and that was the last I saw of them both." Her voice trembled slightly, betraying the fear that gripped her heart at the thought of losing Sirius forever. Unspoken emotions swirled within her, undeniable and raw.

"This is Sirius we're talking about," Jonathan interjected, a hint of levity in his tone, trying to lighten the heavy atmosphere. "The same guy who beat me in a battle of our own. If that's not tough, I don't know what is."

Airella managed a brief, genuine laugh, the tension momentarily lifted by his attempt at humor.

"What's going on over there?" a guard's gruff voice interrupted their conversation, sending a jolt of panic through Airella.

She quickly feigned sleep, her breaths slow and even, until the soldier's footsteps receded into the distance. With a sigh of relief, she carefully concealed the glowing necklace back beneath the fabric of her shirt.

"Jonathan," she whispered once more, her eyes shut tightly against the harsh reality of their circumstances, "we have a lot of planning to do."

The necklace adorning her neck glowed with a soft azure light each time Jonathan spoke, a manifestation of the unwavering faith she held in Sirius's strength.

"Sirius is resilient, Airella," Jonathan whispered. "He possesses a fortitude that can withstand even the fiercest of foes, including Father."

36

"You're a fool," Sirius growled as he got to his feet, now in the blackened world.

Duran drew his sword as Sirius gave his scythe a twirl, the metallic blade catching the dim light that seeped through the eerie atmosphere.

"You and I had a deal when I first set foot in this kingdom. Now I intend to keep my promises." Sirius threw his scythe to the side, and reached his hands out towards Duran.

Just by trying to examine the world of Limbo, its twisted forms and ghostly figures haunted Duran, leaving him still confused. All around them, human-shaped souls stood, their empty eyes fixed on the unfolding confrontation.

"Where are we? Where have you taken me?" Fear consumed Duran as he yelled in anger. Beads of sweat formed along his forehead, glistening in the surreal light that bathed the desolate landscape.

"Isn't it obvious? This, my friend, is your grave. It would cause quite the commotion if our living audience were to see the aftermath after I'm finished with you." Sirius inched closer, his movements deliberate and menacing. Every step Sirius took towards the man cowering in fear was mirrored by Duran with a quick step in the opposite direction, a dance of predator and prey in the shadowy realm of Limbo.

"Miscreant! Let me free of your vile world. Now! I demand it!" Duran pointed his sword towards Sirius. The weapon rapidly shook in his hands.

"Oh, no. You don't demand it. You need it. You're scared. I can sense the fear seeping from your pores." Sirius continuously stepped in Duran's direction until his back finally hit the wall of the ballroom. A twisted smile played on Sirius's lips as he inched closer, his eyes glinting with a sinister light. "It's been far too long since I have had a taste of a fresh soul."

Sirius drew even closer, taking almost no notes of Duran's sword until he grabbed the blade with his hand, the sharp edge cutting into his flesh. Gold blood oozed from the wound, staining the weapon and the floor beneath them.

A sudden sensation of no control washed over Sirius's body, his movements no longer his own.

"Get out of me!" Sirius screamed as he stumbled back from Duran, his eyes wide with shock. It was as if he were speaking to someone else, a presence within him taking over. Sirius shook his head, the realization dawning on him. Father.

"You keep trying to ruin everything for me, don't you, Sirius?" The words spilled from Sirius's mouth, his voice hollow and distant. Panic surged through Sirius as he struggled against the invading force.

"No." He cried out, his hands shaking as the gold blood from his wounded hand trickled down his face. His will faltered, but a flicker of defiance remained. "Get out of my body, Father."

"What the hell is going on?" Duran fell to the floor in terror, his heart pounding in his chest as his eyes widened in shock.

The sight before him was so unexpected, so jarring, that it took a moment for his mind to register the gravity of the situation.

"Oh, I'll tell you what's going on." Sirius's voice dripped with a sadistic tone that seemed to permeate the very air around him, sending chills down Duran's spine. It was as if the words were not truly coming from Sirius, but from another entity entirely. It was Father speaking through Sirius, his features contorted by an unseen force. The realization struck Duran like a physical blow—Sirius had been possessed.

"Isn't it simply astounding? The overwhelming power that resonates within you... It's truly exhilarating!" Father chuckled, all sense of control absent from Sirius's gaze as his eyes met Duran's.

Amidst Sirius's clenched fists and a menacing smirk, Duran retreated to a corner. Slowly advancing with his scythe poised, just as the moment hung in the balance, Sirius's gaze shifted to his own hand. With a smile playing on his lips, he reached out to Duran, his touch transitioning from a casual caress to an abrupt grasp of the chin, drawing their faces drastically close.

"Mortals! So interesting... to cower in fear, yet hold no interest in what they truly are. How pathetic," the possessed Sirius remarked.

As he shifted his hand, a faint aura surrounded him, pulsating with a malevolent energy that seemed to sap the very essence from the air. Fixing his gaze upon Duran, his eyes, once vibrant, now bore a hollow emptiness that mirrored the fading hues of sunset. With a haunting grace, Duran's form withered, each breath escaping him a feeble whisper in the room's vastness until he collapsed with a disturbing crunch.

"Ah, yes. We have a ship to catch, don't we?" The false Sirius sneered, a cruel smile twisting his features as he strode towards the towering doors of the palace. With each step, the shadows seemed to coil around him, his figure shrouded in darkness that devoured the feeble light struggling to pierce through.

"It seems the five ships have already set sail," the possessed Sirius mused, his gaze drifting towards the distant town where the witch's presence lingered in his memory. "Witches know everything. Isn't that right, Sirius?" His words, laced with a dark amusement, hinted at a twisted connection that transcended the boundaries of the living and the dead.

"Teleport me to the ship," Sirius demanded, his voice filled with urgency as he slammed his fist against her alchemy table. Odelle, the old crone, remained composed, though her heart raced. The ingredients scattered across the table, a reflection of the tension in the room.

"Why would I, Dark Beast?" she responded calmly, her gaze steady. "You are not the emotionless Miscreant I met earlier. Who are you?"

A hint of amusement danced in his eyes. Leaning closer, he observed Odelle's reaction, noting the concern that flickered momentarily across her face as she glanced at Duran's still form beside him.

"Teleport me now, and your death will be merciful. Perhaps I'll even spare you."

Left with no other choice, she raised her arms and chanted the ancient spell, the words weaving a mystical tapestry around them. A portal shimmered into existence before Sirius, a gateway to his next move.

Sirius pushed Duran's lifeless body through the portal first.

He had plans to store his body in Limbo to use as a vessel for later. After all, no one but him knew he was dead.

"You won't prevail, Dark Beast," Odelle warned. "They will defeat you in your own twisted game."

Sirius turned back to face her, his expression a mix of amusement and challenge. "What makes you so sure that will happen, Crone?"

"That girl has strengths beyond anything you have," Odelle stated firmly. "I saw it in her. I know it's there. It's a remarkable power for a young girl to possess."

Sirius took a step back, a wry smile playing on his lips. "We shall see, Crone," he remarked in a tone laced with defiance. With a deliberate wave, he bid her farewell and crossed the threshold of the portal.

As his foot landed on the other side, a swift glance around revealed that he had materialized in the dimly lit cargo hold of a ship.

Pondering his next move, Sirius raised his scythe thoughtfully, his eyes alight with a glint of mischief. "Limbo," he mused to himself. Yet, a sudden pause interrupted his train of thought as doubts crept in. "Why conceal it? I am the harbinger of fear. They will all tremble at my very presence," a soft chuckle escaped him, a trace of self-amusement coloring his words. "And where could that elusive girl be hiding now—"

"No." A voice, laden with determination, cut through his musings. The real Sirius fought against the malevolent force that sought to control him. "I will not let you harm her."

The sinister figure known as Father smirked, his grip tightening until his hand bore the golden stain of blood. "But you see, Sirius, your resistance is in vain. With you removed from the equation, along with the half-breed and the troublesome soul she carries around her neck, the scales tip in my favor," he proclaimed, his eyes ablaze with malice.

"Who's there?" A guard's voice boomed through the tense silence as he pivoted to face the shadowy figure of Sirius. "Show yourself!" His demand echoed in the dimly lit surroundings. With deliberate slowness, Sirius locked eyes with the guard, who visibly trembled in fear. The guard's grip tightened on his sword, his knuckles turning white with tension. "You're the wanted criminal."

"Criminal? No. Miscreant? Yes." Sirius's voice cut through the air as he lunged forward. The swift arc of his scythe descended, meeting its mark with a sickening thud. A crimson gash opened, and a gut-wrenching scream pierced the stillness as the guard staggered, blood spilling from the wound on his neck. Desperation etched across his face, he tried to stem the flow, but the pain overwhelmed him, and he crumpled to the ground.

"What was that?" Another guard's alarmed voice shattered the eerie quietude of the darkened cargo hold.

Sirius moved deliberately, his footsteps echoing softly on the creaking floorboards as he ascended the stairs to the helm of the ship. Two guards, unaware of the impending threat, stood conversing by the wheel.

"Hello," Sirius's tone was taunting as he swiftly drove the blade of his scythe through the chest of the guard on the left. The guard's eyes widened in shock before his body slumped lifelessly. In a fluid motion, Sirius withdrew the blade, his gaze locking with the remaining guard. The guard raised his sword as he lunged forward with a fierce battle cry. Sirius sidestepped the attack with ease, seizing the guard by the collar in a swift, practiced move.

"Nice try. But, just not good enough." With a casual strength, he flung the man over the edge of the ship. The sudden gasp of horror from Airella nearby punctuated the scene with an eerie intensity.

In that moment, everything had slowed down to a crawl. Airella's piercing gaze bore into him, making him turn sharply to meet her eyes.

"Hey there, half-breed. Let's have a chat," he stated coolly.

Airella's voice faltered, "Sirius?" His demeanor was chillingly brutal. Glowing yellow eyes locked onto her, seeing through every layer of her being.

"That's not Sirius," Jonathan murmured softly, a faint glow emanating from beneath Airella's white top.

Sirius smirked, his grip tightening on a handful of Airella's blonde locks as he brought her face to face with him. She gritted her teeth, a fierce struggle clear in her every move as she fought against his hold.

"Why don't we find a quieter spot for a little chat?" he suggested, his voice carrying an unexpected softness that clashed with his actions. With a swift motion, he severed the chains binding her to the other prisoners, yet the cold metal cuffs remained fastened around her wrists as he led her, still gripping her hair, towards the nearest cabin.

By now, the sorcery that possessed Sirius had cast a spell of slumber upon the ship's occupants, rendering them unconscious. Airella recognized this enchantment from her past encounters with Sirius and Father—the power to lull individuals into deep sleep, selectively choosing who remained awake.

Guiding her into the confines of the dimly lit cabin, Sirius swiftly secured the heavy oak door behind them. As he turned to face her, a subtle air of mystery seemed to shroud his every move.

"What have you done to Sirius?" Airella's voice cut through the tense silence, her body weak but her spirit unyielding as she used the rough wooden wall for support.

"Oh, don't fret, my dear Airella. Sirius lives. His existence is tethered to my whims," he remarked with a chilling smile, the dim light glinting off his eyes. "After all, I am his creator."

"Please, just let us be. Why are you tormenting us?"

"Humans, my dear, are but sustenance to us. A vital link in our dwindling food chain," he explained. "Their absence has disrupted the delicate balance of our existence on this island, posing a challenge to our survival and prosperity."

"What are you not telling me?" Airella met his gaze, her eyes searching for truths hidden beneath his cryptic words.

He let out a chuckle, the sound echoing through the room. Airella found it hard to adjust to the fact that Father was inhabiting Sirius's body.

"Smart girl. You see, the greater the number of beings we gather back on the island, the more power I will amass from their souls and auras. I will flourish once more. Yet this time, I plan not to exterminate every single one of the mortals. Last time, things spiraled a bit out of control," he concluded, a self-satisfied smirk playing on his lips.

"What do you mean?" Airella instinctively took a step back as he drew closer.

"Ah, that feeble Miscreant hunter village. They were so audacious. My power was adhered to by a barrier they erected. They transgressed against our kind. And there was this one girl..." He pressed Airella against the wall, deftly twisting a strand of her hair around his finger.

"And then?" Airella's voice trembled, but her curiosity was piqued and her anticipation grew. She could hear her heart pounding in her chest. The narrative felt eerily reminiscent, as if she had encountered this tale before.

"Emmaline." His voice turned raspy and ominous as he breathed the name into Airella's ear.

That name resonated deeply within her, for it was the same name as the girl she had glimpsed in her previous flashbacks while in Limbo. It was the identical name that Sirius had mentioned there, too.

"I take it you may have heard of her," he said with a smirk, taking a step back from her. With a nonchalant air, he turned around and walked away. A sense of relief washed over her as she watched him, finally able to draw in a deep breath.

Confusion and curiosity intertwined within Airella as she clenched her fists, her mind filled with questions. "Who is she? Where is she? Why did I see visions of her in Limbo?"

Sirius, upon hearing her words, abruptly halted in his tracks. In a swift motion, he pivoted back towards her. "So, my suspicions were not unfounded. Even your blood carries the same essence as hers," he declared with a chilling laugh, his gaze shifting to the metal cuffs that had dug into her skin, leaving marks of distress. "Emmaline, the legendary Miscreant hunter, the first to birth a true hybrid demon. Zol's mate, a Slayer's daughter, and just one of the many casualties under Sirius's reign."

As the pieces of the cryptic puzzle fell into place, Airella felt a surge of realization. The enigmatic connection between her and the mysterious Emmaline was slowly unraveling before her eyes. She absorbed Father's words, each revelation adding a layer of complexity to her already tumultuous emotions.

"You bear an uncanny resemblance to that woman. Yet, in you, I sense a strength far greater than hers," he mused, his voice tinged with a mix of admiration and malice. "Emmaline was but a pawn in the grand scheme of things, a mere mortal for my younger self to toy with. But you, you possess a potential beyond measure. A refined iteration of your esteemed predecessor."

Airella's mind raced, grappling with the weight of his revelations.

"I would like to offer you a proposition," he said with a sly smile playing on his lips. His gaze lingered on Airella, assessing her from head to toe. "How would you like to access more power than you could ever overcome on your own? To be respected, to gain riches, and to even have enough power to reunite with those you've lost?"

"I want nothing from you," Airella retorted, her voice laced with defiance as she bared her teeth.

"I can allow you to access your inner Miscreant. Rule by my side and become my next apprentice," he continued persuasively. "In return, I will bring your dead friend back from the afterlife and return him to his original body. I will also set Sirius free, and he will never have to hear from me ever again." Extending his hand towards her, he presented the tempting offer. "What do you say, child?"

Airella stood there, her eyes widening in astonishment. The promise of bringing Jonathan back from the dead and restoring him to his true self, of shielding Sirius from Father's retribution —it all seemed too good to be true. Yet, as she contemplated the offer, a nagging thought crept into her mind. What about the fate of the people aboard the ships? Should she agree to this bargain, they would be nothing more than mere sustenance for the beasts roaming the isle.

However, if she were to say no, Father could end her life right there and then. The implications would be grave; Sirius and Jonathan, along with the rest of the humans aboard the ships, would meet their untimely demise. Opting for his proposal might offer a chance for Sirius and Jonathan to intervene. Perhaps wielding the power he hinted at could even lead to a reversal of fortunes against him.

Airella hesitated for a moment, weighing the options, before finally reaching out and clasping his hand, signifying her choice. He held on firmly, a sinister grin spreading across his face before erupting into maniacal laughter.

"Foolish girl." His laughter subsided, replaced by a chilling gaze fixed on Airella. "There are a few crucial details I may have omitted..."

The realization dawned on her as his expression turned malevolent, filling her with instant regret.

His grip on her hand tightened as he sent a wave of shock through her arm, a jolt that ripped through her body like a surge of electricity. The intensity was excruciating, wrenching an agonized scream from her lips that echoed through the small cabin of the ship. Airella's eyes, veiled in tears of torment, blazed with such ferocity that she yearned to claw them out to escape the searing pain.

Crumbling to the ground, she instinctively grasped her scalp with a free hand, feeling a peculiar, scorching ache as twisted black horns sprouted from the sides of her head. The torment intensified as a sharp, piercing sensation coursed through her, heralding the emergence of two pointed ears. With two luminous blue eyes ablaze, hands quivering with an unearthly force, she beheld her metamorphosed form.

Sirius, his possessed expression twisted in a sinister smile, released Airella's hand and forcefully ripped the blue pendant from her neck, shattering the chain that bound them.

"You have so much to learn," he taunted. "Every Miscreant knows that once your physical form is extinguished, it is lost forever. Did Sirius teach you anything?" His words hung in the air as he crushed the glass pendant in his fist, the shards falling to the ground with a poignant clatter.

Airella, sprawled on the cold floor, watched as tears streamed down her pallid cheeks.

"Jonathan!" she screamed. "How could you?" The searing pain of the transformation continued to spread like wildfire, each pulse sending waves of agony throughout her body, making every movement an excruciating challenge.

As he strode towards the cabin's exit, Sirius paused, his gaze locking onto her once more. With deliberate slowness, he lowered himself to her eye level, his eyes gleaming with an unsettling intensity.

"When I reshaped Sirius into who he is now, I lacked the strength to control his free will. But times have changed. Over the centuries, I've grown immensely in power. You, my dear, are now under my complete dominion. You've struck a bargain with the devil." His lips curled into a menacing grin.

"But… what about Sirius?" Airella struggled to push herself up onto her knees, her fingers bleeding as she grasped the shattered remnants of Jonathan's pendant.

"Sirius will never leave my side. Not for anyone, or anything. And as for you," His tone turned chillingly casual, "your internal transformation is far from complete. Brace yourself for unrelenting pain for the rest of this journey." With a mocking laugh, he strode towards the door. "Now that both you and Sirius are no longer a concern, my power will ascend to unimaginable heights. Stronger than ever envisioned. I had planned to eliminate you both, but this outcome surpasses my wildest expectations." His laughter rang through the cabin.

"This is not over. I will make sure you regret all of this," Airella retorted sharply, her voice laced with bitterness as she remained on her knees, defiance burning in her eyes.

With a final contemptuous look, he turned on his heel and strode out of the cabin, each step echoing with an air of finality. As the heavy door slammed shut behind him, a strange, shimmering enchantment seemed to settle over it, sealing her in with an eerie aura of isolation.

Airella's chest constricted with an unbearable pain, a sensation unlike anything she had ever felt before. It was as though icy tendrils were coiling around her lungs, each breath escaping from her lips in a visible puff of frost. The chill seeped into her bones, leaving her trembling uncontrollably as she fought against the cold that seemed to emanate from within her.

As Airella lay on the creaking wooden floor of the cabin, she felt as though every ounce of vitality had been drained from her. She lay still, her gaze fixed on the ceiling above, her body limp and unresponsive. It was a surreal sensation, as if she were merely a shell of herself, devoid of any feeling or warmth. In that moment of profound stillness, all that remained were the haunting echoes of her thoughts, swirling in her mind with a haunting emptiness.

She glimpsed at the shattered mirror propped against the wall. Struggling to sit upright, she observed her reflection—her once rosy complexion now drained to a sickly pallor, icy blue eyes staring back, and her locks transformed into a striking platinum hue. Not to mention the recent additions—two ominous spiraling horns curving from her temples. She resembled a creature plucked from the darkest recesses of a nightmare.

37

As the days crept by, Airella's world grew colder, the chill clinging to her since the day Father had transformed her into this monstrous form. Despite the initial shock, she gradually acclimated to her altered existence. Strangely, she sensed an unfamiliar sensation stirring within her, a subtle shift that hinted at something inexplicably evolving.

While deep in thought, she caught the distant echoes of joyful voices.

Airella's gaze lingered on the sturdy door, locked by an enchantment that her inner voice warned her not to approach.

Memories flooded her mind—the warmth of sunlight, Arii, Sirius, and Jonathan, all distant echoes in her isolated reality. Since her transformation began, Airella had been trapped in this lonely existence, finding solace only in the fleeting sounds of distant merriment.

As hours passed and the echoes of people's cheers faded into silence, the door to Airella's cabin creaked open, the enchantment slowly dissipating. A soldier stood before her, a mocking sneer on his face as he watched her struggle to rise.

"So, you've finally found your strength," he taunted with a chuckle. "You made it sound excruciating."

Airella met his gaze, sensing the familiar presence of Father, the entity that had taken control of another body once more.

"Cat got your tongue?" the soldier jeered, amusement lacing his words as Airella attempted to respond, only to find her voice stolen by an unknown force. Panic gripped her as she realized her inability to speak, her hands instinctively rising to cover her mouth.

"Oh, don't worry, my child," he reassured in a calm yet cryptic manner. "Your kind has different ways of communication. Welcome back to the isle," he stated, his tone laced with a hint of mockery as he sneered once more before pushing the heavy door open.

The sunlight poured in, its brilliance almost blinding. Airella instinctively shielded her eyes from the unexpected intensity.

"You will remain at my side, no matter the circumstance, understood?" His words carried a weight of authority, tinged with a veiled threat. "Otherwise, you'll lose a certain someone that is dear to you."

The mention of someone dear stirred conflicting emotions within Airella. She contemplated the concept of caring or loving for another, a sentiment she had long buried during her weeks spent in isolation. In her mind, she pondered the implications. Arii? Sirius? Jonathan's memory briefly crossed her mind. Alas, his presence was no more, leaving Airella with a sense of resignation.

Faced with his commanding presence and the implied consequences, Airella felt a sense of helplessness. She found herself bound by an invisible leash, compelled to comply with his every directive.

Father, still concealed within the guise of a soldier, reached for Airella's cloak—the same one the soldiers had previously confiscated from her—and draped it over her head. "Wear this. Stay hidden among the humans until further notice. When they realize you're gone, they'll assume you've fled, prompting a search that shouldn't interfere with my schemes. It's in your best interest to comply unless you have a penchant for your death sentence."

Airella longed to inquire about Sirius but found herself mute, overwhelmed by the inability to speak. The unanswered question lingered in her mind as she trailed Father from the cabin to the upper deck. Her vigilant gaze swept the surroundings—all five ships rested ashore, passengers dispersing onto the sands. They busied themselves with setting up camps and orchestrating plans.

"You'll look suspicious wandering around in the open," Father stated firmly, his expression unwavering. "So, just like any of my weapons, you'll stay in my tent until further notice. I've meticulously laid out plans for the Miscreants living on this island. As night falls, the humans will find themselves entrapped, destined to live out their days on this land. They will flourish once more, catering to our needs by providing sustenance for us Miscreants." They both peered down at the shoreline below. "This moment of solace with you is quite pleasant; having someone to confide in, sharing everything, all the while knowing you are powerless to act. Much like Sirius was after all these years—what a shame that it has to end like this." With a chuckle, he descended the ship's staircase, leaving Airella with no choice but to trail behind him.

As they navigated through the bustling crowds of people, Airella couldn't shake the feeling of a specific pair of eyes tracking her every step. Peeking out from under her hood, she caught sight of Duran's stern gaze fixed upon her from afar. The tension between him and Sirius lingered in the air, a mystery she doubted she'd ever unravel.

Guided by Father into the tent, he left with a command for Airella to remain inside. Airella's thoughts raced, her anticipation heightened by the sound of approaching footsteps that seemed unnaturally clear to her ears.

Duran's entrance interrupted her musings, his demeanor oddly unfamiliar. Something about his expression struck her as off.

"Remove your hood," his voice cut through the air, his eyes fixed on Airella, demanding compliance.

Airella displayed no emotion as she dragged down her hood, revealing her spiraled horns and platinum-colored hair cascading over her shoulders. Duran's eyes widened in profound shock, his expression a mix of disbelief and concern. Airella's transformation left him speechless.

"Airella..." his voice quivered, the softness of his tone contrasting with the intensity of his emotions. Awkwardly, he drew her into a tender embrace, his arms encircling her with a mix of protectiveness and anguish.

Airella, her thoughts a jumble of confusion, stood unmoving, her arms hanging limply at her sides, trying to comprehend the whirlwind of emotions surrounding her.

"Airella, it's me," his voice cracked with unshed tears, his hold on her tightening as if afraid she might disappear. "What has he done to you?" he murmured, his fingers gently tracing one of her horns, a sign of recognition and longing intertwined in his touch.

Jonathan? The thought flickered in Airella's mind like a distant memory, a name tied to an elusive past. Yet, despite the familiarity, she remained detached, unable to stir any emotion within herself. She strained to feel something, anything, but the void within her remained unyielding, leaving her adrift in a sea of emptiness.

"Airella? Aren't you going to say anything?" He grabbed her

by the shoulders, his hands trembling slightly as he peered into her now icy-colored eyes, searching for a glimmer of response.

Airella found herself at a loss, unsure of how to react in this moment of turmoil.

"You can't speak, can you?" His expression shifted to one of devastation upon realizing her inability to respond.

She gently shook her head in agreement, causing a wave of emotion to wash over him. The weight of recent events seemed to crush him as he struggled to contain his emotions.

"I don't know what to do anymore. Sirius vanished without a trace. Father is out for blood, and now... you. You're no longer human." During his emotional outburst, he fell to his knees, the ground absorbing the impact of his fists in a display of pain and frustration. After taking a moment to calm his frustration, he rose to his feet, a determined glint in his eyes. He took a slow, deep breath. "Don't worry, I'll find a way out of this. We'll restore your true self and locate Sirius. Father will face the consequences of his actions and we'll get these people off of this island. Together."

With a newfound resolve, he turned to depart, but paused before taking another step. "And one more thing," he presented Airella with a sizeable wooden box he had discovered on one of the ships. "I stumbled upon this aboard the vessel. I think this will hold some significance to you." A faint smile graced his features before he exited.

Airella gazed intently at the small crate. Placing it carefully before her, she lifted the lid. The contents sparkled in the dim light, captivating her attention.

Her fingers brushed against the familiar golden chest plate that had accompanied her on past adventures. Atop it lied Dawnbreaker. Memories flooded back—the clashes with Sirius, the encounters with Father—each etched into the metal's surface. With a wistful smile, she removed the armor from the crate and put it on, glad to be out of the clothes she had been stuck in for the last three weeks.

Settling onto the tent floor, Airella's mind wandered through a tapestry of recollections. Images of Sirius, Arii, King William, Jonathan, and others intertwined, painting a vivid portrait of her journey. Amidst the hushed surroundings, distant commotion gradually stirred.

Airella sat up straight, her heart pounding in her chest, as she listened intently to the panicked screams and yells of the people outside. The urgency in their voices sent a shiver down her spine, and she knew she had to act despite the risks.

As she grabbed Dawnbreaker and stepped outside of the safety of the tent, the dimming light of dusk revealed a scene of chaos and despair. The once tranquil campsite was now a frenzy of motion, with people running in all directions, their faces contorted with fear and confusion.

The acrid scent of smoke filled the air, stinging her nostrils and obscuring her view. As she turned her gaze towards the shoreline, her heart sank at the sight of the five docked ships engulfed in raging flames. The crackling of the fire mingled with the cries of the terrified onlookers, creating a cacophony that reverberated in her ears.

While many around her were paralyzed with shock, Airella stayed composed, processing the unfolding disaster with an unreadable expression. Ash floated like black snowflakes around her.

Airella suddenly heard a sound that pierced through the chaos, a voice calling her name. At first, it was a mere whisper in the tumult, but it grew louder and more insistent with each repetition. She felt a strange compulsion to follow the sound, to unravel the mystery of who was calling out to her amidst the turmoil.

"Airella!"

The voice was unmistakable now, resonating with familiarity and urgency. She turned towards the flaming ships, her eyes scanning each vessel in search of a clue. The question lingered in her mind—which burning ship held the voice that beckoned her?

Airella sprinted her way towards the docked ships, her black hood falling from her head in the rush. She tried her best to follow the mysterious voice that had guided her here, its whispers urgent and compelling. As she trudged through the shallow water, a gust of salty sea breeze tousled her silver hair.

Without hesitation, she climbed aboard the second ship in the row, the wood creaking slightly under her weight. Airella's heart raced, but strangely, a calm determination filled her. She knew she should have been terrified by the sight that greeted her—the deck was ablaze, flames dancing hungrily across the timbers, engulfing everything in their path. Yet, an eerie sense of detachment settled over her, as if she were an observer in her own body. It seemed as if she could do anything, as if the flames held no threat to her.

She ran through the raging fire, the crackling flames casting dancing shadows all around her. Following the mysterious voice that echoed through the chaos, she navigated her way to an untouched cabin door perched on the upper deck of the ship. Airella, with unwavering determination, clenched her fist tightly, ready to forcefully knock the door down. However, as her hand collided with the door, a wave of excruciating pain shot through her arm, weakened by the dark enchantment cloaking it. Despite the agony pulsing through her, she gritted her teeth and continued to throw her body at the door, each strike etching strange black symbols onto her skin.

With every blow, the weight of the enchantment bore down on her, threatening to crush her spirit. Not only was the dark magic draining her strength, but the relentless heat of the flames seemed to sap her very will to persevere. Gasping for air, she mustered the last dregs of her resolve and summoned her remaining energy for one last strike against the door. The wood splintered and crumbled under the force of her blow, yielding to her unwavering determination in the face of adversity.

She rushed into the room, her heart pounding as she laid eyes on Sirius's motionless body sprawled out on the floor. He had endured a severe beating, most likely inflicted by Father. The lingering smoke from the fire only added to the grim scene, hinting at the extent of the damage. Airella's instincts kicked in, and without a moment's hesitation, she hoisted Sirius onto her back, feeling the weight of his battered form as she left the crumbling ship.

Navigating through the chaos of falling debris, she reached the edge of the deck, the wood slippery beneath her feet. With adrenaline coursing through her veins, she made a split-second decision to leap, her heart pounding in her chest. Gripping Sirius with all her might, they plunged into the dark waters, the cold enveloping them like a shroud. Airella's lungs burned as she struggled to keep them afloat amidst the relentless crashing waves, the acrid scent of smoke filling her nostrils. The burning ships loomed ominously, flames dancing in the night sky around them.

Gasping for air, she finally felt the solid ground beneath her feet as she reached the shore. With determination blazing in her eyes, Airella tightened her grip on Sirius, and together they sprinted into the forbidding depths of the nearby forest. The dense canopy overhead cast eerie shadows in the night's darkness, the rustling of leaves adding to the sense of foreboding that hung heavy in the air.

Having ventured deep into the heart of the woodlands, she carefully lowered the unconscious Sirius to the ground, her eyes tracing the intricate black lettering that marked her skin from the mysterious enchantment. A pang of discomfort shot through her as she pondered the unknown magic. Sitting beside Sirius, she contemplated ways to counter the enchantment's effects, to soothe the burns that marred her skin. Yet, as she watched in awe, the dark lettering faded, gradually vanishing as if by some unseen force.

She blankly continued to stare at Sirius, her gaze fixed on his unconscious form. The intense heat of the burning ship singed his clothes and left marks on his skin. Soot and ash smudged his face, and his hair was damp with sweat and seawater. Despite his disheveled appearance, there was a certain calmness in his features, as if he had found peace in unconsciousness.

Father had finally achieved his goal—a new human civilization. With a sinking feeling, she knew that now that he had what he desired, he would have little interest in her and Sirius. Now, they were mere inhabitants of the island, while the humans were left stranded without their sole means of escape.

Airella's mind raced as she pondered their predicament, finding solace only in the presence of the person who had been her unwavering support, the one who had safeguarded her fragile existence up to this point—Sirius.

38

$\mathcal{S}$irius had finally felt a sense of humanity, a feeling that wasn't tied to pain, magic, or anything of that sort, but a connection he discovered through Airella. Without her, he would have remained lost in a cycle of soul-consuming obedience to Father's commands. His determination was singular—defeat Father.

"Airella?" Sirius's eyes snapped open in a sudden jolt, his body throbbing with pain. Despite the agony, he summoned the strength to rise to his feet, surrounded by an all-encompassing darkness reminiscent of a forsaken forest.

A chill ran down his spine as he glanced at his side and caught sight of her presence. The golden armor she wore gleamed under the dim light, a stark contrast to her appearance when they last parted ways at the ball. Her once golden blonde locks had transformed into a platinum cascade, while her eyes shone with an ethereal, icy blue hue. Two elegant and curved black horns now adorned her head, marking a stark departure from her human origins. Yet, Sirius's concern was not her altered form but the fact that she was alive, Miscreant or human.

Sirius lunged for her, his heart pounding with a mix of emotions, and embraced her tightly as she sat there in surprise, feeling the warmth of his hug enveloping her. She slowly lifted her hands, hesitating for a moment before returning the gesture. Tears welled up in Sirius's eyes and rolled down his cheeks, a rare display of vulnerability that spoke volumes.

Airella's heart stirred with a muted mix of emotions, memories of the past resurfacing like gentle waves crashing against the shore. The feelings she had buried deep within her resurfaced, tugging at her heart with a bittersweet ache.

Concern etched in his voice, Sirius growled softly, "Father did this to you?" But Airella remained silent, her gaze downcast as if wrestling with inner turmoil. "Airella? Are you okay?" he pressed, his worry palpable in the air.

Airella raised her eyes to meet his, a veil of emotions clouding her expression as she struggled to find her voice. With a solemn shake of her head, she conveyed her inner turmoil, a silent admission to her pain and struggle. Unable to speak, she gestured towards her throat.

Realization dawned on Sirius as he pieced together the puzzle of her condition, a surge of anger rising within him towards the one responsible. Casting a quick glance around, he spotted a sturdy stick nearby, a makeshift weapon to aid him in his weakened state, since his scythe went down with the burning ship.

"We need help, Airella," Sirius implored urgently. "We can't go back there. It's going to be risky, but we need to find Zol. He's the only Miscreant I know that might match Father in power. We need him on our side." The weight of their mission pressed heavily upon him, yet he felt an unwavering resolve to locate Zol. With an unyielding sense of urgency propelling him forward, Sirius braced himself against the daunting odds.

Airella regarded Sirius with a mixture of disbelief and concern, her expression mirroring the tumult of emotions within her as she shook her head vehemently.

"I know, I know. You don't like it, but we need his help." His voice trailed off, a flicker of apprehension crossing his features as he contemplated the impending encounter with Zol.

As they ventured deeper into the dense woodlands, Sirius's unease grew palpable. The rustling of leaves and the whisper of the wind added an eerie backdrop to their clandestine mission, heightening the tension that hung in the air.

Minutes ticked by in tense anticipation until a sudden commotion in a nearby bush disrupted the silence. Sirius instinctively raised his makeshift weapon in defense, bracing himself for an unknown threat lurking in the undergrowth. As the tension mounted, a figure emerged from the shadows, revealing Duran with outstretched arms lunging towards Sirius.

"I finally found you!" Duran exclaimed with a mixture of relief and joy, enveloping Sirius in a tight embrace. His words carried a sense of genuine concern, underscoring the gravity of their predicament. "I thought you were dead."

The sudden realization took aback Sirius. Hadn't he successfully defeated Duran when Father had taken control of his body?

Glancing at Duran and Airella, Sirius noticed the absence of the pendant around her neck. It all came flooding back to Sirius —when he inadvertently shattered the necklace, freeing Jonathan's soul. With Jonathan's soul released, it had presumably ventured into the realm of Limbo, seeking the closest available body to inhabit, which evidently turned out to be Duran's.

"Sorry," Jonathan began hesitantly, his gaze shifting towards Airella, "your brother... he is very fortunate." Stepping from behind Jonathan, Arii revealed himself to the group. The young boy appeared visibly shaken as he stood there, his eyes fixed on his older sister.

"Air…?" his voice trailed off. "Is that really you?"

Arii cowered back in fear as he examined her. A look of disappointment overcame Airella, her brows furrowing slightly as she lowered her eyes towards the ground, the weight of sorrow and frustration evident in her gaze. She could feel the heaviness in her chest, a lump forming in her throat. Perhaps Jonathan had caught her brother up to speed, and she hoped with all her heart that he wouldn't be fearful of her or the fact that Jonathan was now inhabiting Duran's body. Memories of that fateful night flooded her mind, the screams, the chaos—the last time Arii saw Duran was when he had slaughtered their mother. The pain and horror of that moment had left a lasting scar on both of their souls.

"So, is there a plan?" Duran, or Jonathan, questioned Sirius, a hint of skepticism in his voice as he shifted his weight from one foot to the other. "I mean, we can't exactly get back to Eldaraya without a ship. All the ships have been burned. It was Father's doing, no doubt. He's going to do everything he can to keep us here."

"There's a plan, but you're not going to like it," Sirius replied. "Remember that ice hellion we ran into the last time we were here?"

"How could I forget?" Jonathan crossed his arms.

"We need to convince him to help us," Sirius continued, his words measured and deliberate, trying to convey a sense of urgency without causing panic.

Even though Jonathan was inhabiting Duran's body, his response was just as expected—overly exaggerated and dramatic. His eyes grew wide, mirroring the shock that contorted his features as his jaw dropped.

"Are you insane? Are you forgetting how that demon almost killed us, not just once, but twice?" Jonathan waved his arms in the air.

"Thanks to you and Airella," Sirius expressed gratefully, his eyes reflecting a sense of relief, "I've felt more human than I ever did serving Father. That's how I know this is our only option. This has to work."

As he moved forward, Arii remained steadfastly by his side, Jonathan trailing close behind, while Airella, her voice lost in silence, followed suit. Concern etched on Sirius's face, he cast a fleeting glance over his shoulder at Airella, silently ensuring her well-being. They trudged through the icy terrain, the cold seeping into their bones.

"What do we do once we find him?" Jonathan's voice trembled with apprehension. "We can't risk the kid's safety by keeping him with us."

Sirius's expression darkened slightly. "We won't find him. He will find us, no matter where we tread in his domain. This frozen wasteland belongs to him, but with luck—"

"Does this mean that the ice hellion from my sister's tale is real?" Sirius's gaze lingered on Arii as he spoke.

"Yes, but don't worry. We will shield you from harm," Sirius murmured softly, ruffling Arii's hair in a reassuring gesture.

Suddenly, a chilling voice pierced the air, sending shivers down their spines. "Żînčœvēłí! Get out!"

"Get Arii and Airella away from here, and stay out of sight until this is over!" Sirius demanded, then watched as Jonathan took Airella's hand and carefully carried Arii by his waist into an iced-over brush.

Sirius turned with determination to face the towering ice hellion, a creature of frozen fury. He unsheathed his twin daggers, and his eyes blazed with a fierce resolve as he locked gazes with the monstrous being.

"Who are you?" The ice hellion's voice, though strained, struggled to form the words in English, its tone laced with confusion and primal anger.

"I am Sirius, the Miscreant that brought death to your beloved Emmaline." his voice carried a weight of history and regret.

Sirius leaned on his wooden staff. Zol lowered his daggers, the fierce gleam in his eyes softening as a wave of memories and emotions flooded his being. The pulsating glow in his eyes subsided, and the once menacing figure of the ice hellion simply stood. Zol clenched his massive fists at his sides, the ice crackling with an icy fury that mirrored the turmoil within his frozen heart.

"Emma? You? You... YOU!" he cried out in a mix of shock and anger, his voice trembling with emotion.

Just before he lunged at Sirius, his eyes filled with a fierce determination. With a swift movement, he tossed his daggers aside, the metallic clatter echoing in the tense silence of the forest. Grasping Sirius by the collar, he hurled him forcefully against the nearest tree, the impact reverberating through the air.

Zol held Sirius in a vice-like grip, his strength and fury palpable as ice encased Sirius's legs. Despite the cold seeping into his bones, Sirius felt a surge of fear and desperation. Zol's hand tightened around his throat, cutting off his air supply.

"I'm sorry... I took her from you..." Sirius gasped out the words, his voice strained and hoarse.

Zol's growl rumbled low in his chest as he exerted more pressure, pushing Sirius harder against the rough bark of the tree. The wood creaked under the strain, threatening to splinter.

"You took Emma from me!" Zol's voice was a dangerous hiss. With each word, the grip around Sirius's neck tightened, the world around him fading into darkness at the edges of his vision.

"And that is something... I will regret for the rest of my days... but, there is one... Miscreant that you can... let your anger out on. The Miscreant that was behind it all," Sirius's plea was desperate, his fingers clawing at Zol's obsidian skin, seeking any leverage to loosen the hold around his throat.

Zol hesitated, his gaze flickering with a mix of conflict and curiosity. As Sirius's words sank in, a glimmer of interest sparked in Zol's eyes.

"Explain," he demanded, his voice commanding yet tinged with a hint of uncertainty, a crack in his previously unwavering facade.

"His name is Conivx, a shadow Miscreant. We seek your help in reaching him, as he remains beyond our grasp in this reality," Sirius said between coughs, his voice strained from the recent choking episode.

Zol, with his intimidating brute-like appearance that cast a dark shadow over Sirius, seemed to consider the request. After a moment of silent contemplation, Zol gruffly released Sirius, showing his reluctant willingness to assist.

"Zol no like you, but I'll help. There are more here?" he inquired with a deep, rumbling voice.

"It's okay to come out now," Sirius called out.

First to emerge was Jonathan, followed closely by Arii, and last, Airella stepped into view. Airella's expression shifted as her gaze met Zol's intense stare. Despite the helmet concealing his true feelings, Zol's unwavering gaze remained fixed on her.

"Çœæmöïlï? Çæváñ... Zol," he uttered in a gravelly tone, his voice resonating with an unspoken history.

Sirius glanced back at Airella, who returned his surprised gaze with a look of recognition.

"Vækïźáïi kœvïqî ćæmïz, Airella," she responded smoothly,

no longer mute. Her words flowed effortlessly, as if the language was second nature to her, hinting at a deeper connection to this mysterious encounter.

To Airella, the prospect of encountering Zol once more seemed surreal. This enigmatic being had once posed a threat to their existence, yet here he stood, calmly engaging with her in a manner she could never have expected. The words effortlessly spilled from her lips, a newfound sense of confidence enveloping her.

With a tremor in her voice, she introduced herself, "My name is Airella." Speaking in his native tongue, she left Sirius, Arii, and Jonathan bewildered by the exchange.

"Zol," the ice hellion identified himself, a mysterious aura surrounding him. His presence captivated Airella, her mind racing with questions yet unable to form any coherent thoughts.

"You have changed since we last faced each other. You are no longer like Emmaline." Zol observed, drawing closer to inspect her altered appearance. "You have evolved. We are the same."

Airella's mind buzzed with intrigue as she contemplated the implications of this revelation. Was it possible that she was unraveling the threads of her own ancestry?

"I don't have all the answers yet, but I believe you may be my ancestor." The notion rooted itself in her consciousness, causing doubt in everything she had been led to believe.

Zol locked eyes with her, a silent understanding passing between them in the timeless span of a few heartbeats. Airella turned to the others, breaking the connection with Zol as she grappled with the weight of these newfound revelations.

"Airella, tell him we need to create an army of our own," Sirius ordered urgently, a hint of desperation in his voice. "Not to harm the humans, but to stop Conivx. To stop all of this." She nodded in understanding and turned back to Zol, her eyes reflecting the weight of their mission.

"Üñdęrè ttÿèç hûbdér, jœł ßéåçèñ," Airella spoke fluently in the odd language, her words resonating through the tense air. Zol hesitated, uncertainty clouding his features as he processed her request.

"I can't do that," he answered abruptly. Only she could understand the depth of his reluctance, the unspoken burdens he carried.

"Why?" Airella's voice held a mix of curiosity and concern, her eyes searching his for answers.

"The Miscreants on this island have been waiting for human arrival for the longest time. If anything, they'd obey Conivx at all costs. I know of him. He rules the shadows. He's power hungry," Zol finished explaining.

Disappointment flushed through Airella, a pang of sorrow tugging at her heart. "The least you can do is try. Lives are at stake." She clenched her fists.

"Human lives have been at stake since the moment they arrived centuries ago. I've already learned that lesson," he expressed with sorrow in his tone. As sadness rushed through him, he gazed downwards briefly, contemplating the weight of his words. "However," his voice regained strength as he lifted his gaze, eyes ablaze with a fierce resolve, "I will still seek my revenge on Conivx. He will pay for all he's done. He doesn't deserve his place." The intensity of his emotions manifested as rage coursing through him like a torrent, visible as icy shards erupted through his helmet in a dramatic display.

Observing Sirius, Airella acknowledged his unspoken agreement with a subtle nod, signifying a united front with Zol now firmly on their side.

As the snowflakes descended upon the group, blanketing them in a soft white layer, an aura of chill enveloped them. Despite the cold, Zol and Airella appeared unfazed, displaying a peculiar resilience to the wintry weather.

Airella stole a glance at Arii, noting his apprehension as he sought comfort near Jonathan. She found solace because he was now under her protection, a responsibility she embraced wholeheartedly.

Suddenly, a shadow seemed to creep over their surroundings, casting an eerie darkness that sent a shiver down Airella's spine. Puzzled by the sudden change, she scanned the area, her keen eyes searching for any signs of danger amidst the encroaching gloom.

"What's going on?" Jonathan's protective stance around Arii mirrored the unease that gripped the group.

In a hushed tone, Airella muttered an ancient phrase, "Hüth étæn," a whisper that carried a weight of foreboding.

"He's found us."

39

A powerful gust of wind suddenly burst through the dense trees, causing Airella's hair to flutter wildly in all directions. Amidst the rustling leaves, a haunting howl echoed in the distance. Father was not alone in this secluded forest; it seemed he had an entire legion at his command.

From the dense foliage emerged a towering figure, a six-foot-tall wolf-like creature with an eerily humanoid appearance, followed by an array of other mystical beings.

Airella glanced around as she and her companions—Zol, Sirius, Jonathan, and Arii—formed a protective circle, weapons in hand and their backs pressed tightly together. Trapped in the heart of this chaotic scene, it felt as though escape was an impossible feat.

"Look there," Jonathan's urgent voice broke the tense silence, his gaze fixed on a shadowy figure advancing towards them.

"I offered you all a swift end. Airella, I even presented you with a chance to evade this fate," Father's voice boomed. "Yet it appears you persist in obstructing my designs. Thus, I must now bring about your demise with my own hands. Let us conclude this swiftly, shall we?"

"You can dream," Jonathan retorted defiantly, his hand instinctively reaching for the hilt of Duran's sword.

The ground below them turned dark, as if it had become a shadow itself. Without warning, it pulled the team in like quicksand. They all struggled to free themselves, but to no avail. It simply just made things even worse. In that moment, Airella knew they were all done for. The thought of failure had set in her mind. She supposed this was it.

Airella gave one more glance around to the others that she cared so deeply about, now waist-deep in the shadowy tendrils that pulled them in deeper.

"Arii!" Sirius grabbed hold of the boy. He clasped his and Jonathan's hands. They would be the only mortals to face Father and survive.

Meanwhile, Zol's struggle against the oppressive shadows was intense. He summoned every ounce of his strength and focused his mind, channeling his inner energy to repel the darkness that enveloped him. With a fierce roar, he broke through the shadowy tendrils, forcing them to retreat with a burst of light. He turned to Airella with a face etched with determination.

The shadows' cold, unyielding grip still trapped Airella, entwining her limbs. Zol didn't hesitate; he lunged forward, his hands glowing with a brilliant icy light, and tore through the shadows binding her. Airella gasped for air as the darkness dissipated, her eyes widening with relief and gratitude.

But their moment of triumph was short-lived. As soon as they were free, a horde of miscreants descended upon them. Zol and Airella barely had time to brace themselves before the onslaught began. They fought valiantly, side by side, but the overwhelming numbers left them at a disadvantage.

Sirius, Jonathan, and Arii watched in horror as their comrades battled the swarm. They were helpless, unable to assist, and the looming presence of Father cast an even darker shadow over them.

"Look at you. I never thought I'd have the delight of witnessing you so enraged," Father sneered, lifting Sirius's chin with a menacing glint in his eye. Sirius strained against the encroaching shadows. Every muscle tensed in futile resistance, but the darkness seemed almost alive, coiling tighter around him. "I want to savor this," Father declared, his grip tightening as he seized Sirius by the throat, yanking him out from the engulfing abyss.

Fury contorted Sirius's features into a mask of defiance as he locked eyes with his tormentor. Anger flowed through him, and he felt his helplessness raw and palpable as Father paraded him like a trophy, using him as a pawn in his sadistic game. Airella and Zol, embroiled in their own desperate battles, were oblivious to his plight.

In that moment of harrowing vulnerability, Sirius found a fleeting connection to his humanity. Emotions surged within him, heightened by the distant, concerned glances of Airella and Zol. Tears welled in his eyes, his cheeks aflame with a mixture of searing pain and indignation. Father's oppressive grip seemed to crush his very soul, leaving him gasping for air amidst the chaos.

"Airella!" Sirius yelled, his voice echoing through the chaos surrounding them. He hesitated, torn between the desire to express his feelings and the knowledge that she might be safer without him. Memories of their dance at the ball in Eldaraya flooded his mind, intensifying his internal struggle.

As he extended his hand towards her, a sharp, crushing pain enveloped his head, intensifying with each passing moment. The eerie howls of the lycans, the bloodcurdling roars of the bloodsuckers, and the ominous presence of other malevolent beings seemed to converge, all seemingly in allegiance to Father, the force slowly consuming him.

With desperation, Airella's eyes widened with fear and sorrow. Her heart ached as she watched Sirius struggle, the being she cared for slipping away. She could see the torment in his eyes, the battle he fought within himself, and it shattered her soul.

With a gasp, Sirius met Airella's gaze, his eyes filled with a mixture of longing and resignation. Her expression mirrored the turmoil within him, her icy tears contrasting with the fierce grip on Dawnbreaker. The feelings they shared, the dreams they had, all seemed to crumble in that instant.

"I..." His voice was strained as the world around him slowly blurred. Airella's image wavered, fading into obscurity as he felt himself disintegrating into ethereal gold particles. The surreal transformation unfolded before Airella, leaving her stunned as she witnessed him dissipating further and further until he was no more.

Airella screamed, falling to her knees, her hands reaching out in vain to grasp at the shimmering remnants of Sirius. Her cries echoed through the desolation, a haunting lament that seemed to pierce the heavens. A gaping wound formed in her heart, tearing it apart and rendering it unable to heal.

His essence scattered into the unknown, leaving behind a faint trail of shimmering gold remnants that soon faded into nothingness. He was gone, leaving Airella alone in the cold, cruel reality, with only the memory of his touch and the sound of his voice to haunt her dreams.

The world seemed darker, emptier, and the weight of her loss was unbearable. She clutched Dawnbreaker and vowed to avenge him, even as her heart cried out for the love she had lost forever.

40

Airella's shock turned to a torrent of emotions, her grief and anger manifesting in a luminous blue glow that radiated from her eyes. She let out a scream of desperation as the ground beneath her quivered as icy spikes emerged, impaling the malevolent beings in a display of raw power and fury. The vivid transformation marked a turning point in the unfolding chaos, a moment where her resolve solidified amidst the surreal events transpiring around her.

Arii's cries echoed loudly, his voice breaking into screams that seemed to pierce the air. Jonathan, feeling helpless, tried his best to soothe Arii's overwhelming emotions. The situation spiraled out of control, a sense of chaos filling the space.

"Sirius!" Jonathan's voice trembled with fear and desperation. "Where did he go? What have you done to him?" His accusatory gaze landed on Father.

"He's gone. Where? I can't say. I never seem to know where they vanish to, but one thing is certain: He won't return." Father's words were cold.

Airella stood in disbelief, processing the sudden turn of

events. Sirius, a steadfast companion who had stood by her in the face of countless challenges, was now lost to the unknown. Their shared adventures and unwavering support now relegated to bittersweet memories that lingered in the shadows.

"No!" she cried out in anguish, her voice trembling with despair. "Please, don't leave! Sirius!"

The overwhelming sense of loss and sorrow triggered a profound change within her, unlocking words that had long held captive. No longer silenced by her grief, her voice resounded with a newfound strength.

"Don't you dare abandon me." Her cries resonated with raw emotion, tears streaming down her face. Casting a fierce gaze towards Father, a sudden shift in her demeanor was palpable. "You. You're going to pay for this. I may not know how, but I swear I'll bring you down!" Her command of their language had fully returned, her words dripping with fury. As her rage intensified, a chilling transformation took hold—icy shards formed on her skin, her complexion paling with each passing moment.

Raising Dawnbreaker, she lunged towards Father with a vengeance, but to no avail. The spectral figure remained untouched by her blows, a mere apparition in the face of her wrath. Undeterred, she swung her weapon repeatedly at the elusive shadow, each strike punctuated by her heart-wrenching cries.

"Where did you send him?" The words tumbled from her lips in a torrent of anguish, her sorrow reverberating through the empty expanse.

"Airella!" Jonathan screamed at her as he used a thick, gnarled branch to pull both him and Arii out of the shadows that ensnared them like invisible tendrils.

Bloodsuckers, vile creatures of the night, took their time, savoring the scent of the duo's blood before making their sinister move.

"Stay back!" Jonathan's voice echoed through the eerie silence of the dark forest as he clutched Arii protectively. Together, they pressed against the rough bark of a towering tree, their backs to the solid trunk, seeking refuge from the encroaching darkness.

Airella, once vulnerable and uncertain, now stood amidst the chilling winds that wrapped around her like an icy embrace. She attuned her body to the freezing temperatures that encased her. With a steely resolve, she felt a surge of power coursing through her veins, freeing her from the shackles of doubt and restraint. Airella's gaze, fixed upon Father, held a fierce determination that belied the chaos swirling within her.

"This power, you don't know how to harness it!" Jonathan's voice echoed through the gusting winds. But the blizzard, stirred by Airella's unleashed power, intensified. "Airella!"

"Hüè gœttø!" Zol repeated urgently as he dashed to Airella's side. With determination etched on his face, he grasped her shoulder. In a mysterious twist, it appeared he was drawing power from her, amplifying the blizzard's intensity twofold with his own energy.

"I always knew you'd defy me. But, oh, how mistaken you are about who has the upper hand!" Father's voice boomed as he conjured a radiant purple gem out of thin air, his shadowy form hovering above the ground. "Don't tell me you've forgotten about our lovely time spent onboard the ship. When I said you're under my control, I meant it." The island resonated with his words as he brandished the gem for all to see, its glow captivating onlookers. Squeezing it tightly, Airella crumpled to the ground, struggling for breath, feeling the pressure on her chest intensify.

"What sorcery is this?" Airella uttered between gasps.

Jonathan and Arii observed helplessly from a distance, encircled by Miscreants, while Zol remained steadfast by Airella's side.

"This is what I'm capable of," he chuckled, a twisted glint in his eyes. "I give an order, and you'll do as I say. Otherwise, I'll break this gem and you'll be miserable for centuries to come due to the awakening of the hellion within you."

Airella, her heart pounding in her chest, clenched her teeth together. "You've already gotten what you wanted. The humans are stuck on this island, and Sirius is dead."

"Yes, but why stop there?" he mused with a chilling smile. "I'm on the path to becoming a god. You will all bow down to me, and you all will become prey and servants to all the beasts who walk this earth. I am capable of anything, don't you see?"

"You just sound power-hungry and selfish," Airella retorted, her fists clenched tightly at her sides, ready for whatever may come next.

"You just wait, you'll be begging me for mercy," Father menacingly uttered as he raised the purple gem to his shadowy lips. With a whispered command, the purple gem ignited in a radiant glow, casting an eerie light that mirrored the new violet intensity in Airella's eyes.

As the mysterious power enveloped her, Airella felt a profound transformation taking place within her very being. It was a struggle to resist the overwhelming surge of strength coursing through her veins, as if her essence was slipping away, replaced by something unknown and formidable.

"Kill them," Father's bitter voice pierced the charged atmosphere, his command targeting Jonathan and Arii, the unsuspecting victims of this dark power play.

Airella's body seemed possessed by an unseen force as a new presence, deep and commanding, resonated from her. With swift and unnerving agility, she lunged towards Jonathan. Gripping him by the collar, she effortlessly hurled him against a nearby tree, leaving him gasping for breath amidst the crimson splatters of blood.

The malevolent presence within Airella's form shifted its focus to Arii, a wicked grin playing on her lips as she seized him by the hair, lifting him with an unsettling ease. Before she could unleash her wrath upon him, a sudden impact sent them crashing to the ground, disrupting the unfolding chaos.

"Airella, stop!" Zol pinned her to the dewy ground, dampening the scent of earth as Arii sprinted to Jonathan's aid. She defiantly kicked Zol off her, his weight sending him skidding across the grass. "You're strong," Zol spoke through his thick accent.

"What did you expect?" The defiant hellion girl chuckled, a mischievous glint in her eyes.

Jonathan wheezed and leaned on the sturdy trunk of the oak he was hurled against, using it as leverage to regain his footing. "Airella! Can't you see that you're being manipulated?"

Airella's lips curled into a sharp, almost predatory smile, revealing a glint of something primal within her. The being before them was no longer Airella, but a manifestation of the enigmatic essence that set her apart from mere mortals.

Zol's gaze darted towards Father, who held the glowing pendant in his outstretched palm. Reacting swiftly, he lunged towards him.

"No, no," Father chided, the corners of his mouth turning up in a sly grin. "Unless you wish for your friend's metamorphosis to be irreversible, I suggest you think twice before making any rash moves."

"I care not for your threats," Zol growled defiantly, an icy aura emanating from his obsidian helmet, crystalline spikes forming around him like a fearsome halo.

"That's the spirit." Father applauded mockingly.

"You killed Emma." Zol's words were strained, laced with

grief and accusation. His eyes, filled with a mix of anger and sorrow, locked onto Father.

"Oh, yes. She was quite the hassle, along with the rest of her people. But that's in the past now, so I believe it's your turn to die," Father retorted callously. "Airella, take care of this saucy fellow."

Airella gave a dark smile. With a swift motion, she delivered a ferocious punch to the center of Zol's chest, the impact leaving a visible crack in his obsidian armor. Zol staggered backward, collapsing into the pristine snow, his hands instinctively reaching for the source of searing pain.

"I'll make this quick," Airella declared, her resolve unwavering as she raised her foot above his head, poised to deliver a final blow.

41

Sirius's eyes wandered, but he had yet to figure out where he was. The last thing he remembered was telling Airella—

That's right.

From what he could tell, he was floating in a void of darkness. Countless souls hovered around him, their spectral forms gradually solidifying into humanoid shapes. Each ethereal figure bore the weight of those Sirius had devoured many years ago. As he floated through the black expanse, the souls' collective outrage pierced the silence. Their cries of anger, disbelief, and sorrow bombarded him, evoking a tumultuous mix of emotions within him. Desperate to drown out the cacophony of anguish and curses, Sirius covered his ears, seeking solace. Suddenly, his movement ceased before a solitary soul stood out from the others.

Emmaline.

She was the one soul he regretted devouring the most. A look of serene forgiveness graced her features as she extended her radiant hand towards his cheek. Before any further interaction could unfold, a voice resonated from the shadows behind him, shattering the eerie stillness.

"Don't trust these souls, Sirius. They're welcoming you to death."

Sirius turned sharply, his pulse hammering as he locked eyes with the dark-haired stranger. A stranger who wasn't a stranger at all. His face.

Alikad.

The reaper—the one he was supposedly cloned from by Father's hand—stood before him, watching with an intensity that sent a cold shiver down Sirius's spine.

"You can't die, Sirius," Alikad continued, stepping closer. "We must merge if we are to defeat Father. You need a new body. Take mine." His golden eyes burned with conviction. "We are the same person."

Sirius hesitated, his thoughts spiraling through the tangled web that connected him, Alikad, and Father. The air between them crackled with tension, the weight of unspoken truths pressing down on him.

"Before I even consider that," Sirius narrowed his eyes, voice firm, "I want answers. Why did Father clone you to create me instead of just using you?"

Alikad's jaw tensed. A flicker of something unreadable crossed his face—pain, bitterness, regret. Then, he exhaled slowly, his gaze hardening.

"He stripped you from me because I couldn't be controlled," Alikad admitted, his voice laced with anger. "So, he took the part of me that could be—the part of me that was compassionate and kind."

Sirius's breath hitched.

"The part of me he took," Alikad pressed on, his golden eyes burning into Sirius's, "*was you.* That was all he needed to wipe out humankind on the isle—to rule over the Miscreants. You may be my clone, but you don't share my memories. You were made to serve him. But you don't have to."

Sirius clenched his fists, his mind reeling. Everything he had been told—every sliver of identity he thought he had—was unraveling before him. His very existence was the product of Father's manipulation.

Alikad stepped forward, extending his hand, urgency sharp in his gaze. "Trust me, Sirius. Your friends need you right now."

Sirius hesitated, past uncertainties clashing against the dire need of the present moment. His heart pounded in his chest as he stared at Alikad's outstretched hand, the final tether to the truth.

Then, with a sharp inhale, he grasped it.

The moment their hands met, an overwhelming surge of power ignited through Sirius's body. Light and darkness collided, fusing into something ancient and whole. A radiant glow enveloped them both, their forms pulsing with raw energy as their souls converged.

Sirius was no more. He was Alikad, fully realized. Whole.

A transformation overtook him—his body shifting, morphing into something more than either of them had ever been. His obsidian hair cascaded past his shoulders, wild and untamed. His golden eyes glowed like twin suns, fierce and unrelenting. A cloak, tattered yet ethereal, swirled around him like living shadow. Strips of fabric, resembling ceremonial bandages, wound around his torso and arms, and trailing behind him like unraveling threads of fate.

Then, with a sharp inhale, skeletal wings burst from his back, stretching wide like the remnants of a forgotten god. Pain flashed across his features, but he gritted his teeth, standing tall as the newfound strength coursed through him.

Through the haze of transformation, his gaze fell upon Emmaline. Bound. Helpless.

His fingers twitched at his side before he moved toward her, his calloused hand reaching out to brush gently against her cheek. His touch was tender, hesitant, a promise unspoken.

"When this is over," his voice was a low vow, "I will set you all free."

A shiver of determination ran through him as he straightened, lifting his hand. The air crackled with power. From the void, a mask materialized—its intricate carvings twisting into the shape of a raven's skull. The sockets glowed, empty yet full of something ancient and knowing.

With slow deliberation, Alikad placed it over his face.

A shift in the air. A presence rising.

A scythe coalesced in his grasp, its dual-bladed edges gleaming under Limbo's eerie moonlight. Black feathers, shimmering with an unnatural glow, adorned the handle, beads catching the light with every subtle movement. It was no ordinary weapon. It was his.

The weight of it settled into his palm like it had always belonged there.

Without hesitation, he swung the blade. A rift tore through the air before him, an opening to the world beyond.

A way out.

As he stepped forward, the cacophony of anguished screams and guttural growls filled his ears, but they no longer unnerved him. He was not the prey anymore.

Toweringly tall, eclipsing even the group of cowering Miscreants before him, Alikad raised his scythe high above his head. With a deft stroke, he brought the blade down, a whirlwind of motion that cleaved through his foes with ruthless precision. The aftermath left a chilling scene, with severed limbs and splattered blood painting the once pristine snowy ground in macabre hues.

He felt eminently stronger than he had originally. The

newfound strength coursing through his veins gave him a sense of invigoration he hadn't experienced in quite some time. As he reveled in this newfound power, a sudden burst of laughter echoed through the air, catching his attention.

Turning towards the source of the laughter, he saw Arii and Jonathan being tossed to the ground.

Alikad placed a hand over his head, feeling a strange cloud of shadows descending upon his mind. It was as if his memory was being toyed with, elusive and fleeting. With a swift and purposeful movement, he made his way towards the bloodied duo, his steps barely leaving an imprint on the snowy ground.

Alikad arrived just in time and deftly caught both of them as they descended from their next shove. Arii trembled in fear as Alikad gently set him down.

"Who are you?" Arii's voice quivered with uncertainty.

Ignoring his question, Jonathan swiftly positioned himself protectively in front of the boy, drawing his sword in a defensive stance.

Alikad tilted his head in confusion, his golden eyes reflecting a mix of disbelief and curiosity behind his raven skull mask.

Slowly, he cautiously approached them, his shoulder-length black hair swaying with each step. As he neared, a sense of wariness lingered in his gaze. With a hesitant motion, he raised his slender hand towards them, his pale skin almost glowing in the dim light.

Before he could fully process his next move, a sudden motion disrupted the air. Jonathan's sword sliced through the space between them, severing Alikad's hand in a single, precise strike. Shock rippled through Alikad, his eyes widening as gold blood gushed from the stump where his hand once was. Yet, strangely, he felt no pain, only a surreal detachment.

Alikad, amidst a blurred world, stooped to inspect the detached hand on the pristine snow. Gently placing his scythe aside, he calmly lifted the severed limb. With almost nonchalant grace, he realigned his hand, and the limb seamlessly mended itself.

Arii shuffled nervously behind Jonathan, his wide eyes fixed on Alikad. Tentatively, he approached the enigmatic being, offering a handkerchief as a gesture of peace. The fabric trembled in his grasp as he reached out, his small frame trembling in the cold.

Alikad observed Arii's actions with a mix of surprise and curiosity, his eyes never leaving the young boy's face. Gently, Arii wrapped the makeshift bandage around Alikad's wrist, his touch gentle against his icy skin.

Looking up at Alikad with a tentative smile, Arii murmured softly, "You won't hurt us, will you?" The question lingered in the frosty air, a silent plea for understanding and acceptance.

"Arii! Get away from it! It could kill you!" Jonathan growled as Alikad pulled the boy protectively to his chest.

Alikad wasn't exactly friendly, not as much as the young boy had hoped. However, it quickly became apparent that Alikad wasn't directing his stand-off demeanor at Jonathan; instead, it was aimed at the shadowy figures ominously encircling them.

"Jonathan, look out!" Arii yelled as Alikad's wings thrust forward.

With a swift movement, Alikad pulled Jonathan closer, and in a stunning display, his skeletal wings detached from his body, weaving together to form a cage of bone that ensnared both Arii and Jonathan within its confines to seal them from the oncoming Miscreants. As Alikad twirled his scythe and brought it down with force, a shockwave of dark mist emanated from the impact point, rapidly enveloping the area. The ground trembled beneath them, causing the boy and the soldier to stumble within the bone enclosure.

"Who is this?" An ogre-like Miscreant sneered as it drew closer to Alikad.

In response, the reflection of a lycan against the gleam of Alikad's raven skull mask growled fiercely in defiance. "I thought the only reaper on this island was the one the shadow beast just killed."

Alikad tightened his grip on his scythe, his voice a low whisper. "Kill the Miscreants," he commanded.

A strong vibration rippled through the air, causing a sudden jolt of fear in the Miscreants standing before Alikad. Among them, a large, green, and grotesque werewolf with rotted fur leaped ferociously at a bloodsucker, sinking its decayed fangs deep into the victim's throat. The Miscreant's piercing screams swiftly morphed into gurgles, their desperate attempts to hold on to life futile.

As the fallen Miscreant lay lifeless, Alikad fixed his gaze on the other encroaching figures, now retreating in horror. The gruesome werewolf, its maw stained with fresh blood, exhibited bits of flesh and sinew dangling from its gory teeth.

A sudden, piercing scream reverberated through the forest. Emerging from the shadows of the woods, pale and decaying husks of Miscreants slithered forth, their movements hauntingly slow yet purposeful. Like a macabre ballet, they descended upon the living Miscreants, a symphony of agony unfolding as bites and screams resonated from every corner, painting a gruesome tableau of carnage.

Alikad, now the puppet master of these undead horrors, orchestrated the grim dance of death, the souls of the fallen Miscreants becoming his dark currency. The forest bore witness to a chilling spectacle of darkness, where the line between life and death blurred amidst the chaos and despair.

"Wait, Sirius? Is that you?" Jonathan yelled over the deafening cacophony of war.

The name caught Alikad's attention immediately, prompting him to pivot towards the source of the shout. As he began striding purposefully in their direction, a menacing troll barreled straight at him. Yet, with a swift and precise motion, Alikad cleaved the Miscreant's body in two with a single swipe of his scythe. The metallic scent of blood filled the air as crimson droplets splattered across his face.

Having reached the protective barrier he erected around Jonathan and Arii, Alikad's presence exuded both strength and resolve. As he deftly swung his scythe through the air, the bones composing the structure shifted seamlessly, returning to their original formation on his back. This action not only secured their safety but also created a portal leading to the ethereal realm of Limbo. Gesturing towards the shimmering passageway, Alikad ushered Jonathan and Arii to step through it for their own safety.

However, just as Jonathan paused on the threshold before entering fully, he withdrew his leg hesitantly, fixing Alikad with a resolute gaze. "If you truly are our friend, help Airella, she's in danger," he implored, his voice tinged with urgency. With those words hanging in the charged atmosphere, Jonathan proceeded through the portal, leaving Alikad to confront his foes alone.

As Alikad raised his scythe, preparing to engage the encroaching horde of Miscreants, a sudden memory pierced his consciousness, causing him to grimace in discomfort. In his mind's eye, he stood before a shadowy figure of immense stature that loomed ominously over him.

Conivx is my true name, the figure intoned cryptically, its voice resonating with dark authority.

The name echoed through his mind relentlessly as he skillfully sliced through each Miscreant that crossed his path. Blood stained the once pristine snowy ground. It appeared he was wading through the densest concentration of the vilest of creatures, their twisted forms no match for his swift justice. Limbs tore asunder, causing lifeless bodies to crumple to the earth as their essence fled their monstrous forms. Alikad, now a figure cloaked in darkness, consumed the fallen souls with a voracious hunger for retribution.

A surge of rage coursed through him, his wings swatting aside any Miscreant foolish enough to attempt an ambush from the shadows. Emerging from the throng of horrified adversaries, Alikad surveyed the aftermath of his onslaught. A significant number lay dead, reduced to mere piles of flesh and bone amidst the chilling silence. The haunting growls and howls of the undead, drawing nearer, spurred Alikad into action.

$\mathcal{L}$eaving the surviving Miscreants to confront their own fates, Alikad embarked to uncover the source of the malevolent laughter that had pierced the air. His brief journey led him to a desolate expanse ravaged by ice, where his gaze fell upon a fierce battle between ice hellions.

"We are not alone," whispered the shadow from behind Alikad. Father's physical force was powerful for something that was physically untouchable.

Alikad quickly dodged his attack, jumping back as his boney wings dug deep into the tree behind him. He pulled himself free and gripped to his scythe firmly.

"Now what?" Airella turned her attention to Alikad and away from Zol. Her eyes glowed a piercing bright blue overwhelmed with a hypnotic purple haze,.

With calculated precision, she firmly placed her foot on the chest of the male ice hellion below her. Blood oozed from her victim's chest, contrasting against the frozen landscape.

As Alikad continued to observe her, a sense of familiarity tugged at the corners of his mind. Then, in a sudden rush, the floodgates of remembrance opened, engulfing him in a torrent of past adventures, battles fought, and names—Arii, Jonathan, Duran, Father—echoing through the labyrinth of his mind.

"Airella!" Alikad roared, turning his attention to Father in a blinding rage.

The air crackled with tension as Alikad's hand shimmered, gradually taking on a transparent quality akin to the shadow looming before him. With an intense surge of power, Alikad seized Father, only to feel his own energy swiftly ebbing away, leaving him weakened and vulnerable. The force of Father's impact forced Alikad to his knees, his grip faltering as he released his hold on the malevolent figure.

As the ethereal grip dissolved, Alikad's arm regained its solid form, but a sharp, searing pain shot through him, causing him to cry out in anguish. Alikad's back forcefully collided with the sturdy trunk of a nearby tree, resulting in the tree being abruptly uprooted. With a swift, fluid motion, Alikad regained his footing, his gaze fixing on Airella, whose expression betrayed a twisted pleasure at the pain she had inflicted upon him.

"What have you done? What have you done to her?" Alikad's voice reverberated with a mix of fury and desperation as he confronted the shadowy figure clutching the purple stone.

"Who are you?" Father's chuckle dripped with malicious delight, provoking Alikad to advance menacingly towards him. In a deft move, the shadowy Miscreant sidled closer to Airella. "Another of your old acquaintances, Zol?" Father taunted the male ice hellion, his words laced with a sinister edge.

"Guess again." Alikad's voice reverberated through the air, resonating with a newfound depth and strength that hinted at a concealed power. Feathers cascaded from his cloak, drifting to the ground as he lifted his hand towards the concealing mask that veiled his true identity.

With a swift motion, Alikad swept his hand across his face, causing the mask to dissolve into nothingness, unveiling a pair of piercing yellow eyes that seemed to hold the weight of centuries within their gaze. Amidst the shadowy strands of his now charcoal hair, a few wisps of ashen white stood out, a subtle yet significant detail that sparked a realization within Father.

A blaze ignited within Alikad's eyes, an inferno of defiance and resolution that burned brightly as he faced his once mentor. "You can't extinguish the life that has already been stolen, Father." Alikad's words cut through the tension, each syllable dripping with a mixture of sorrow and wrath. "You underestimated the consequences of your actions. With every Miscreant that falls, their essence fuels my strength. Consider my words a curse upon you, a wretched seeker of power and shadow." Pointing an accusatory finger at Father, Alikad's gaze bore into the very core of his being. "You shall meet your end, Father. I stand by my vow from our encounter aboard the ship. Should you ever bring harm to her, I will pursue you relentlessly, even if it means facing death and resurrection a thousandfold." Alikad's emotions boiled over, consumed by an unyielding rage towards the shadow that had once been his guide and tormentor.

Father's look of shock slowly transformed into pure, maniacal laughter. Airella followed suit, her expression mirroring a mix of surprise and amusement.

"You're telling me you merged with that wretched boy, Alikad? How disappointing," Father remarked with a tinge of bitterness. Turning to Airella, he added, "Be a dear and eliminate him for good. He's bound to exhaust his energy at some point."

Airella responded with a nod. She lunged towards the reaper, Dawnbreaker clashing against the hilt of his scythe.

However, Alikad swiftly intercepted, seizing her arm and deftly hurling her aside. Clearly, she wasn't his focus.

Alikad, now fixated on Father, made a decisive move. His hand reached for the purple gem clutched close to his chest. Despite his impressive speed, Airella matched his pace. Her hand wrapped around his ankle, spinning him around effortlessly. Regaining his balance, Alikad propelled himself skyward with a powerful flap of his wings, morphing his silhouette into that of a shadow.

He dashed at Father once more, desperately reaching for the shard he held. Alikad couldn't hold this form for long. It drained him of energy much too quickly. As an unfortunate result, he transformed back to his physical form once again, the strain clear in his weary eyes and trembling hands. He pulled one of his wings forward, the feathers ruffling in the rush of movement, where the tip of his left wing shot for the purple shard. With a swift motion, he knocked it away from them both, the shard clattering faintly as it fell to the ground.

Father took a moment to comprehend what had just happened before he rushed to his search for the stone.

Before Alikad could even consider joining the search, his wings swatted Airella from her ambush with a forceful motion. However, with a strength that belied her appearance, she managed to take hold of his wing in a sudden twist of events, her grip unyielding as she snapped the bone in two with a resounding crack that echoed through the icy forest.

Alikad winced in excruciating pain as gold blood spurted from his fractured bone, the agony searing through his body. With a desperate lurch to the side, he dislodged his assailant from his wings, only to collapse to the unforgiving ground. Despite the torment gnawing at him, Alikad's fingers scrabbled towards the glimmering purple shard, a mere breath away from his grasp.

In a cruel twist of fate, Zol's heavy boot descended upon his outstretched hand. The chilling gaze of Father met Alikad's anguished eyes as his muffled voice emanated from his helmet.

"I don't think so, my boy. Once you relinquish your will to fight, she will dance to my tune as your replacement," taunted Father.

Every nerve in Alikad's body screamed with pain as Airella kneeled into his spine and wrenched his arm back. Through gritted teeth, Alikad cast a defiant smile at Zol, a flicker of resilience shining through his suffering. A fleeting chuckle escaped Alikad, though he buried his face in the snow to veil his tumultuous emotions.

"You underestimated Zol. He can never truly be possessed." Alikad's voice rang out with a mixture of defiance and triumph, challenging the malevolent spirit that had usurped Zol's form. As Father, the puppeteer of Zol's body, kneeled to meet Alikad eye to eye, the tension crackled in the frigid air.

"His stubborn will and extreme hatred for you give him more willpower than anyone else here," Alikad remarked with a sly grin, observing the fierce struggle unfolding before him. "You'll be kicked out of his body. He's a full-blooded demon. It would take something much stronger than you to possess the likes of him." The ominous threat hung in the air as Father's agonizing roars filled the clearing, a testament to the intense battle of wills taking place.

Alikad chuckled tauntingly as Father writhed in pain from the internal conflict. Suddenly, a shadow shot forth from Zol's form, revealing the true Zol as he turned to face the unfolding drama. With a swift motion, he retrieved the shimmering purple gem and tossed it to Alikad, a silent exchange loaded with unspoken significance.

Airella, consumed by a fiery rage, launched herself at Zol once more, her fury palpable as she pinned him against a gnarled tree, her clenched fist connecting with his obsidian helmet in a resounding impact that echoed through the forest.

"I need you back," Alikad declared solemnly, his voice tinged with urgency as he pressed the gem to his lips.

The gem's ethereal glow dispersed, revealing a pulsating core of energy within, which he deftly extracted and hurled towards Airella, a shimmering cascade of light merging with her being. In a moment of stunned realization, Airella faltered, allowing Alikad to swiftly crush the now lifeless shard beneath his heel, a decisive action that sealed the fate of the fallen gem.

As the dust settled, Alikad gathered Airella in a protective embrace, her form slumping with exhaustion. Yet, amid this fragile equilibrium, a new threat emerged. Father's sinister laughter reverberated through the clearing, a new dark purple shard pulsating with malevolent energy clutched in his outstretched hand.

Alikad's gem, a harbinger of unknown perils yet to come, cast a foreboding shadow over the unfolding saga of light and darkness.

"You still have that?" Alikad yelled as he gently laid Airella down alongside Zol. His heart raced with a mixture of shock and confusion, memories flooding back to the day he thought it was gone forever. "But I watched you break it. You shattered it out of frustration years ago because you weren't able to control me with it."

"Calm, Alikad. No need to be that way," Father replied, his voice soothing yet tinged with a hint of sinister satisfaction.

With a mysterious air, he whispered into the purple shard, the words barely audible to anyone else present. The shard emitted a strange energy that surrounded Alikad, providing him with a cloak of tranquility that he found both comforting and disconcerting simultaneously. As if under a spell, Alikad involuntarily dropped to his knees.

"Yes, I shattered the shard, but after my recent time spent on the mainland, I was able to grow immensely in power thanks to the countless human souls I had access to. Thanks to this, I was able to create these new shards. With this stronger power of mine that I'm able to channel through these human souls, I will control anyone and anything now. Including you. I may not have the half-breed anymore, but I will always have you," Father declared, his words laced with a chilling sense of control.

Alikad felt a strange sensation creeping over him, his eyes widening in disbelief as the world around him seemed to blur. His gaze locked with Father's, and in that moment, something shifted within him. His eyes, which were once a piercing yellow, transformed into an ethereal shade of shifting purple, mirroring Airella's own enchanting gaze when she became ensnared by the same mysterious power.

Struggling to find his voice amidst the turmoil of emotions and revelations, Alikad lifted his head, his voice barely a whisper as he stammered, "No... How?"

"Oh, Alikad. I know what it's like to live in eternal isolation. Why not have something that is practically immortal, just like yourself?" The shadow's voice was filled with a mix of longing and desperation. "This way, I will never be alone again. As for the half-breed, she is still mortal. She is capable of death. You, however, *are* death. You control everything that dies! You resemble him so much..." As Father raised his hands into the air, a chill ran down Alikad's spine, his mind racing with questions and uncertainties.

Him? Alikad thought, his thoughts a jumble of confusion.

"You could be the most powerful Miscreant on the isle, Alikad. Remember all those years ago, when you were all but a boy? You pledged yourself to me, remember? You never disobeyed me. You were loyal to me until you got old enough to ask questions." Father's words carried a weight of authority.

"Fortunately for me, this gem is intricately linked to your very will. Now you're going to be loyal to me for eternity."

With a swift motion, he raised the shard up to his shadowy lips, whispering incantations. He writhed in agony as the dark magic took hold, a battle raging within him as he struggled against Father's insidious influence.

With desperation etched on his face, Alikad fought against the invisible chains that bound him. As his mind clouded with confusion, Father kneeled beside him, a twisted smile playing on his lips.

"Why fight it, Alikad?" he taunted, his voice a mixture of cruelty and persuasion. "You're mine, and yet you resist. What do you cling to with such determination? There is nothing left to save, Alikad. Your companions have met their fates, and your resolve only weakens you further."

With each word, Father's influence seemed to tighten its grip, a web of manipulation encircling Alikad's wavering thoughts. "I am your sole ally, Alikad," he whispered. "All you require is me, and nothing more."

Alikad hesitated, his hand trembling as he tried to grasp the purple gem tightly held by Father. The weight of his decision bore down on him. Destroying the gem meant freedom, yet the thought left him paralyzed. As he struggled with his inner turmoil, his grip on his will weakened, slipping away like sand through his fingers.

Finally, unable to bear the weight of his choice any longer, Alikad collapsed to the ground, his body surrendering to exhaustion. The commanding presence looming over him demanded his obedience, and with great effort, he rose to his feet. In the background, Airella's soft groans filled the air, a reminder of the turmoil surrounding them.

The manipulated and demonic appearance within her had vanished alongside the gem's destruction and the physical exhaustion. She no longer bore the two spiraled horns or the silver hair. In her place stood the familiar blonde girl whom he'd grown to care for, stripped of the mysterious aura that once shrouded her. Her eyes were back to their multi-colored state, one green, and the other an icy blue. Alikad realized that the hellion within her was not a creation of the gem but an inherent part of her being, a revelation that dawned upon him with newfound clarity.

"Alikad?" Airella's shocked voice broke the silence, her gaze fixated on his presence.

"Sirius? Where is Sirius?" Airella was in a state of confusion and had no awareness of all that had just occurred. She was oblivious to the danger he had yet to bring. Zol's hand then grabbed her ankle, keeping her from getting any closer.

"Sirius is no more, girl. They merged. Now, Alikad. Kill her," Father ordered, raising the gem, which forced Alikad into action.

Without question, he picked his scythe up from the ground. He slowly turned to Airella as he popped his broken wing back into place. He took a few deliberate steps toward her, his eyes fixed on her, calculating his move. With a sudden burst of speed, he dashed towards her, the scythe cutting through the air as it sailed towards her. Airella's instincts kicked in, and she swiftly dove out of harm's way, narrowly avoiding the deadly weapon.

Before she could fully process the unfolding events, Airella found herself suddenly face-to-face with her attacker. The intense shade of purple cast an eerie glow in his eyes, hinting at the danger she was in. As he extended his hands menacingly towards her throat, a surge of inhuman strength surged within her. With a swift and forceful motion, she pushed him away, using the nearby tree for support as she regained her footing.

The entire encounter had taken its toll on her, leaving her feeling physically drained and weaker than she had ever been before. Coughing up blood into her trembling hand, Airella's gaze met Alikad's, who had stumbled but quickly recovered his composure. In a blur of movement, he closed the distance to retrieve his scythe, fixing her with a chilling glare.

As a tear trickled down Alikad's stern and stoic face, he uttered a single word.

"Run."

mixture of defiance and resignation welled up within Airella, her fists clenched tightly at her sides. Tears welled in her eyes as she raised her head defiantly, a newfound resolve taking root within her.

"I won't run anymore. I refuse to be a coward, always fleeing from the inevitable. No longer will I cower in fear." With a sudden surge of determination, she met Alikad's advancing form head-on, ready to face whatever awaited her.

Alikad jabbed his scythe at Airella's head repeatedly, but she agilely dodged left and right, like it was a choreographed dance of death.

"Father, why do you avoid facing me directly? You aspire to ascend to godhood, do you not?" Airella's voice echoed through the confrontation.

In response, Alikad swiftly turned his scythe horizontally, using its bar to press Airella against a nearby tree. She strained against the bar, the threat of choking looming just inches away.

This encounter felt markedly different from their initial meeting; Alikad had evidently grown immensely in power now that he and Sirius merged. A sinking feeling formed in her gut. Did that mean Sirius was gone forever? Do he and Alikad share those memories?

Heart pounding and breath ragged, Airella's voice trembled with both fear and unyielding love. "Sirius, I know you're in there somewhere," she cried out, her eyes searching Alikad's. "I love you, Sirius. I always have. Please, fight him. Fight Father from within. Remember who you are, remember us!"

Alikad's cold eyes flickered momentarily, a brief falter in his relentless assault. Airella's words seemed to reach some hidden part of him, some fragment of Sirius still alive within.

"You and I—we shared dreams, hopes, and feelings that even the darkest powers cannot destroy," Airella continued, her voice growing stronger with each word. "Come back to me, Sirius. We can still defy him together."

For a fleeting moment, Alikad hesitated, the grip of the scythe bar loosening ever so slightly. Airella seized the opportunity, pouring all her heartfelt emotions into her plea, hoping that her confession could reach the Sirius she knew and bring him back from the abyss.

Airella couldn't help but long for the demonic presence that had previously overtaken her, feeling its absence with a deep sense of loss. While her demonic form had been something she initially struggled to accept, it granted her a physical prowess that was incredibly helpful in battle. The power, the agility, the sheer might—it was all so much more than her human form could ever provide. Yet now, she was utterly exhausted and uncertain if she could even shift back into that form again without Father's intervention.

Airella did not know how to initiate the transformation on her own. The process remained mysterious, and without Father's guidance, Airella felt hopelessly adrift. She had tried to remember the sensations, the triggers, anything that could help her replicate the shift, but it seemed elusive. The gap between knowing and doing loomed large and insurmountable.

Stuck in her usual human form, Airella felt a profound weakness that gnawed at her confidence. The strength she had once wielded seemed like a distant memory, a dream she couldn't quite grasp. The roles had reversed, and now she faced the daunting task of overcoming Father without the demonic strength she relied on. Despite this, she had already strategized, formulating a plan to face Father. But the uncertainty of her ability to transform left a lingering doubt—could she truly succeed in her current state?

"You're nothing but a coward, Father, delegating your battles to others to avoid facing them yourself." Airella's words dripped with defiance as she strained against Alikad's hold.

In a moment of desperation, she swiftly ducked under the scythe, causing the tree supporting her weight to shatter in response to the force of his weapon.

Airella, her heart pounding, slowly pushed herself up from the forest floor, Dawnbreaker in hand. Her eyes fixated on the shadowy figure before her.

"Who are you, really?" she questioned. "You've yet to inflict any true physical harm upon any of us but Sirius. All you've done is resort to manipulation to evade direct confrontation. Are you lacking in strength, or is there more to your tactics than meets the eye?"

Just as she finished her words, a commanding female voice pierced through the tension.

"Shadow, return to me."

Out from the darkness of the surrounding trees stepped a figure cloaked in dark robes. Her complexion was as fair as porcelain, her locks a deep black cascading gracefully, and her eyes shimmered violet, holding an otherworldly allure. There was a distant, almost ethereal quality to her presence as she regarded Airella.

Airella's gaze narrowed at the newcomer, a scowl forming on her face as she anticipated the next move. With swift reflexes, she dodged Alikad's incoming attack, the rush of movement stirring the surrounding undergrowth.

The elegant woman's crimson lips curved into a serene smile, her shadow, whom they'd originally known as Father, coiling protectively around her arm.

"So, you've pieced it together," she remarked, a hint of amusement in her voice. "You are perceptive, indeed. You are the first to uncover my centuries-old secret." A soft chuckle escaped her as she maintained her composed facade, a mask of friendliness concealing deeper intentions.

Airella met the enchantress's gaze with a mixture of defiance and wariness. "What? Like it was hard?" she retorted boldly, her stance unwavering despite the tension crackling in the air.

The enigmatic woman's tone shifted, a subtle undercurrent of power lacing her words as she teased, "Shall I offer you a reward for your insight?" Her voice held an almost hypnotic quality.

"Who are you?" As Airella braced herself for the impending revelation, a sudden jolt of pain lanced through her. She cried out as Alikad's attack grazed her forearm, serving as a stark reminder of the perilous dance she was entangled in.

The woman's eyes sparkled with a mischievous glint at the sight of Airella's blood, a cruel smile tugging at the corners of her lips.

"My name is Conivx," she purred, her voice tinged with a hint of darkness, "a sorceress of no small talent. You were but a pawn in my shadow's game. He dances to my tune, a puppet to my will." With a flick of her wrist, she summoned her sword from its sheath, the dark blade gleaming ominously in the dim light. "Manipulation," she declared with a sly grin, "is an art I have mastered. Shadows, minds, the very fabric of reality—all playthings in my hands."

Airella winced, her grip tightening on her wounded arm as Alikad lunged forward, his attack relentless. Desperation fueled her resolve as she struggled to stem the crimson tide, her eyes locked on Conivx's malevolent form.

"Wait," Conivx murmured, her voice a velvet whisper that seemed to echo in the air, lifting the enchanted purple gem that rested in her hands.

Instantly, Alikad froze, his movements stilled as if by an unseen hand.

"Now, my dear," Conivx taunted, her laughter chilling, "you were spoiling for a fight, weren't you? Bravery and foolishness often walk hand in hand." With a mocking twirl of her jeweled sword, she circled Airella, her steps graceful and predatory.

Airella knew she was outmatched, and she could feel her strength ebbing with each passing moment. The toll of the battle weighed heavily on her shoulders, her human form ill-suited for the conflict that loomed before her. Yet, with a fierce determination that belied her weakened state, she raised Dawn-breaker, steeling herself for the inevitable clash.

"That's the spirit!" Conivx cheered as her shadow seeped from her arm, a dark, ethereal mist swirling around her. "No worries, I'll play fair. But first, I must thank you for bringing me these fresh human souls. I would've done it myself, but I am tied to this forsaken island. It's as if invisible chains bind me here, preventing me from venturing beyond its shores."

"And why's that?" Airella exhaled.

"My heart beats at the core of this island, darling. I am intricately linked to its very essence. All of those years ago..." Conivx's voice trailed off, a mix of nostalgia and mischief dancing in her eyes as she reminisced. She suddenly broke into a fit of laughter, the sound echoing through the eerie landscape. "It's quite a long story, filled with twists and turns that I'll have to regale you with another time."

"There will be no next time, at least not for you." Airella's eyes narrowed, a flicker of determination masking the fear that gnawed at her core. The two women circled each other, a silent tension hanging heavy in the air.

"I think you'll find it extremely difficult to end me, dear Airella. I've honed my swordsmanship over centuries, and my immortality grants me a resilience you can barely comprehend." Conivx's grin widened, a mixture of arrogance and amusement playing on her lips. "Your only glimmer of hope of defeating me would lie in turning my magic against me. But let's be honest, have you taken a good look at yourself? Your powers are but a flicker compared to mine. It's almost comical, really!"

Airella gritted her teeth, her heart pounding in her chest. She dashed at Conivx, Dawnbreaker raised high, ready to strike. However, in a sudden blur, she vanished from sight, leaving Airella bewildered. With a sense of unease creeping over her, Airella spun around frantically, only to find Conivx standing calmly behind her, her back turned. Conivx stood in a poised stance, as if she had just completed a forceful attack, lowering her sword with a confident air. Airella's eyes widened in shock as she noticed the lower half of her golden hair cascading to the ground, cleanly severed just above her shoulders.

"Look at all that beautiful golden hair. Such a waste," Conivx remarked, facing Airella with a taunting smile.

"When did you—"

"Don't underestimate me," Conivx retorted with a smirk, swiftly closing in on Airella once more, vanishing at an astonishing speed, and ending up behind Airella in the exact position as before. Airella found herself frozen in place, unable to react in time.

This time, Airella's armor was effortlessly sliced from her body, collapsing with a heavy thud on the ground. All that remained on the blonde warrior was fabric and chain mail.

"Your sword..." Airella voiced her shock.

"Oh, this old thing? It has a name. Umbra. I forged it myself many years ago. Quite handy, isn't it?" Conivx replied casually, a cunning smile playing on her lips. "Alright, I've had my fill of amusement. It's time to end this." With a deft twirl of her sword, she lunged at Airella once more.

Like before, Airella had no time to react.

With a swift, calculated movement, the elegant woman thrust her dark sword through Airella's stomach, her eyes gleaming with a sinister intent. The blade twisted cruelly, igniting a searing pain that tore through Airella's body, setting every nerve ablaze with agony.

She crumpled to the ground, clutching her gaping wound, her fingers slipping on the slick, warm blood that poured from her stomach. The blonde coughed violently, her breath catching as the sight of crimson blood splattered around her.

"Welcome yourself to the underworld," Conivx's voice dripped with a venomous mix of mockery and twisted admiration. "Be proud that you solved my mystery and live on in the afterlife." Her laughter echoed hauntingly through the air, a chilling sound that seemed to mock Airella's suffering. Conivx turned on her heel, her graceful steps carrying her towards Alikad, leaving Airella writhing in unspeakable pain behind her.

Airella fought desperately against the encroaching darkness, her vision blurring as she struggled to stay conscious. She knew that giving in to the seductive pull of sleep would mean risking never waking again in this twisted reality. An urgent sense of survival gripped her, urging her to keep her eyes open no matter how heavy they felt, to keep fighting against the pain that threatened to consume her.

Meanwhile, Conivx stood next to Alikad, her movements eerily tender as she reached out to caress his face with enticing hands.

"Oh, my darling," her voice was soft, laced with possessiveness, "how I've longed for this moment." She planted a gentle kiss on his forehead, her touch betraying a history filled with dark complexities and unfulfilled desires. "To hold you like this is what I've been waiting for. I've watched you transform into a full-fledged reaper... You're all mine, and now you're finally whole. My dearest, you're only mine." She colored her words with a twisted devotion, promising an unbreakable bond and the eternity they would share. "Together, we shall be unstoppable. We will conquer death itself—"

Her sentence came to an abrupt halt as a sudden, excruciating pain tore through her being. A blade had found its mark in the center of her body, slicing through flesh and bone with merciless precision. Conivx's eyes widened in shock and agony, her breath hitching as she looked down at the blood-soaked blade protruding from her chest.

And there, standing amidst the chaos, was Alikad. His face was a mask of grim determination, his eyes cold and unyielding. Without a moment of hesitation, he yanked his scythe from her body in a fluid motion, spraying blood in a grotesque arc. The silent declaration of defiance and resolute determination was clear in his every movement.

"How?" She fell backward onto the damp ground, crimson blood seeping from her wound. "The gem... instead of attempting to defend yourself, you snatched it from me. You're not as feeble as I thought. You have... turned my manipulation magic against me..."

As she drew her last ragged breaths, the life force drained from her body, causing her eyes to glaze over with an eerie stillness. With a final, agonized exhale, she succumbed to the inevitable.

At that moment, the island itself seemed to mourn her passing. A chilling decay spread rapidly, like an unstoppable plague, through the once vibrant plants and trees surrounding the group. Leaves shriveled and fell like autumn's last breath, flowers wilted, their colors draining away to nothingness, and the lush greenery turned brittle and lifeless. The air grew heavy with the scent of death and decay, as if the very heart of the island had ceased to beat. It was a tragic, dramatic end, marked by the island's swift transformation into a barren wasteland.

Airella's fingers clutched tightly to the shimmering purple gem, its glow dimming as she continued to bleed out. Despite witnessing the island's descent into lifelessness, she found solace in the belief that everyone else was unharmed.

With trembling hands, she whispered a final plea to the pendant, "Alikad, come back to me." Each word pained her to utter. Airella lay there motionless, gazing up at the dawning sky, resigned to her fate.

$\mathcal{A}$likad snapped back to reality, his eyes locking onto the mysterious, darkly clad woman before him. Her dark hair cascaded around her pale, flawless skin like a cloak of shadows. Bewilderment clouded his features as he struggled to place her amidst the chaos. Taking in the decaying forest, he sprang to his feet effortlessly, a newfound clarity washing over him. Arii and Jonathan's safety weighed heavily, reminding himself that he sent them to Limbo before his mind went dark.

It took Alikad a moment to fully view his surroundings. Fear filled his mind as he took in the scene. His vision pulsed and blurred as he rubbed his head, seeking comfort from a major headache that seemed to intensify with each passing second.

That moment of disorientation passed swiftly as his gaze fell upon the blonde-haired girl gasping for air on the ground before him. The metallic tang of blood hung heavy in the air, saturating the area around her as she tightly clutched the wound on her stomach, her fingers slick with crimson.

"No!" Alikad's voice cracked with urgency as he scrambled to her side, his heart pounding in his chest. "No, no, no, no,"

With trembling hands, he reached for one of hers, his touch gentle yet firm as he applied pressure to the grievous wound. Sitting on the ground beside her, he cradled her in his arms.

With quick thinking born of desperation, Alikad summoned a reserve of strength and used a weak swing of his scythe to tear open the fabric of reality, creating a shimmering portal to the realm of Limbo. Within moments, Arii emerged from the otherworldly gateway, his eyes wide with shock and concern, followed closely by Jonathan. They had witnessed the unfolding tragedy from the vantage point of Limbo's dimension.

Sadness weighed heavily upon them all as Alikad wept, his tears mingling with the bloodstains on her torn clothing. Placing his head against hers, he whispered words of reassurance, his voice choked with emotion. As she weakly opened her eyes and gazed up at him, a glimmer of recognition and gratitude shone in her gaze.

"Sirius… are you in there…?" Blood trickled from a corner of Airella's mouth.

"Shhh! Don't speak. I remember everything, Airella. Sirius and I are one now. Just wait, I—I can fix this," Alikad's eyes widened as her breathing slowed. Yet, in truth, he couldn't fix this. He knew he couldn't. The wound was too deep, and he knew nothing of healing, only death. The closest thing he could do to help Airella was to remove her soul like he did Jonathan and find her a new body, but he couldn't bring himself to do it. He had nowhere to keep her soul, and he loved her far too much to send her to the dark depths of Limbo, as he knew that's where her Miscreant soul would linger for eternity, never truly succumbing to death.

Alikad's heart ached at the thought of losing Airella, a pain so deep it felt like a physical weight on his chest. He couldn't fathom a world without her by his side, her presence filling every corner of his being with warmth and light. The love he held for her was unlike anything he had ever known, a love that anchored him in a sea of uncertainty. He, or more like Sirius, never took the chance to tell her these things, and now she'll die without ever knowing.

"I… I don't know what to do." Alikad growled, clenching her hand. His voice trembled with the raw agony of impending loss. To lose her would be to lose a part of himself, a part he never knew he had until she entered his life. Every fiber of his being rebelled against the idea of her absence, the mere thought of it creating a chasm of emptiness within him.

The memories they shared played out like a vivid tapestry in his mind, each moment a precious gem in the treasure trove of their bond. The fear of losing her consumed him, a relentless storm raging in his soul. In that moment, Alikad faced a choice no one should have to make—to save the one he loved at the cost of the unknown or to let her slip away into the shadows.

Alikad clung to her hand as if holding on for dear life, his grip tight with desperation and love intertwined. The minutes felt like hours, the seconds like an eternity. Her breaths came shallower, each one a cruel reminder of her dwindling time. He couldn't imagine a tomorrow without her laughter, without her presence. The thought of waking up to a world without her was a nightmare from which he couldn't wake.

"Airella, please stay with me," he whispered, his voice breaking. Tears streamed down his face, mingling with the blood and dirt on his cheeks. He wished he could stop time, capture every fleeting second they had left, but reality was a cruel mistress, pulling her further away with each passing breath.

"I can't do this without you," he choked out, his heart breaking with every word. The world around them seemed to fade, leaving only the two of them in a cocoon of shared pain and love. Her eyes met his, filled with a mixture of pain, love, and acceptance. At that moment, they both knew the inevitable truth. Alikad leaned closer, pressing his forehead against hers, their breaths mingling as one.

As Airella's eyes closed, Alikad felt a part of himself shattering. The silence that followed was deafening, filled with the echoes of their shared past and the void of a future that would never come. His soul cried out, a silent scream that resonated through the very fabric of his being.

Alikad gazed down at her, observing the tight grip she had on something in her hand. Upon closer inspection, he recognized it as his precious gem. With a sense of dismay, he watched as her fingers gradually slackened their hold, allowing the gem to slip from her grasp and clatter onto the icy ground below. Turning his attention to the dark-haired woman lying motionless a few meters away, Alikad felt a surge of conflicting emotions. Clutching his gem tightly, he realized that if he wished for Airella to live, he must depart to unravel the enigma of the woman before him.

Alikad, consumed by the weight of guilt and grief, pondered striking a desperate deal with Conivx, who seemed to possess an otherworldly power. The idea of bargaining for a chance to resurrect Airella, his beloved companion lost to the cruel hands of death, weighed heavily on his heart. The realm beyond Limbo, a place where the veil between the living and the dead grew thin, tantalized his thoughts. While the afterlife beyond Limbo remained a distant and elusive concept, out of reach even for the most skilled reapers, Alikad found a flicker of hope in the possibility that Conivx, with her enigmatic abilities, could somehow breach that ethereal barrier.

Conivx, like Alikad, was a Miscreant and wielded immense power. As a dark enchantress, she fed off the power of others, growing stronger with each life force she absorbed. Perhaps, if Alikad could offer her his own power to feed off of, she could be brought back to life. And in return for this life-giving force,

Conivx might do him the favor of bringing Airella back to life as well. The very notion of such a feat seemed preposterous at first glance, especially considering that it was Airella herself who had made the ultimate sacrifice to break him free from Conivx's grasp.

Now, burdened by the haunting memories of her sacrifice and the void left in her absence, Alikad knew he must do this one thing, even if it meant risking everything to bring her back from the abyss of death. Conivx's death had already taken its toll on the island, causing it to wither and decay. The once lush and vibrant landscape was now a shadow of its former self, struggling to sustain life without the enchantress's powerful presence. The life of the island and Conivx had an intrinsic connection, with her essence intertwined with every living thing.

As a great sorceress tied to so much life, Conivx had the potential to bring back Airella. But if she refused his request, Alikad was prepared to offer anything, even pledging to stay by her side for eternity. He would do whatever it took to get Airella back, no matter the cost. The thought of Airella's return, of seeing her smile and hearing her laughter once more, was the only thing that kept him going. Alikad was ready to face any challenge if it meant bringing his beloved Airella back to life.

45

"You're going to hate me again..." Alikad whispered into Airella's ear, gently stroking her cold cheek as Jonathan stared at him with a mix of concern and disbelief, his brow furrowed in worry. "Really, really hate me..."

"What? What are you going to do?" Jonathan's voice rose with desperation.

Arii's sobs of sadness for his sister grew louder, his hands trembling as he watched Alikad's intense gaze fixed on Conivx's lifeless form.

"Hopefully with me at her side, she could bring Airella back and leave you be." Alikad's words hung in the air, filled with both determination and sorrow as he continued to stare at Conivx, a sense of regret flickering in his eyes. "I can't save Airella. She's already long gone. She's... dead. However, Conivx feeds off of power. If she can feed off of mine, maybe I can convince her to bring Airella back to life." Alikad's voice cracked with emotion as he held her limp body tighter, the weight of his helplessness bearing down on him. "I can't save her, but maybe Conivx can."

"You can't be serious! You want to bring Conivx back from death to save Airella? That's beyond reckless." Tears welled up in Jonathan's eyes, and he moved closer to Alikad, empathy and concern etched on his face.

Alikad's frustration boiled over, his fist slamming into the icy ground, cracks spreading out as a physical manifestation of his inner turmoil.

"It's the only way!" Alikad exclaimed passionately. Conivx had achieved her goal—the humans now resided on the island. With a pointed look at Jonathan, Alikad continued, "She won't bother you anymore if you play it smart. She has everything she desires, except for one crucial thing. Me." His words were laced with determination as he recounted the island's history. "Mortals vanished here long ago as we failed to safeguard them from dwindling too quickly. But now, there's a thriving community. Should Conivx seek me, she shall have me. Besides, just look around you. When Conivx died, so did the isle. It's withered away. How will your people survive here? I have to bring her back. I have to try." With a last glance at Airella's resting place, Alikad strode purposefully towards Conivx's still form.

He kneeled beside her, placing his hands on her chest. A dark mist enveloped her, a desperate attempt at rejuvenation. Though lacking healing abilities, Alikad knew the consequences of her draining presence. A Miscreant of her caliber could drain others to heal themselves when in dire need. He felt himself grow weaker as his essence was stolen from him. The wound inflicted by Airella sealed itself as the mist dissipated from Conivx's body, her breath deepening.

Alikad, taking charge, pulled her to her feet, the greenery around them blooming once more as he held her arm firmly. The island had come back to life alongside Conivx.

A slight gasp resonated from her mouth as she gave Alikad a cocky glare. "You should have left me, my dear," she threatened.

Alikad raised the blade of his scythe to her throat.

"Don't test me, Conivx. Bring her back," Alikad demanded, his gaze unwavering as he locked eyes with her violet ones. "Do it, or I swear on my life I will brutally end you just to bring you back again, over and over."

She chuckled softly, a mischievous glint in her eye while nonchalantly brushing the dirt from her shoulder. Her gaze shifted from Airella's lifeless form to Alikad, a sly smile playing on her lips.

"What is in it for me? If I bring this troublesome girl back from the dead, what shall I have in return?" With a teasing gesture, she raised her hand as if to caress Alikad's face, but he instinctively pulled away.

"I brought you back to life," Alikad stated clearly, his voice tinged with frustration.

"I want more. I want you." Conivx gazed into his golden eyes, her tone dripping with malevolence.

"Why? Father was always doing your dirty work, I see that now, but why keep me locked up for centuries?" Alikad demanded, his confusion morphing into anger.

"I love you, Alikad. You were always meant to be mine." Conivx spoke honeyed words, yet they carried a sinister undertone.

"Then why never show your face?" Alikad asked, bewilderment clear in his voice.

"I could never get you under control. You were uncontrollable, and almost still are. But now that I have all these human souls, Father grew strong enough to control you and create your gem." Conivx's confession was as chilling as it was revealing.

With many questions still lingering, Alikad knew he was running out of time. He also knew the rumors about Conivx's power—how her life magic was intertwined with the life of the island. Airella's only chance lay in Conivx's twisted hands.

"Okay. I'll go with you." Alikad's voice carried a hint of regret, belying the complexity of his emotions. She met his gaze with an evil grin, relishing in the power dynamics at play. "However, there will be ground rules." With a decisive tone, Alikad pushed her away, his demeanor firm. "First, no harm comes to the humans, at least not until this island is well populated. Second, if anything ever happens to Airella, Jonathan, or Arii, death will come to you. You are to never harm them. Ever. Do you understand?"

Conivx silently nodded in acknowledgment of the pact being formed, but her eyes sparkled with a sinister glee. She then made her way over to Airella. Softly, she chanted unfamiliar words as she delicately placed her hands on Airella's chest, as if weaving a delicate thread to reconnect her soul with her body. A wave of relief washed over Alikad as he witnessed Airella's chest rise with a breath once more.

Yet, the tension between Conivx and Alikad was palpable. He could sense the malevolence behind her every move, the beauty she wielded like a weapon. Alikad's eyes never left her, his heart pounding with the realization that he had made a deal with someone who could turn on him at any moment. Conivx's power was undeniable, but so was the danger she posed. Alikad's mind raced with the possibilities, each one darker than the last, as the fragile pact they had formed hung in the balance.

In a rush of emotions, Alikad dashed to Airella's side, his heart pounding with a mix of overwhelming gratitude and deep concern. With a swift and decisive movement, he pulled Conivx away from Airella and then kneeled down to embrace her limp body in a tight hug. Relief washed over him as he felt the soft rise and fall of her chest.

"You're okay, Airella. You're okay," Alikad whispered, his

voice trembling with emotion. He pulled her closer, kissed her forehead tenderly, and rocked her gently in his arms. Tears of joy streamed down his face as he realized she was unconscious but breathing. She was alive, and that was all that mattered.

In that moment, a realization struck Alikad like a bolt of lightning—he should have destroyed the gem that Conivx tightly clutched in her hand when he had the chance. But right now, all his focus was on Airella. The depth of his feelings for her became undeniably clear; he loved Airella and had never found the courage to tell her.

As Alikad held Airella, a heavy silence enveloped him. His eyes met Conivx's gaze. The speed at which Conivx had acted was remarkable, as if she possessed an otherworldly grace. But beneath that grace, he saw something else—jealousy.

Conivx's voice broke the silence, dripping with both power and envy. "That, or I can have you and do as I please with them. You'll be at my side forever and nothing can stop us. Why care for a mortal?" She cradled the gem close to her chest, her eyes darkening with jealousy as she watched Alikad's tender reaction to Airella.

Alikad's resolve hardened. He gently stroked Airella's short hair, his heart swelling with love and a newfound determination. It was all thanks to Sirius. He felt everything he did. He would protect her at any cost, and when she woke, he would finally tell her how much she meant to him. However, now that he's made his promise to Conivx, that day may never come. For now, he held her close, knowing that in his arms, she was safe.

Alikad's voice hardened with resolve, his loyalty shining through his words. "My friends are honest and kind. Airella is honest and kind. I'm doing this for their sake, but if that's what you're planning, I'll just have to kill you." Alikad's growl echoed with determination, momentarily forgetting the threat of

Conivx possessing his gem as he took a step closer to confront her.

"Now, now, who's in charge here?" Conivx waved the gem in front of Alikad's face.

With an unexpected jolt, Jonathan jumped at her, his hand outstretched to reach for the gem before Alikad lost his will once again. Yet, with a swift and eerie grace, Conivx's shadow—once known as Father to Alikad—materialized and seized Jonathan by the throat, hoisting him high in the air as if he weighed nothing more than a feather. Panic flashed in Alikad's eyes, realizing the gravity of his mistake the moment Conivx regained her stance.

"The last time you walked free without the constraints of Limbo, you did as I commanded. Now you will stay that way for as long as I please," Conivx's voice dripped with authority and malice, each word laced with power.

Alikad might have made a grave mistake by resurrecting her. Now, the consequences loomed over him like a dark cloud. Airella remained in a slumber, her presence a haunting reminder of the tangled web of fate woven around them. He gently rested Airella's head on the ground and stood.

Alikad, now caught in the clutches of Conivx's manipulative schemes, was to be easily molded to fit her whims and desires. His loyalty, a double-edged sword, bound him to her will without question. He was a pawn in a game of power and control.

"Just abide by the rules I've set, and then I'm all yours. You don't have any interest in them. You have what you want. Leave the mortals be," Alikad's voice quivered slightly as he tentatively stepped forward, his gaze shifting between Conivx and the group of allies—Jonathan, Arii, Zol, and the unconscious Airella —a silent plea for mercy hidden beneath his facade of obedience.

"Very well, my dear. Your deal shall and will be kept, but just so you won't get any nasty ideas about betraying me again, I will keep you under my control until you can prove yourself to me," she said, her words echoing through the icy forest.

Alikad, feeling a pang of shame, lowered his head in silent agreement, his eyes reflecting a mix of emotions.

"Sirius, I know you're in there somewhere. Don't do this," Jonathan cried out in despair.

Conivx's shadow engulfed him, forcing him to the ground with a swift and powerful motion.

Conivx, with an air of anticipation, whispered into the mystical purple gem, "Let's be off."

Alikad's gaze shifted back to its emotionless purple hue as he retrieved his scythe. Jonathan tried to intervene, but his efforts were futile against Alikad's strength and resolve.

"Oh, how I've longed for this moment," Conivx murmured softly. "We will live forever together, my dearest Alikad." With a tender touch, she kissed Alikad's forehead, her lips then seeking his, drawing him into an unexpected embrace. As their lips met, an unspoken connection seemed to bind them closer. Alikad's dark eyes glistened with an otherworldly violet intensity.

Turning to face Jonathan once more, Conivx flashed a seemingly sadistic smile, a hint of triumph in her gaze. Alikad, with a swift and resolute motion, raised his scythe, slicing through the air. The portal to Limbo materialized, setting the stage for what was to come.

"Yes, we shall," Alikad said blankly, his voice echoing in the otherworldly space. His emotions were tumultuous, a tempest raging within him as conflicting desires warred for dominance.

Despite his inner turmoil, his outward demeanor remained stoic, a mask of obedience concealing his emotions within. He glanced back once more at the unconscious blonde girl, a pang of regret tugging at his heart for the compassion he once felt towards her. Her slumbering form appeared serene, unaware of the impending events that would shape their destinies.

Suddenly, Airella stirred, her eyelids fluttering open. She looked dazed and confused, her eyes struggling to focus on her surroundings. When she finally locked eyes with Alikad, a spark of recognition flickered within her.

"Alikad? What's going on?" she asked, her voice trembling. Although her head was throbbing, her memories rushed back. Alikad, Conivx, the battle, everything. She observed Conivx leading him into a portal. "Please, don't leave me. Stay."

Her words pierced through Alikad's resolve, creating a crack in the walls he had built around his emotions. He hesitated, his heart heavy with the weight of his duty and the burgeoning feelings he couldn't entirely suppress. For a brief, fleeting moment, he allowed himself to absorb the raw vulnerability in Airella's multicolored eyes, a silent plea that stirred something deep within him.

It was just before Conivx whispered into the gem again that Alikad mustered one last smile, a bittersweet expression laden with unspoken regrets and resigned acceptance.

"I'm sorry, Airella," he murmured softly.

With a heavy heart and a sense of duty weighing upon him, Alikad prepared himself to follow Conivx's command. Airella's outstretched hand reached for him in a desperate attempt to hold on to the connection they shared.

As the final echoes of his last words lingered in the air, Alikad stepped through the portal's shimmering threshold, leaving Airella's heartbroken gaze lingering where he once stood. He disappeared into the swirling vortex of light and shadow, embarking on a journey from which there might be no return.

EPILOGUE

The isle had not changed in fifty years. Its jagged cliffs stood tall, unyielding, while the wind that swept across the land whispered the same songs it had since the beginning of time.

Much like the isle, Airella had remained unchanged, suspended in a cruel version of eternity. Her ageless face reflected none of the years that had burdened everyone else. She still looked the same as she had the day Alikad disappeared—frozen in time. She stood on the precipice of a towering cliff, her gaze locked on the churning waters below, the salty air tangling in her hair as it always did.

But while her physical features showed no signs of the years that had passed, Airella's heart bore the weight of every second.

It had been fifty years since Alikad had stepped through the portal. Fifty years since he had struck the deal with Conivx, the dark enchantress who had bound him to her will. Fifty years since Airella had been ripped from death's grasp and thrust back into life—forever altered.

Airella's chest tightened as she stood in the same place she had countless times before. Here, where the cliffs met the sea, she had always felt closer to Alikad. Closer to understanding why he had made the choice that had taken him from her.

But there were no answers. There never had been.

Behind her, footsteps crunched on the rocky path. She didn't need to turn around to know it was Arii. Her younger brother had grown old, his once blonde hair now silver, his strong figure now hunched slightly with the weight of years. And yet, despite his age, there was still strength in his steps. Ryder, Arii's son, walked beside him. He was tall and strong like his father once was, his face filled with the youth that matched Airella's.

Ryder was a reminder of the passage of time she had stopped feeling, of what she had lost. His bright green eyes, so much like his father's, always seemed to watch her with an odd mixture of curiosity and something deeper—something Airella could not place.

"Another year," Arii said softly as he approached, his breath visible in the cool evening air.

Another year without Alikad.

Airella nodded but didn't speak. What was there to say? The anniversary of his disappearance was always the hardest. Fifty years without a word, without any sign of him. She had no answers, only the questions that plagued her mind each time this day arrived.

Ryder came to stand beside her, his broad shoulders towering over hers. He, like the rest of the village, had grown up knowing the story of Alikad—the reaper who had vanished after the final battle in Zol's icy domain. Ryder had heard the stories his whole life, of Airella and Alikad, the demon within her, and the sacrifice Alikad had made to bring her back.

"You should come to the village tonight," Ryder said, his voice gentler than his father's. "There's a gathering. For you."

Airella shook her head. "I don't want to be the reason for another reminder of what was lost."

"It's not about that," Arii said, stepping forward, placing a weathered hand on her arm. "It's about remembering what we've survived."

Airella's gaze dropped, the weight of his words sinking into her. She had survived, yes—but at what cost? The demon inside her had been awakened, whispering in her mind ever since that day. It begged to be released, and while she had never spoken of it to anyone, the voice had grown stronger over the years.

But the people here didn't know the burden she carried. They saw her as their protector, the ageless warrior who had fought to keep the village safe from the Miscreants that roamed the island.

"I'm not sure I can," Airella murmured. "Not today."

Ryder exchanged a look with Arii before stepping closer. "It's been fifty years, Airella. Alikad... if he were coming back, wouldn't he have done so by now?"

Airella's jaw tightened at Ryder's words, the unspoken truth cutting deep. She had spent every year hoping—waiting—for any sign of him. But there had been nothing. Only the silence and the empty space where Alikad should have been.

"Do you think I don't know that?" she replied, her voice sharper than she intended. "Do you think I haven't spent the last fifty years wondering where he is? Or if he's even alive?"

Arii stepped forward, his eyes searching Airella's face for a moment before he spoke. "I know you have. But you're not alone in this. We all miss him. We all lost something that day."

Ryder's face softened, his eyes filled with understanding. "It's alright to move forward, Airella. You don't have to carry this on your own."

Airella turned away from them both, her heart heavy with the weight of her guilt. How could she move forward when so much of her past still haunted her? She was trapped in the present, ageless and unchanged, while everyone else had moved on, aged, lived.

"Maybe I don't want to move forward," she whispered.

The wind howled around them, filling the silence that followed her words. Arii looked as if he wanted to say something, but Ryder shook his head slightly, signaling him to give Airella space.

"We'll be in the village if you change your mind," Ryder said quietly, stepping back. "We won't push you, but you don't have to face this alone."

Airella didn't respond as they turned and made their way back down the path. She stood alone once more, the sound of the waves crashing below echoing in her ears.

Fifty years. Fifty years of silence. She had told herself she was waiting for him, but perhaps Ryder was right. Perhaps it was time to accept the truth—Alikad was gone, and he wasn't coming back.

But as she stood there, staring at the horizon, the faintest whisper brushed against her mind, the voice of the demon inside her stirring once more.

He's not gone, it hissed. *Let me out, Airella. He's waiting. And so are you.*

Airella's hands clenched at her sides, the battle within her far from over. Perhaps the others had moved on. Perhaps the world around her had changed. But deep down, she knew that something—whether Alikad or the darkness he had disappeared into—was still out there.

And one day, she would find it.

Centuries before Airella's story began, the isle was ruled by shadow and betrayal. Discover the tragic love story of Emmaline and Zol—a tale of forbidden love, deadly secrets, and the dark magic that shaped the isle's fate.

Keep reading for an exclusive preview of

ISLE OF LIES AND LEGENDS

$$1$$

ISLE OF LIES AND LEGENDS

The sea was a monster with no mercy.

It roared and foamed, an endless maw of churning black water, swallowing everything in its path. The ship was gone—splintered, devoured. The wreckage bobbed like shattered bones upon the waves, the storm still raging overhead.

Conivx's fingers ached as she clung to a jagged piece of debris, her knuckles bloodless, her body screaming with exhaustion. The salt stung her raw skin, filled her nose, her mouth, as the ocean dragged her down, again and again, like a beast playing with its prey.

A strangled cry barely reached her ears over the howling winds.

"Vespera!"

She twisted, heart hammering. Through the slashing rain, her sister's form flickered in and out of sight, tossed like a broken doll amidst the waves. Her amber eyes, wide with terror, locked onto Conivx's.

"I can't—" Vespera gasped, her fingers clawing at the water, reaching.

Another wave rose like a towering wall, crashing between them, stealing her away.

No.

With a guttural scream, Conivx lunged forward, slicing through the freezing water, her muscles burning, lungs seizing. She kicked, pulled, fought. The sea was an unrelenting force, dragging her back, pressing against her like a living, vengeful thing.

But she wouldn't lose Vespera.

Her fingers brushed wet skin, then bone-thin wrists. She grabbed hold, her grip iron, just as the next wave crashed over them.

The world became a violent nothingness—foam and darkness, salt and pain.

Down. Down.

Pressure crushed her ribs. Her lungs screamed for air. Vespera's wrist began to slip.

Not this time.

With every ounce of strength she had left, Conivx kicked upward, dragging them both toward the faint, fractured light above. The ocean fought her, pulling them back, unwilling to give up its prey. But she was done losing.

Just when her vision blurred to black, the sea spat them out.

The impact was a shock—jagged rocks, wet sand, the raw burn of air in her lungs. Conivx barely registered the sting of scraping flesh before she collapsed onto her hands and knees, coughing up seawater, sucking in oxygen like it was the first breath she'd ever taken.

For a moment, there was only the ragged sound of her breathing, the distant roar of the tide.

Then she remembered.

"Vespera."

Her voice was hoarse, barely a whisper, but she forced herself to move, to crawl toward the unmoving form beside her.

Vespera lay sprawled on the wet shore, her golden-brown hair tangled with sand, her skin deathly pale.

No. No, no, no—

Conivx grabbed her by the shoulders, shaking her roughly. "Vespera!"

A heartbeat of silence. Then—a violent cough, a sharp gasp.

Vespera turned onto her side, hacking up seawater, her body shuddering. Conivx slumped back, breath hitching between exhaustion and relief.

"Conivx?" Vespera rasped, blinking up at her.

A lump formed in Conivx's throat, but she swallowed it down. "Who else would I be?"

Vespera attempted a weak smile, though it faltered as she took in their surroundings. "Where... where are we?"

Conivx followed her gaze, unease curling like a snake in her stomach.

The coastline stretched in either direction, jagged and uninviting. The sand was dark, almost gray, littered with driftwood and broken shells. Beyond the beach, the land rose sharply into cliffs, shrouded in thick, rolling mist. The air carried a biting chill, though the season should have been warm.

Something about this place felt... wrong.

Not just unfamiliar. Not just dangerous.

Wrong.

Conivx pushed herself up, muscles trembling from exhaustion. "I don't know," she admitted.

Vespera, still weak, reached for her hand, seeking reassurance. "At least we're alive," she murmured. "We'll figure this out together, won't we?"

Conivx nodded, but a hollow feeling gnawed at her.

Together.

Vespera had always been the beloved one. The one people trusted, admired. Even now, half-drowned and trembling, she looked untouchable—like something out of a legend, a tragic heroine who would emerge from this stronger than before.

And Conivx?

Conivx was the reason they had been exiled from their kingdom.

Her magic. Her ambition.

But there was power here. She could feel it, pulsing beneath her feet, coiling in the mist like a living thing.

A rustling in the undergrowth made Conivx stiffen. Her pulse quickened as shadowy figures emerged from the mist, their weathered faces flickering between caution and curiosity.

"By the gods," a gruff voice murmured. "Survivors."

The word felt like an accusation rather than relief. Conivx's dull eyes narrowed, assessing the newcomers with quiet suspicion. Beside her, Vespera, ever the peacemaker, offered a trembling smile, her damp curls clinging to her face.

"Please," Vespera said, her voice hoarse from salt and exhaustion. "We've been shipwrecked. Can you help us?"

An older woman stepped forward, her silver-streaked hair wild from the wind, her gnarled hands outstretched in an almost maternal gesture. "Of course, dears. You poor things look half-drowned. Come, let's get you to the village."

Conivx fought the instinct to recoil as rough hands reached to steady her. There was something wrong here—something in the very air, a quiet hum beneath her feet, a presence thick as the mist curling between the trees. A weight pressed down on her chest, not unlike the moment before a storm broke.

"Where are we?" she asked, her voice measured.

The villagers exchanged uneasy glances. Finally, the old

woman answered, her voice thick with something unspoken. "This is the isle."

Conivx arched a brow. "The isle?"

"That's all it's ever been called," a younger man added, his hollow eyes unreadable. "It doesn't need another name. Few who come here ever leave."

Vespera hesitated, glancing at Conivx. They had no choice but to follow.

The path twisted through an ancient forest, the riot of the shore giving way to an unnatural silence. Conivx exhaled slowly, steadying herself. She had lost everything—her home, her status, her place in Aurian. But maybe, just maybe, she could rebuild something here.

Ahead, nestled in the valley, the village emerged from the gloom. Ramshackle cottages leaned against one another, their thatched roofs sagging under years of disrepair. Dim lanterns cast long, twitching shadows across the cobbled paths.

The old woman turned back to them, a tight smile stretching her lined face. "Welcome to your new home."

Home. The word rang hollow in Conivx's mind.

But this place was something else entirely. Something waiting.

Power lurked beneath the surface of this land.

And this time, no one—not Vespera, not the gods, not fate itself—would stand in her way.

As they stepped into the village center, the mist curled around their ankles, damp and clinging. The air felt heavy, thick with something unspoken. The villagers stood in wary clusters, their faces shadowed by flickering lanterns, their gazes a mixture of curiosity and unease.

Vespera, ever radiant despite their ordeal, stepped forward with a warm smile. Even with her damp curls clinging to her face, she looked composed, grateful.

"Thank you all for your kindness," she said, her voice smooth and soothing. "We're so grateful for your help."

The villagers' rigid stances eased. A weathered fisherman, his face lined with years of hardship, stepped forward hesitantly.

"Aye, lass. It's not often we see new faces 'round here," he said, though his gaze flickered past her to Conivx—cautious, uncertain. "Especially ones that survive the journey."

Conivx said nothing, her dark eyes scanning the crowd, noting every whisper and hesitant glance. She stood apart, her pale skin ghostly in the dim lantern glow.

"Tell me," she finally spoke, her voice measured, almost too calm. "What exactly lurks beyond your village borders?"

A heavy silence fell over them. The villagers exchanged uneasy looks, but before anyone could answer, Vespera laughed lightly, diffusing the tension with practiced ease.

"My sister, always the curious one," she said, gently touching Conivx's arm as if to pull her back from the edge. "Perhaps those tales are best saved for when we're rested, hmm?"

Conivx stiffened at the touch. Always the peacemaker. Always stealing the moment. Even here, even now, she was the one they trusted.

As Vespera continued talking, drawing them in as she always did, Conivx remained silent, watching. The air here was thick with something old, something powerful. She could feel it humming beneath her feet, coiling in the mist.

Power.

She would find it.

A hunched old woman stepped forward, her clouded eyes unreadable. "We've a small cottage on the outskirts," she rasped, pointing toward a narrow, winding path that disappeared into the mist. "It's not much, but it'll keep you dry."

Vespera's face brightened. "Oh, that's so kind of you! We couldn't possibly—"

"We accept," Conivx cut in sharply, her gaze locking onto the elder's. A slow, knowing smile played at her lips. "Your generosity won't be forgotten."

The old woman gave a slow nod.

As they walked the misty path, the village faded behind them, swallowed by the thick fog. The silence between them stretched.

Vespera's easy acceptance of charity grated on Conivx. She acted as if kindness alone could mend their broken fate, as if they hadn't lost everything.

The cottage loomed ahead—a squat, weathered structure of stone and thatch. Inside, it was sparse but dry. A small hearth, a rough-hewn bench, a single bed.

Vespera let out a soft sigh of relief, brushing damp strands from her face. "It's not so bad, is it? We can make this work."

Conivx prowled the room, running her fingers along the uneven walls. "Make what work?" she asked, her voice edged with bitterness. "Our exile? Our fall from grace?"

Vespera flinched but didn't back down. "Con, please," she said. "We're alive. We're together. That's what matters."

Conivx gave a cold, humorless laugh. "Is it?" She turned, meeting her sister's eyes. "And how long before your new adoring public comes knocking, desperate for more of your boundless optimism?"

Vespera's face fell, hurt flashing in her amber eyes. "Why do you always do this?" Her voice wavered. "Why can't you just—"

"Just what?" Conivx snapped, stepping closer. "Pretend this is some grand adventure? That we haven't lost everything? That I didn't ruin us?"

Silence.

Vespera swallowed, her throat bobbing. "We haven't lost each other," she whispered.

For a moment, Conivx felt something stir—a flicker of something raw. Regret, maybe. A memory of what they had once been.

But she crushed it.

Ambition rose like a tide, drowning everything else.

She turned away, her voice barely more than a whisper.

"No," she said. "I suppose we haven't. Yet."

ACKNOWLEDGMENTS

Writing a book is never a solitary journey, and I owe so much of this story's creation to the incredible people who walked beside me.

First and foremost, to Cristian—your unwavering support, love, and belief in me kept me going even when the road got tough. Thank you for being my constant, my anchor, and my biggest cheerleader.

To my family, who always encouraged me to dream big and pursue my passions, thank you for nurturing my love for story-telling from the beginning. Chewy and Leia, my fluffy writing companions, your presence brought me comfort on countless late nights.

A huge thank you to my ARC readers and the early supporters of Isle of Beasts and Shadows. Your feedback, excitement, and kind words helped shape this story into what it is today. You took a chance on a new author, and I will forever be grateful for your belief in this world and its characters.

To my book club girls (big shout out to Haley Rogers, Carly Frasier, Ashley Belt, and Paige Fuller) and the readers of roman-tasy everywhere, you inspire me to keep writing stories filled with magic, love, and strong female leads. You are the reason this world exists, and I hope it sparks as much joy for you as it did for me while creating it.

And lastly, to you, the reader. Whether you stumbled across

this book by chance or have been with me since the beginning, thank you for taking a chance on this adventure. I hope it sweeps you away into a world of legends, beasts, and shadows.

AFTERWORD

Writing has always been a part of my life. I remember scribbling my first stories on notebook paper back in elementary school—tales of vampires, werewolves, fairies, and anything that had a touch of the supernatural or fantasy. Maybe it was the influence of a certain popular vampire movie at the time, but those worlds captured my imagination and wouldn't let go. My friends, back then, would read my short stories and encourage me to write more. So, to my little 4th-grade friends, you had no idea what you were starting, but thank you for igniting that creative spark in me.

I started writing Isle of Beasts and Shadows when I was just 14 years old, never imagining how much this story would evolve or how deeply it would become a part of me. At 19, I self-published the original version, The Forgotten Isle: Destined to Be Legends, without any editing or proper formatting—just pure, unfiltered passion. Now, years later, I've had the opportunity to revisit that story, give it the attention it deserves, and reintroduce it to the world the right way.

And this is only the beginning. There are more stories waiting to be told, already written, just waiting for the right moment to be shared.

I hope Airella's journey has taken you on a heart-pounding adventure, and I can't wait for what comes next.

ABOUT THE AUTHOR

McCayleigh is a Texas-based author, voice actor, and lover of all things fantasy. As a proud Texas A&M University former student, she's all about that Aggie spirit. Gig 'em!

When she's not writing epic tales of romance and adventure, she lends her voice to characters in audiobooks, bringing stories to life with her rich, captivating narration.

She enjoys spending time with her husband Cristian and their two beloved Shih Tzus, Chewy and Leia. She also shares her home with a sulcata tortoise who keeps life grounded amid her creative flights of fancy.

McCayleigh is dedicated to telling empowering, female-led stories within the realms of fantasy and romance. She hopes her work inspires readers to embrace their inner strength, fight for what they believe in, and never stop believing in magic.

FOLLOW THE AUTHOR

To stay up to date on future books, announcements, and exclusive content, visit www.mccayleighdaniels.com.

Don't forget to follow McCayleigh on social media for the latest news, giveaways, sneak peeks, and behind-the-scenes updates.

Instagram, Threads, & TikTok: @mccayleighdaniels

PLEASE LEAVE A REVIEW

Thank you so much for joining me on this adventure through Isle of Beasts and Shadows. If you enjoyed Airella's story, I would greatly appreciate it if you could take a moment to leave a review. Your feedback not only helps me grow as an author but also helps other readers discover the book. Reviews are incredibly important in spreading the word, and your support means the world to me.

Where you can review:
    Goodreads
    Amazon
    Barnes & Noble
    Books-A-Million
    Storygraph
    and more!

Don't forget to share your review on social media using the hashtag #IsleOfBeastsAndShadows.

Thank you for being part of this journey!

TRIGGER WARNINGS

- **Violence:** Includes physical fights, battles, and combat scenes, sometimes graphic in nature.
- **Death:** Death of key characters and mention of past deaths.
- **Dark Magic/Supernatural Themes:** Themes involving demons, dark magic, possession, and the supernatural.
- **Blood and Gore:** Descriptions of blood and injuries during combat and other violent situations.
- **Steamy Moments:** However, all 18+ scenes are closed-door.
- **Emotional Manipulation:** Characters experience mental and emotional manipulation.
- **Loss of a Loved One:** Grief and emotional turmoil surrounding loss.
- **Torture:** Implied or brief references to torture or suffering.
- **Mental Health Struggles:** References to hearing voices and internal struggles with one's identity.
- **Betrayal:** Themes of betrayal by trusted individuals.

Please be mindful of these elements before continuing, and take care while reading.